Miscreations

GODS, MONSTROSITIES, & OTHER HORRORS

EDITED BY DOUG MURANO
& MICHAEL BAILEY

Westminster Public Library
3705 W 112th Ave
Westminster, CO 80031
www.westminsterlibrary.org

MISCREATIONS: Gods, Monstrosities, & Other Horrors
© 2020 by Written Backwards

Anthology edited by Doug Murano & Michael Bailey
Cover artwork / illustrations by HagCult
Cover & interior design by Michael Bailey
Foreword © 2020 by Alma Katsu
Individual works © 2020 by individual authors, unless stated below.

"Spectral Evidence" first appeared in *Ploughshares*, © 2017 by Victor LaValle

"Resurrection Points" first appeared in *Strange Horizons*, © 2014
   by Usman T. Malik

Written Backwards
www.nettirw.com

ISBN: 978-1-7327244-6-4 / Hardback Edition
ISBN: 978-1-7327244-7-1 / Paperback Edition
ISBN: 978-1-7327244-8-8 / eBook Edition

Miscreations

GODS, MONSTROSITIES, & OTHER HORRORS

Foreword

ALMA KATSU

Psst, Gentle Reader. Yes, you, the one holding this book, trying to decide whether you'll take it home with you. You're looking for a good, long read, something to crack open as you settle into your favorite chair, a glass at your elbow. But a collection of stories about monsters? Is that likely to help you wind down in the evening, wash away the detritus of another long day at work? You waver; do you *like* stories about monsters? Not for you, dark scary tales about the boogeymen who haunt our dreams and daylight hours. Life is terrifying enough, you think. You don't need any more monsters in your life.

But that's not true.

Man and monster, monster and man: We are inseparable, twined together like ivy. If you dwell on it, the logic is obvious. Monsters couldn't exist without man to will them into existence. Monsters are (nearly always) man's creation, sprung from man's mind. (We'll get back to that parenthetical aside.)

We blame monsters for the terrible things that happen in our lives. Monsters are responsible for the fright that comes out of the blue, the noise from the uninhabited basement, the weighty presence in the darkness at the top of the attic stairs. We're told from childhood that monsters exist, in fairytales and in big, colorful picture books; in cartoons on television and in movies; in reality shows that hunt for ghosts and Bigfoot; even in commercials and advertisements. Before long, we don't need anyone to tell us they're real. We know it down to the marrow in our bones, and we're afraid to look under our beds or in the recesses of our closets. In the darkest corners of the forgotten, old stand-alone garage or the very back of the cellar behind the furnace. In the farthest reaches of our mind.

They're waiting for us. Always waiting for us. Faithfully, even.

But that's not the only kind of relationship we have with monsters. No—we love monsters, too. Admit it. After the initial fright has worn off, the fascination remains. We are drawn to them; we're curious about them. How did they get to be the way they are? How do they live with it, day in and out, knowing that everyone is afraid of them? They will never know the contentment of hearth and home. For them, only mobs with pitchfork and torch, baying hounds forever on their trail. Do they ever get lonely?

We know that the monster has a story, too, and if only we knew that story, we'd come to understand the monster. See his side of things. That's the story of Frankenstein's monster: both the book and the movie portrayed the creature as sympathetic, a figure that didn't ask to be made, and certainly not as his creator made him. He longed for his creator's love and mankind's pity, and when he got neither, turned on the weak and judgmental man who doomed him to an eternity of unhappiness. What heart, on hearing such a story, could still scorn the monster?

We have, in *Miscreations*, many references to the king of the monsters. In Stephanie Wytovich's "A Benediction of Corpses," for instance, a modern-day Frankenstein's monster comes to terms with what she is. And in Ramsey Campbell's "Brains," an intellectual is hounded by the angry mob into showing his monstrous side in this love letter to the movies of Frankenstein's monster. Theodora Goss brings us back to the tale that started it all with her delightful "Frankenstein's Daughter," which shows why hubris is a sure indication of monstrosity.

If not Frankenstein's doomed creation, might we talk about other monsters of lore? We have a smattering of famous monsters in our collection. Take, for example, "One Last Transformation," a wonderful werewolf story from Josh Malerman, whose narrator, a beguiling charmer, swears he's ready to give up the Curse ... or is he? Like many an addict, he claims he can stop anytime he wants, but it's not clear whom he's trying to convince here, the reader or himself. And for those who itch to make their own monster, we learn how to make a golem in Lisa Morton's "Imperfect Clay," from a woman who, with a track record of disappointment, refuses to accept anything less than perfection.

Do we love monsters because they are more powerful than us, and we can turn to them to protect us, to vindicate us? In our collection, we have stories about the marginalized in society who make themselves into monsters in order to stand up to their oppressors. In these stories, the protagonists are weak and helpless, while the ones in charge are so strong. When those in power only use that power to victimize and torture, making yourself into a monster might be your only recourse. Brian Hodge gives a perfect example in "Butcher's Blend," where the powerful are running things, and feel free to make examples of society's outcasts. They didn't expect the outcasts to fight back. Similarly, in Usman Malik's "Resurrection Points," a peaceful boy is driven by the angry mob to use his inherited gift to raise the dead to defend the weak and the persecuted.

And, of course, we can learn from monsters, too. We can learn to be heroic, such as in the heartbreaking and yet chilling "You Are My Neighbor" by Max Booth III, where a neglected boy elects to take the place of the monster in the cellar if it means he'll no longer be alone. After reading this story, you don't know whether to be utterly creeped out or to cry.

Monstrosity can also serve as a cautionary tale, can teach us what not to do, how not to behave. Such is the case in Bracken MacLeod's "Not Eradicated in You," where a girl emancipates herself right into the loving arms of a demon because her mother is a waking nightmare. Or Joanna Parypinski's "Matryoska," where a woman learns of the terrible bargain the women in her family have made—for generations. Or Victor LaValle's brilliant "Spectral Evidence," which shows that even the best of intentions can have tragic, unintended consequences.

There are also stories in the collection that defy categorization, that draw on emotion and imagination and dare to tap into the wellspring of weirdness that exists in all of us. Such is the case with Michael Wehunt's meta "A Heart Arrhythmia Creeping into a Dark Room," and Laird Barron's witty, trippy fantasy piece, "Ode to Joad the Toad." Mercedes Yardley's "The Making of Asylum Ophelia," M.E. Bronstein's "Sounds Caught in Cobwebs," and Kristi DeMeester's "Umbra Sum" which all make you wonder about the role of the victim in his/her victimization. Scott Edelman's thoughtful "Only Bruises are Permanent," and, because for some people, sex will always be the monster in the room, we have Lucy Snyder's "Her Knowing Glance."

There is still another aspect to the monster story, one that is less accepting, more judgmental. Sometimes, when confronted with a monster, don't we wonder what it did to deserve it? Through this legacy of our puritanical society, we are taught to believe that misfortune is deserved. That it's a punishment. To be monstrous is an indelible sign, proof of wickedness and failing for everyone to see. Linda Addison's poem "One Day of Inside/Out" is a powerful depiction of our craving for justice—of our belief that, in a just world, a monster would not be allowed to remain hidden.

Another story where monstrosity is a punishment for the wicked is "Paper Doll Hyperplane" by R.B. Payne. In it, a math professor—and aren't all math professors villains, really, gleefully torturing the rest of us?—gets what's coming to him after he reveals his utter inhumanity. It's a cerebral puzzle box, a lovely bit of unconventional storytelling, so good it deserves to be enjoyed with a glass of your favorite beverage.

And there are more delicious stories of comeuppance. In addition to Goss's aforementioned tale, there's Christina Sng's poem "The Vodyanoy," one of two of her works in the collection, which tells the tale of a woman who creates a monster (or has she merely trapped a monster?) through a violent and murderous act, but can any act that monstrous be justified?

Monstrosity is such a complicated topic.

Which brings us back to the question I posed earlier: do monsters exist, or are they only stories we tell ourselves? To frighten ourselves, console ourselves? To explain aberrant behavior?

Let me tell you a little secret. For many years, I was an intelligence analyst, working for one of the government agencies you know so well. For a while, I covered operations other than war (which is, ironically, the title of Nadia Bulkin's story in this collection, which shows that what's a monster to one person is a savior to another). In the 1990s, this usually meant humanitarian operations—peacekeeping and humanitarian missions—and a subset under this, genocides and mass atrocities.

It was a decade of mind-numbing inhumanity. Bosnia, Rwanda, the names everyone thinks of, but also Sierra Leona (where drugged-out rebels chopped off both hands of thousands of people as punishment for voting for the wrong man). Sudan and Uganda and the Democratic Republic of Congo, where thousands of children were torn from their homes and forced to become child soldiers. Anywhere neighbors who had lived peacefully for years and years suddenly believed that everyone who wasn't like them had to be wiped out.

Following genocides and mass atrocities taught me a few things about men and monsters. First, no one, no matter what crimes he's committed, believes he's a monster. He justifies his behavior, dissembles, denies. It's not his fault: he was driven to pull his neighbors from their house, unarmed and defenseless, and leave their bodies to cool in a mass grave. Or, he was in fear for his life, and that's why he chopped up the bodies of children and grandmothers he'd murdered and let to rot for ten days in the sun before going back to hide whatever was left so the UN peacekeepers wouldn't find them. *They brought it on themselves. They're not people, they're vermin, they're insects. They're monsters.*

Are monsters real? This is why I always answer yes.

And that's why we need stories like these, and why these stories need to be read.

Alma Katsu
Washington, DC
September 2019

Contents

A Heart Arrhythmia Creeping into a Dark Room

MICHAEL WEHUNT

The sun lowers until it's caught and torn on the mountains and I'm caught watching it, through a filthy window, thinking about how I have never been able to plan my stories out before I write them. They come in floods, lifting the surprised boat of my mind on their sudden waves, or they come stubborn as sap from a longleaf pine. I have two weeks to write this one. From the carpet near my feet, my dog makes a noise in her throat for my attention. I nearly always give it to her, but these days I am supposed to be regaining my momentum as an author. "In a minute, little bear," I tell her. In a minute she'll break me, and I'll be on the floor with her.

The story is for a book called *Miscreations: Gods, Monstrosities & Other Horrors*, and the loose theme is the Frankenstein myth. When Doug and Michael, the editors, invited me to write something for it, I said yes because I trust their vision and because I assumed life would have "turned around" long before now, the deadline drifting toward this streaked window and blocking out its view. I was over halfway through a year and four months of no stories when I said yes. There was no room inside my cluttered, stressed head at the time, and so I told myself I would miscreate a monster later; there would be plenty of time. Plenty of sunsets.

(And life did end up turning itself around, to a degree. I started working for a new company, fixing words, tuning content to the right frequencies. My breath, most days, grew easier and filled the lungs more. But I didn't consider the creative rust, the clumsy decay that had set in. I assumed the exhaustion carried home every day on my shoulders would be no heavier than it had been in the past. I assumed the fear I had grappled with would break apart like a ghost I no longer allowed to draw my eye, and would not seep into my heart. I thought my pride would have scabbed over.)

A scratched Bartók record is playing at a low volume, managing to sound like these American mountains, ancient things in a land we pretend is new. It's a concerto I found in a thrift store, and I've always felt it must have spent too much time in the sun. I picture a windowsill with open curtains, ambient heat seeping into someone else's room. The record kept out of its sleeve by an inconsiderate listener. There's the mildest warp in the vinyl that causes the needle to rise and fall like a buoy on a black sea. It could be a symbol, fore-shadowing that this story will break into a flood. Coupled with the saltwater static the needle reads in the scratches left by its former owner, the imperfection of the concerto moves me. The flaws bring me closer to something.

The Appalachians are flawed, from a certain perspective. They sit like old, worn teeth coated in moss, rooted in the earth's jaw. I can see three eroded peaks from my desk, as their distant tree lines rake through the egg yolk of the sunset. The broken light turns from an aged yellow to a purpled orange, as though blood swirls in. What will my monster be like? What will fill its veins?

My dog loves her neck to be scratched beneath her collar. I lean forward and take care of this important task and my heart palpitates for the first time today—it skips a beat, pauses a beat, then stumbles back into its rhythm. I straighten in the chair, breathe deep in frus-tration, and look out the window for the fortieth time as the color of night leaks down. Calm leaks back into me with less grace. I half-chant the list the ER doctor counted off on his fingers four months ago, afraid to lose the force of its litany: heart enzymes good, electro-lytes good, no clots, blood pressure OK, rhythms textbook strong, no atrial fibrillation or arrhythmia. And the coda, lighthearted for a heart heavy with fear: Try cutting back on caffeine.

The dog puts her front paws up on my knees and stretches her nose toward me, concerned and offering comfort for her Boy. Her left ear never straightened, and I stare at how it flops over before closing my eyes. I am as aware of the squirming organ in my chest as an owl is aware of the animal it snatches into its beak, the texture of warm flesh, the movement of the small bones down its throat. The owls are waking in the mountain foliage any moment now. The presence of my heart is as incongruous as a panicked fly trapped in a closed hand. I spill similes across the carpet. I meditate for a minute, but meditation has always eluded me. It, too, comes in a rush or like sap from a narrow tree, never the holy middle ground.

My monster must be as inconstant as my heart. If it were a viola—another middle ground—in this Bartók concerto, it would be played vibrato, or perhaps in between the still lake of a legato and the skipping stones of staccato. It would corrupt the rhythm in a way that would need several measures to discern. I lower myself to the floor and a rough, warm tongue greets my face. The opposite of a monster—though we call her a monster often—pounces on me, licking my nose, my eyes, my cheeks until I tell her that's enough.

(Later, a week after I thought I was having a heart attack at the office but wasn't, I canceled an appointment with a cardiologist after memorizing the ER litany, lovely excuses strung on a line, a comforting weight of words. I cut my coffee down to one cup a day and missed the other four terribly. The palpitations came less often, less thunderously. The panic attacks that erupted alongside them eased into manageable anxiety. The pair of hospital bills hurt, even with insurance, and I couldn't add to them just yet. It is too easy to ignore sickness in this country.)

My monster could be a heart attack—the fear of a heart attack, a heart attack that hasn't caught up with me yet—brought to flesh. The things I can't deal with. A disease of the heart walking upright, something I can see looming over me when my eyes open in bed, around a corner when I look behind me in the supermarket. A disguised creature parting the crowds toward me without public alarm, its long fingers able to grasp my head full of excuses. It could reach me at any moment and with any audience, like the seismic stopping of a heart.

I picture its face as I begin to create it. I see it as so much like a man's face, with beautiful features and quiet, cold green eyes, a face to stare out of billboards. The beauty does something to my pulse, it sends a trill through the blood. But something is wrong with the face, soft and handsome though it is. It is slightly too large. And it is in the moment of beginning to slip from its anchor of ligaments and tissue. If the face spoke—if it were not biding its time—the voice, like my heart, would carry an uneasy glissando that turns the stomach. It is an arrhythmia of nature.

It will come down out of the mountains, ancient and new as the land. Can it crawl on its legs and arms? Most of its limbs are folded up inside the clothes it wears to follow me out into the world as the semblance of a man. The four limbs I see in my mind could unravel to their true lengths from sleeves and cuffs. Its clothes are nicer than mine. Like its face, they speak of money that can solve problems. The monster would be so tall if it were ready to show itself to me. Its arms would drag behind it on the floor of the detergent aisle, in the gutters of the streets. The limbs I can't see must be freed from their buttoned container, so that it can come after me like a spider in the end. For now, it smiles at me from a distance. Its beautiful face slides into the corner of my eye.

The door sensor beeps twice as my partner comes home from work, and the dog, surprised that she didn't hear her Girl outside while distracted by my need, barks once and sprints from the office. I hear my partner's voice climb two octaves as they greet each other, reunited again. I hear the clatter of nails on the hardwood, and my heart eases. It beats a sober drum. I put on my not-worried face, and it, too, seems poorly anchored by its ligaments and tissue. I stand and look out the window again and the sun is now just a stain on the mountains—for a moment it brings an early fall to their coloring.

How will my monster fit into this world? I must assemble it, give it sinews and lungs and something like its own heart, and it will give me a story. Tonight, when the palpitations come, I'll pretend I am woken by the sound of scrabbling on the roof above us, though the dog will look at me with her eyes shining in the dark instead of giving a warning bark, and I know I'm always the last of us three to hear things, anyway.

Why do we create monsters? The mad Dr. Frankenstein, as we see him in films, wanted to play God. In the novel, he wanted to do so less theatrically. Horror authors answer this question differently: to frighten readers. It could be to make a buck; it could be to hold a mirror up to the world, in more ambitious cases.

I've written creatures before that were for readers as much as they were for myself, if not more. I wrote them in the hope that what unsettles me would be a universal thing. But if I create a monster for myself, to coax toward the only heart it is made to haunt, to give voice to fears I won't allow to bloom inside a stethoscope or an electrocardiograph, how can I frighten others? How can I honor the trust placed in me by the editors of this anthology? If the monster were to break free of this tether and appear on bookstore shelves, how could such a terror hope to translate? Perhaps the sign of a true artist is to make people afraid of things they didn't know they were afraid of. But the reader has only to say—*This is a story about a writer writing a story. I am holding* Miscreations, *so the writer lived to tell me the story. From the start he is pulling back the curtain to show me the smoke and mirrors, the innards of his monster.*

(Sometimes, too, there's a tightness near my left shoulder, like the blood I need is trying to squeeze into my heart around an obstruction. I sometimes skim articles about angina and convince myself all the symptoms but the squeezing aren't present. It's only indigestion, I must be swallowing air as I eat. I remind myself the palpitations have improved. My partner reassures me, and the look in her eyes tells me she means it. Though I keep many of these thoughts from her and recite the ER litany to myself, familiar enough to hum under my breath as though it were the first measures of a concerto.)

Mid-mornings at work are the hardest. It's when my belly is full and indigestion—what I tell myself is indigestion and the only root of this pressure—expands inside me. But more than that, mid-morning is when I thought I was having a heart attack that day but wasn't. Mid-morning is a nudge for my palms to sweat, for my breath to become shallower than it needs to be, for my heart to gasp in my chest. Mid-morning is when I'm trapped in an office fifteen traffic-clogged miles from home. A panic attack is less likely these days, but if it's near, this is when its teeth will come out.

Today I go to the restroom and splash my face with cold water, looking up at the mirror in time to see a too-long arm retracting through the closing door, down near where the carpet begins in the hallway. I didn't hear the door open. There was no one in here when I came in. A monster I made would do this exact thing, to let the protagonist know it is near and push the story a step further into horror and a heartbeat closer to confrontation. It's a reminder that the uncanny is insinuating itself into what has been mundane.

Since the monster is half-made, I spend my lunch break writing this list of components, the parts I will stitch together:

Organic and of the same atoms as my body. In another story, the protagonist would drive up into the mountains, wade through the dusk, and cut a palm open. Squeeze blood onto moss cushioning a dead oak, for the symbolism of it, the amateur witchcraft. In this story, my heart aches to be quieted.

Twelve appendages, long & pale & many-jointed for folding, the pair below the face ending in ten growths that are almost fingers. In another story, the protagonist would have a terror of spiders. I do not—mine is of wasps, but I have no wish to build a creature from a wasp's blueprints, either. This would place my fear in the wrong box. The extra limbs remove it from any taxonomy I know, and will cause my gut to churn in unease, giving me another excuse to blame all of this on indigestion.

Hairless torso with distended belly & caved, sagging chest. In another story, the monster would have slept long beneath the mountains' quilt of nature and eons, waiting for the moon to shine through a hole eaten by a rare beetle in a leaf upon a certain tree. The line of moonlight would strike the earth at an ordained angle above the creature's open eye. The monster, the god has waited for this beetle to begin its hungry life. Somewhere a cult convenes, unaware that the benign moon has found something they have roamed the earth in search of. Its belly would be full of things that burrowed into the soil to offer themselves to it. In this story, it is the mere bloat of gas, and above it the breathless cavity searching for something to fill it. My worried heart.

No tail because this would suggest a demonic or religious nature. In another story, faith would be a consideration. Something to cling to, an icon to hold up to evil. Faith would carry more light than a chain of words spoken in an emergency room. In this story, the sermon is given behind a sternum and the ribcage pews are empty.

Nine feet tall fully upright, its many arms opening to embrace me. In another story, the monster would tower over the protagonist in the dark. It would snatch him up and bear him away to some unspeakable end. I don't know why the monster must be so tall, or why I feel the need for my horror to gaze upward. I suppose it's because awe tends to come from a great height, and I look up so rarely. But I will be left in my bed, I believe, in the end.

A long withered neck, a stem holding the gorgeous face of a twenty-five-year-old Adonis, too large a face, careless brown curls draping the forehead, a wet plump mouth. In another story, such beauty would elicit worship, as it does in the cult that has been roaming cities and townships and poring over old books. In this one, I cannot fathom why this creature must be so handsome. Perhaps there is too much ugliness in the news and I can't bear to build more of it. Or it is the reverse—how much evil has crawled on the skin of this world with a pleasant pale face?

A voice box with no voice, the root of a tongue that never grew (my self-complicit silence). In another story, it makes an awful, awful noise, a burring clicking choking garble. But if I turned to my partner and told her my thoughts, if I used my own voice, perhaps the monster would have a tongue, or perhaps the monster wouldn't exist at all.

I can picture this thing clinging to the side of our house and peering through the top of the window, crouched in the vacant cubicle next to mine, bundled in the hatchback of my little black car. I can imagine it—I can almost feel it on my skin—creeping into our bedroom in the crease between night and morning. It's bent over staring into my face. Its eyes glitter with a distant beauty. It drags the tips of its fingers through the sparse hair on my chest, above my heart. All of its legs are out and flexing in the dark air. And I can see my partner lying beside me, but not the dog—where is she? How could I bring the idea of something like this into the lives of my two loves?

How could this creature scare anyone other than me? Many authors say they write for themselves, but it's not enough. I waste the rest of my lunch hour staring out a window, into a parking deck, and see something moving in the shadows between cars. I make it through the rest of the day. Traffic home is thick, an orange paste of taillights and sun glare, and my car is an oven. The air conditioning can't keep up and my blood pressure must be elevating. I worry about hypertension. I recite the emergency room benediction. My eyes keep darting to the rearview mirror, in case something is hiding behind the back seat. But it's not ready yet. Neither is its maker.

We take it for granted our hearts will keep beating, and when they shudder out of their clockwork, we stare down at ourselves in disbelief. We feel our bones, the density of them, with a new clarity, we feel the tendons creaking between them. We feel the organs stammering inside of us. The spark of life glows brighter in a desperate confusion. We are made aware of the machines of us, and we find we don't know them after all—the synchronicity of all these gears is suddenly frightening. And when we survive these interruptions, we build meticulous architecture with our minds and hope our hearts will settle into the new rooms. We exercise. We lock the bourbon away. We salt our food less. We let time pass.

On Saturday, I take a nap and press my chest into the mattress when the day's first palpitation comes. My pulse lurches, then grows tranquil until I am lulled to sleep, then sputters again. Late in the afternoon, I buy a used elliptical from an online marketplace and begin doing cardio for the first time in my life. I start slow, feeling my heart slam like an uninvited, furious fist on a cheap door. I tape a note beside the display screen that reads WITH A HEAVY HEART.

The exercise seems to help. My heart thinks it's stronger and so it is. Sunday there are no palpitations, and we pull up poison ivy outside in the wet blanket of heat, our arms and hands covered in protection against the vines that are monsters, too, in their invasiveness. The mountains are hidden behind a screen of our pines and a neighbor's sprawling oak, a sluggish creek bisecting our properties. We eat roasted chicken Monday night, dinner salads Tuesday, and I push my heart on the elliptical, a few more minutes each day. A drop of sweat jumps from my face onto the note, causing the AR in HEART to run, the ink blossoming from the paper. I hope and I worry that my monster is dying against this new determination.

Perhaps the deadline for the story will become its own creature—it crawls behind me, ten days left, seven, three. Doug and Michael send a mass email reminding the solicited authors that they're looking forward to reading our takes on the Frankenstein theme. I remember Doug telling me last year that we can interpret it loosely—war is a monster, I thought then, the president is a monster, division is a monster, we made these monsters—and this looseness becomes its own little prayer I repeat. After all, I have committed to the fear of my own heart.

Evenings I sit in the office with my laptop and watch a handful of suns drown in the trees through the window. The mountains like teeth, the sky a gullet, but the monster begins to swell in my imagination and my fear subsides in the blank face of such vastness—a cosmic Lovecraftian god cannot stir the creative hairs on the back of my neck anymore. My dog goes back and forth between the living room and the office, unhappy that her pack isn't in the same room. "When I finish the story," I say to her, "just a little longer." She licks my face and later I take her out back so she can patrol the fenced yard in the dark, protect us from what creatures she would make up in her own mind.

We are caught in the rhythm of our workdays, there is something like peace, we watch our regular shows on TV. My skin doesn't grow hot with panic at the office, and nothing dark trails behind me through the herd of cubicles or the parking-deck gloom. I begin to go long minutes without thinking of my heart, as it opens itself up to the future, locked in its steady voice: *believe, believe, believe*—

But, of course, this must be a horror story. Halfway through Friday evening's walk with the dog, the dark falling and the humidity reluctant to follow it, my heart stops beating. I stagger and count to what feels like three but can't be that long, until my heart swerves back into rhythm, runs pounding up a flight of stairs to catch up with the rest of me.

My partner asks what's wrong, a note in her voice that tears at me. I don't answer. "Was it a palpitation?" I tell her yes, I thought the exercise had helped, and she tells me precisely the thing I need to hear—that I have to give it time, a week of cardio isn't going to be a miracle. She's right, but ahead of us, in the overgrown lawn of the empty house where the road curves, I see the shape of my monster crouched in knee-high grass. A cloud of gnats writhes above it.

And it comes to me tonight, for the first time, after my partner has fallen asleep. As though it, too, has forty-eight hours to finish the story. A click comes from the bedroom doorknob, then the soft whine of a creaking hinge as the air we have been breathing escapes into the rest of the house.

I listen to it creep into the dark, until the beautiful face slides over the lower rim of my vision, staring down at me. Its expression could be mournful or studious. My heart trips beneath my chest, kick drums falling out of line, and the creature moves to my right, passing around my side of the bed. It is naked, with its appendages freed. Four of them unfold above its head, and I still won't move my face to allow more of it into my sight.

But the dog is not making a sound—I jerk my head away from the monster and there she is, her head on her paws, her eyes open with a hint of streetlight gleaming off them from the blinds. She hasn't shot to her feet with a volley of barks. Her silence tells me the story isn't real. Beside her, my partner turns toward me on her side, her face soft in sleep.

I look to my right and the creature isn't there. I wait to see if it is inside of me, twitching itself around the heart attack that has taunted me for months, long before I gave it a face. The dog stretches and puts a paw on my leg. Turning back to her, I see that she has closed her eyes. A weight lifts from me. I muddy the story further by sleeping without dreams.

I have proven what Dr. Frankenstein knew—that the trickiest part is animating the flesh, the flickering of the brain stem into sentience. And I have realized that 4,200 words into this, the deadline quickening like its own heartbeat, I have no tangible agency as a storyteller. These machines—the heart, the brain—are stimulated by electricity. What current can I tap into to bring the monster off the page?

My heartbeat has slipped three times today, and I am standing at a pine tree in the hills that crest up toward the mountains. I have pricked my right thumb and smeared blood on the dusty bark of the trunk, where a spigot might be driven in. But even if there were a spigot, it would have dried to a syrupy crust. My story is due tomorrow. The creature will return to our room tonight, and the final seizing of my heart feels like the only ending that's left.

My pulse judders a fourth time. A pressure builds near my left shoulder. I speak to the tree: "Heart enzymes good, electrolytes good, no clots, blood pressure OK, rhythms textbook strong, no atrial fibrillation or arrhythmia." The words have gathered a sort of music into them these last few months, their constant striving toward the calm legato. They will keep me alive. The rough tongue of my dog will keep me alive. The arms of my warm partner will keep me alive. The old hum of the mountains will keep me alive. The deadline will pass, the story won't end. Above me the sun burns through a sheer haze of clouds, its heat squeezing everything until it is forced under these green breakers again.

"Night, love," my partner says. She'll fade into sleep within a minute, so I kiss her hand as she rolls away from me. I hug the dog so long she tries to worm out of my arms. Though I'm tired from an extra fifteen minutes on the elliptical, I wait for the monster, counting the soft lines of light the blinds reach across the ceiling like fingers.

I hear it clutch at the doorknob a few minutes past one. The hinge moans, and I see the shape of what I made filling the threshold of the dark room. Its shadow drops and the ends of its twelve legs scratch across the floorboards. My heart wheezes as the ambient streetlight catches the carved marble of its face, as it moves around the bed to me, as it rises up, limbs twitching out.

I hear it for the first time as it leans down over the bed, a crackling drone, arrhythmic with the straining root of its tongue. Only now do I notice it has no scent—I never gave it one. I think of the smell of my parents' basement the year it flooded, the moldy cloud that took months to get rid of, but the monster doesn't take the assigned odor into itself. Then a whimper rises, a sound I would know before any music, and the dog is suddenly not on the bed. I slide up onto my elbows and see her crouched in the corner of the room, by the closet, her eyes wide enough to show the rings of white around the dark brown irises, staring up at the creature. She's terrified, and now I do smell something: the tang of her urine on the floor.

"What—" my partner calls out. "What is it?" And the monster's arm lowers to me, the growths that give it a hand spreading to grip my chest. The dog makes a noise that is terror and protection and heartbreak, my love makes a noise that is the low beginning of a scream, and I can't do this anymore.. I can't bring this into their lives. It wasn't supposed to be real in this way.

I picture a man, my age, darker hair, murmuring the same assurances of an emergency room doctor. I sketch him in my mind with a blunt pencil, all in a moment. The replacement protagonist—David—reaches up and pulls the monster into an embrace. Its hand meets his chest, it pushes through the sternum and tears out his spurting heart. David's girlfriend—Ana—shrieks until the monster turns to her. Then she is silent, and the dark thickens in the house. The night falls upon the night, and hides the twelve legs scrabbling out into the dark, the crickets falling as silent as Ana, the mountains poorly drawn silhouettes in the distance. It clutches its prize and a trail of blood follows it into the world. There was never a dog in the room. David and Ana don't own a pet.

I have to send the story to the editors today, but my trick with David—drawing him up in an instant of panic, giving him rudimentary likes and dislikes and a familiar horror of what his heart is doing at every moment inside of him, channeling a kind of electricity through him—isn't the ending I wanted. It's an ending a reader is likely to feel cheated by. I fell back on the timeless author's trick, pitting an evil I created against an unwitting character I created. David saved me.

My dog comes over to the chair and tucks her head under my arm and lifts. She wants me to scratch her magic spot, so I do, grateful last night has faded from her mind. And my partner's—I swore she'd had a nightmare, nothing more, and she believed me just enough.

But the monster isn't finished with me—it wants blood, not David's pixels. When the book is published, the ink in David's veins won't be enough. I turn back to the laptop, this narrative with no resolution—unless—until the monster returns, the arrhythmia creeps into the dark room, and your eyes open at the creak of the door hinge. Your wife, partner, husband, boyfriend, dog, or children lie sleeping next to you, caught in their warm dreams. The face, beautiful enough to haunt us all, regards you. Its eyes glitter in what could be moonlight, if you want it to be. Its limbs reach out and flex along their many joints.

Again, you have only to say, *This is a story about a writer writing a story. I am holding* Miscreations, *so the writer lived to tell me the story*. But take a moment to imagine the organs filling your body. Focus on your heart, think of how you take it for granted that it will keep beating. Feel its rhythm, feel what happens when it stutters out of true, feel one of its valves close incorrectly, and gasp open again, feel the disbelief that the machine of your body has betrayed you. Your heart has always been there, unnoticed in moments of calm.

Focus on it until the calm slips. Feel it palpitate right now and feel it gallop to reclaim the grace of its gait, fighting the abrupt illness of its rhythm. Feel the ugliness of it squeezing blood out and slurping blood in.

Take a moment to listen for your heartbeat, slow your breathing until you hear something behind you, crawling closer along the carpet or floorboards or blanket of pine needles.

I made David up, and in that fiction he canceled out the monster. It needs something real to claim. David couldn't take my place because he wasn't real. But you are real, and I have pulled back the curtain to expose your heart.

Matryoshka

JOANNA PARYPINSKI

My childhood was filled with dolls. Painted, bright shawls, red flowers. Lined up on the mantle. Smiling with their rosy cheeks.

Matryoshka.

Ludmila, my mother, collected them. I was never to touch them, even as a girl—a girl who liked to mother dolls and small creatures, whose play was in nurturing. Thinking if I could nurture, I could be nurtured, too.

Seeing those dolls staring out at me again, in this dingy house so immaculately kept if not for its irreversible age, cramped in on either side on the minuscule lot, sent me back to my childhood. Their painted eyes and rounded heads, bulbous against the tacky floral wallpaper, ran back the clock 'til I was ten again, spiteful, collecting bugs from the yard—opening a nesting doll, peeling back its onion layers, closing a beetle in place of the seed. Poisoning one of my mother's precious dolls.

"Open it," said my mother.

The Russian doll felt heavy in my lap, and I was weary. "Later, Mama. I appreciate the gift, but I'm tired. I just want to take a hot shower. Have a drink. Go to bed."

"All right," she said, giving me her iron-gray stare, hard as slate. Even the deepening grooves in her face did not diminish her. "But the daughter I raised would not fall to pieces. She would find a solution. And if she could not find a solution, she would make one."

The burning in my eyes, the taste of tears in the back of my throat, infuriated me almost as much as the fact that she could still do this to me. Could still make me feel like a weak, incompetent child. Maybe I was. My mother had raised me alone, working two or three jobs to make ends meet, never complaining. But she had too much of the old country in her. Even though Ludmila moved to the U.S. before she could talk, Grandma Inga had instilled in her the virtues of hard women in a hard country. I was too far removed, perhaps, from that experience; too soft.

"What solution?" I snapped. "There's no fixing it. I'm just broken." I choked the words out, hating that my mother was making me go through this again—explain to her my infertility, the revelation of which came after months of trying and the slow dawning realization that something was wrong. As it turned out, *I* was wrong. It was me. And after my doctor confirmed it, I couldn't believe Carter's utter lack of resentment. He was almost cloyingly gentle, at first—minimizing. I wanted him to slam his fist against the wall or go on a bender, but he only held me and told me it wasn't so bad. "There's no solution that will fix this," I told my mother. "Carter thought so and now look at us."

The picture of a crumbled marriage: my inconsolable swollen-eyed grief, the disconnect of his misunderstanding, heated arguments, muttering frustrations into cups of coffee, the black well of despair. And like a kettle set to boiling, it finally shrilled its surrender: I packed my suitcase and came here, to my mother's.

Carter thought adoption was the answer. "Think about it: How many kids are orphans, or unwanted? We could help them, Tasha," he had said only *hours* after we got the news. Only hours, and maybe that hurt more than anything.

But how could I tell him? All I had ever wanted was something of my own. A child of my own flesh. I didn't *want* someone else's child. A terrible, selfish thing. Perhaps. And yet.

Seeing our impasse, my mother fixed me a hot toddy.

"When I was your age, my mother gave me a matryoshka doll."

"I know. The one above your bed?"

"It is very special to me," she said, nodding to the doll in my lap. "Open it."

Knowing better than to refuse my mother a third time, I pulled apart the two halves to reveal the slightly smaller doll inside—and on until the smallest one came apart in my hand. At its core should have been the seed: the tiny wooden piece carved whole. But it was empty.

I threw down the doll in disgust. Its hollowness was inside me. Mocking me. "How could you?" The dolls lined up on the mantle stared. "You knew it was empty."

My mother reached over and took my hands in hers, wrinkled and knobbed with age. I thought of my own hands growing gnarled, growing old, alone.

"So fill it," she said.

"With what?"

Her smile, as it had ever been, was thin and wooden, did not quite reach her eyes. "A piece of yourself."

Pressing my lips together, I reassembled the doll with its hollowness inside. How many dolls, plants, insects, clumps of cloth had I poured my love into as a child? "I'm not *playing*."

"It isn't play. It will help." She stood, took my empty glass. Behind her, the fire crackled. "Maybe it is an old wives' tale." She shrugged, the fire dancing behind her. I could not make out her face in shadow. "But maybe not."

I half-expected Carter to call, to check in, but the phone kept quiet.

The house was quiet, too. My mother didn't like TV. She preferred embroidery, crossword puzzles, polishing her collection of dolls. Watering the droopy plants which didn't receive enough sunlight inside, where the few dusty windows were crowned with ugly valances.

In the quiet, I could hear faint restless scratching in the attic, the scrabbling of claws. I looked at my mother, busy with her embroidery. "Rats? Still?"

"They don't cause any harm," she said without looking up.

"Mama, you can't just let rats live in the attic." The scratching sound clawed at my ears, sent knives up my spine. "I can't believe you *still* haven't taken care of it." There had been rats in the attic since I was a kid. It was why I never went up there. At night, I dreamed of dark little creatures scrabbling around, their dull beady eyes red with the reflection of dim light. Burrowing into the wood floor and walls, nesting in cardboard boxes of old clothes.

"I've always taken care of things around here," she said sharply. "Have I not?"

I thought about offering to help, reminding her that she was not so young anymore, and that so many years of manual labor had aged her beyond her sixty years. Reminding her that I, too, was capable of taking care of things. Instead, cowed, I said, "Yes, Mama."

"Have you planted your seed yet?"

Casual, off-hand; clearly she was not as bothered by the scratching above as I was, sharp little claws on my nerve-endings.

"What am I supposed to put inside?"

Finally she set down her hoop and linen, looked up at me. I saw she was embroidering a rose embraced by its own prickly stem. "What are *you* willing to sacrifice for your child?"

"I don't know."

"Then maybe you are not ready," she said, returning to her work.

Sacrifice? The word followed me to work the next day, drawing my mind inward on itself, plunging deeper and deeper until I was so ensconced in layers of rumination my colleague had to rouse me from the depths by putting a cup of coffee right in front of my face, draw me back to the surface. I knew having a child wasn't easy, but I'd always thought of it as gaining something—an addition, not a removal. Did my mother see me as a sacrifice?

When I came home, I asked her what I should have asked when she first posed the question. "What were you willing to sacrifice?"

Puttering about the kitchen, she turned, lifted the hem of her house robe, and carefully toed off her left slipper; a calloused foot with yellowing nails emerged, missing its pinkie toe, a subtraction that had always stopped her from wearing sandals in public.

"I don't understand."

She dropped her robe and managed to get her slipper back on with her other foot; she had a bad back that prevented her from bending over.

"You'll have to decide," she said, picking up a wooden spoon and returning to the boiling pot on the stove. "Then you can plant your seed."

Despite the warm smells of cooking, my stomach turned. I had to leave the kitchen, had to move to keep my own revulsion at bay. I did not understand. I did not *want* to understand.

I found myself in my mother's bedroom, a place I'd hardly been allowed as a child. Even now, it felt like a small rebellion to be in here alone.

On her headboard sat the old matryoshka doll she cherished most, polished but faded with age, the eyes nearly rubbed off into white smudges. The rosy cheeks gone gaunt, almost gray. I picked it up, felt the heft of its many hidden layers, wondered at my mother's secrets.

Why couldn't she have just held my hand and told me, yes, this is terrible, this is the worst thing that has happened, and you have every right to grieve? Why couldn't she have told me that Carter was being an imbecile, so let's turn up the radio and have a few extra drinks? Maybe eventually I could even come to accept my barrenness, if only everyone would stop trying to invalidate the feeling that I've plummeted off a cliff. But then, what did I expect from her? None of my grievances, growing up, had ever been enough to stir her remotest sympathies.

A flash of impotent rage sent the doll flying from my hand. Its outer shell shattered against the wall, the inner dolls rolling onto the floor still intact.

Regret soured in my mouth. I picked up the broken pieces. What would my mother say of this childish outburst?

I brought the pieces to the kitchen to tell her I would mend it, I would glue it all back together, but as soon as I stepped in the doorway I dropped the pieces again.

My mother lay on the floor.

Her arms and legs twisted at the wrong angles; her skull was cracked, red lines separating her head into three pieces; blood pooled into the grout between tiles. Milky white eyes stared off in different directions, gauzed with death. She was a jumble, a ruined puzzle.

I struggled to breathe, stumbled away looking for my phone, my memory a pale void. The pot on the stove boiled over, and I shut off the burner, trying not to taste the tang of blood in the air, the vomit rising in my gullet. *Murdered.* She must have been murdered. How else could her body lie so irrevocably broken? Thinking this, I blindly grabbed the first solid object my hand touched when I opened a drawer—a meat tenderizer—and clutched it to me as I crept into the hall, my ears ringing.

A sudden scratching, and my heart pirouetted—*just the rats in the attic.*

The shifting groan of a footstep. *My imagination, surely.*

The squeak of a door swinging on its rusty hinges, opening like a yawning maw.

With a cry, I lunged in the direction of the sound, the meat tenderizer raised high, ready to bring it down on the figure who stood in the doorway of my mother's room, the shadow stepping out into the hall—

The figure switched on the light, momentarily blinding me, setting me off-track; and when I looked again, I saw it was my mother.

My head swam. "You ... you ..."

The woman came closer. I recognized the hard slope of her nose and the slash of her crooked eyebrows; the slight droop of her left eyelid; it was *her.*

But her iron-gray hair was threaded with chestnut brown; lines in her face had smoothed, like God sweeping his hand over rutted sand. Her hands lacked their grooves and liver spots.

It was my mother, but it wasn't.

I recoiled. "Who are you?"

Ludmila smiled, and it did not reach her eyes. "You don't know your own mother?" She took the meat tenderizer from my hands. "What were you going to do with this? Smash me, like you smashed my matryoshka doll?"

"I'm sorry," I said at once, blundering into my own faults and away from the inexplicable sight of my dead mother standing, alive and youthful, before me. "I'll fix it."

"It's too late for that." There was an edge to her voice, sharp as when she'd found the beetle I'd hidden inside one of her dolls and slapped me, scolded me, sent me to my room without supper. Such harsh words for such a small thing, but nothing was more precious to her than her dolls. Nothing.

"Is this how I've raised you?" Ludmila said, frowning at me. Disapproving, disgusted. "You behave this way, a child of my own flesh. Destroying what is mine, after all I've given you."

"What have you given me?" I shrieked, keeping my eyes open, for if I closed them I saw her body in the kitchen and wondered which one was her.

"Go to your room."

I'm not a child, I wanted to say, but she looked just like she did when I *was* a child, so maybe I was wrong. I went to my room and sat on the lumpy twin bed. I listened to her walk down the hall to the kitchen, listened to the scrape of her picking up the broken pieces and dropping them in the trash, bending over effortlessly. Was the body still there? Had I imagined it? Was I losing my mind?

As she cleaned, I snuck back into her room and found the doll, bringing it back with me and shutting, locking the door.

She cared more about this doll than anything, and all I wanted was to care more about something, some creature that needed me, than anything. And yet *she* was the mother. I was just a hollow, barren thing. A toy.

I opened the next layer of the doll and cracked it under my heel. A splintering sound in the kitchen, like cracking bones. What exactly was she cooking in there?

Then, footsteps, but from the wrong direction—from my mother's bedroom.

The doorknob rattled.

"Tasha?" It was the voice of a young woman, someone my own age. The door shook. "Tasha, you are being a naughty child. Open this door."

"You're dead!" I called through the wood.

"Do I look dead to you?" The knob jiggled again, insistently. I could see the shadows of her feet beneath the door. "Open this door and see for yourself how alive I am."

"You're not my mother."

"Of course I am," said the voice of the young woman. "You are of my own flesh. Just as I am of my mother's own flesh. She knew what to sacrifice, and planted her seed. Just as I did."

I shook my head, clutching the doll in my hands, trying to breathe. "No."

"Infertility runs in our family, Tasha. I should have told you sooner. All the women of our line have been barren."

I thought the hungry black hole in my gut would devour me. "Which one is it?"

Silence on the other side of the door.

"Don't I have the right to know which one is mine?"

"I was going to give it to you," young Ludmila's voice came through. "But now I'm not so sure you can be trusted with it. You've already broken two very precious, fragile dolls. You'll have to be punished for that."

Punished. I had always feared she would put me in the attic, to spend a night with the rats. She never did, but the threat still hung, unspoken, in the air. I leaned against the door. Placed my palms flat, felt its reverberations. And wondered if I was part wood, too. If I rubbed my eyes, would the paint smear? Would I smudge my pupils? Would the rats eat my eyes from my skull?

I pictured my mother sitting at her embroidery, when she was still gray and aging, not young and unfamiliar, and her bones made of wood knocked hollowly together, and somewhere under her face lay a wooden skull, carved and polished, gnawed by termites—

The next layer of the doll came apart in my hands and I destroyed it.

I had to steel myself to open the door and step over Ludmila's young, broken body, had to force myself not to look. I made it as far as the living room, where I collapsed onto an armchair before the blazing fire, which was the only light in the room, convulsing against the shadows that webbed the line of dolls upon the mantle. My face was wet. The matryoshka dolls watched me, and I wished I had never touched one. I thought of mothers who want children, and daughters who cannot help but have mothers. The house reeked of death and dust.

Then, from down the hallway came a small figure. A young girl, no more than a child, with chestnut hair; a silhouette. She stepped into the light, looked at me, and her eyes were stormy, her eyebrows sharply slanted. Horror clawed its way up my throat. She held out her hand for the small doll in my lap. "You're making a mistake," she warned.

And the sight of her reaching out for the doll—not for me, not to comfort her daughter, but to take back what was hers—made me open it and throw the outer pieces into the fire.

The girl erupted in flames: curling over her skin, bubbling it black, eating her away. Flames burst through the cavities where her eyes had been, through her gaping mouth.

Without putting out the fire, I stumbled away, blinded by tears, gasping in untenable breaths. Distantly I heard my phone buzzing, wherever I'd left it—*Carter*, I thought, with longing—but then I heard, too, the sound of a baby crying.

Still clutching the tiny doll in my fist, I found the infant on my mother's bed, stretching its pink fists toward the moonlight and scrunching its blue-gray eyes as it wailed. Numb, I picked up the baby, bounced it in my arms until it calmed. Its flesh was warm, cradled against me. Just a helpless little creature who needed love. I felt my heart unwinding, my tension unraveling. My tears drying.

What if, I wondered ... *What if I just raised my mother as my own child?*

She was, after all, of my own flesh. A piece of her was inside of me, buried deep. A planted seed.

But what would happen when she grew old enough to speak? Would she remember that I was not her mother, but her daughter? Would she resent me, as I had resented her for so many years?

I put the child back down on the bed and wondered what I would sacrifice for my own child. What bloody piece of myself I would be willing to part with, to carve away and offer up.

An ache in my gut. I couldn't think of anything.

I took the last little nesting doll—the one that held the seed, the soul of this many-layered being—and carefully pulled it apart.

Inside was a lump of putrefied flesh, withered, whorled with wisps of hair. Part of an ear. Part of Grandma Inga's ear.

JOANNA PARYPINSKI

The baby stirred, coughing wretchedly—hiccupping, seizing, and finally a chunk of rotten flesh burped up from the baby's mouth, and the child fell still.

For a time, I considered finding my own matryoshka doll, the one containing my mother's pinkie toe, and destroying it all at once. Have done with everything. I knelt beside the bed, my face pressed into the comforter beside the body of the baby, soaking it with my grief. I coughed on my tears until I realized that the air was acrid, smoky. The fire in the living room was wild, untamed, unmoored from the hearth, and I wondered how much it had destroyed already. If I found my doll and tossed it into the fire, would all my selves unravel as we burned, or would it just be me, would they stay inside of me? The air was warm and smelled of burning cloth. I thought of my mother's embroidery.

Should I try to get out?

I heard scrabbling overhead. The rats in the attic must be getting hot, must be panicking as the smoke curled its way up through the cracks in the floorboards. At least it would kill them. Good riddance.

The heat growing unbearable, blocking me from the living room and the front door, I realized the only place to escape was *up*. I pulled down the hallway ladder, stared up into the black square, the mouth of the attic. And, hearing it now without the barrier of the ceiling, I realized the scrabbling was too loud, too large, too singular to be a nest of rats.

I remembered my mother taking the matryoshka doll with the beetle and stashing it in the attic, where I could not get it.

Perhaps this was what I deserved. I wondered if Carter was worried that I hadn't answered my phone. I wondered if he would come, would find the house in ash, would find what I had birthed unknowingly in the attic: something monstrous, not of my own flesh but of my own creation.

Could I love such a thing?

Slowly, I began to ascend the ladder as the fire made its way down the hall toward me. I did not know what was up there, but as I listened to the scuttling of many legs, the clicking of oversized mandibles, I wondered if what I found there would have my eyes.

Butcher's Blend

BRIAN HODGE

This was mostly the same speech to the cowed and corralled that Annie had heard before, and the time before that, and the very first time they'd locked her up. But not identical. It had undergone refinements. Three years into these hidden pogroms, the speech was still a work in progress.

"It gives me no joy to welcome you here … any of you … but especially those of you who have been through this opportunity before. Because it's obvious you chose to learn nothing."

The standard lead-in from the woman at the microphone, Aryan tall, which she would've come by naturally, but the Aryan blonde part, that brittle looking shit came from a bottle. During the most recent of Annie's in-betweens on the outside, she'd seen a verified picture, an early one, high school yearbook or college, and the woman had started off as mousy brown as a watered-down turd. Still had the crazy eyes, though, even back then. Like she might've been looking your direction, but Jesus had just stepped up right behind your shoulder, and she was certain she was the only one who could see him.

Blessed like that, you know.

Mother Constance, was what she went by now. That took some nerve. Over the years, Annie had known the soothing touch of some world-class earth mothers, and not one of them had looked anything like this, all starch and creases in her slacks and a perpetual glare of aggrieved disappointment that simmered all the way to the back of this bare-bones auditorium.

Definite ice-MILF material, for those who went for that sort of vibe. This had to be strategic. Dowdy crones were easier to turn into background noise. A woman who looked like she could leave you a paraplegic in the bedroom, not so much.

She informed the newcomers, and reminded the recidivists, there was a word for them: They were the Disinvited. It didn't get any more upside-down newspeak absurd than that. Of the thousand or so in her captive audience, nobody would've had the option to decline. The snatch teams may have sounded polite and professional when they came for you, but they made sure you saw the Tasers.

"If you don't know what Disinvited means, let me make it clear for you ..."

Up on the stage, amplified by the PA system, Mother Constance looked as comfortable as any woman possibly could when flanked by armed guards and others ready to turn fire hoses on an unruly crowd. They would spray whatever they needed to keep order.

"To be a Disinvited is the worst fate you can bring upon yourself, because it's so selfish. You have rejected your place in a society that wants to hold you in its loving embrace. You've said no to the party, so your invitation has been withdrawn. The good news is your place will be waiting for you when you choose to accept correction."

Oh, for the courage to shout the obvious: *Bitch, just call it like you see it. We're your undesirables. And nobody's getting corrected here. All you're doing is weeding out the ones you can break from the ones you decide one day you're going to have to kill. Not just an example here and there. Whole cities' worth of us.*

That was what came next. Go back forever, and it was always what came next.

"What we're doing here is God's work," Mother Constance said. "If I may be so bold, we're *improving* on God's work. Because, judging by surface appearances, without looking deeper, even God can get a little sloppy now and then."

Among the audience, you could tell who was hearing this for the first time, from the ripples of their gasps and murmurs. These aren't your father's zealots, kids.

She basked in it, did Mother Constance. "I've listened to your claims. I've patiently heard you out a thousand times. You are as God made you. You love who you love because that's how God made you. You think what you think, and do what you do, because God gave you free will. Your life, and the way you've chosen to live it, is God seeking to know himself through the variety of his magnificent creation. I've heard it all."

She had a way of strolling about the stage and stopping to glance up at Heaven's teleprompter as if it was all coming to her on the spot.

"I've heard, and I don't even disagree. We can see eye-to-eye on this. But that doesn't *excuse* you." Her voice sharpened on cue. Every time. "You are still mistakes, and we, here, are charged with the task of correcting the mistakes that God has made so abundantly."

Annie shifted, cheek to cheek. Beneath her, the bench was hard and unforgiving, bolted to the concrete floor, a seat made for proving your devotion to listen for as long as it took.

The most uneasy part of this? The projection screens on either side of the stage. With an audience of a thousand, there was no need for them. Mother Constance didn't need camera zoom-ins to command attention. There had to be worse coming, already. It was a kick in the gut: They were starting the examples early this time—the very first night.

"Now, how can it be that a perfect God is prone to making mistakes? Isn't this a contradiction? Not at all! Even mistakes are a part of the grand design that we're here to help you see. Our perfect God makes mistakes because it is a part of his perfect plan to do so."

Annie glanced around at her neighbors to see how they were taking this in. Who was rolling with it, who was getting steamrolled by it. Pay attention, and you could always find somebody who could use a friend for the next two weeks.

"Why? Why would he do such a thing? Why would God go to such lengths and allow you all to endure so much suffering, crushed by the burden of what you are? It's because we ..." She spread her arms as if trying to wrap them around her goon squad. "... *we* have been given an even heavier burden. It's so those of us with the clear vision to see his mistakes can assume the responsibility for correcting them ... and in our quest for perfection, we are all drawn closer to God."

That yanked Annie's attention back to the stage. This last bit was definitely new. She would've remembered a thing like that. The rationalizations, getting more elaborate. The self-aggrandizement, layering on more and more crazy. The urge to vomit, dialing up and up and up.

Call it the Gospel According to Mother Constance: And on the eighth day, God looked at all that he had made, and said, "A little help here? I kinda fucked up some. But I meant to." And this lanky bitch gave every appearance of believing every word. Why not—it was perfectly self-contained, watertight in its internal logic. Sit her down for a hundred years and you couldn't come close to talking her out of it. No cracking that shell. It was true believer stuff—the rest of you ignorant defectives wouldn't understand. Because you were denied the capability.

Trust us.

It went on, of course, the condemnatory harangue delivered in a wrapper of love, sticky and coated with dead flies.

Back to her fellow undesirables. There ... the bench in front of her, four seats to the right. The poor kid was looking around as if he were about to drown and getting desperate for someone to toss him a rope. That was the trouble when everyone around you was just as scared: lots of hands but no lifelines.

Annie held her gaze until he felt it, as sure as she'd tapped him on the shoulder. He stared back and she gave him her best reassuring smile. He had a long, thin face, and wide eyes, and straight black hair down to his Adam's apple. It drooped across his face from left to right. A few years ago, she would've found it annoying, the frequency with which he twitched his head to flip it out of his eye. Now? Now she just found it endearing, the nervous tic of it. There was probably a time when he thought it made him look nonchalant, didn't give a fuck 'bout nothing.

First time? she mouthed. She'd been blessed with a wide mouth, all the better for lip reading.

The boy nodded.

You'll be fine. Okay?

Again, he nodded. An easy sell. He wanted to believe.

She checked the stage again, saw who was coming out.

It's about to get bad. Don't watch. But don't let them see you not watching.

The boy gave her one last nod, tentative at first, then more confident. *Thank you.*

Onstage, Mother Constance was wrapping up her main spiel in a nice big ... bow? Hardly. Tourniquet, more like it. Watch and learn, she commanded them all. See the price for choosing not to learn. See where your transgressions could ultimately lead, if you continue to stubbornly refuse correction. God's word couldn't have made it any plainer: If thy eye offends thee, pluck it out. If thy hand offends thee, cut it off.

A lot of implied leeway there. These people could find so much about the body that caused offense.

As for the man who'd come onstage to make examples of those adjudged no longer worthy of leniency ... until she'd seen it for herself, Annie would never have believed someone could know so much about cutting, about plucking. It seemed that a man with these capabilities could only have existed in legend. Yet here he was.

Legend was where he should've stayed.

Three more of Mama C's beefed-up enforcers dragged out a struggling fellow, somewhere in his middle years but his voice screeching as high as a middle schooler's. On the close-up screens, his face streamed with so much sweat Annie wondered how slippery the rest of him was getting.

He was, according to Mother Constance, an incorrigible and unrepentant developer of role-playing games, which had been found to have a corruptive influence on those who played them ... young minds especially. To pretend to meddle with spellcraft was to open the soul to engaging in actual spellcraft.

The punishment hardly ever seemed to fit the crime here. Cutting the offending hand off a thief made a medieval kind of sense, yet during Annie's prior detentions, she'd never seen them deal with those sorts of wrongdoings. But: When all you have is a hammer, went the old saying, every problem looks like a nail. And when all you have is a fourteen-inch carbon steel butcher knife, even thought crimes come down to soft tissue and joints.

And the man who wielded it? She'd yet to hear him called by anything like a proper name, only titles. The Blade of God. The Lord's Butcher. The Master Carver. His rubber apron, dark green, looked like serious business. The expression on his face, anything but. He hardly seemed to be there at all, balding and bland, with a look in his eyes that in any other context might be called dreamy.

Mother's goons took a far more active satisfaction in their work. It required two of them to hold the game developer steady despite his struggles, and the third to stretch out his left arm, away from his sleeveless shirt. The Carver inspected the naked arm; wrapped a hand around the elbow; probed here and there with his fingers and thumb.

With a single deft stroke, jiggling slight changes of angle in the middle, he drew the knife all the way through, from the inside of the elbow to the outside. The holder let go of the wrist, and the lower arm dropped to the stage in a gout of blood. At first the developer scarcely realized it was gone, until he staggered and wailed while they held him upright as the tourniquet was applied and tightened.

At the uproar, Mother Constance motioned for quiet and calm. "Hard to watch, I know, I know!" she cried. "But necessary. It will make him think next time. It will make you all think. And thinking … saves … lives."

The Carver stepped back, placid, beatific, to await the next. And there would be more. He could do this all night and never tire. But how? He put some weight behind the stroke, but it was far from the brutal swing of a katana, broadsword, or scimitar. Just a handheld knife. She knew the legend, but still didn't comprehend the *how*.

Annie looked down toward the boy she'd tried to reassure, and found him frozen on his bench in a too-rigid posture and, she guessed, soft-focus eyes.

But he'd seen enough.

His name was Patrice, she learned the next afternoon, when he sought her out in the mess hall and plopped down across the table with his lunch going cold on his tray.

"Last night, you told me I'd be fine," he said. "Which meant a lot right then ... but how can you tell me that when you don't know? You can't promise me that, not after what I saw them do."

"Your first time," Annie said. "They don't do anything like that to you your first time through. They'd rather have you a fully so-called productive member of society than an amputee. So, first times, they're hoping it's enough to scare you. Scar you on the inside, maybe, but you go home whole."

"A scar on the inside is still a scar."

"Those buff out easier. Ask Mr. Game Developer which he'd rather go home with."

Patrice looked unconvinced but too tired to debate the point, his eyes ringed from lack of sleep. Same as everybody else's. Four hours a night, that's what you got here. It kept you alive, kept you sane, but softened you up, started opening cracks they could widen to get inside. Correction was a round-the-clock business, just about, from class to class, work detail to work detail, diatribe to mandatory diatribe. *Motherfuckers, just stop yelling at me for five minutes and let me catch a nap, and I'll be whatever you say.*

"How many times have you been through this?" Patrice asked.

"This is my fourth."

Those wide brown eyes popped wider. "Aren't you scared, that many?"

"Hell yes I'm scared. Every minute of every day, and in most dreams, too."

He peered deeper, hunting for the cracks. "You don't look it."

She glanced down at her plate of mac and cheese, then flashed him a grin. "Maybe the parts inside that would let it show are scarred over already."

"Innncorrrrigible," he said, playing with the word, stretching it out, a lilt in the middle. Not a bad impression of Mother Constance. "Why are you here? What's their problem with you?"

"Indecision, mostly."

His expression went adorably blank. "I don't follow."

"I like men. I like women, too. Seems a shame to have to decide. So I don't. But there's only one approved decision anyway, so it's not like they're badgering me to pick one or the other."

He gave her the first smile she'd seen out of him. "Then I've got you beat there. I'm all the way in the wrong. I just like guys."

"And I can completely understand that." Annie leaned closer. "I'm also one of those tree-hugging dirt worshipers they disapprove of so much. But I keep my feet washed, so I think I should get credit for that."

"Cleanliness, godliness, you totally should." Patrice gave her another once-over, as if he were a sketch artist tracking every detail. Maybe it was something he really did on the outside. He lingered at the top of her head. "You look like you should have dreadlocks."

"'Til about twenty-four hours ago, I did."

"They *cut them off?* I didn't think that's how it worked here, when they process you in."

Normally it wasn't. It wasn't like the Army, or some prisons, shaving you down. The goal with reeducation wasn't to erase your identity. They didn't want to draw a distinction between what you looked like in here and what you looked like on the outside. If they did, their theory went, you'd be more likely to backslide into your old ways once you started looking like your old self again.

But sometimes they just couldn't help themselves. Looking her over on intake—fourth time? Something needs to change here. One of them smirked and went for the clippers, tossing off a comment about the rats nest on her head, so mark it down as a hygiene issue. They made it sound like they were doing her a favor: *Foul thoughts find it easier to take root in such an untidy head.*

"I can still see them, almost. Your dreads," Patrice said. "Really, I can. It's how I thought they should be there in the first place. Big fat ones, weren't they?"

"Well. Bless your spooky little heart." She wanted to believe him. "You're like that experiment with the leaves."

He didn't know about it, so Annie shared as much as she remembered: a series of trials that suggested life, matter, organized itself around energy fields. The researchers had photographed tree leaves via spectrums of light human eyes didn't normally see, to reveal a glow in the shape of each leaf. When they snipped away a portion of the leaves and took new photos, the glow was still there, as if they could cut away the matter but couldn't break the field. The leaves still knew what they were meant to be.

Patrice hadn't eaten a bite yet, still sitting hunched over his tray and looking scared to get into what he really wanted to know.

"Who ... who *was* that guy last night?" His voice, quiet to begin with, dropped to a hush. "I wouldn't have ever thought it was possible, the way he did that. How easy it was for him. Like cutting through butter."

"Some real *Star Wars* lightsaber shit, isn't it?" she said. "About that ..."

Yes. About that.

Once upon a most ancient time in China, Lord Wen-hui stopped to watch the butchering of an ox and marveled at the display of skill he saw. Every move of Butcher Ding and his knife—rhythmic and fluid, free of hesitation—was like that of a ritual dance. And so, before the delighted gaze of his master, Butcher Ding did his dance that was not a dance, and a cascade of meat and bone fell away from the carcass.

None of which Annie had ever heard of until her second stint through correction. Not in any class, and not from Mother Constance's stage, but on the sly. Because people talked, people shared. Over a meal here, three seconds in a corridor there. They talked to make it through another day. They talked to better understand the enemy. You never knew when the softest whisper might land in just the right ear. Someone who needed to hear it; someone who might be in a position to do something more about it.

So on those occasions when Mother Constance extolled her praise for the Master Carver, saying he showed how even the teachings of godless lands could be turned toward the greater glory of God, there were those among the Disinvited who were onto her bullshit. They recognized the sources; understood what moved the man who whittled down the ability of so many to live the lives they wanted, or carved them out of life entirely.

As for Butcher Ding, and how he did it …?

He no longer saw oxen, no longer saw meat at all. His skill was so great he had transcended skill. Butcher Ding let his knife be guided by something beyond expertise; beyond even what he could be sure of knowing about any given carcass. Without thought, he followed nature's contours, let himself be guided by structure and cavities. Even in the densest joint there were spaces between, and the edge of his knife was honed to nothingness. He had but to slip the nothingness into the gaps, and as he worked it through, it would part the rest aside.

He did without having to force. He tried without trying. His hand, and the knife it held, simply followed the Way. In nineteen years, Butcher Ding had never needed to sharpen his blade, yet it remained as keen as it was when it had last left the grindstone.

And for Lord Wen-hui, life was never the same. Because at last he knew its most sublime secret.

So went the hours, and the days they made. Annie had been through this before, but it never got easier. The only easy day was yesterday. As the sleeplessness piled up, it got hard to tell which was worse: being screamed at, or being told by cooing voices how much she was loved. Was she really worthless, her existence an insult to the world? Or was there goodness in her worth saving, that yearned to be free of the shackles of her ignorance and sin? *Motherfuckers, make up your minds.*

They were all about family, but questioned how much your family could truly love you if they accepted you as you were. Real love meant judgment. Nurturing meant voicing objections. Benevolence and discipline went hand in hand. And family need never be permanent. An unsuitable family could be cast aside in favor of a new one, a family that would never hesitate to show you the Way.

They were all about love, too. They loved everybody in the abstract but hated individuals by the thousands. They were all about compassion for humanity but willing to see half of it dead, to leave more room for the other half to thrive, no longer disturbed by reminders of how degraded their fellows could be. They were all about the sacrifice most of all, as long as it was someone else.

Sometimes it was tempting to see it their way. Would it really be so awful a thing to renounce the past that had brought her here? She loved women as much as men, but had she ever found a woman she'd loved more than her own arms and legs? She loved the world and its elements—earth, air, fire, and water—and the trees that grew across its surface, loved them root, bark, and spore. Would it really be such a capitulation to pledge her devotion to their version of the god they said created it?

Go along to get along.

Go along to get some sleep.

Instead, she just kept going.

She caught up with Patrice whenever she could, but the schedules they kept everyone on were never less than erratic. A few minutes at mealtime, then she might not see him up close for two days. She worried. He wasn't made to last here. Annie knew a look of erosion when she saw it.

Early in the second week, he fell in beside her during one of the daily marches. She found this the strangest of the regimens. The guards would pick a couple hundred or so at random, then send them outside to trudge around the perimeter of the camp for an hour or two. Exercise, they called it.

Maybe it was. Or maybe it was actually to reinforce how isolated they were.

"Where are we? Do you know?" Patrice's voice was ragged and weak, just the way they liked it. "Where in the actual fuck *are* we?"

"I have no idea. It felt like it took about eight hours for me to get here, but I could be way off on that. And I don't know which direction it was."

Beneath the low and sullen clouds of a late autumn day, a sky that spit freezing rain, the camp was a cluster of buildings and lots, like a small army base. Beyond those was a double row of high fencing triple-crowned with vicious coils of razor wire. Beyond that were featureless plains and, in the farthest distance, what looked like a ridge of hills or mountains. Big sky country.

"I don't do well in places like this," he said. "If I don't have enough pavement and reflective glass around me, I get weird."

"There's an easy fix for that. Just break. Give 'em what they want for the next sixty, seventy years of your life. You'll never have to worry about this view again."

Wherever this was. Every camp she'd been in had taken varying numbers of hours to reach, riding blind like cattle in the back of a semi trailer after a night in a holding cell. Every camp different, and every camp the same, too, with a whole lot of empty waiting on the other side of the razor wire in case by some miracle you made it over. She supposed this was strategic. Liberators couldn't come for you if they couldn't pinpoint a moving target.

Sixty years ...? Patrice tried to get the words out but deflated halfway through.

"This can't last that long," he whispered. "It can't."

"Says who?"

March, two, three, four. Trudge, two, three, four. Maybe this wasn't exercise at all, but their idea of walking meditation. Around and around, contemplating your past, present, and alternate futures.

"I don't understand how this ... happened."

"You didn't see it coming? Not even in hindsight?" she said. "You must not have been catching your minimum daily dose of escalating ugly shit these last few years. You must not have noticed all those amateur goon squads getting away with it, before they got the chance to turn pro."

He bristled, and it was good to see. A little fight after all. "No, I did. I did. But I have rights. We have rights."

"Oh. Those. Well ... you got the right to remain silent. You got the right to be invisible. You got the right to be made an example of, if somebody decides they're sick of you being you. Those the rights you mean?"

Plod, two, three, four. Patrice didn't seem the type to cry alone. He needed somebody with him to let it out. He needed trust. Apparently he trusted her.

They had the right to an expedient death, too, and if they got it, they'd go to their unmarked graves never knowing who was behind it. The prevailing theory was that it wasn't the government, not directly; more likely some devil's bargain with a private contractor, free to do as they saw fit with maximum autonomy and minimum oversight. Pay us on time and we'll make a better world for you, and try to ask as few questions as possible ... because do you *really* want to know the answers? Some pols would, of course. Some would salivate over every gruesome detail, as long as they were assured it was the right people who were getting hurt.

Stumble, two, three, four. When they passed the rounded Quonset hut that served as the auditorium, her gaze lingered on the bin behind it, looking a bit like a dumpster, but it wasn't. Not with that biohazard logo and stenciled lettering on the side, marking it as medical waste.

If she looked inside, what would she see? A story for every severed piece, a life permanently altered. They'd kept the Carver busy on a nightly basis, letting it all accumulate in the cold before it would go to an incinerator. He lopped off the hands and arms of those who'd written criticism. He took legs from those who'd tried to mobilize. He sliced off ears that listened to the wrong words, cut out tongues that spoke them, peeled away tattoos deemed to defile the skin and offend the righteous eye. He left scars in place of pride—a cheek taken from a beautiful face, the Achilles tendons sliced from an athlete accused of being too boastful of how fast he could run.

Stand tall and keep going, two, three, four.

"I don't know what to do," Patrice whispered.

She scuffed along a few more steps before she spoke. "Here's one thought. Show 'em what they want to see. Contrition, they love that, and you've got the eyes for it. Get your freedom back. Then learn to hide. Look for a few others as scared as you. And if you see a chance to get away with the right kind of murder, take it."

He snorted a laugh, full of snot and doubt, as if she were talking about someone else, someone he could never be. "Contrition? When's yours gonna start showing?"

"I got no more contrite left in me. I'm done with that shit."

"Don't say that, you're scaring me. You're the only person here who will really talk to me."

They scraped a few more steps over the cold, hard dirt. "Look at me. What do you see? Can you still see where my dreads used to be?"

He flipped back that lank sweep of hair and peered at her with his bleary eyes. "A little. Some. But it's faded. A lot."

She believed him. Believed that he could see, somehow, past surface, to spirit. That he could see potential and promise; could see what had been beaten down and excised and negated, because something of it remained beyond the touch of blades.

"That's what I was afraid of," she said. "Fading. Like those leaves I told you about. They'd keep shooting pictures after they cut away the pieces. That glow, the field where the missing piece used to be? It wouldn't last forever. Give it time, it would fade back to match the new shape. I can't have that."

Whatever, two, three, four.

Even then, Annie supposed she knew there were eyes on her. Sensitive that way—some people were, had a primal awareness of being watched. Stick those grimy peepers and bad intentions in my field, you bet I'm gonna feel it.

The question was: How could you make that work for yourself?

So when they came for her at the end of the second week, all boots and body armor, she wasn't surprised.

When they locked her in a holding room for a few hours, she knew where this was heading. Fourth time through, she'd been on thin ice the whole time. Incorrigible. Her value, Mother Constance must have decided, had shifted, now worth less as a commodity on the outside and more as an example to the rest who would go back to it. Watch and learn, ye able-bodied. Teach your children the importance of obedience.

They were playing the long game here.

When they took her from the last little jail she would ever have to endure and escorted her onstage to meet the Carver, she thought of how things had changed in just two weeks. Gone was the horrified silence that met the making of a new example. Gone were the tears of shock, the moans of empathy. They booed and they jeered now. They gave back what was expected. She squinted into the lights hoping for a glimpse of Patrice, so she would know that they all couldn't mean it.

Use me, she thought.

And when they held her in place before the Carver, he was every bit as blandly blissful up close as he'd looked from farther away. Not a single thing about him she found interesting other than the lies he must've told himself.

Use me, she sent out, a prayer to whatever might be listening from the wild layers of the earth, the force that made trees grow and rocks congeal from sand and lava.

They stretched out her arm so the Carver could probe it with his fingers, seeking the spaces between, divining how the meat wanted to come apart.

Use me. I got hate enough in me for who's earned it and love enough for the rest. So use me.

She looked the Carver in the eye until he felt it, to seize his undivided attention.

"Most of me never wanted to get close enough to you to have words," she said, and her voice didn't quaver too bad. "But there was a little part of me that did. So's long as we're here ..."

He raised an eyebrow, just a degree, holding his blade at the ready, but stilled. He wanted to hear. He couldn't resist. This should be interesting.

"That Butcher Ding parable—yeah, we're onto you, we know what makes you tick—you got it wrong, took away all the wrong things," Annie said. "Just like you people always do."

His brow began to knit, a ripple of annoyance across the tranquil pool.

"Bet you didn't even know that, at the time the story came from, butchering oxen was a reviled profession. In everybody else's eyes, a man who did that was down with the lowest of the low. Didn't matter to Ding. He devoted himself to doing the best job he could.

Until it made him wise enough that even the lord of the land felt privileged to be his student for the day."

One of the guards snorted, impatient to get on with the good stuff. Pearls before swine, you know.

"It's not about the glory of mastery or setting yourself apart," she said. "It's about the raising up of the lowly, the despised. Because they got things to teach, too."

When his knife flashed, it still seemed to move in slow motion, as the edge honed to nothingness led the way through flesh and fat, severing nerves and slipping the gristle, finding its way through the gap between bones, then out the other side, as the chilled air flowed through her, touching places it had never been, and the lower half of her arm thudded to the stage.

Beyond the lights, they cheered.

There wasn't nearly as much blood as she would've expected two weeks ago. She'd either learned to control that much, or it wasn't her at all.

Use me.

She made her stand and looked the Carver in the eye until she saw all the rage behind it.

"Motherfucker, turn that knife on yourself next, why don't you," she said. "You think you're free of pride? You got more pride than anyone here."

He kept going, no stopping him now, and she held on, and onto as much, for as long as she could. His anger made him sloppy. She'd known it would.

What to call it now? Not waking up, certainly, nor coming to. Awareness, maybe that was the key. She was *aware*. In defiance of all the reasons she shouldn't be, a reason for every piece of her cut from the rest, she was once again aware.

But now it no longer felt localized, her head and maybe her heart, her gut. It was over there, in that first forearm to go. And over there in the corner, the upper arm that followed. There, too, in the arm taken straight from the shoulder. In the legs, from the severed knees to the bunions that were started to be a problem. She lay where they'd flung her, good riddance, and in every part of herself she was aware … and though in the dead of night it was purely dark inside the waste bin, it didn't matter. Not now. In a spectrum beyond the sight of human eyes—or most of them—every piece and scrap of her remained aglow with the memory of what she had been.

And she was not alone. Beneath her, around her, lay the cold fragments that had come before, many still fading, the rest gone out entirely. So many. Struggling to be heard, they knew their own.

Use me. All of them, close at hand, and farther away: *Use me. Use me. Use me.*

She began with herself, drawing herself back to wholeness, welding with hate, melting with love, until she was no longer aware of any distinction between what had been hers and what hadn't. They were all one now.

Use us.

As the first light of dawn began to line the gap between the lid and the lip of the bin, she threw it open like a hatch, and clambered out behind all her arms, then rose tall on her many legs, alert to the slightest sound with her myriad ears. All this extra bone, she would figure out the most punishing ways of wielding it as she went.

Bitch, make an example out of me, and I'll make sure you get back a nightmare.

She stooped to lower herself through the nearest doorway, so they could finally start dealing with what they had wrought.

Operations Other Than War

NADIA BULKIN

Noah Quint said that his father was a hero who had earned his medals protecting the freedoms of everyone who lived in New Birmingham in the war against Kursattar, and Noah Quint was right. His father came to his class to talk about the war and he was so noble, so calm and gentle with his rumbling voice and easy laugh. He was like every dad in every Christmas movie, the way he paused to check that his jokes were landing, when he clearly knew they were. He said it was important—very important—to know when and what to sacrifice.

Tom Mortensen's father had made a lot of sacrifices, or so his mother said. But then, his mother said a lot of things, especially on the phone with his grandmother. When Tom saw his father, he saw a man he wouldn't trust to protect anything or anyone, curled up like a conch shell, hands forever clenching a blanket beneath his chin as if he was the child afraid of the dark.

Tom's father spent most of his time in a medicated sleep. But when he was awake, Tom asked him about the war, and when Tom asked him about the war, his father spoke of a monster.

The monster was a giant. A mechanical giant like the kind in Iron Force that went to war against equally giant grotesque lizard-men. A giant with dead eyes and steel limbs the size of air tankers who could reach up and crush planes, who repelled missiles like a cow's tail swatting flies. Every time Tom's father shut his eyes, he said, he saw the monster's face rising out of the sea in a wash of froth, a face large enough to serve as a small helipad. The sound of its arrival, his father said, was the sound of the earth coming undone. Splitting open. Like a headache.

It confused Tom, because the mechanical giants he saw in Iron Force and other knock-off cartoons were always heroic—large, blocky heroes, wielding giant swords. They'd only been built that big because the villains they had to defend humans against were themselves so large, big enough to tear down bridges and knock over buildings. Fight fire with fire, the engineer characters always said, with brave determination. Those giants were called things like Earth's Defender. And Tom did not know why his father would be fighting against one.

"Did you fight against a giant monster in the war?" he asked Noah Quint's father.

"The enemy had some truly wild weapons," said Noah Quint's father. "Thank God our men and women were braver."

"So the monster was real?" Tom asked impatiently, and then the teacher said that was all the time they had for questions. But Tom saw Noah Quint's father giving him a stony look, the kind of look that he'd seen adults give each other when they were pissed but couldn't say so.

This confirmation served as padding when Noah shoved him while he was standing in line for the bus and said that his father was a drug-addicted loser who didn't know anything. Drug-addicted loser, he could believe. But Tom knew his father knew things. Only people that couldn't lie about the world's truth ended up like his father, held captive and soiled by their own thoughts in a dark room—or so his mother said. The liars, she said, ended up like General Quint.

By the time Tom was in college, the truth had come out—there were eyewitness accounts, declassified satellite images—that Kursattar had built an all-terrain defense system in the shape of a man. They called it SOLAT. Some technical acronym. They insisted that it was deactivated, as part of the peace treaty that they'd been made to sign. The U.S. military corroborated their account, promising that UN weapons inspectors were making regular checks on SOLAT. And then it was as if no one had been lying about anything. The existence of SOLAT became one of many things that had only been kept secret as a matter of national security, which was the one great reason that could never be questioned.

SOLAT had been forcibly disabled, they said, by an ingenious young pilot named Amy Dee, who figured out the machine's weak spot and crashed her airplane straight into it. No suicide dives had ever worked on SOLAT before, they said—they did not elaborate on how many had been tried—but Amy Dee's did. And then, like a spring from a stone, a monument to Amy Dee was unveiled overnight: The Purity of Sacrifice, it was called. Tom looked it up online. She looked like a child in that marble. But she was a soldier like his father.

Before it had a name, Tom used to have nightmares about the giant. He'd be on a boat, slowly rocking toward some lush green island, when the skies would blacken and the earth would moan and the water would rise to the height of mountains until, finally, dropping like a curtain in a thunderous crash, revealing a wall of metal still steadily rising behind. He assumed these nightmares had been passed down from his father, like his high school girlfriend had inherited her mother's migraines.

So Tom was anxious to tell his father he wasn't crazy, to vindicate his fears, even though his mother said never to raise the war with him at all. Tom hoped that by giving it a name, he'd be able to rid his father of the hold the monster had on him. SOLAT was just another weapon, after all, like stealth planes or weaponized drones. Nothing nightmares should be made of.

"You were right, Dad," he whispered in his father's dark bedroom. "It was real. Its name was SOLAT." And it was then, when he heard the name, that his father started to howl.

The bomb in his father's soul was not deactivated, even if SOLAT was. Some things, Tom's mother said, were so contrary to the way of God that there is no amount of truth that can make them light. Black holes. Which made Tom wonder if his father, too, was one such abyss. If that room that he never left anymore wasn't just another swallower of light.

Tom meant to heed his mother's words and his father's darkness, to avoid SOLAT and the war while he was at school. But he kept fixating on mentions of poor defeated Kursattar—the church kids asking for aid after yet another natural disaster, the food truck out by the gym. And he'd watch new movies with giant robots—except now, the giant roots were no longer heroes like Earth's Defender but villains, killer contraptions made by mad scientists that threatened the freedoms of little towns like New Birmingham—and remember when those robots wielded swords of glory, held high and gleaming above their heads.

So he took a class with Professor Gordon Chalmers on the present and future world order, and waited anxiously for the syllabus to turn to Kursattar. To the war. To its weapons.

"It wasn't a war," said Professor Chalmers when a student asked him what lessons future war-planners could draw from the experience. "It was an assault. And we were the assailants."

Assault. Such a loaded word. Assault, an attack with the purpose of incapacitation. Assault that was more one-sided than a fight, or a war. An operation other than war. Tom had attended enough political science lectures, by then, to have heard about those—assassinations, extractions, sanctions, embargoes. Not all displays of power are war, even if all you see from the headlines are two giant beings whaling at each other, like a pair of Punch and Judy puppets.

We were the assailants. Tom thought of his father creeping through the bushes, black paint on his face, rifle in hand. "My father was in the war," Tom was used to saying, but if he wasn't in a war then what was he doing in Kursattar? Some nights when Tom couldn't sleep, he'd start seeing the monster's ghost again: the face rising, breaking the water. A giant metal body, moving without a heartbeat. The realization that the pounding that sounded like the very pillars of the earth falling was in fact his own heartbeat.

"He was their hero," Professor Chalmers said of SOLAT. "Their defense system. No, more accurate to say their self-defense system.

It's inappropriate to call him—and yes, I said *him*—a weapon. He was built to be an umbrella."

Sometimes, Tom saw Professor Chalmers in his drab, brown coat walking past the young anti-imperialists agitating for the end of unfair trade practices. With his glasses slipping down his nose, he looked like one of those engineers in Iron Force who had to decide when to activate Earth's Defender, who ground their teeth and said, on every episode, *"This is our last chance."*

A semester before graduating, Tom finally went on a date with Vida Mair. They had been in the same discussion section of Political Economy and she was very sweet and smiley, but always seemed to have somewhere better to be. Always rushing ahead of him. When they ran into each other at dorm parties she was a little more chatty, a little more languid, but still folded in on herself. She always needed to care for a drunk friend, or call home. She was here on a student visa for a reason, and that reason was not love.

But they were both stuck on campus during their final winter break—him because he did not want to be in a decrepit house with his father the black hole, her because she did not celebrate Christmas anyway—and one day after walking her home from a library study session, Tom convinced her to get dinner with him at the cute little Chinese hole-in-the-wall down the road that Tom thought had the best dumplings in town.

Vida was small and dark and pretty, and looked nothing like the girls Tom grew up with in New Birmingham. She could carry on conversations about medical dramas over iced coffee like she was just another co-ed in blue jeans, but she was not; there was a panoramic, technicolor otherness about her that suffused every square inch of her skin. Vida had seen things with her black eyes few girls on campus could imagine, even if they cited it in a paper. Vida was the world—weather-beaten, delicate, colorful, hurt, wronged. And just like men are driven to climb mountains, there was a distance between them that Tom always found himself wanting to cross, because he was from New Birmingham, and Vida was from Kursattar.

She did not talk much about it, even when he asked her direct questions. All he picked up through their first month of dating was that she was from the capital city and her father was some kind of businessman and she had a younger brother who had been sent away to boarding school. She was quick to insist that she had not struggled like the children in those sad charity posters—her home had not been destroyed, she had not starved. But she did not like to talk about her mother's death, or why she had not had the meningitis vaccine. She did not like to talk about why her father decided to send her to attend college in the land of the victorious enemy.

He asked her sometimes: Did she resent Americans? Was she homesick? Was it strange for her to walk the streets of the country that had defeated hers? Because it would be strange for him, in her position. Professor Chalmers had assigned him plenty of post-colonial theory by then, and he had read enough of it to understand post-war humiliation. He was proud of the fact that he tried to be considerate of it with Vida. To not take it into bed with them.

But Vida never seemed to find it strange. "There's opportunity here," she'd say flatly, as if refusing to see anything but opportunity. Opportunity was her answer for everything. Opportunity was why she was majoring in economics. Opportunity was going to save the world. It seemed woefully naïve. A product of her privileged upbringing, he supposed.

"Why are you always trying to make me angry?" Vida asked once. "You want to see me lose my temper? I know we lost the war. You don't have to rub it in."

"Of course not," Tom said, surprised, although he did in fact question why she wasn't more angry at the likes of him—if it was just the gentleness of her spirit or the brutal rationality of "opportunity" or what. The poor wounded doe. "I just want to understand. I'm just curious."

"So I'm a curiosity," Vida said, shaking her head. After that she was cold to him for several weeks, and only when the thaw gave way to springtime did she return one of his calls.

"I want to explain," he said. "I was told nothing about Kursattar when I was growing up. My father came back terrified of some monster that guarded the island, that's all I knew."

For an uncomfortable moment she was quiet, so still that Tom had the uncomfortable sensation that time had stopped around them, frozen Vida on the other side of the gulf. "Some monster," she repeated, smiling sadly. That was when Tom remembered, too late, what Professor Chalmers always said—that SOLAT was Kursattar's hero. *As much a hero as our fighter jets.*

Professor Chalmers was off in the Caucuses, collecting stories for a book on cargo cults. Tom had tried to beg his way onto the trip, but Chalmers opted for a PhD student instead.

Tom apologized. "Your self-defense system, I mean. The thing that keeps—*kept*—you safe." A little chill bubbled down his throat at the implication: Vida wasn't safe.

"He is a monster," Vida said, quietly. "And he also kept us safe." Then she straightened her spine and added: "But he's deactivated. They made sure of it. It's for the best."

"So it really is that dangerous," Tom said. Professor Chalmers always said that SOLAT's capabilities were overblown, that its power was largely symbolic, the rare force capable of generating both inspiration and existential fear.

"Nothing scares the world more than a little backwater country with a weapon," she said, in the first time he'd ever hear a hint of national pride in her voice. There were always rumors, always quashed, that the United States was trying to build its own SOLAT, stronger and faster and equipped to throw American-made Hellfire missiles. Religious groups were always very vocal in their objections, threatening to withhold support for any candidate who did not foreswear the idea. Idolatry, they called it. God did not suffer cheap imitations.

He might have said something else, but Vida turned to look at the television. Smoothly turned her smooth, luminous face toward the great blue light, as if swiveling her head on an axis.

Vida did not want Tom to go to Kursattar. They weren't dating by then, so she had very little say over his decisions, but when he told her over a weekend coffee, she was still unafraid to show her displeasure. "Why would you go there?" she asked, "What are you looking for?"

But those were the very questions he was going there to answer. He did not know why the coordinates he saw when he closed his eyes were Kursattar's, why he felt compelled to see if the rumors on the dark web were true and SOLAT lay defused on a beachside military base. His mother thought it was perverse, an attempt to confront—or maybe *thank*—the thing that broke his father. But he didn't think there was that sort of emotion attached to it. Nothing so personal. It was just so fucking unbelievable, the way he imagined people must have felt when they first discovered dinosaurs to be real. That the immense horror of this thing had broken his father's brain only made it that much more compelling.

"I don't know what I'm looking for," he told Vida, who sighed and sipped. She was working at the World Bank now, calculating the aid that should be allotted to countries like Kursattar. The sort of thing that Gordon Chalmers would have said was just another arm of empire, had he come back from the Caucuses alive. Now that everyone was dead, the world was an untapped oil field. Full of potential, yet barren. Tom left for Kursattar the week after.

He arrived with his passport and his credit cards and a few changes of clothes into a roiling pit of humidity and humanity. His passport earned him no sour looks, no visa trouble—maybe not in and of itself surprising, since the United States was busy jawing about the respect it was due, trying to goad its rivals into a missile shoot-out—but he almost wished it had registered more of a reaction. He wished he saw more fight from a vanquished people. More resentment. It was the same gnaw he'd felt since he put on pounds the summer before junior high, came looking for Noah Quint, and discovered that the jackass had moved away.

Instead, he saw something else. Indifference. Disregard. The small immediacy of life.

The country was struggling without SOLAT. Without the monster's protection, there was nothing it could do to make assailants stand down, to extract better terms from the IMF, to kick out predatory corporations, to kill any foreigners who brought any drugs within its zero-tolerance borders, free of all but the softest of pressures. Now Kursattar fluttered in the breeze, frayed and faded. The over-inflated currency—tens of thousands for a taxi—still boasted of their long-gone days as a force of global rebellion—the proletariat pride, the forward motion—but that was the stuff of fantasy now. The old factories that had welded together the parts that would make SOLAT had been shuttered and condemned, if not torn down for mall space.

Roadside vendors with missing limbs did still sell vintage posters issued by the defunct propaganda office, and Tom bought several to unroll in the privacy of his hotel room, but the SOLAT that towered in the corner of those posters was so unlike the old satellite images. That SOLAT was mechanical, an armored soldier blown up to a thousand times the size of the fleshy, disposable kind—faceless, skinless, inorganic. The SOLAT in those posters was just a very large kindly guardian, one who might scoop up a drowning child on the beach. It certainly had a face.

Kursattar's national history museum claimed that SOLAT's menace had been greatly exaggerated by a hysterical Western media. One plaque even said SOLAT had been the size of a clocktower, not a skyscraper. Was it even real, Tom wondered, or had his father lost his mind over a walking clocktower? Maybe his poor old man had always been feeble-minded; he was too young to remember otherwise. Or maybe the only "monster" his father had seen in Kursattar was the one in the mirror. He'd never know what his father had done after his boat made landfall.

While Tom was sitting near Ode to Freedom—the last remaining tribute to SOLAT—eating shaved ice and feeling sorry for himself, he was approached by a local middle-aged man who asked him if he had come to Kursattar to see SOLAT.

"Yeah, I saw your statue," Tom said, glancing over at Ode to Freedom.

"Not the statue. The real thing. It isn't junked, you know."

A beat of hope thumped in his heart, but he quickly tried to collect himself. "I know it isn't," said Tom. "It's deactivated, it isn't junked." Did this man think he knew so little about that legend-ary Kursattar pride, whatever magic they'd cultivated that gave them the nerve to build a steel giant to ward off the American empire? Oppressive dictatorship or not, even an American had to admire that sort of daring. "They would never have just junked it."

"That's right, we wouldn't have." The man tilted his head thoughtfully, as if to look at Tom in a marginally different half-light. "Would you like to join a pilgrimage to see it?"

By then, his father was dead; General Quint was as well. Only one of those men got a motorcade through downtown, but he tried not to let this bother him. What mattered was that all the barriers of that old reality were lifting. It was nice to think that he might yet have the chance to live in a world that was still in the making instead of a page in a textbook, a world that breathed and moved as it willed. A world that warred. Was that why he loved SOLAT so much? Because its war gave him meaning? Because he still needed Earth's Defender to be good?

Time to start the world over. He stood up, crumpled up the cup of melted shaved ice in his hand, and said, "Yeah."

SOLAT was as horrible as it had been in his dreams. Not the thoughtful daydreams of his post-doc days—not that one dream he used to have about going home to visit his father and seeing a small fallen robot lying in his bed, like a silver mannequin—but the visceral nightmares of his childhood. The face rising from the water. The sound of the splitting earth.

The pilgrimage had only taken a day, but it had felt like a week. On the bus there were grandparents with grandchildren, couples holding hands, solo travelers who spoke to no one and stared out the window with tears in their eyes. Tom plugged in his earbuds and listened to the new president promise a new world on Voice of America. He hadn't voted for this platform, so he didn't know what this meant—it seemed to include a lot of deployed warships—but the hint that the world was about to come alive, even in a terrible fashion, still gave him a blood-rush. Though he'd originally intended to catch up on sleep, he felt every minute that passed.

In the evening, they reached a western beach, and there they walked through fields of weeds toward a military base that lay dark and quiet by the surf, a long bullet-shaped tomb. A guard was at the gate to greet them and take their payments—hundreds of thousands this time—and absently jerked his gun at Tom. "What are you doing here, American?"

Why don't you want to see it, he always asked Vida. With her back to him, her voice always answered: *Why do I want to see a thing that will guarantee a war if it ever wakes up?*

Why do you want to see it?

The guard took them into the base. Around him the other pilgrims were starting to weep, to sing, to take out little white sticks that he quickly realized were chalk. More than a few times Tom felt himself tripping over his own feet, only to be buoyed forward by the push of the murmuring crowd. He knew in his gut that to see where this crowd was taking him was to see the thing that he had come across the world to find, so he tried to answer Vida's question with what little time he had left before everything changed. But his mind was completely blank, save for a deep demand from every blood cell of his body for everything to change.

He didn't know what he expected to see behind the last door that the guard unlocked. Maybe a vaguely humanoid submarine submerged at the bottom of an Olympic swimming pool. Or a kingly statue that didn't look like it could ever have moved at all, carved in the likeness of a paladin and lying in state. Possibly nothing. But he did not expect to see a giant steel man kneeling as in prayer. With knees to floor and head to knees, SOLAT was perfectly folded up in what Tom recognized from Vida's yoga classes to be "child's pose." The world's largest and oldest child, now rendered at rest. Passive. Sleeping. A dead battery. But that was the difference between man and machine, wasn't it: A battery could be recharged. Dead to the world and yet …

Humming. An unmistakable steady hum of a machine that was not actually off.

Tom looked at the guard. The guard looked back at him, across the same stretchy bridge of indifference that he had never managed to cross with Vida. There was so much he wanted to ask, but he knew those eyes. He knew now that they'd never open for him.

The other pilgrims were using their chalk to write on SOLAT's legs, the only part of his enormous body that they could reach. Tom had brought no chalk and was in too much shock to ask for one, but one small child saw him standing, looking lost, and gave him a stick of chalk as her grandparents carried her away. It was with this tiny blessing that he walked up to SOLAT, Earth's Defender, and reached out to touch it. He tried to make out some of the other messages etched, weakly, into the giant's skin, but he could only make out stray words in the steel. "Health" and "job" and "love." The small immediacy of life, on so large a being.

Part of him wanted to scrawl a screeching obscenity. Maybe "USA," just to get a reaction. He had a fantasy of waking it to life with his rage, watching it lumber to its feet, looking for enemies to crush. Swimming to New Birmingham, leveling the whole town flat. Maybe he'd run out to meet it before it disappeared into the water, wave his hands, yell, *take me*.

Kill me.

But he decided he didn't want to die. So, instead, he searched for the great, charred wound where Corporal Amy Dee had crashed her plane, and wrote his father's name upon SOLAT's ankle. Then he leaned his head against SOLAT's skin, and listened for the sound of his heart.

One Day of Inside/Out

LINDA D. ADDISON

Most believed it was a special effects hack,
    videos of people shrieking in pain while
    skin flash-burned to muscle and bone, within
    seconds healed to grey, leathery epidermis,
leaving horrible, naked creatures in human shape.

Behind locked doors, others' skin instantly flayed
    then closed in thick ropey scars, resulting
    in living things with useless hands and feet,
    writhing on tiled, carpeted, wood floors,
mouths twisted open, incapable of denying their past.

Cameras dropped, onlookers froze as leaders, court
    rooms, events witnessed eruptions of flesh,
    splitting with mottled purple infections, leaving
    limbless nightmares behind, out-of-control egos,
now resembling squirming, hideous movie creations.

No one knows what caused the Day of Reckoning,
    permitting remorseless ugly insides to erupt out,
    carving deep in dermal stratum repercussions of
    previous actions. No science could fix the living
malformations that remained—proof of free will misused.

One Last Transformation

JOSH MALERMAN

Full moon means you gotta decide.

Always been that way; that's how it is. Of course you know it's coming and you got time to make up your mind, but, just like the coat you think you're gonna wear to the party isn't the coat you wear to the party, you don't really know what you're gonna do 'til the night of.

I've transformed into a wolf six hundred and thirty-four times. From about age nineteen into the sixty-one years since, I've decided yes much more often than I haven't. Still, there's close to a hundred moons I've said no to, a thing I take great pride in. Am I slowing down? Do I say no more often than I used to? Damn right I'm slowing down. So are you. Don't matter how old you are, you're not as quick as you were last year. And changing ain't as easy as jogging a lap around a track. It's something more like exerting yourself to the brink of insanity, pushed as far as you can think, 'til you worry your bones might break, your brain might pop, you might actually lose something in your head. But once you decide to do it, you're a different person than you were when you hadn't yet made up your mind. Something like the alcoholic who says you know what, one more, and, for a while at least, believes he's made the right decision. That's how it is, how it's always been. I've never known a wolfman to chain himself up or lock himself into a room, even if I've only known a dozen or so other wolves in my eighty years of living. If you decide to do it, you're doing it. And you're temporarily insane by that choice. You feel thirty, fifty years younger. Your hair feels fuller, your body feels tighter. You actually crack a smile. Cause you know what's coming, for better or for worse.

It's like falling in love. Falling in love with the moon.

Every time.

We're not pack animals for this very reason. Who seeks love in a pack? And just because the inner half of us travels that way doesn't mean the outer, the man, feels any loyalty to that instinct. We're about as loner as it gets, I'd say, and the locales in which I've crossed paths with others were as remote as any you're liable to find on the planet. Saw one across a tundra once, he on all fours, me on the same, two silhouettes feasting on villagers, and all we did then was nod. Not a word. Not a growl. Not a howl. I didn't look for him in town the next day and I'm sure he didn't look for me either. Same with the one I ran into—physically ran into—in the northern forests of Canada, way up, chasing a young man who'd decided to write about roughin' it. I know what the man was up to because I took the time to read what he'd written after I swallowed the fingers he'd done the writing with. But before catching him, I chased him. And as I chased, I took turns in the woods, quiet as I could bring myself to be, too quiet perhaps because the other didn't hear me and he must've been thinking the same way cause I didn't hear him any either. We rammed heads out there. The clunk alone shoulda sent the writer into hiding. But I suppose he took the sound for a natural wonder. The other and I exchanged a look. I didn't piss any territorial stamp and neither did he. I believe his head got the worst of it and, without any exchange of words, certainly no how-do-you-do, he went his way and I continued on mine. Did I wonder what food he found that night, under that northern moon? Only insomuch as one fisherman contemplates whether or not the dots in the distant boat got anything of their own. No more.

We don't travel in packs.

And I've no idea how many of us are out there.

I can guess, maybe. Based on news reports and stories and just how afraid people actually are of the werewolf. This changes through the years, different when I was twenty. People are piqued again nowadays, after a long period of not worrying so much at all. I don't know enough about the real world to tell you why. Maybe it has something to do with feeling like you know all there is to know or feeling like there are still the unknown, elusive truths to be had.

But people are scared of us again. Just enough so anyway. You can see it in their eyes, in the way they look over their shoulder a minute or so after laughing about the idea of a werewolf. I bring it up all the time. Usually in hotel lobby bars. I'll make a joke of it to the man or woman sitting next to me, say something like, *Not unless a werewolf transformed in here and ate us all.* Without fail, people laugh. But some, more recently now, they'll look at you for a second, silently asking, *What did you go and say something like that for?*

I like scaring people. It's something of a snack, you could say, compared to the feast I have to decide on every month of my life. Scaring people is fun. And any werewolf who tells you he or she isn't in the scaring business, that it doesn't feel good to see true horror in the eyes of the to-be-feasted-upon is lying. How many have I killed? Every moon I've changed but one. One unfathomably hungry night in which my stomach became something with teeth, it seemed, like it had begun eating the rest of me from inside. But that one horror-show night aside, I've killed under every moon. That means I've seen the eyes of every one of them, as they realized my kind are real, as they realized, too, they themselves had reached the end of things. Most look to your claws first, perhaps determining the odds. In my case, they almost all look to my chest, to the name there, my name, tattooed fifty-three years ago in Finland, a drunk thing I did to remind myself I'm more human that wolf. Way I saw it, on the nights I had to decide, I'd go check myself in the mirror. Read my own name on my chest. *Johnny.* Remind myself to consider the moon, not to rush. But I know now that doesn't work. And the only thing that tattoo added was people knowing the name, the human name, of the creature that killed them.

I don't feel like a Johnny anymore. Don't feel like a Jonathan either. Feel more like a J. That's right, J Dennis Allan. Old enough to go by initials if only because my life, and the guilt inherent, has chipped away at the very letters that must look so powerful and gigantic on my wolf's chest as I rise to full height before the people I kill.

So it's up to you, see? Up to me, anyway. My kind. And ain't that the kicker? Ain't it cruel? Not only is that monthly carrot wagged in front of you, not only does it feel good to change, to do it, to kill, but then you don't even get the consolation of saying you had no choice. You can't shrug your shoulders and carry on, believing you're a good man who happens to be more than a man. Nope. I'm responsible for every one of those deaths. For having acquiesced. For having said yes to over six hundred moons.

I met a man once, long time ago, much older man, who told me he'd figured out how to say no every time. This man I met on the tracks, train-hopping from Detroit, Michigan to Seattle, Washington. That's where he had his mind set to go. Told me he'd heard of others like him out there. Men and women who had figured it all out. He told me it didn't get any easier month to month, as it should have (his words, and I agree), he said a day didn't go by when he didn't thirst a little for the blood in the bodies he passed. But he cited "moments of clarity," see, brief bursts throughout those same days in which he understood, wholly, that he was *good*. I asked him if it was worth it, briefly believing himself to be good versus satisfying that everlasting love for the moon? He didn't answer. Said he didn't know. But he told me I ought to go with him to Seattle. And I thought about it. All the way into the Dakotas I thought about going the distance with this man, meeting the others he said he heard of. I thought about learning from him, learning more, getting myself together like he had. But day before the moon of that month, I snuck off the boxcar in the early, dark hours. He noticed me at the car's ledge and called to me from the recessed shadows. He said,

It's not too late to change, Johnny.

But I knew it was. I knew there was no way on heaven and earth that I could refuse this moon with a mind to refuse every one to come. I leapt from that train, hitting gravel hard enough to strain a shoulder, an injury that persisted for weeks, but that seemed to clear up just in time for the moon after that one.

And as goes the man in the car, Angelo Hanks, I never forgot him. Never forgot a word he said. And so he was fresh in my mind when, six years later, I saw his picture on the television set. Saw that he'd been arrested in Tacoma, Washington for having tore a woman's arms from her abdomen, for having eaten half her legs.

This from one who'd figured it out.

The report said the woman survived. Do you believe that? And do you think Angelo Hanks still lives guilt-free?

It's amazing how news works, you know, how you might feel strongly one way or another about a tragedy but if the same tragedy happens to you, you suddenly relate to a different song. I suppose you could say I've been able to live with myself because this is myself. And isn't that what any violent man or woman can say? Wolf or not-wolf? Isn't that the argument being made in a thousand apartments in a thousand cities right now … men and women running for the brandy in the cupboard, crying out,

This is me, dammit. ME.

Yep. Feels horrid to admit it now, but that's been me my whole adult life. For good reason, some might say, as I've lived through extenuating circumstances. But again, that decision thing …

Full moon means it's up to you.

I feel compelled to tell you about last night. That's right, my own story, as recent as it gets. I won't tell you where I am now. For obvious reasons, I'd like to keep that to myself. But the thing is, I'd been telling myself I'm too old to transform for a long time now. And these days I say no as often as I say yes. These days my head hurts worse.

So do the thoughts, the memories of what I've done.

I gave it up. Last month. I told myself that was it as, the day after, my body felt as though I'd been in a fight. Even my bones felt sore, bones that have no nerve endings of their own. My chest hurt and my breathing was labored and, if I'm honest, I started thinking about death. I'm an old man, you see? An eighty-year-old werewolf walking the roads of small town X____, muscled, sure, full head of hair, yep, but wrinkled and white as the next one. I know most people think I'm a Navy man, and maybe the tattoo on my chest, visible through the tank top that is my only shirt these days, adds to that. Or maybe it's the look in my eyes, not of having survived war but violence nonetheless. People can tell, see. You're all much smarter than you think you are. Here's a tip: If you see a stranger in town, man or woman, and you find yourself thinking of the wolf, chances are your instincts are right. There's a wolf in town.

You can tell by the coupling of the violence and the guilt. Navy man doesn't have that the same way.

Did I tell you I killed a schoolteacher in Ohio in 1965? That I tore her face from her head and sent it spinning through the sky until it landed upon a knot in a tree, the bud of the trunk through the eye socket? I left it there. Even the day after, having changed back, I left it there.

I understand why we kill, but why do we carry out these smaller cruelties, these mean details on the way? I left the schoolteacher's face on the tree just as I left the father of three's head on the roof of his car in Indiana. I tore a young woman from a park bench in New Mexico as the man she sat with knew not what to do. I squatted in a field in Vermont, waiting for the same hippies who had invited me to the outdoor party not two days before. I waited in the kitchen of an old woman, older than I am now myself, and when the woman entered the room and saw the beast I am, I showed little mercy, tearing first the photos that hung on the wall above the sink, as if letting her know that her life was over, set to be erased, chronologically from the past up to now.

Why?

It's the demon in us, Angelo Hanks said on that train. The wolf is not only addicted; the wolf is unkind. And the reason we abide, Angelo said, his voice rocky from the speed of that train, is because the wolf has convinced the man there is more depth in the taboo than the accepted. But is this true, Angelo asked? Is the guilt that follows more profound, more telling, more of a teacher, than the joy of turning it away? I asked him if it was a matter of maturity, him being much older than I was at the time. He considered this, for an hour I'd say, silent in the black corner of the car. Then he told me something that's followed me to this day. Perhaps it's why I've decided to quit.

The body grows old. Philosophy matures.

I guess that meant it was up to me. And isn't that the whole of the werewolf existence? All always ... *up to me?*

Full moon means you gotta decide. That also means you got the days between the moons to think. Here you weigh what you've done, often fooling yourself into believing you may as well continue the carnage, if only to prove to yourself that this is who you are, and there ain't no stopping it. Because if you *did* stop ... wouldn't that mean there was something to quit? And wouldn't that then imply what you were doing before was a terrible thing to do? I don't need to know other wolves intimately to know that half the reason they sally into the swampy shadows under the bright midnight sky is because *not* doing it would be admitting *wrongdoing*. And the wrong-doing of a wolf is a lot worse than yours.

So we keep going.

Until, perhaps, a certain maturity *does* arrive. See, I think Angelo Hanks was wrong when he finally changed his mind and said maturity was in the mind of the beholder. I think it does come. It's come to me. And if I'm honest with myself, and therefore honest with you, I'll admit I'd been wanting to quit the life for a long time now. Ten years? Yeah. About that. But quitting takes time, you know. Especially quitting something you've long believed to be *you.*

Last month, I quit what was me. A particularly messy scene not a hundred miles from where I stand now. And because I quit, that put a spotlight on last night.

The full moon last night.

And full moon means you gotta decide. Every time.

Why was I so confident I'd quit? Was it because I'd said no to full moons before? I suppose it was something like that. Angelo has been on my mind a lot lately, despite his ignoble end. Something like that, too.

Time was up, far as I could tell, despite the fact that I'd noted the nightly routine of a farmer named Ivan, a young man, the head of a young family, who walked to and from town about an hour after midnight, every night, in order to retrieve fresh water from the town bar as the well out by Ivan's farm had gone bankrupt.

Now hear me out. I understand that my watching him was a bad idea. That my knowing his routine by heart was even worse. But haven't you heard of the man who quit smoking by keeping cigarettes in the breast pocket of his shirt? Way he saw it, that horrid desperation, that feeling of being so far from what he longed for, would never come to pass. Rather, it was right there, at his fingertips if he so desired. And while desire it he did, he could wait, knowing where it was.

You see? Different ways of doing things is all.

I knew where Ivan was. Every night. It got to the point where I could play drums on my thighs to the sound of the water rocking in the wood bucket he carried back to his farm, a gift from the town bar. Water to start Ivan and his family's every day.

I don't know the name other wolves have for this process, Angelo and I didn't speak of it, but "stakeout" certainly works. How many had I spied on? How many lives have I known in this way? Did I tell you that the schoolteacher once sat in a chair in the woods and prayed to God for money? Did I tell you that a woman in Louisiana walked her cat on a leash the same six blocks every night until the night she met me under a moon so gorgeous I think of her still?

You get to know the routines like most people know the traffic lights, the street names, the signs. To us, it's the routines that make up the town. Not the laws.

So what if I knew the owl would hoot twice before Ivan's shoes could be heard in the distance? So what if I knew that same owl would hoot a dozen more times before Ivan could be heard return- ing, the water sloshing in rhythm with those shoes? And so what if I knew the owl would catch, at last, the mouse he'd been waiting for just as Ivan went out of earshot again, as I, eighty years old and sore from crouching in the tall grass beside the road, finally stood up to see the kill?

I'd already quit as far as I was concerned. I'd already given up the life, my life, the life that, at times, was as profound, inversely, as Angelo's descriptions of "brief joy." The first step to quitting is wanting to do so, so they say. And I was well past wanting.

My body said no. My mind said no more. I was done.

Then, last night. The test, one might call it, though I don't like the idea of either passing or failing the moon. It's a hard thing to explain, that bit there, but I imagine it'd be something like putting a score on your love life. Can you quantify how you've fared in love? Can you say whether or not you've won or lost, day to day, month to month? If you keep a record, that's on you. But me? I'm elastic in my feelings for the moon. My nature won't debase her with a number.

I'd already told her I was finished. In that same tall grass, as Ivan sloshed home the night before last night, I stood and turned my face to the moon. Face, not snout, a rare sight for her to see.

Thank you, I said, *for all you've given me. Thank you for the virility, the action, the blood. Thank you for the feasts that perpetuated my life, that brought me sustenance in a way no restaurant menu and no home cooking could fulfill. Thank you for the chase, the hunt, the run. Thank you for the light to see by, the slants of glorious reflected unseen sun.*

For, in an effort to wean himself off the moon, Angelo proposed that what we really worship is the sun. Why, isn't it the light of the latter that guided our hunts? I smiled at this attempt, me in shadows, sensing Angelo might not find peace in Seattle, the way he was talking in Illinois. Because I knew (as every werewolf must know) that it wasn't the light we idolized, but the face suspended in the sky, the eyes and chin, the nose and snout and teeth, there floating in the darkness, so big and profound that it denied the sun, that it *refused* the sun, *using* it for us below, taking something so kind and, by way of repurposing it, exploiting the darkness therein.

Don't you know, sun worshipers? Haven't you heard? The wolfman hunts by the same light you dance to.

I love you, I told her. But the truth of it is, each moon is her own. And while I've loved over six hundred, I'd already decided to turn my back on this one. Still, isn't that some form of love? Perhaps the highest. To resist killing in her name. Bound to her forever, for her being the one you quit by.

I thought of my parents then, them being the only real coupling I'd ever bore witness to, never having human, daily love of my own. They loved, oh did they love. Uninterrupted, as they never knew the beast they'd birthed.

I left home three years prior to my first transformation (oh, what a moment, oh, what an era). I could feel the horror on its way. At first it confused me. How could I not wonder at the coming monster that had sprung from them, they being so honest, so mindful, so dear? I was far from them for my first change. Alone in a bathroom, if you must know. And, in the coming months, I snatched more than my share of lovers without once thinking of what the same fate would mean to my mother or father. I can still hear one woman calling,

Gene? Gene?? GENE?

But Gene was deep in the dark of night by then.

I can still see the horror in all of their eyes, scanning the horizon for their other half, so recently by their side. Perhaps the smell of fur kept them searching. Probably they knew something much worse than abandonment had occurred.

Is what I did to them worse than abandonment? Or am I now doing worse to the moon?

These thoughts and more, last night, a night of a moon.

Poor Ivan, the farmer, with three mouths to feed. Yes, I knew his family, by sight, as I followed him the first night I heard him, followed him all the way home. There he had a wife and a daughter, a dog and two cows, a goat. I kept Ivan in my breast pocket, so to speak, within reach.

Now, as you know, I've turned down moons before. So why should this one be any different? Is perspective, point of view, so profound a thing, even to he who is guided by the body, the change, the thirst? I wasn't worried. I was sad. Yes, me, eighty years old and weeping for the life I'd left behind. For behind it truly was, even as, last night, I crouched under that moon I'd said goodbye to and waited for the sound of Ivan's shoes, the empty bucket in his hands.

Do you find me foolish? Do you think me so bad?

I've been foolish before. I snatched a man from a parade. Desperate, I was only twenty-two and he not much more than that. Nobody heard him screaming as I stole him from the very back of the crowd and dragged into an alley. I hardly heard him, what with the music. Last night, Ivan's shoes made me think of that music, the beat of it, eclipsed, for me, only by the beating of that man's heart, clenched between my upper and lower jaws.

Ah, it all sounds so dark, doesn't it? Hard to explain to someone who hasn't lived it. Am I an animal who can talk? Who can tell you how guilt-free it is to chase down a deer and burrow my snout in its chest? Or am I a man, here to confess? I've tried not to think of these things, through the years, the decades. I've tried to ignore my own mind. And that leaves the body, I am living, and therefore reliant on these muscles and bones. At eighty, they've begun to betray me. And me, last night, knowing I had no need for Ivan the farmer under that mournful moon, I rose to and entered the deep woods behind me, where the mice tried to avoid the owl.

In there, I thought of the busted motorcar on the side of an Alaskan highway. This was, what, fifty years ago? Forty? Hard to know, though these incidents do leave an imprint, rings on a tree, wrinkles in skin, a watermark that someone a little more studious than I might pinpoint. In any event, I was much younger, and foolish enough to have found myself possibly hungry for the second time, for a second moon. At the sight of that moon, I'd decided to transform, to take hold of the night. I remember feeling particularly free about it. I remember assuming there would be food to feast.

But that's no way to wolf.

A plan is knowing the routine of the farmer Ivan as he passes, as you yourself are deep in the shadows of the woods, as you hear his steps upon the road and the sound of the bucket clacking against his belt or thigh.

That Alaskan night, I had no plan. But the moon provides. Mostly, the moon delivers on her promises, though I won't be the one to say she owes you any. Still, you tell her you love her and she gives you a broken vehicle with a single passenger, a middle-aged woman with a briefcase full of pills and papers. Who am I to guess what the woman was doing out there? Who am I to know? I'm just the one who descended from the incline of evergreens dwarfing her car. I'm the one who, when she looked out the driver's side window, made her scream.

Is it too much? Yes, of course it's too much. But don't you see? Denying one moon is the equivalent of saying yes to a hundred.

Because there's nobody to tell you not to. No second wolf to direct your decision. You've got you and you alone out there, in all the world, all that night. So I felt okay, last night, for having denied the moon. For having said no, at last, to the life.

I heard Ivan's footsteps vanish toward town.

I left the woods then, returning to the grass. I stood there in my jeans and white tank top, the grass to my waist, the letters of my name jutting up over the dip of the shirt's collar.

And I looked up at the moon.

I'm leaving you, I said. But I smiled because I guessed she knew I wasn't angry, that I couldn't be, that we shared a bond no two humans could understand. And as I gazed upon her, I saw her smile back, something beyond the light, of course, the *real* her, the rise of half a lip over the side of a her cratered snout.

You're awake, I said. But of course she was. What I really meant to say, but was too worried to voice was, *You see me.*

I was certain she did. Sure she was looking directly at me, me of all below her, me of all the wolves in the world. I couldn't look away, as the memories of two dozen kills crossed my mind. Turns in Florida and Wisconsin flooded my mind, as if they were near on the map. And I knew why: It was in both these states that I stole men who reminded me of myself. I was particularly brutal to both.

I recalled a blonde man in Utah. A runner in Oklahoma. A woman from the patio of a restaurant in Denver, as life went on behind the glass walls of the dining room inside. I recalled them all, every one, as I prided myself for having turned down the life, denied the moon this time, and every time now, retired. I removed my shirt as I walked toward the road, hearing in the distance the shoes of Ivan the farmer, the young man, husband and father, and I told myself,

By letting this one go, you are absolved for taking all others.

I believed this to be true. Because isn't it about learning? Isn't it about improving upon our pasts, what we've done? At eighty I'd done it all, and had determined what was best in the end.

Yet, there I stood, shoeless and shirtless in the dirt road, facing the darkness from which Ivan would no doubt soon be stepping.

My eyes still on the moon, still on *her* eyes, my history rotating through my head like pollen falling from the summer trees I could not entirely see. And what wind propelled said pollen? I ask because I felt it. Winds swirling behind my eyes, sending my thoughts sailing.

The intoxication of the moon.

Ivan's presence grew louder, and the sloshing in the bucket was off rhythm with those steps. This was unlike him. Was he hurrying? I wished he was. I suddenly wished he was moving so fast I would see only a streak in the darkness.

Then the words, bad words perhaps, crossed my mind:

One last transformation.

It's so easy to equate us to drunks, isn't it? It's so easy to imagine a man two months sober, his life in order, his partner beaming with pride. It's ready-made, the image of this man, his suit and case, the car carrying them both, diverted from the main road home, taking the shallow drive to the local roadside bar, perhaps a place he's never been, half the reason for stopping at all. If I can see him, you certainly can.

But we're different. My kind. Because I *have* denied the moon so many times before. And because a transformation is more taxing than even twenty drinks. The stress on the bones, the body ...

... the mind.

I looked up the road, expecting Ivan already. I imagined the nod I'd give him, the how-do-you-do as he passed me on his way to his wife and little girl. But without him yet there, I looked up again to the moon, *our* moon, ever changing, yet always somehow that singular face, looking down, eyeing us, eyeing *me*, as if the shafts of illumination, the light upon me, were coming directly from the craters of her eyes.

One last transformation.

I could feel the electricity, the charge, rip through me. Hadn't I already denied her? Hadn't I done told her goodbye?

I worried about my shoulders, my knees, my body that still ached from crouching in the grass, a thing I used to do for hours on end, eyeing the lights of a distant village, waiting for who went to sleep last.

I denied her again then, last night, with effort. I turned my face from the moon, turned instead to face the long dirt road that ran along the heavy woods, the woods from where the owl hooted, once, before I saw not Ivan, but a mouse of my own.

Ivan's little girl carried the bucket out of the darkness.

Not Ivan but his daughter, struggling to carry the wooden bucket with both hands.

There I was, shirtless and tattooed, white-haired and wrinkled, no doubt a vision to her in the shaft of moonlight fit so snug to my person.

She saw me as sudden as I saw her. And there she stopped. Ivan's child. Young Zoya having gone to fetch water on the full moon.

I almost spoke her name. I almost said,

Zoya, go back to town.

Yes, I knew her name from having spied on Ivan in his farmhouse. Knew she was seven years old. Too young to plow the field but old enough to fetch water if ever Ivan wasn't able.

The moon showed me her in full. Zoya, her small face barely big enough to hold her enormous eyes, eyes fastened upon me facing her in the road. And me, just an old man, standing.

Had she caught me looking at the moon? Maybe she saw the decision was still active after all.

I felt a swirling within me yet, images of so many dead, my dead, and me, too, on the nights I'd denied the moon, the nights I lay in a bed or a hayloft happy for proving something, anything, to myself; that I could change in more ways than one. Than I didn't repeat myself month to month. That maybe, one day, when I was old, as I am now, I would be able to quit the moon.

I saw Angelo Hanks in that moment: his vision, a life with no more transformations.

But the thing about quitting is that there has to be a *last time you do it*, too. And that last time ought to mean something to the quitter.

Zoya set the bucket at her feet and raised a hand, a single finger pointed at me.

Shouldn't a man know it's his last time as he does it? And did I know, last month, that I was done? Had I given myself the proper sendoff? Had I given the life its due?

Zoya opened her mouth. She spoke.

Am I safe?

Of all the things to say. And who taught her to fear an old man in the middle of the road? Who explained how to sense a wolf?

I looked up to the moon and I said,

I've already said goodbye.

I closed my eyes and I saw it all again, the unfathomable number of dead bodies and the incredible variety in which I made them so. Was I an animal, bent on death by any means? Or was I a man, creative in his passionate pursuit?

I looked to the road again, just in time to see Zoya had halved the distance between us. The bucket behind her in the dirt. She pointed to my chest and said,

Johnny.

In that moment, my name spoken, I could no longer hold back the guilt. How long had I been rationalizing this life? Perhaps this was what Angelo meant by clarity.

Brutal, unkind, and true.

For in that beat, the little finger pointing my way, I remembered the man I was, *before becoming the wolf.* I recalled my parents and the love they bestowed upon me. I remembered the draw to the taboo as I feared for their safety, as if my own makeup were on a ship, close enough in a far distance to hear. Yes, I remembered *hearing* my own future approaching. The very reason I left mother and father behind.

I knew then what I was and what I was on my way to doing.

I saw youth in Zoya, how could I not? And I saw youth, too, in who I once was.

Johnny.

Would I have stolen Johnny from the parade? Would I have taken him from a broken car in Alaska? I knew his parents, knew the effect I would have had on them.

How many people had I really killed?

Yes, I said to Zoya, my smile bending the path the tears took down my face. *Johnny.*

But in that I lied, for I was no longer the man who had yet to change into a wolf. I turned from Zoya then and looked up once more to the moon. In the face there, in its shining eyes, I saw it watched me and only me in all this darkness below.

I looked back to the child and I thought,

You've already said goodbye.

But when I reached out toward Zoya, to plant my hand upon her small shoulder, I saw the budding tips of black claws beginning at the tips of my fingers.

One last transformation.

And why not? Doesn't a man deserve to know when it's the last time? Even half a man such as me?

Am I safe?

I shook my head no. As my smile grew to a size that no doubt would have fractured her adulthood, had Zoya any adulthood ahead.

Full moon means you gotta decide.

Last night I decided I deserved to know it was the end. I deserved an ending. I decided upon one last transformation.

And as I changed in front of the girl, as she fell, frozen, to her knees in the dirt, I felt the moon. And as I slashed her eyes into the woods and heard the owls descend upon them, as I buried my snout in her belly, I felt the moon.

I saw it, too, reflected in the water I lapped from the bucket still sitting in the road.

Do you find me foolish? Do you think me so bad?

Today is the first day of my quitting. I've been given the ending I deserved. Now, here, on a boat, I look down into the water rushing past, seeing no longer the reflection of the moon, but rather that of an old man leaving another town, heading toward a new one again. And who could have known—how could I have known—that all my travels would bring me there, where I will no doubt deny the moon, having resolved, at last, to say goodbye?

𝕭𝖗𝖆𝖎𝖓𝖘

RAMSEY CAMPBELL

From the Filmy Eyed online group:

PHIL MEEHAN: May I pick everyone's brains? I'm trying to fix something in my mind. Cast yours back to James Whale's *Frankenstein*. When Colin Clive learns Dwight Frye brought him a criminal brain to put in the monster he does a double-take Oliver Hardy might have been proud of. But they've already pinched a body from the gallows, and Frankenstein complained he couldn't use the brain because the neck was broken. Wouldn't that brain have belonged to a criminal as well?

KARLOFFANN: Have you got nothing better to do than poke fun at a classic? Just because the make-ups aren't as gory as they make them these days doesn't mean you have to laugh at it. Some of us can do without seeing people's eyes gouged out and their entrails everywhere, thank you very much. Mind you, I can think of people who deserve it, the ones that make those films. I'll stick with good acting the way it used to be and films that left a bit to your imagination.

MY FRIEND FLICKER: He's not just poking fun, he's spoiling it for everyone. Like he's so clever for spotting stuff that's never bothered anyone for nearly a hundred years. Oh look at me everyone, I've got a better brain than yours because I saw someone with a wristwatch in a medieval epic. And look, someone's got a mobile phone in that Shakespeare play. People like him want us all seeing that crap instead of enjoying the films. I go to be entertained, me, not pretend I'm better than whoever made them.

PHIL MEEHAN: Apologies to both of you. I'm just after inspiration. You carry on appreciating films how you like. For the record, I like *Frankenstein* a lot, and other Whale films too.

EDDY TING: weve got your permission to watch movies how we like, have we? thats big of you, in fact its monsterous. maybe youd of let us if youd kept your shit to yourself.

LIGHTS, GAMERA, ACTION: I love monster films, my screen name is the book I'm writing about them, and I don't want Mr Meehan to stop posting. Have you got any more quirky ideas about monsters, Mr Meehan?

PHIL MEEHAN: Most people think *The Bride of Frankenstein* is misnamed because Elsa Lanchester plays the monster's mate and not the scientist's, but I think it works with the gay subtext where Ernest Thesiger is Colin Clive's bride and they have an unnatural daughter. Remember Thesiger seduces Clive away from his wife with whom he had a son at the end of the first film. Now they don't have one, because the film has turned time back so the narrative can deviate.

LIGHTS, GAMERA, ACTION: Why do you have to bring perverts into it? They're everywhere now, but they weren't allowed then. You said you didn't want to spoil films and now you have. You're trying to make it dirty when it never was. We watch monster films to get away from all that, so why can't you leave them alone?

PHIL MEEHAN: I don't believe I put anything in. James Whale was gay, which gives us insights into several of his films. His friend Thesiger made no secret that he was and used to sell his needle-work while they were filming *Bride*. They made *The Old Dark House* with Charles Laughton, Elsa Lanchester's husband, who was gay as well. In that film Thesiger's called Femm, and he lives up to the name in both.

KARLOFFANN: So your point is what exactly? Who are you trying to smear? Don't you dare say that about Boris. He was happily married and a gentle-man. I think these people who want us to believe everybody's homosexual only ever have one reason, they're it themselves and want the rest to join them.

PHIL MEEHAN: I'm as straight as the edge of your screen, and my lady is as well. Your sexual-ity shouldn't dictate how closely you look at a film. You just need to be prepared to see what's in front of you and while you're at it have a second look.

GETAGRIP: What do you know about her screen? Better not be spying on us or we'll hunt you down. Watch out we don't think you're as homophobic as you're trying not to sound. You don't know arse about her sexuality either. Or maybe you want us thinking you're a phobe so we won't know you're gay. Bit confused, Phil? Make up your brain.

LIGHTS, GAMERA, ACTION: I think Mr Meehan is trying to confuse us. I watch films to see the characters, not who they really are or people like him say they are. Have you finished making things up about films, Mr Meehan? Haven't you got anything to say about *Son of Frankenstein*?

PHIL MEEHAN: It's the last one where Karloff keeps his brain.

GLENN STRANGER: Sounds like youre losing your's.

PHIL MEEHAN: I think I'd better take it elsewhere before someone steals it or my ability to think.

KARLOFFANN: Don't go till you've said what you meant about Boris's brain in *Son of Frankenstein*.

PHIL MEEHAN: After he and Ernest Thesiger split up Colin Clive must have had a son who's grown up to be Basil Rathbone. Karloff learned to speak in *Bride* but now he can't, because being struck by lightning leaves you speechless. Bela Lugosi lost his chance to play the monster in the first film, but now he's the monster's friend, and later they'll get closer than you'd believe friends could. After this film things get monstrously complicated.

KARLOFFANN: You still haven't told us about the brain, and what are you trying to say about Boris and Bela?

PHIL MEEHAN: In *Ghost of Frankenstein* the monster's turned into Lon Chaney Junior, but Lugosi's as much his friend as ever. He could be recognising his old friend's brain inside a new head. I'm saying they were friends, since they worked on several films besides the Frankensteins, but I expect you all know they were rivals as well. Cedric Hardwicke is yet another Frankenstein, and Lionel Atwill's his assistant in charge of brains, but Hardwicke's also the ghost of the original monster maker and tells himself to put a better brain in the monster. Lugosi wants it to be his, but the monster's after the brain of a little girl he befriended, presumably to make up for throwing someone like her in a lake in the original film. That would have had to be the first sex change operation in Hollywood. Hardwicke means to put in the brain of an assistant the monster killed, but Atwill tricks him into using Lugosi's. When the monster comes round he has Lugosi's voice, and we can hear Bela's triumph at being the creature at last. Only the operation has blinded him, as if whenever the monster comes back he has to leave a sense behind.

LIGHTS, GAMERA, ACTION: I'd say you've lost yours. Why did you need to bring a sex change into it? They'd never have had ideas like that back then. You might as well say Lionel Atwill grew a new arm because the monster pulled it off in *Son of Frankenstein*. And while you're at it why don't you say Dwight Frye came back as a villager in *Ghost of Frankenstein* because he'd had enough of being killed off as for helping Frankenstein in *Frankenstein* and then in *Bride* as well.

PHIL MEEHAN: Sorry for the sex change, and thank you for the extra notions!

GETAGRIP: What are you thanking him for? He was having a joke, you brainless clown.

LIGHTS, GAMERA, ACTION: I'm not a him. Girls have brains as well.

KARLOFFANN: You bet we have, bigger than a lot of men's. They could do with having ours.

PHIL MEEHAN: To be fair, we can't tell gender from a name like LGA. I was thanking her for inspiration, because I've been thinking aloud on here, trying out ideas to give students. Thanks to everyone who indulged me.

GLENN STRANGER: Your saying your a teacher? Thats like gamera saying hes a girl.

LIGHTS, GAMERA, ACTION: Not just saying. What are you trying to do to their brains, Mr Meehan?

PHIL MEEHAN: To make them look again at films they think they've finished with and have fun.

LIGHTS, GAMERA, ACTION: Have you finished having your fun? Four films to go. Let's hope you've run out of twisted ideas or you haven't seen them.

PHIL MEEHAN: I have, and they get more complicated. For a start, in *Frankenstein Meets the Wolf Man* Ilona Massey is Frankenstein, but we won't say anything about gender change. Lugosi is the monster, but now his brain has brought his body with it, which means Lon Chaney's has to find another role. He's the wolf man who was killed at the end of his own film, and now he's resurrected by the full moon. Come to think, Rathbone played Wolf von Frankenstein in *Son*, so he was a wolf man too. And thanks for reminding me about Frye and Atwill. Dwight is a villager who's grateful to get some dialogue, and Atwill is the burgomeister, having come back to life after Chaney with Lugosi's brain killed him last time.

LIGHTS, GAMERA, ACTION: At least you didn't bring in sex change, except you did. Have you still not finished?

ALL TO REEL: Obsessed with sex change, aren't you, Gam? No wonder you hide your name.

PHIL MEEHAN: *House of Frankenstein* brings in extra monsters. Last time Dracula showed up on the screen he was Lon Chaney, who was either the count's son or the man himself. Now Chaney can't stop being the wolf man, and so John Carradine has to be Dracula, since presumably Lugosi's brain is still in the Frankenstein monster's head, though he's turned into Glenn Strange when he's found where he was buried under the castle at the end of the last film, along with the wolf man. Karloff has graduated from monster to scientist in charge of brains, but though he promises hunchback J. Carroll Naish that he'll find him a better body he never transfers a single brain. Lionel Atwill has got his police job back, but there's no sign of Dwight Frye, because he's definitively dead.

LIGHTS, GAMERA, ACTION: That's awful. You shouldn't be a teacher if you make a joke of people dying.

PHIL MEEHAN: I'm not a teacher, you should have seen I'm a lecturer, and I rather think students can cope. Anyway, Frye died long before I should think you were born.

LIGHTS, GAMERA, ACTION: You don't know how old I am and you won't be finding out either.

ALL TO REEL: Don't let the sissy shut you up, Phil. You carry on sharing your brains with us.

PHIL MEEHAN: *House of Dracula* reunites the monsters and keeps some of them the same. Now that Karloff has reclaimed his brain he's gone elsewhere, leaving Onslow Stevens to carry on the operations. Stevens means to cure the wolf man by brain surgery and give Dracula blood transfusions to turn him into a man. They're Chaney and Carradine again, and Glenn Strange shows up in a cave under the doctor's castle. Though he's still the monster, some scenes turn him into Karloff or Chaney, and you have to wonder whose brain has ended up in him. Atwill has kept his police job but he's changed his name from Arnz to Holtz. Hunchback Carroll Naish is now hunchback Martha O'Driscoll. Are these films really about the impermanence of personality? That's how they seem to fit together.

GETAGRIP: No they aren't and no they don't. Rather play with films than stand up for people, would you, Phil? If you're supposed to be a lecturer you're meant to look after them.

PHIL MEEHAN: I've already told you I'm better than supposed, and who am I meant to be defending against what?

GETAGRIP: Too busy pumping up your brain to read what someone else said about sissies? It isn't homophobic just to say it, not caring is as well.

ALL TO REEL: There's no fucking homophobes round here. That's just what your lot call anyone that wants to stay normal.

PHIL MEEHAN: I didn't realise the comment about sissies was intended to be homophobic, which I'm absolutely not. I thought it was about sensitivity even if it wasn't called for.

KARLOFFANN: Don't say any more or you'll be tying your brain into a bigger knot. You've got no more ideas, so go away. Even you couldn't make anything out of Abbott and Costello.

PHIL MEEHAN: I'll have to disagree with that. This time the brain surgeon is Lenore Aubert, who plans to transfer Lou Costello's brain to Glenn Strange's head. Chaney is the wolf man and tells Abbott and Costello they're in the house of Dracula, perhaps thinking he's still in the last film. Lugosi is Dracula but forgets at one point and shows up in a mirror. Costello turns into the wolf man at a masked ball. Perhaps Aubert is Frankenstein, since the film is *Abbott and Costello Meet Frankenstein* and she's stored his research in her brain. Enough for everyone?

KARLOFFANN: You're getting desperate, aren't you, crippling a comedy so it'll fit your brain. If you've got any students I hope they're laughing at all this.

PHIL MEEHAN: Anyone can laugh. I said it was about having fun.

LIGHTS, GAMERA, ACTION: Then stop trying to ruin ours. Like Karloffann says that's a comedy, so don't try making it something else.

PHIL MEEHAN: Let me point out that it was filmed as *The Brain of Frankenstein*, which fits my thesis.

LIGHTS, GAMERA, ACTION: It's a thesis now, is it? I thought just students did those. I think you've made that title up like a lot more you've been saying.

PHIL MEEHAN: I've made nothing up. Try searching for the title, and then you might apologise.

LIGHTS, GAMERA, ACTION: I don't need to search to know I don't believe you, and I'd swap brains with you before I'd apologise. I don't even believe in your name.

PHIL MEEHAN: That's quite a laugh, Miss Gamera, considering what you call yourself. I ought to have acted like the rest of you and made up a name.

LIGHTS, GAMERA, ACTION: Just so everyone knows, I searched for your name and it isn't listed as a lecturer anywhere. What's it meant to be? Film Me Ann or Fill Me In? I believe you're laughing at us for missing the joke.

PHIL MEEHAN: It's no joke. It's me and I'm it. I'm afraid it looks as if the joke's your name and the book you claim you're writing. You ought to realise it isn't original. It's all over the internet, where I expect you found it even if you didn't realise. The net is part of everyone's brain.

LIGHTS, GAMERA, ACTION: My brain's nowhere except here in my head. What are you trying to make me think?

PHIL MEEHAN: I'm saying your name and that title is everywhere, but I think the book is only in your brain. If I'm wrong do prove it. Post a chapter or a few as evidence.

LIGHTS, GAMERA, ACTION: I'm not putting anything on here for anyone to steal.

PHIL MEEHAN: Somehow I didn't think you would. You can't prove anything is real by hiding it, you know. If you won't post any chapters, how about a few of your ideas? We've seen none except the ones you didn't mean to give me.

GETAGRIP: Maybe that's what Phil He Mean wants us to believe. Maybe he's inside your computer like we thought he could be.

GAIL LLOYD: Excuse me, could you all stop disturbing my daughter?

PHIL MEEHAN: May we know who you're talking about and who you're saying you are?

GAIL LLOYD: I'm Ann's mother, the girl who's been posting as Lights, Gamera, Action, and I want you to stop bullying her.

PHIL MEEHAN: You're the girl, are you? You're saying you're her. Do you share a brain by any chance? It doesn't seem to be functioning too well. Is Ann short for FrAnnKenstein? There's already one Ann here, and I wonder if there's only one.

GAIL LLOYD: I think it's your brain that needs some attention. Just so you know, she's vulnerable and you're doing her no good. I can't believe you're bullying her over such trivial things either.

PHIL MEEHAN: At least I don't talk about myself in the third person, and you're the one who's been inciting me, Miss Gamera. Gail, would that be ILGA mixed up? And is Lloyd short for Cellulloyd? That's a joke.

ALL TO REEL: Sounds more like Gay fucking Lloyd to me.

GAIL LLOYD: I don't play games with words and films like you, Mr Meehan, or whatever your name may be. And just so you're aware, Ann isn't as strong as she likes everyone to think. She's sixteen and she's in a wheelchair.

PHIL MEEHAN: You know my name perfectly well. I don't pretend to be anyone I'm not. She isn't a hunchback as well by any chance, Miss Gamera? Did you piece her together out of your own head? Isn't one body enough for you? Would you like it to be in a film? I'd better stop before you accuse me of bullying.

GAIL LLOYD: You're a real monster, aren't you? I can see how much you enjoy it. You aren't affecting me, and you'll have to find another victim, because my daughter won't be here any more. I hope you're proud of driving her off somewhere she thought she'd find minds like hers.

PHIL MEEHAN: After brains, was she? If you want me to feel guilty you'll have to show me why. Let's see you prove who you are, Ann Lloyd.

GAIL LLOYD: I shouldn't even have posted her name, and I'm certainly not giving you any more details. People like you need to be kept at a distance.

PHIL MEEHAN: People like what? What are you saying I am? I've only been responding how I've been made to respond. I'm sending you a private message in case you really are who you say. If I show you who I am I hope you'll do the same for me.

GETAGRIP: Been quiet for a while, hasn't it? Maybe they've switched their brains off.

GLENN STRANGER: Looks like Filmy Ann and Gay Lloyd must of got together somewhere else, except more like theyre both him.

PHIL MEEHAN: I'm back and I'm nobody else, but I have to apologise. I was wrong about Ann Lloyd and wrong to harass her. She's disabled as her mother said. I'm leaving the group now, but I hope she'll give it another chance. If she does I hope you'll all treat her better than I did.

GLENN STRANGER: Your giving up pretending to be her and her ma, more like. Maybe you was trying to involve us in the arguments you made out you were haveing and it didnt work. Maybe your tired of sharing your brain round till you want to be Gammy again. Theres a good name for somebody that says theyre in a wheelchair.

PHIL MEEHAN: All right, I'll stop pretending so that nobody can mistake the truth. I was never a teacher or a lecturer. I tried to teach but couldn't cope, and then I put in for lecturing but my ideas got laughed down. At least that's giving me time to make them into a book. That's the honest truth, and I've told it about Ann Lloyd as well.

GLENN STRANGER: Writeing two books now, are you, Gammy? Better do one before you start the other. Dont try telling us how to act, though. Dont bother showing up as your mammy either, Mammy Gammy. If you come saying youre Gammy youll get treated like it, and if you cant cope like you said you couldnt then piss off.

PHIL MEEHAN: For christ's sake, I'm exactly who I say. Can't you see I've given up pretending? And you know their real names now and what they are. Can't you believe in anything?

GLENN STRANGER: Yeh, I believe your like youre monsters, always turning into someone else.

PHIL MEEHAN: I'm. Ban. Ging. My. Head. A. Gainst. The. Screen. Am. I. Get. Ting. Through. To. You? What. Do. I. Have. To. Do. To. Get. Some. Sense. In. Side. Your. Head?

GLENN STRANGER: Trying to play monster, are you, Gam? Watch out you dont hurt your brain. Youd hurt for real if we ever met. Thats a promise.

PHIL MEEHAN: I'd look forward to it. Somebody wouldn't be walking away from it. Just tell me where you are and we'll see who's the real monster.

GLENN STRANGER: Message on it's way to you right now, Gammy.

KARLOFFANN: Have we lost someone again? It's quieter than ever.

GETAGRIP: I'd say the topic's died on us.

EDDY TING: feels as dead as all them actors.

PHIL MEEHAN: So did Glenn.

KARLOFFANN: That's your latest joke, is it? You're not in on it, are you, Glenn?

PHIL MEEHAN: He won't be answering even if I didn't get his brain out. I think I touched it, though.

KARLOFFANN: What a nasty thing to say, even as a joke. Don't let him use you for it, Glenn.

GETAGRIP: That's right, Glenn, don't you let him pretend. Just give us all a shout.

EDDY TING: come on glenn, youve shut up long enough, you dont want anyone believing him.

PHIL MEEHAN: I thought you all liked monsters. You've created one and now you don't believe in him, so he'll have to hunt you down. You won't be really gone, because he'll keep you in his brain. It's as near as you'll come to fame without being in a film. If you're reading this and you don't believe, he'll find you. Glenn would say so if they put him back together, and it's his tongue that's talking. It's saying use your brains while you can.

You Are My Neighbor

MAX BOOTH III

I used to break windows. One window in particular, really. Our neighbor had a basement and we didn't, and I always thought that was unfair. Growing up, all I wanted was to live in a basement and invite all the kids from school to come hang out and drink beer with me while listening to Black Sabbath. But we didn't have a basement and nobody ever came over because Mom was too embarrassed of how messy the house was and Dad was paranoid someone would swipe their oxys while he was asleep.

He always accused me of taking them, but I never once dared. One night, around two in the morning, I woke up to his hand squeezing my throat and he was above me, tears pouring down his face and splattering against my own, and he demanded I tell him what I did with them, and the way he looked at me I could tell he didn't want to be doing what he was doing but something beyond human consciousness had him under its control, and I had to beg and beg for him to let me go, that I didn't have his pills, and eventually Mom stumbled in and reminded him they'd already finished off their stash the night before.

So, sometimes, I broke the neighbor's basement window, the one at foot-level along the side of their house half-hidden in dirt. It was a thing to do while Mom and Dad were down for the count and I was bored because I couldn't invite anybody over and I wasn't allowed to walk along the interstate to visit anybody so what the hell was a kid to do besides break windows?

The first time it happened, it was just about twilight and every-body next door had left. I'd watched all four of them pile into their tan station wagon and drive off. Who knew where? Maybe to go get ice cream or watch a movie. Stuff families did together on TV. The household consisted of a mother and father and son and daughter. I didn't know any of their names, but they always seemed busy doing bizarre activities. Having barbecues in the back yard and going on vacations and playing catch in the street for the whole wide world to see. The shame of it all just about killed me.

I was sitting on our porch as the family next door drove off, all smiles and bubblegum as the station wagon disappeared beyond our little subdivision. The anger in me bubbled like a welt. I stomped across our front yard and maneuvered around the fence separating our property. One glance at the basement window along the side of their house made me tremble with rage. Musings of what could be beyond the glass did not occur. The fact that it existed here and not in our house spoke plenty of the situation.

From the grass, I unearthed a fist-sized stone and hurled it at the window. It bounced off without inflicting any damage, like it was mocking me, laughing at the pathetic boy too weak to even break a window.

On the second throw, the rock shattered it to bits.

The noise echoed far and loud. Scared me so bad I fled back inside our house and hid in my bed. Through my bedroom window I could hear the neighbors return home several hours later, although none of them seemed to notice the damage I'd inflicted upon their property. Perhaps it was simply too late and they'd immediately succumbed to exhaustion. I waited all night to hear a scream that never arrived.

Two days later, the window was fixed. Almost like it'd never been broken, like my actions were meaningless. No one had even come to talk to me about it. I stood near our fence, unable to stop staring at the flawless fixture. Behind me, the school bus pulled away and the other kids in my neighborhood laughed and shouted, relieved to have finished another day of education. I could not share their excitement. All I felt was the certainty that my existence didn't mean anything and nothing I did would ever alter this truth. I could break every window in the world and within a week they'd be replaced with new ones.

I fled inside our house and found my parents on the couch, entwined together like the infinity symbol. The oxys had already knocked them out. I sat on the floor in front of the couch and leaned my head against an empty space on one of the cushions and closed my eyes and visualized glass shattering and reforming over and over until sleep came knocking.

I woke up to a stinging sensation across my face and Dad standing over me, still naked, pointing at me like I'd been up to no good.

"What'd you do with it, you little shit?" he said.

"I didn't touch them. I swear."

He shook his head, the sound of his teeth grinding loud enough to penetrate my own skull. "The Xbox, goddammit. It ain't in your room."

A proper response failed me. Paranoia raised the question of whether or not this was a test. Either way, he didn't like my answer. Slapped me so hard my head just about performed a three-sixty. I felt like a cartoon character without an audience, no laugh track or anything.

Dad grabbed my shoulders and leaned his face in real close to mine and demanded my Xbox. Behind me, still on the couch, Mom rolled in her sleep and groaned for us to keep the noise down. Instead of giving him an answer, I started weeping, which only pissed him off more. The reason he wanted my Xbox was he hadn't gotten paid yet and they were already out of oxys, so he'd drop the Xbox off at the pawnshop and go restock their pill supply. The only problem in this plan, which I couldn't find the courage to tell him, was he'd already pawned my Xbox last month. He wouldn't have believed me even if I did remind him, and if he did remember after the fact, he sure as hell would have never admitted it. So, instead, he squeezed my face and screamed for something I couldn't give him and then eventually he got bored and got dressed and stormed out of the house. The sound of his car screeching from the driveway relieved an enormous weight from my chest and I settled back against the couch. Mom shifted again and asked me to fetch her a cup of water. Her mouth was dry.

The second time I broke the window came a couple weeks later. I had decided to do it the night before. Nothing specific prompted the decision. I had simply been lying in bed, listening to Mom and Dad arguing in the living room, when the thought crossed my mind. *Tomorrow, I will break the window again.* It generated not as a question but a fact. Tomorrow, I would break the window, and when tomorrow arrived that's exactly what I did.

Sunday mornings always mystified me. We'd never been a church-going family, never discussed religion or the possibility of deities. Kids at school referenced Christianity as if it were a common limb attached to everybody's bodies. Weekly visits to wooden pews. God and Jesus and all that trash. Waking up early dressed like rich folks. What a scam. But our neighbors, they fell for it every Sunday without failure. That specific morning, I sat next to my bedroom window early enough to beat the sun, waiting for them to pull out of our subdivision. Eventually they emerged from the house wearing clothes our family could never hope to afford. All four of them smiling and enjoying each other's presence. It made me want to break all the windows in the world.

But I'd settle for the one in their basement.

At least for now.

This time around, I came prepared with a baseball bat resting along my shoulder. The aluminum rattled against my palms with each contact it made against glass. It took five good swings for the window to spiderweb, another two for it to completely surrender. A coward might have fled at the sound it made, but I was no coward. I feared nothing.

I knelt in the dirt and stuck my head through the window, careful to avoid slicing my throat open with the remaining shards sticking out along its sides. Sunlight reflected off the broken glass on the floor below. Winking at me. Inviting me inside. Instead of accepting its offer, I scanned the rest of the basement from my vantage point outside. The interior disappointed curiosity. Boxes covered with sheets were lined up against the wall. A wooden staircase led from the floor to a door several feet up, into … what? The kitchen? This was the first basement I'd ever seen in real life and out of all the emotions I expected to feel, I had foolishly omitted "boredom" from the list. Now that the window was broken, nothing further seemed to offer much excitement.

Then I saw it.

On the opposite side of the basement, nearly swallowed by darkness: a door.

But not only a door …

… a door with a padlock attached to it.

The rest of the week moved at a glacier's pace. Whenever I closed my eyes, I saw the door in our neighbor's basement. The mystery followed me like disease. What awaited beyond it remained an intangible black hole that irritated my flesh and clogged my concentration. At night I rolled around in bed fantasizing the myriad secrets hidden inside their locked room, imagination running the gamut of potential treasures. Money, of course, but money seemed too obvious. Gold, too, offered nothing for me. What kind of secret could a family keep that would require a padlock? Locks kept things from escaping. It seemed logical to assume whatever was in that room could be alive. Could be dangerous. A prisoner, but why?

Several days after the second window breaking, I asked Dad about the neighbors. He was in the kitchen sprawled out on his back, halfway under the sink with a wrench as he attempted to fix a leaky pipe.

"No," he said in the midst of struggling, "they don't talk to me, and I don't talk to them. If you was wise, you'd do the same. Nothing good ever happened from letting goddamn strangers in on your business."

"Did they live here when we moved here, or did they come after?"

Dad sighed and slammed the pipe on the floor and sat up. The look in his eyes was the same look he always gave me. It was the only look.

"Do you think I have the kinda time to sit around paying a single goddamn second to who lives in this neighborhood? I worry about me and my family and that's it. The hell's got you so interested in this shit, anyhow?"

I shrugged. To admit the truth would be the same as issuing a death sentence upon myself. "Nothing. Never mind."

"You ain't been fucking around, telling people things that's no concern to them, have you?"

"No."

"Denny …"

"I promise."

He stared at me for several seconds before returning to the sink. The moment he broke eye contact, I fled to my bedroom and shut the door.

The next day, I found the courage to sneak back across our property line. Someone had boarded up the window. What had our neighbors thought, coming home to find the very same fixture shattered again? Would they bother replacing it a third time, or instead stick with wood and nails forever? I did not want to break wood. I wanted to destroy glass. I wanted to hear the sound of something shatter.

Before I could process the actions of my limbs, I was already standing on their front porch and ringing the bell.

WHAT AM I DOING WHAT AM I DOING WHAT AM I DOING, my brain screamed.

The door opened and before me stood the residence's father figure, sometimes referred to as "the man of the house" on TV. He smiled down at me. Although he was not dressed for church, his clothes still seemed infinitely nicer than anything my family could ever dream of owning. "Hello there, son. How can I help you?"

My throat threatened to close. *Son?* He had called me his son. Why had I come here? This was never part of the plan. *What plan?* No such thing existed. I was here because I was meant to be here. I opened my mouth to speak but words refused to form beyond a soft croak. The man of the house stepped back, his initial welcoming posture rapidly deteriorating.

"Son, is something wrong?"

He knelt so we were eye level and clamped a hand upon my shoulder. The contact weakened my knees and I nearly collapsed right there on his front porch. Memories of the last time an older man touched me exploded like lightning. Dad squeezing my throat, both of us crying, screaming loud enough to rupture the universe.

I swallowed.

Took my time.

Then said, "Sugar?"

"Excuse me?"

I pointed behind him, into the house. "My mom needs to borrow sugar. Can we borrow sugar?"

"Sugar?" He hesitated, chewing over what I said, still kneeling, then smiled. "Your momma fixing a cake, son?"

I nodded, enthusiastic. "It's my birthday."

"Today?"

"Yes."

The man's smile morphed into pure excitement. "Well, how about that!" He ran his hand through my hair. "Come on in, son."

I followed him into the house and shut the door behind me. It felt good to lie. Almost as good as breaking windows. My heart started beating like I'd been sprinting through a field. I wanted it to beat so fast it'd explode through my chest and paint the neighbor's kitchen with my blood. The ultimate shattering.

The inside of their house looked just as fancy as their church clothes. I wanted to burn it to the ground. I wanted to live there forever. The man fetched a bag of sugar from a cupboard and asked how much we needed. I stared at him for several seconds, trying to decide how much sugar a cake could possibly need.

"A lot," I finally said. "A whole bag."

He cocked his brow. "A whole bag?"

"Yes."

"How much cake is your momma making, son?"

"A lot."

"Well." He hesitated, glancing at the bag of sugar in his hands then back at me. "Okay, I suppose since it's your birthday and all, why the heck not?"

"Where are your kids?" I asked.

"What?"

"Your kids."

"Oh." He bit his lip, the warmness to him briefly evaporating before returning. "They're in the basement, with my wife."

"The basement?"

"Yeah." He nodded, completely unaware of the concert of noise thundering inside me. "They're playing."

"What are they playing?"

"Say, son." He touched my shoulder again. This time a little tighter, a little rougher. I thought of Dad again. "Don't you think it's about time you went back to your momma? Otherwise, how else is she gonna make a birthday cake for the birthday boy, right?"

He led me back through his kitchen and living room and out the front door. He stood on the porch and watched me walk back to my house. Something told me, even after I entered and closed the door, he remained out there, watching …

… waiting …

That night, curled up in bed, I dipped my finger in the bag of sugar and sucked it dry. I kept repeating the action until a headache emerged, then I did it a few more times just for the hell of it.

Next door the family had been playing in their basement. *Playing what?* I didn't just want to know. I *needed* to know. Playing in the locked room, surely. Playing with whatever they kept hidden from the rest of the world. Playing with someone or some*thing?*

I did not have a clock in my room to obsess over so instead I watched the headlights shine against my wall through the window. Cars passing in the dead of night to places I could not imagine. None of them knew the truth. None of them knew they were driving past a house with a locked door in its basement. None of them even cared.

I cared.

I cared so much.

It was easier to sneak outside than I anticipated. All I had to do was tell myself I had fallen asleep and everything that followed was simply a dream. In dreams, consequences did not exist. A person could do anything in a dream and it always ended the same. You woke up and after a couple minutes you forgot it ever happened.

Turned out wood made much less noise than glass when it broke. No special tools required, either. I sat on my butt in the dirt and gave the board one mighty kick with both feet and it fell to the basement floor. It created a loud thud upon impact, but nothing too distressing. Nothing that would alarm the floors above—or at least I hoped. I slid through the window and let gravity drag me down several feet to cement. I hadn't expected the drop to be so high and it was a miracle I didn't break my ankles. It only occurred after infiltrating the basement that I'd neglected to form an escape plan. But that was okay. I would worry about that later.

After I discovered what was behind the door.

All the nights I'd spent fantasizing about being in this basement, and the moment had finally arrived. The aged scent made my eyes water and nostrils twinge. I moved slowly across the dusty cement, taking my time, enjoying every second of my limited time here.

I'd brought the baseball bat with me, intending on using it to bash open the padlock. Of course I was aware of the noise it would make, and what that would mean. The family would wake and come downstairs to investigate. I didn't care about being caught. As long as I made it inside the room first. As long as I saw.

Something shiny gleamed in the corner of my eye as I neared the room, a small key winking at me from the edge of a table. I didn't want to feel disappointed, but if I could control my emotions then I wouldn't have been down in this basement in the first place. Finding the key felt wrong. Like it'd been waiting for me. I set down the bat and held up the key, feeling its various ridges before giving up and inserting it into the padlock. The mechanism popped open.

Maybe this really was a dream, after all.

I opened the door.

Inside the room I was met with total darkness. The odor shifted from a strong musk to something … rancid. Like meat that'd sat out too long. I gagged, shot both hands up to my mouth, terrified of breathing in whatever awaited inside. The time for retreating had expired. I stepped forward and felt around the wall closest to the door. Eventually a light switch materialized in the darkness. One flip and a dim bulb dangling from a chain in the center of the room buzzed to life.

A dim bulb, dangling directly above a small figure.

At first, I mistook the shape for a mannequin. Like something displayed in a shopping mall. Except … it was hard to tell at first, but the thing's chest had a steady rise and drop to it. I assumed the figure was a child based on its height, which nearly matched my own. As to its sex, I could not venture a guess, as its entire body had been wrapped in an old, mildewed cloth material. Even its face had been confined in the stuff. The nearer I approached, the worse its stench became, but I would not allow something as trivial as a horrid odor prevent me from fulfilling what I'd set out to accomplish tonight.

We stood inches apart from each other in an otherwise empty room. No toys, no books. There wasn't even a goddamn mattress. How long had the family kept this child here, and for what purpose? Something sinister. Something evil.

"Hello," I whispered. "My name is Denny."

The child did not react to my voice.

Could it see me?

I raised a hand, palm out. *I'm friendly*, the gesture represented. *I come in peace.*

"You are my neighbor," I said, and softly touched the child's shoulder.

Somewhere from behind its face wrap: a gasp.

Then the figure jerked forward, wrapping its arms around me.

Hugging me.

I tried to jerk away but its grip solidified like concrete. I stopped resisting and embraced the situation. It wasn't hurting me. I felt nothing but desperation from its touch. A plea for help.

"Okay," I finally whispered in where I assumed its ear was

YOU ARE MY NEIGHBOR

located, although who could tell for sure with the cloth wrapped around its head? How could it even breathe like that? "Okay, okay, okay. Let's get you out of here."

I led the imprisoned child up the basement steps and through the house. We moved slowly, careful not to bump into anything in the darkness. I expected the father of the family to be waiting for us somewhere upstairs, somewhere in the shadows. But he never showed. We slipped through the front door without incident. I led the child across the property line and into my own house, not thinking about my parents until I saw them in the living room, passed out on the couch. Crushed up pills all over the coffee table. Empty beer cans discarded on the rug. I was relieved the child couldn't see any of this. The embarrassment would have killed me. Gripping its hand, I whispered for it to follow me, we were almost there, and up the stairs we went to my bedroom.

I kept the light off and the door locked. After some guiding, the child sat on my bed. Somehow its stench had started to become tolerable. I could live with this smell. Live with it? Already I had fantasized a life with this stolen child in my bedroom. I would share my meals with it, read it bedtime stories, raise it as my own. We'd be best friends, forever and always. Someone I could talk to and share my deepest secrets. This could work. This could actually work.

I snuck a glance out my bedroom window. The neighbor's house still appeared dark. Nobody was awake. Nobody had noticed a goddamn thing. My heart wouldn't stop racing and I never wanted it to stop. I sat on the bed next to the child and tapped it on the thigh. It didn't react.

"Can you hear me?" I asked.

Nothing.

"How long have they kept you prisoner?"

Nothing.

"What ... what were they doing to you?"

Same response, rinse and repeat.

I wasn't going to get anywhere using words. I reached up and touched the thing's face, intending on peeling off its wrapping, but couldn't locate the end of it. I trailed my hands along its body and came up with nothing to grab. The child wasn't wrapped in anything.

This was its flesh.

"Oh my god."

I tried to leap off the bed but the child lunged at me, wrapping its arms around my shoulders again. It lay along the bed, dragging me down with it. I did not resist. Together we spooned in the darkness. My body still tense, expecting the door to burst open any second, either Dad or the next-door neighbor; I couldn't decide which possibility I feared most. Despite the anxiety, the child's embrace felt comforting. I never wanted it to let go.

I fell asleep in its arms and woke up the same day.

When I rolled over, I had to bite my lip to prevent screaming.

Its no-face had morphed into something somewhat resembling a human being's. Like its skull had been made of clay and someone had pressed their fingers against it, molding the template for eyes and a nose and mouth.

"What the hell," I said, reaching up to touch them.

Its face felt hot.

Overheated.

"What are you? Oh my god, what are you?"

My neighbor continued to hug me and I was left with no choice but to stay in bed. Its grip tightened, like it was restricting my lungs from breathing properly. I had slept most of the night, yet I was still dog-tired.

I woke up before I realized I was even going to sleep.

The child's face had continued evolving. Now it had pupils, and teeth, and pores.

And hair.

No longer an *it*, but a *him*.

I'd seen this face before.

Chills trickled down my body.

My body, which felt drained of all energy. I couldn't have gotten up now if I wanted to. There was nothing left.

This thing was doing something to me.

Emptying me.

Of what?

Goddammit, *of what?*

Before I could give it any more thought, I was asleep again.

Next time I woke up, I thought I'd melted into the mattress. I tried to move something as simple as my toe and failed. I couldn't talk, either. I couldn't do anything.

The boy was smiling now.

"Hello," he whispered into my ear. His voice sounded like metal. "My name is Denny." He hugged me tighter. "You are my neighbor."

I woke with just enough energy to stand from the bed. If I turned my head to the side, everything became dizzy, so I kept my focus straight ahead as I stumbled downstairs. In the living room, I stopped in front of a mirror and confirmed what I'd already expected.

I found my parents still on the couch. The crushed-up pills had disappeared from the table. Sometime during the night they'd woken up, snorted them, then passed back out. The boy sat on the floor next to them, legs Indian-style, staring up at me.

Smiling.

"Go home," he told me. "It's time to go home."

If I had still had a mouth, I would have told him okay.

I would have told him good luck.

Instead, I walked outside and headed next door. The bottom floor was still empty. Either they were asleep or had left for the day. I moved down into the basement, one step at a time. Despite no longer having eyes, somehow I could still see. Everything was blurry. Like a camera lens contaminated with a fingerprint. If I'd walked any faster I would have fallen, but there was no need to rush. I was where I was supposed to be. Where I was always supposed to be.

I entered the empty room and closed the door behind me and stood under the dangling lightbulb and waited.

Eventually, my family would come down to check on me, and together we would play.

There were no windows here.

The Vodyanoy

CHRISTINA SNG

I keep you in a tank
By the washing machine
Where I watch you bob
Up and down in the water,

Like an old buoy by the harbor,
Adrift and forgotten after
A lifetime of ill-gotten gains,
And great, terrible adventure.

I remember so clearly the day
You seized me from my family,
Butchering each one of them
While you made me watch,

Screaming till my voice was gone,
My home and everyone
I'd ever known and loved
Burned to the ground.

You took me back to your world,
Kept me as your property and pet,
Paraded me to your family and friends
Despite your people's obvious contempt.

I returned the favor to you
At your 40th birthday bash,
In the chocolate ganache cake
I made for all of you.

Watching your people choke and die,
Bleeding to death from the inside,
Was my greatest joy
In the endless years I lived with you.

I fed you the antidote,
Paralyzing you,
Transporting you home,
Far from everybody's eyes,

Placing you in a tank
I custom-built to keep you,
Floating like my lost foetuses
In the jars you filled with glue.

Often, my daughter asks,
What kind of monster are you?
I tell her you are a vodyanoy,
An evil water creature

Who loves to enslave girls
And destroy worlds.
We keep you here to ensure
Humanity is safe from you.

She likes that answer
And much later,
As a world-class mythologist,
Immortalizes you.

You've always wanted to be famous,
Boasting about how great you are
For the better part of twenty years.
Now you live in a museum.

Don't say
I've never done anything for you.

Imperfect Clay

LISA MORTON

What I've discovered:

We're all born broken.

My name is Ariché Stone; my mother's mother was from Chihuahua, and my first name means "dusk" to her people, the Rarámuri. My friends just call me Ari. I'm a twenty-five-year-old, heteronormative, cis-female magician, like *mi abuela*. I've had two year-long relationships with men; neither ended well.

You're probably more interested in hearing about my vocation, though.

I'm a magician, but not the kind who performs card tricks for drinks or produces doves from scarves. I'm only five-foot-three, and my hands are too small to palm anything larger than a grape. I also don't enjoy appearing in front of large groups of onlookers scrutinizing my every move in hopes of discovering my secrets.

That won't work, anyway, because my secret is that I'm a *real* magician, as in, I can perform severe alterations in matter by thought, willpower, and spellcasting. My particular specialty is working with organic material. Hand me a scarf, and I won't just show you a dove, I'll produce a small dragon that might set your hair on fire.

I'm in my third year of apprenticeship, and my master is the renowned Dr. Jameson Charters.

I don't like him much. Certainly, he's a genius at what he does, and I'm lucky to be studying *under* him (I know that because I hear it so often). But he takes a little too much enjoyment in making sure that I know I'm under him.

In case you're wondering why you've never heard of any of this, if you're thinking that I'm full of shit, just some new age believer gone too far, or maybe I'm a few meds short of sanity, let me assure you: Magicians (we call ourselves the Gifted) are real and we're all around. Sure, we don't advertise what we do; the first spell most of us learn is erasure, so you won't remember our miracles. Why? Because most of the history of the Gifted's interaction with humans consists of us being shunned, tortured, hanged, and burned. Maybe you've even met me and don't remember.

Anyway, I'm glad that I'm coming into the concluding year of my apprenticeship. For the last three years, I've shared a small apartment near the Charters Institute in Los Angeles; my roommate, Mackenzie, is also a third year apprentice but she's studying alchemy with Kristina Ling. She adores Kristina; they sometimes have coffee together after sessions.

Jameson is likelier to make me bring him coffee and then tell me to leave. Kristina teaches her students in a lovely, airy, wood-paneled studio behind her home in Brentwood. Jameson's lessons are learned in a dingy university lab, unpleasantly lit by overhead fluorescents that only add to the greenish pallor already provided by the color of the walls.

Fourth-year apprentices are required to create and complete a major project of some kind. It's the final test of everything they've learned, the Gifted's equivalent of completing grad school. Mackenzie's project will be to create a ship from seawater. She's always enjoyed the beach.

I'm going to make a man.

The final project must be something that will take at least six months to create. Mackenzie's ship, for example, will have to be a fully-functional vessel, with a solid hull and engines and navigation system and crew quarters and guest rooms and decks and everything else a ship needs to travel the ocean. When it's complete, she and Kris will take a cruise; if the ship is found satisfactory, Kris will approve Mackenzie as a journeyman magician, and Mackenzie will theoretically have a number of jobs to choose from. She's hoping someone will hire her to make underwater cities.

Me, I want to be a healer. I'd like to go from studying under Jameson to employment in R&D with a biotech firm.

If I survive Jameson. And if I can create a man.

It's a notoriously difficult project. Other students have tried and failed. There was a story (it sounds like an urban legend to me) of a young man named Nick Hronis whose attempt to make a woman resulted in a quivering blob of sentient jelly that pulled him down into its hot red essence, where he suffocated.

"Do you think you can do it?" Mackenzie asked.

"Do you actually think you can do it?" Jameson asked.

I told them both I could.

Mackenzie's next question was, "Why that?" When I didn't answer right away, she added, "Is this because of Devonté?"

"No," I blurted out, but after a few seconds I added, "Maybe a little ..."

I said that I'd had two year-long relationships; Devonté had been the last one, and I was lying slightly because we'd actually been together only nine months. Nine months: long enough for me to realize we were not pregnant with future potential. Devonté wasn't a magician, but a musician, so we understood each other well enough. Surely the creation of a song, made up of individual notes pulled from nowhere, is a form of magic.

My favorite evenings with Devonté were the ones we spent together at home, either mine or his (a guest house behind a beautiful if slightly tumble-down old Victorian in Silver Lake that was probably kept standing by a few spells Mackenzie had secretly cast). On those nights, I'd study and practice my magic, while Devonté, working with a laptop and a plug-in four-octave keyboard, would create his music. We'd occasionally look up at each other and smile. At some point we'd come together, kiss, grapple, fall into bed.

The evenings I was less fond of were when we went out. I've never been good at parties, but Devonté didn't help when he'd forget to introduce me to his friends. At restaurants (which he chose), he'd order for me. In small groups, he never even noticed how often he cut me off in mid-sentence.

I accepted it for a while, blinded by his many gifts, but then he started asking me questions about working with Jameson. The questions got more aggressive ("Are you sleeping with him?"), and Devonté got angrier. He'd throw open the door to his guest house and stride furiously around the backyard. This, too, I accepted for a while, but it was Mackenzie who finally got through. "You're not happy, Ari," she said, one night over frappuccinos, "and I hate seeing you like this."

So I worked up my courage and told Devonté it was over. He screamed for a while, apparently believing the decision to end it should have been *his* choice. He stopped calling after a week, especially when Mackenzie intercepted one of the calls and told him she could change all of his equipment into blocks of granite.

I, of course, could have done far worse to him. But *mi abuela*, who'd also been a healer, had taught me well.

Mackenzie was a little bit right, though: I *did* want to create a man in part because of Devonté (and Tom before him, and my father before him, and Jameson now). I would create a man who was a true partner, an equal in every way.

Mackenzie smiled at me. "I think my boat's gonna be easier," she said.

I told her I'd never been interested in easy.

So it began:

The ancient texts all indicated an order to the creation of a living being. First, a half-body was created from clay, to serve as the shell. Jameson—who had assured me over and over that I would fail my final project—gave me my own workshop room. It was small, just large enough to hold a steel table and a few counters, but it was fine for my needs. I set up two webcams; I might be working with unseen powers and eldritch magicks, but I would need to provide modern documentation to Jameson.

I started by choosing a name. I wanted my creation to be perfect, angelic. The thought of making him musical amused me, so I named him Gabriel.

It took weeks to mold the clay into a six-foot-long hollow form, only the open bottom half. The clay had ash from the tomb of an ancient Mycenaean priest mixed in, and some of my hair and blood.

The next step was bones. These I formed from cedar branches, laid carefully into the clay half-body.

Then: muscles from strong hemp fiber. Veins from cotton threads. Nerves from spider webs.

I was into the fourth month of Gabriel when I began work on the major organs. Jameson appeared from time to time to check my progress. At first his lip curled, but as the weeks wore on his expression became sober, his tongue silent. I thought he was no longer amused but impressed.

In Month Six, Mackenzie finished her ship. I rode on it with her, parting the waves of Santa Monica Bay on a glorious early spring day. We cried at the beauty of it all, and laughed, and hugged. It far exceeded her plans. For her graduation, Kristina gifted her with a fifteenth-century grimoire, still bound in the original vellum. Mackenzie received multiple job offers.

Gabriel, meanwhile, was nearing completion. Stomach, liver, kidneys, had all been placed. The brain had been crafted from the trunk of a 300-year-old oak tree that had just been cut down for a housing development. The heart was the purest mother-of-pearl, ground and mixed with a piece of dried skin that had once belonged to the body of a great hero. Jameson had reluctantly granted me that item from his own store of materials.

The last touch was something that none of the texts or records talked about, something that no other magician had—as far as I knew—ever tried. If it worked, I would be not just be a full magician and free of my apprenticeship to Jameson, but even famous.

The last touch was to place one of my own ribs into Gabriel.

I had performed simpler surgical procedures; I'd set broken bones and sealed cuts. Once, when my brother was five and I was eight, he'd been bitten by a rattlesnake, and I'd extracted the venom and smoothed out the bite marks. The biggest thing I'd ever done was remove a grapefruit-sized tumor from my Uncle Danny. Working under Jameson (always *under*), I'd assisted with psychic surgeries; I knew how to transplant organs, graft bone, and restart hearts.

I'd never tried any of these things on *myself*.

I knew I could ask Mackenzie for help, but I was afraid she'd stress out, try to talk me out of it. I thought the whole thing over and over for days, until I was convinced I could do it.

The time came.

I'd already prepared a replacement rib from some of the same cedar wood I'd used for Gabriel's bones. I would remove my clothing and lay down on the floor below Gabriel; I would clear my mind first, as I did before more difficult healings. When I was centered, I would use my right hand to reach into the left side of my chest; my fingers would move through the skin easily. The bone would be more difficult, but I knew my concentrated effort would finally allow me to press my fingers together through the bottom (floating) rib like I was pushing through butter. I would then remove the rib (about four inches of it), and immediately replace it with the artificial one. I expected pain, I expected a few hours of recovery as the cedar transformed, aligning with my marrow and osseous tissue.

And Gabriel would be born from a part of me.

It was, of course, agonizing, as this kind of labor should perhaps be. Removing the rib tore fascia that was not easily repaired. Because I needed to stay awake, I couldn't apply any unconsciousness spells. The pain nearly overwhelmed me, causing my vision to fail. I clung on to awareness and life, barely keeping hold. I felt the heat of blood smearing my body, smelled it bubbling up from within as well. My shuddering fingers found the replacement, shoved it in without caution or finesse. I had to turn it inside, each movement causing fresh waves of red excruciation. I bit back screams, choking.

At last I felt the new bone align, meshing with the existing me under my fingers. The wood changed, knit with the surrounding tissues. I extracted my hand, massaged the skin, healing. The blood dried beneath my touch.

I passed out.

When I awoke, it was a day later. I was weak, famished, still covered in dried blood, but alive and whole.

I placed my rib within Gabriel. His interior was complete. It took me three days to recover. I moved on to the final stage.

In another month I finished the upper half of the body, and then began the process of instilling life. For seven days—a span of time I'd not specifically planned, but which I recognized as rich in meaning—I chanted over my creation, invoking the most ancient energies. I paused only for my own basic needs. As the enchantments flowed from me, I watched the clay of his body take on the suppleness of skin, turning to a hue of dark bronze; the hairs I'd mixed in to the material of his head grew, becoming ebony, luxuriant waves. The features of the face took on definition, day by day molding themselves ala the most revered expression of classical beauty.

On the night of the seventh day, Gabriel took his first, trembling breath.

I leapt from my cross-legged position on the countertop and stood over him. He struggled for the second breath, then the third. I put my ear to his chest and heard the beat of his heart. Placing my hands on him, I focused my energies and he breathed easier. Soon he seemed like someone in a deep sleep.

I made notes, spoke to the cameras, and waited. I had an ice chest full of food, water ready, boxes of adult diapers.

On the eighth day, he opened his eyes. For a few minutes he didn't move, but then he looked at me. What did I see there? He was unfathomable.

"Hello, Gabriel," I said, in the gentlest of tones.

He blinked, uncomprehending.

I'd cast spells of intelligence, treating him as a human computer with a pre-installed operating system and files to draw from, but had I failed? What if he emerged as an exquisite, mindless thing?

He slept again.

On the ninth day, when he awakened, I got him to sit up. It was hard, he had to cling to me, but at last it was accomplished. He needed nourishment, so I held up a carton of almond milk, drank from it with exaggerated gulps. He watched, and I saw the first hint of understanding. I had a jug specially prepared of the milk enchanted with spells to speed his development; I offered that to him, and he reached for it. Working together, he took his first, sputtering sips.

He wanted more.

After that, his growth proceeded quickly. Within another week he was walking, eating everything I ate, and watching videos on a tablet computer. I replaced the steel table with a comfortable cot. He learned to use a bedside toilet.

On the eighteenth day, as I washed him, he stiffened under the cloth. We both looked down, both curious, both something more.

On the twentieth day, he used my name for the first time. "Ari," he said, as my back was to him while I made notes. I turned, saw his erection, saw the wash cloth he held out toward me, the pleading look in his eyes.

I at least turned off the cameras before I pushed him back onto the bed and climbed on top of him.

Maybe you're thinking that was a mistake, that I'd confused my professional and personal goals. Maybe you'd be right. But it was incredible, and when he climaxed inside me, I saw a new spark in his eyes.

After that he progressed even more rapidly. He learned to speak complete sentences; he watched movies and television and news shows on the tablet, he listened to podcasts and music; he took it all in, a ceaseless sponge. He told me one day he wanted to go outside. Dressed in a simple T-shirt, jeans, and trainers, we took a walk out of the dingy university building.

When he saw the sun, he cried then laughed. I cry-laughed with him. Female students we passed stared at him in open awe. He smiled at one, who turned a deep crimson shade.

After an hour, we returned to the workshop room and he slept. I was thankful we hadn't run into Jameson; I wanted his first meeting with Gabriel to be perfectly engineered. Of course he was curious; he took every opportunity to remind me that my deadline was only two weeks away. I told him I wouldn't miss it.

First, though, I wanted a test run with someone else, so I invited Mackenzie to meet him.

I tried to give Gabriel a crash course in morality first. He didn't immediately understand when I told him that he couldn't touch Mackenzie the way he touched me, but he agreed.

Mackenzie arrived at Gabriel's room at the appointed time. I opened the door, she saw him, and her expression froze.

"Hello, Mackenzie," he said, just as we'd practiced, "it's very nice to meet you."

She inclined her head toward me and half-whispered, "Holy shit, Ari, he's *gorgeous*."

The meeting went flawlessly. Gabriel offered her a bottle of water. She took it, and we all chatted mindlessly for fifteen minutes.

The only surprise was the way Gabriel held onto me. He squeezed my hand so hard it hurt. I was recording the meeting and didn't want to give away my discomfort, but it was hard to maintain my composure.

Mackenzie finally gave me a hug, told me how proud of me she was, and left. I did turn off the cameras, then, and asked Gabriel why he'd held my hand so tightly.

"I don't know," he said.

Finally, the time came to meet with Jameson. This, the last and greatest test, I wanted to take place in Jameson's office; I wanted him to see Gabriel walk in with me. We rehearsed the meeting for two days in advance. I felt certain we were ready.

In the afternoon of the thirtieth day of Gabriel's existence, we both entered Jameson Charters' office. I had a bound book of my notes and a thumb drive of all the videos that I deposited on Jameson's battered old metal desk before saying, "Dr. Charters, please meet Gabriel."

Gabriel thrust out a hand. Jameson, his eyes never leaving Gabriel's, rose slowly to accept the greeting. They shook silently, and then Jameson's eyes moved slowly over Gabriel's form, which I'd clad in a simple suit, no tie.

"Well, it's not a puddle of sentient slime, I'll grant you that," Jameson said, never glancing at me, "but can it *do* anything?"

"What would you like me to do, Dr. Charters?" Gabriel asked, smiling.

Jameson looked at me then and nodded.

I was released from my apprenticeship a week later, a full-fledged journeyman member of the Gifted.

Gabriel and I even became minor celebrities within Gifted circles. Of course Jameson tried to take much of the credit, but the real story (isn't it always?) was the one about the relationship between my creation and me.

As much as it hurt, Mackenzie and I gave up our apartment together; she'd taken a job in Seattle, and I had Gabriel now. With Mackenzie gone, he moved into the old apartment. We both began to receive job offers, me in the Gifted-friendly biotech firms I'd hoped for while Gabriel fielded offers to act.

We went to functions almost nightly—parties, networking opportunities, podcast recordings. Gabriel reeled from it at first, but he adapted quickly. He began to develop his own personality, his own likes and dislikes, his own friends and favorites.

One night at a party, I couldn't help but notice his arm wrapped around my waist. At first it felt warm, affectionate, protective, but at some point I realized it wasn't that. He was steering me where he wanted to go. When I disengaged he looked down, frowning. "What is it?"

"I'm just going to get something to drink."

"Oh. I'll come with you."

Day after day, night after night, he stayed next to me. When I sat at home one afternoon weighing three positions with different companies, he pointed at a folder. "That's the one," he said.

I laughed and looked up at him. "Really? I was about to move them to the pass pile."

"But I like them."

He didn't offer an explanation, and I didn't ask.

Two nights later, we had dinner with the firm's CEO and his wife, the latter obviously quite taken with Gabriel. The CEO, a man named Arthur Abrams, had chosen the restaurant, so I asked him what was good on the menu. He told me. When the waiter arrived, Gabriel ordered for me. He didn't order what Arthur had suggested. He was cool throughout most of the rest of the meal. By the end of the evening, I knew I wouldn't be working for Arthur's company.

Later, at home, I asked Gabriel what he'd been thinking. "I didn't like him," he said. "I think he just wants to have sex with you."

This was not the man I thought I'd created.

"You know I just lost that job," I said.

"That wasn't the right job for you."

I didn't sleep well that night. When Gabriel reached for me in bed, I got up, dressed, and left the apartment. I drove through the night, ignoring my phone. I watched the sun rise over Santa Monica Bay, wishing I still shared the apartment with Mackenzie.

I knew what I had to do.

I contacted Kristina Ling, who remembered me as Mackenzie's friend, and asked if I could rent her studio for a week. She said it was available in the evenings, and I could use it for free. She asked if she could meet Gabriel, who she'd heard so much about; lying, I told her she could.

I returned to the apartment, gathered books and equipment, told Gabriel something urgent had come up and I had to help a friend. He followed me with a continuous string of questions. "What's this project? How long will you be gone? Does it involve Arthur?"

I didn't tell him *he* was the project.

I spent the rest of that day going over my notes. Where had I failed? Had it been the hero, infesting the heart? The Mycenaean priest, his ashes poisoning the skin? Surely not the great, wise old oak.

What if it was the part of me, the rib?

Or ... what if it was something so basic to Gabriel's sex that not even magic could deny it?

I called Mackenzie. I cried as I told her about yesterday. "Oh, Ari," she said, speaking from her new apartment in Seattle, "I'm so sorry. What are you going to do?"

"I'm not going to take it."

"Good! I'm glad to hear that. But you can't just leave him ..."

I told her then what I was going to do.

That was five days ago.

Gabriel lies unmoving on a wooden table in Kristina's studio. That's where he's been since I invited him over and gave him an enchantment-infused tea.

Here's what I told Mackenzie: "I'm going to change him."

She'd taken a beat before reminding me that I'd once thought I might be able to change Devonté. This was different, I reminded her. I'd *made* Gabriel, after all.

I've been here for five days, chanting over him, performing purification rituals, invoking cleansing spirits, replacing and renewing.

I'm afraid to awaken him. I'm afraid the first thing he'll do will be to storm out of the studio, tell me I can never do this again.

But if that happens, I *will* do it again. I'll do it until I get it right. We may all be born broken, but some of us can be *un*born and *un*broken.

And our imperfect clay will be changed.

Spectral Evidence

VICTOR LAVALLE

"They think I'm a fraud."

"They think I'm a fraud."

I like to repeat this to myself in the mirror before I go out and do my job. It might seem weird to say something cruel right before I perform, but I thrive on the self-doubt. If I go out there feeling too confident then I don't work as hard. It's easy to get lazy in this trade but I take the job seriously. For instance, the word "psychic" does not appear anywhere in the window of my storefront. I never say it to my visitors. I call what I do "communication."

The other value in staying behind the curtain for a minute is that it gives the guests a chance to sniff around the parlor. They want to peruse the décor. They yearn to leaf through the handful of books I keep on the low shelf by the chairs. They're here for a performance, too. If I stepped out too soon they wouldn't have the chance to reconnoiter and then while I'm talking they're casting their eyes around the room and I have to repeat myself. Or, even worse, we just never make a connection. I'm not here for the ten dollars I charge during the initial visit. That money doesn't even cover the cost of all the coffee I drink in a day. Of course I'm in this for the money, everyone's got to make a living, but even that isn't the real goal. As I said, I am a communicator and when a session works right all of us in the room play a part in the transmission. And at the end I get paid so what's wrong with that?

I like to start work in the morning. Not many others do. Most folks who do this kind of work don't even open their eyes until mid-afternoon. Their days start in the early evening and run through the dawn. But that's not my way. For one, there's too much competition and I'm not part of a family or a crew. For instance, the Chinese work in small groups and cater only to their own. I tried to learn Cantonese for about fifteen minutes but one them took a liking to me and explained that no Chinese person would ever go to an American woman for help so what was the point? I didn't take offense to it. She communicated something important to me. The only thing I can still say in Cantonese is, *Can I have your address?* At least I think that's what it means.

The other reason I like mornings is because it means I mostly get old people coming through the door. You know why they're here? Most of them just want to talk and it turns out I do too. The cards I turn over at my table are secondary. Their loneliness is what blew them into my store. Isolation is as powerful as a gale force wind. There's times when we've been going at it for an hour or three and before they leave they actually force a little more money on me, like I'm a niece who should buy herself a new dress or something.

Which is why, I admit, I'm baffled by the three folks who are in the parlor right now. Can't be more than nineteen or twenty. Girls. They might be drunk. People who are drunk at eleven in the morning are scary, no matter what. They're so far gone they can't even talk quietly. Even when they shush themselves they only come down to about a nine on the dial. Immediately I figure they were passing by and decided to stumble in for a laugh. The best I can hope for is to get them in and out quick, collect a few dollars, then greet my usual morning crowd. I'm already looking forward to hearing about someone's endless concerns for a grandchild compared to corralling three drunks for half an hour. But work is work. They came in and I called out that I'd be there in a minute. Then I gave them five minutes to poke around. I tend to wait until they get to the books. The shelf is low and right by the chairs so if they're reading the titles it means they're probably sitting down.

"*Wonders of the Invisible World,*" one reads aloud. She moves on to the next. "*The Roots of Coincidence.*"

"Just sit down, Abby."

"Where is this lady?"

"It's too dark in here."

They're getting impatient. I give myself one more look in the mirror. I've been trying out this new look, a scarf wrapped round my head, one that drapes down around my neck as well. It makes me look like I'm from the silent movie era, think of Theda Bara in *Cleopatra*. But last week when I came out wearing it the guy in the chair asked me if I was a Muslim and things stayed tense after that. But these are three women and I tell myself they'll appreciate the flourish. More than that, I like the look.

I give the scarf one last touch and whisper the five words to myself. "They think I'm a fraud."

Then it's time for the show.

Two of them want to leave after ten minutes, but it's the third who won't get out of her chair. Abby is her name. Her head is down for most of my reading, hair hanging over her eyes. Her friends find her exhausting, but I try not to be hard on them. After all they haven't left her side. Abby is the only one who doesn't ask silly questions. I know how that might sound to some. Any serious question at a storefront psychic's must be, by definition, "silly." I get it. There's hardly room for all three of them on the other side of my table, it's a little wooden countertop that's really only made for two. But it doesn't matter, only one of them wants to be sitting across from me.

Abby's mother died six years ago, that's what brought Abby here. As soon as she says this I find a part of my heart warming to her. Suddenly she doesn't look all that different than my Sonia. What would she have been like if I'd died when she was twelve or thirteen? Would she have ended up in a place like this, with someone like me, or much worse than me? I find myself feeling even more grateful for her friends, no matter how impatient they're becoming. They will not abandon her, at least not today. I wish I could remember either of their names.

"I just want to know if ..." Abby whispers. Even though she seems tortured I don't think she's going to cry. She sounds resigned. "Is there something ... after all this?"

I have a few things I usually say when people skirt close to this subject, the whole point of being here. But I can't think of them because I've never had someone ask the question so directly before.

"Okay," one of the friends says, rising to her feet. She's the smallest of the three, but the most potent. This one is the sergeant-at-arms when they go out to the bar. She looks at me. "We're going to miss our train back if we don't leave now."

The other friend is in worse shape, she sort of oozes off her chair. For a moment it's not clear if she'll fall flat or stand up. She stands, puts a hand on Abby's shoulder but it doesn't look like comfort, only a way to keep her balance. It looks, for a moment, like she's crushing the poor kid.

Abby nods and finally rises as well. Is it strange that I'm thinking less of Abby and more of her mother? Trying to guess what I'd want some stranger to have said to Sonia if she'd come to them pleading for answers, or at least comfort. I guess the obvious choice is to say something simple and uplifting, but I can't do that about something so serious. Anyway, I can tell that's not what she really wants to hear.

While I'm struggling Abby opens her bag and finds three ten-dollar bills. She hands them across the table to me and of course I do take them. We've been together for a half-hour, exactly like I'd expected. I hold Abby's wrist. What should I say? What should I say? All my talk about putting on a show and I've got no preplanned act that will work for this.

"Yes," I say and squeeze her hand. It's the best I can do. The friends are already at the door, opening it and letting in cold air and sunlight. "There is more."

Abby looks at me directly; chin up. It's the first time I get to see her eyes. They're red from lack of sleep. She cocks her head to the left, seems surprised to hear me being so definitive. Then she pulls her hand free and follows her friends out of my life.

My daughter died a year ago this July. Sonia went to the Turning Stone Casino in Verona and jumped from the 21st floor. We hadn't spoken to each other in almost four years by that point. I hadn't even known she was living upstate. The coroner's office sent me an envelope with her last effects. Inside I found loose change and receipts from the ATM in the casino lobby, a flip phone that had somehow survived the fall, and a broken watch. It had been the watch that tore me open. I'd given it to her when she graduated high school. I didn't know she'd kept it all that time. It's not like it had stopped at the moment of impact or anything, the hands weren't even still attached. In a way that seemed more accurate. For her and for me time didn't stop, it shattered.

It's nearly eight by the time I get home. I've been in this apartment for three decades, raised Sonia here. After Abby and her friends left I welcomed my stream of regulars, but I thought about Abby the whole time. Most of my days are as long as this one. I leave early for work and don't come home until dinner. All I do is sleep in this place now. I avoid it. I should admit that to myself.

I come through the front door with my late night pick up of Thai food and in the kitchen I make a plate. For a little while—all of last year—I would eat the food right out of the container. There were times when I didn't even take the container out of the bag. It got to be too sad. So now I pull down a plate and utensils. I find the white wine in the fridge and pour myself a glass. I even sit in the same spot I've been using since my daughter was old enough to sit up in a chair by herself. She made such a mess when she first learned how to eat on her own and I never acted too patiently about it. Even before she died I found myself fussing at details like that, trying to trace a line from how she fell apart to something I'd done when she was still a child. Somebody is always to blame and most of the world tends to agree it was the mother.

How do I know I'm a true New Yorker? I actually believe the city goes quiet at night. Sonia used to have trouble sleeping because we lived next to the BQE and all night she heard the trucks and cars speeding by, but by the time I had her I'd long learned to tune that stuff out. It was only if I got in bed with her, like if she'd woken up and couldn't get back to sleep, that she'd point out the noise and I'd finally hear it.

Dinner done I wash the dishes and pop the cork back into the wine. I can't even claim I tasted the food. The apartment has one long hallway with rooms branching off from it. I pass Sonia's old room. The door is shut. I never open it anymore. In the bathroom I take a slow shower, putting in the time to wash my hair, a nice way to slow myself down. My bedroom is at the end of the hall. I get in bed and turn off the lamp by my bedside and I listen to the sounds of this city.

"It's too dark in here."

The words came from the hallway, but I don't even roll over. I know who it is.

It wasn't a week after Sonia died that I started hearing from her. She only ever says the one thing. When it began, once I decided to believe it was happening and not just something caused by my grief, I had her body exhumed. I thought that might be what her words meant. She didn't like being buried. But it didn't help. She kept on talking. I begged her to tell me what she meant but I couldn't get her to say more. I kept longer hours at the storefront because I wanted to be around other people. When I'm alone I can't drown her out.

"It's too dark in here."

She's come down the hallway now and joined me in my room. She'll go on like this all night.

A week later I get a walk in first thing. It's a middle-aged white guy, which is pretty unusual for me. He's standing on the sidewalk when I show up at nine. He asks for me by name. I bring him in and ask him to wait. I slip in the back but when he's looking at the bookshelf I take a moment to part the curtains and snap a photo of him with my phone. At least if he kills me the cops will find his picture. This might seem paranoid to some, but I don't care. It strikes me as a completely rational thing to do. I've had more seeing-eye dogs in here than lone middle-aged men strolling in.

I look at myself in the mirror, but this time I don't chant, not trying to charge myself up for a fine performance. Maybe he's a cop, that's the kind of energy he's emitting. They still do undercover operations on storefronts. Two years ago a guy gave away over $700,000 to a pair of psychics in Times Square. I won't put on a show for this one, that's what I decide. No scarf draped across my head and neck. He won't see Cleopatra, only me.

When I get to the table he's already laid out the ten-dollar bill. There's something insulting about seeing the cash before I've done anything. It looks new. Maybe he went to the ATM right before he showed up. Immediately I wonder how many more fresh notes are waiting in his wallet then I feel angry at myself for being so easily enticed.

His hair is white and thinning and slicked back and his sharp nose slopes down until the tip hovers above his top lip. He doesn't seem to blink even as I sit there quietly watching him. There's something predatory about him. Like he's a bald eagle and I'm a fish. I'm used to people looking at me like I'm a fraud, but not like I'm a meal.

"You're an early riser," I say, trying to be chatty.

He holds my gaze. "Where's the cards? Don't you people use cards?"

"We can," I say. "We will. But I like to talk first. It puts my visitors at ease."

He hasn't moved. Still hasn't blinked. His hands are flat on the table but that doesn't make me feel any safer.

"What kind of things do you say? To put visitors at ease."

I look up and count how many steps it would take me to reach the front door. Seven maybe and I can't say I'm in any shape to run. The backroom has a bathroom, but there's no emergency exit. I could lock myself in the bathroom and call the police, but how long would it take for him to smash his way in?

"What did you say to Abby, for instance?"

He says the name with emphasis but I admit I don't know who the hell he's talking about. *Do you know how exhausted I am?* I hardly sleep at night. At this point I just lie there with my eyes closed listening to Sonia. How am I supposed to think of anything else?

For the first time he moves, crosses his arms and leans forward in his chair.

"You don't even remember her," he says. He almost sounds happy about it, like I've confirmed his worst intuition.

"Abby," I say. Then I repeat it. I'm trying to get the gears of my memory to catch. When they do I snap my fingers. Maybe I look like a child who's happy to have passed a quiz. "She came into my store a few weeks ago."

"One week ago." He breathes deeply and his crossed arms rise and fall.

His eyes lose focus and he stares down at the table and the posture is exactly the same as Abby's had been. That's when I recognize him. It's not their faces but the way they hold their bodies.

"Who is she to you?" I ask.

"One week ago," he repeats.

I calculate my path to the door again. Maybe I could make it in five steps. This old girl might have one more sprint in her.

"What did you say to my daughter?" he asks.

I don't understand where this is headed. Is he back to ask for her fee? All this over a few dollars? The story of an overprotective father scrolls before me, the kind who won't ever let his child become an adult. I'm insulted on her behalf.

"She's a grown woman," I tell him. "What I said to her is confidential."

He drops his arms and slips one hand below the tabletop so I can't see what he's doing. Reaching into his pocket maybe.

"You're not a lawyer," he says. "You're just some scam."

The words settle on me heavily, a lead apron instead of a slap. I find myself needing to breathe deeply so I do but it hardly helps.

"Did she report me or something? Are you here with the cops?"

He pulls his hand out from under the table. He's holding a tiny flashlight, like a novelty item, a gag gift. There's a bit of fog on the inside of the protective glass, where the bulb is.

"I gave this to her years ago," he said. "It was still on her keychain when her body was recovered."

The blanket across my chest feels even heavier now. I think I might get pulled down, right off the chair.

"What did you say to my daughter!" he shouts and he throws the flashlight at me. It flies wild, goes over my shoulder and into the back. As soon as it leaves his hand he looks horrified and chases after it. He sends his chair flying sideways and it knocks into the shelf. A few of the books fall to the carpet. He hurtles through the curtain and he's in the back and suddenly I'm alone. I get up to run for the door. I'm sure I can flag down a cop car on the street. But then I hear her.

"It's too dark in here."

Now I plop right back down onto the chair, can't move my limbs. My mouth snaps shut and so do my eyes. What did I say to his daughter?

Yes. There is more.

He steps back through the curtain and he's got my scarf in one hand, Abby's flashlight in the other. I wonder if he's planning to strangle me with the scarf and, for a moment, consider that I'd deserve it. The death of my child was already my fault so why not his as well?

"I thought you would've run," he says quietly. He stands over me, holding the scarf and the flashlight as if he's weighing the two.

"There's nowhere for me to go," I say.

He sits on the ground right there beside me. It's strange to see a man my age cross-legged on a carpet.

"I won it for her at the Genesee County Fair," he says of the flashlight. "It's funny what kids hold on to."

Now I understand why he grabbed my scarf. He's patting at his face, his tears.

"Maybe I said something to her?" he asks. The words come out so quietly that I my first instinct is to lean in closer but he isn't talking to me. I need to get an ambulance for him. I rise up from my chair and slip my cell phone out of my pocket.

"I'm going to call someone for you," I say and he nods softly. Now I'm surprised I thought he seemed angry, when he's only delirious with despair.

After I call I crouch down beside him and wait for the sirens. This makes my knees start hurting instantly, but I can endure it. I grasp one of his hands between two of mine and I remember the way I touched his daughter when we spoke. They have the same delicate wrists.

I'm afraid to tell him what I said to her but not because I fear for my safety. Instead I wonder if Abby thought I meant something hopeful when I told her there was more to existence. If she lost her mother, if she missed her mother, maybe she thought I meant the woman waited for her across the veil, that they'd be reunited in a better place. Why wouldn't she think that? It's the story people prefer. What if I told her father the same thing now? Would he be tempted to try and join Abby? I couldn't be responsible for such a thing so I say nothing and simply hold his hand.

The EMTs arrive and help Abby's father to the ambulance. After taking some information from me they drive off with him then I go back inside the store. For the first time I can see the place like so many others must: the silly dim lighting, the bookshelf of mystic texts. It's such a cliché. No wonder my visitors viewed me as a fraud.

I go to the back and make myself some tea. While the water boils I lift the chair Abby's father knocked over. I gather the books that fell but instead of putting them back on the shelf I got in the back and drop them, one by one, into the trashcan. I find the scarf and leave it in the garbage with the books.

My work changed after Sonia died. There is an afterlife and it's worse than the world we live in. That's what I know. I don't understand why I kept the news to myself.

"It's too dark in here."

The kettle whistles in the other room but I can still hear my daughter. I suppose that will never stop. I make my tea then I sit at the table and wait for visitors. From now on whoever comes to see me is going to hear the truth.

Ode to Joad the Toad

LAIRD BARRON

Interesting times came to the city of many names, namely the Old Capitol.

King Mingy's bastard son, Larry, mounted the throne on the second Friday of the Month of the Dead—nine days of state mourning after the old king succumbed to advanced years and a white-hot iron shoved up his ass.

Long live the King!

Sunday evening, a buxom maid tended the royal instrument while two of her cohorts pinned young Larry's skinny arms. A fourth sawed off the head his Majesty should've been using more assiduously.

Long live the King!

Monday afternoon witnessed a blaze of trumpets and the flourish of banners to commemorate the ascension of King Richard Creely IV to the Lion Throne. Fresh graffiti in Ball Cutter Alley declared, *Dick is King!* Something few would argue. Except for whomever had scribbled, *Off with his head!* and *Kick against the pricks!*

Two figures lurked at the far end of the alley; a popular rendezvous for nefarious sorts. A short man, and a tall, toad-ish, something-other-than-man, at least a broadax haft wide. These worthies regarded the Piss Wall and its timely message.

"The maids are dealt with," the small one said to the wall. Sneaky Bob wore a raggedy cloak and boots, but a fancy doublet and hose beneath. He'd come directly from his apartments above one of the city's finer brothels, which, not coincidentally, had provided the "maids" who ushered King Larry into the Underworld.

"How dealt is dealt?" Walther Neck said. Words emerged from the wattles of his throat as a rusty blade grinds forth from its sheath. As a consequence, while he often spoke at length, he seldom raised his voice and seldom needed to do so.

"Bottom of the bay, chained to an anchor," Sneaky Bob said. "Cut 'em and dumped 'em over the side myself." His smirk projected the idea that he didn't favor women despite, or because of, his close association with them.

"This is good to hear."

Neck's physiognomy appeared toadish because he was in fact an Ur toad, which meant he was a venerable exemplar of toad-kind, yet infinitely more. The gods had gifted Ur (supreme among animals) with speech and reasoning, and empathy toward humanity that did not necessarily equal love. Possessed of the relative mass of a grizzly bear, Neck moved slowly and ponderously, except for those moments when he didn't. He favored a moldering black coyote pelt (skinned from Prowl, King of the Coyotes) and horrid cork boots of amphibian leather, though he required neither furs nor boots. He also carried a notched khopesh forged from a petrified slab of wood. Equally unnecessary unless he wished to fell a small tree or quarter an elk, which he sometimes did.

At the moment, he regarded his human companion and waited with patience honed from eons of cautious observance. Ur were savage as any beast; humans were masters of treachery. One could never be too safe around a man, especially a man who despised his fellows.

Many hands made light work of a *coup d'état*. Sneaky Bob's mitts had gotten particularly dirty. He'd arranged the most intimate details of the royal assassination and several others that followed. High lords decreed the time and place; Bob had selected who and how. Meanwhile, Walther Neck's task in the grand scheme of political reorganization was to resolve delicate personnel matters—mainly overseeing the severance of certain employees. Bob was the last name on Neck's list.

"I pray the seneschal is satisfied." Sneaky Bob referred to the King's right-hand hatchet man, Seneschal Geld. The Seneschal owed Sneaky Bob a knapsack of golden lions for services rendered. Which meant, as the seneschal's agent in this matter, *Neck* owed Sneaky Bob a knapsack of golden lions. Forebodingly, there was neither knapsack nor gold on Neck's person.

"The Kingdom is grateful for your sacrifice." The Ur toad's thin-lipped smile broadened. He rotated his unnervingly prodigious cranium to orient upon his tiny compatriot.

"Twas nothing," Sneaky Bob said. Between one breath and the next, *he* was nothing.

Come rosy-nippled dawn, Neck expelled shreds of a raggedy cloak, fancy doublet, and hose into the gutter of Eyebolt Passage. This alley bored into the mountain spine. The mountain carried the city upon its back. Stalactites oozed evil rainwater. Friezes depicted leering amphibian horrors (exceedingly toad-like) that once dwelt Below. Primitive tribes of men carved them, and worse.

Wind gusted through the alley. Dead leaves from the Royal Park whirled around his shoulders and added their number to the bed of mulch and slime and the fossilized skeletons of animals and men. He waddled forth to get drunk at a tavern and cogitate upon what he suspected to be his own imminent doom.

The Jackdaw Tavern was one of a baker's dozen similarly designated establishments scattered around the Old Capitol. This being the Month of the Dead, and thus against custom to sally forth sans costume, the proprietor assumed Neck's awful visage to be an artfully crafted mask. Neck rented a cell on the second floor. He licked a vat of curds and pleasured himself desultorily. The curds were fermented from the tainted blood-milk of rats that dwelt in the sewers. The rats surfaced at night to steal garbage and strip inebriated vagrants to the bone.

Neck was old as the Ur measure such things, perhaps old as rocks and trees measure such things. He recalled but fragments of his voluminous history. Had his existence always been so squalid?

He committed an array of dirty deeds for meager pay. Hatchet jobs. Murder. Mayhem. Skullduggery. Prostitution. He made a terrible prostitute. His Bidder's Organ followed its own star and Neck was down to mate whenever the opportunity presented itself. Alas, altering sex taxed the Ur-toad and he usually went into hibernation upon accomplishing the deed.

He squatted before a minor altar to Joad, patron deity of toads great and small, and other, less savory creatures of the bogs and swamps. This was a wooden effigy, nothing akin to the colossal mural in the Hall of Doom that depicted insatiable Joad as a behemoth, its tongue drooling down to the dirt, scores of men caught fast in its barbs like flies dying in amber. Not a popular deity, to be sure.

Hours burned away as Neck stoically awaited word from Seneschal Geld as per his instructions. The two had met in the flesh but once, many years gone by when the seneschal swam with the little pollywogs at the court of good King Mingy. Oh, how times changed. A man of Geld's current status did not treat personally with mercenary scum, lest it be by dead of night and in the presence of numerous heavily armed guards. Therefore, Neck anticipated contact with a trusted emissary of the seneschal; i.e., a professional murderer. That's how the great web and its functionaries worked— one man to arrange assassinations and then to murder the assassins; another man to liquidate the first fellow; and a third to take care of *him.*

Where would it all end? With a knock on the door and an envenomed dagger stabbed through his slow-beating heart, is what Neck suspected. Seneschal Geld preferred loose threads to be snipped. The powerful always did.

Shadows of clouds moved against the window. The gray gloom of his niche blackened at the edges and curled inward until only the last trace of light glimmered in the pitiless rhinestone eyes of the idol.

Where will it end, indeed? The altar of Joad whispered from many directions at once. That voice, like the creak of sun-whitened leather, sounded as familiar as Neck's own. *For you, it ends in a pot of bubbling oil and seasonal spices unless divine providence intervenes. Have you been keen?*

Have you said your prayers? I haven't heard from you since that sticky incident with the Croatoans.

Neck had been neither keen nor faithful. The only prayers he attended were those of his victims who occasionally babbled for mercy before their pitiable souls were snatched into the Underworld. He also attended the gurgling of his bowels where damned souls occasionally simmered and stewed.

You've done it now.

"The oppression of Mingy had grown intolerable," Neck quoted the sentiment of nobles and peasants who'd chafed under the old king's increasingly burdensome yoke.

But why, small fry?

"May as well ask why a man peels a scab. It's an impulse."

You're no man.

"Yet, here I squat in his rude habitation observing his customs. Digesting his humor and habit, no less."

Thanks to your meddling, the kingdoms of men shall endure naught but woe. Dick will see to it.

Verily, King Dick represented an existential threat to peasants and paupers everywhere his scabrous hand extended. Cruel beyond the usual measure, even for a mortal tyrant who were forced to pack every conceivable iniquity into their flea-span lives, the king would happily usher in a new dark age of fire and destruction and political whoredom.

"You're welcome," Neck said, drunk on the vile curds and his own rank fatalism. "Consider it a favor. Down with primates, eh?"

Don't presume me any favors. Perhaps "you" bear these primates enmity. I rather enjoy their antics. Joad's altar emanated a suggestive slurp.

Easy for a god older than the mountains to adopt a sanguine view. It had presided when creation was a soupy mess that spanned pole to pole. It had known worms and mollusks and trilobites as supplicants. It would persist for eons after other lifeforms gave way to cockroaches scurrying beneath a reddening sun. Meanwhile, the blight known as mankind spread across the countenance of the earth, virulent as mold through the meat of an overripe peach. Men slew Those Who Came Before or drove them into the low caverns where neither celestial light nor rain were ever felt.

The Ur, such as Neck, risked much to walk abroad. His mostly extinct kind did so only by the forbearance of lords of men. Ur perforce served human princes and kings as advisors and executioners, and, alas, toadies.

You are despised, it is true, the wooden god said. *Those who know their history fear you. Those who know you fear you. Hate you. Even Geld. Especially Geld. Especially Dick.*

"If they only knew how little they know," Neck said to the altar, to himself. A coal ignited in his belly; dull and dim, then rapidly brightening to the incandescent heat of a torturer's best iron. His eyes teared and for the first time in epochs, he heard the north wind sighing through the reeds of his distant home estuary. He smelled the brine of tidal water and he smelled green bird shit.

The altar fattened on liquid darkness and his misery. Long had Neck harbored greedy phantoms of inconsolable yearning and pitiless regret. Long and longer had he suffered guilt and self-reproach like perpetual festering wounds.

When you were voiding your bowels in Eyebolt Passage this lovely morn, did you perchance hearken the clink of a mostly dissolved vial as it vented from your nether port and rolled into the gutter?

"I fancied Bob carried a bottle of scent. My innards smell quite pleasant, I trow."

Bob did NOT carry a bottle of scent. Bob carried a vial of rare and deadly poison called Sanguine Dream Eater, several drops of which he intended to spice your curds at the first chance.

Few natural poisons or venoms upon the gods' good earth could affect the constitution of iron-gutted Neck. He was, so far as he had reason to believe by dint of brutal experience, immune to the worst effects of every foul, toxic material devised by man or nature except ennui. Indeed, when aroused, he exuded a toxic slime capable of inducing a hypnogogic state, nausea, and death. Victims reported an orgy of phantasmal imagery prior to their demise.

"Who would provide Bob such a rare potion for fell purpose?"

Someone who wishes to send you home. Someone wise enough to know you don't poison an Ur-toad, nay THE Ur-toad; you poison reality itself. The ulti-

mate trip! My guess? A king or his seneschal.

"It was a rhetorical question." Neck understood precisely what had befallen him—he'd been commanded to destroy Sneaky Bob and leave no trace. The seneschal, knowing full well the manner in which Neck typically assayed the disappearance of his victims, would snip two loose ends for the price of one. "Are vivid ... hallucinations ... the first stage?" Neck waved his paw and his claws briefly multiplied.

Time is a ring. You will meet the Terrible Shadow on High once more. I am sorry it has come to this.

"That makes two of us. Tell me what I must do, O hopping god." Though it sounded familiar, Neck couldn't remember the precise connotation of the Terrible Shadow on High. The phrase smacked of mystical gobbledygook used to frighten peasants. "Mighty Joad? Hello?"

The altar spoke no more, although a strong reek of bog remained in the garret. Neck vomited a steaming pile of curds. He lighted a candle and blearily contemplated the mess with the concentration of a haruspex.

A distant screech resounded; and again, closer. Green light seeped through the window. Shadows dissolved. The gaseous swampy stench thickened and the ceiling boards creaked. He looked up into the annihilating center of the universe.

A plethora of horrors crept forth to mingle with gentlefolk during the Month of the Dead. Costumes, greasepaint glamour, and expectations concealed the nature of these entities. First, Neck had entered the Jackdaw Tavern, his hideous form unremarked by neither proprietor nor patrons. Sometime later, five Men of the Flat Affect arrived, accompanied by a young woman. The men were likewise treated with affable diffidence despite their most unwholesome physiognomies. Common folk scarcely recognized them for what they truly were, particularly in broad daylight. The White Ones tended to lurk at the twilight margins; given to haunting lakeside cabins, abandoned asylums, and rural knolls popular with lust-crazed teenagers.

None could authoritatively derive the origin of these creatures. Rumors abounded: They had died, as mortal men usually do, then were reassembled and resurrected by the gods of death; they were mortal men, perfectly alive, but enslaved by enchanted masks; or they were an immortal servitor species marooned when their star-faring ship crashed on Earth and now emerged from crevices at the bidding of eminent black magicians such as Julie V, Satan's own bitch, and Jon Foot, erstwhile warlock to the Imperial Court. Whatever the truth of their provenance, Men of the Flat Affect, or White Ones, resembled typical men, except for visages sickly pale as clabbered milk, an unnerving rictus, and shambling gait that covered more ground than an untutored observer might warrant.

The Pale Society, as scholars designated their plurality, was divided between the Ecstatics, whose evil grins permanently curved unto their ears, and the Stoics, who were blank and cold as the very snows. Men of the Flat Affect spoke solely to lure victims from sanctuary and into darkness. They possessed no scrutable motivations save a love of sadism and murder.

This cruelty consisted of three Ecstatics and two Stoics, each yoked in servitude to the aforementioned woman, Delia Labrador. Delia wore a woolen cloak and a gemstone-encrusted domino mask. Her lips were blacked with ash. She sat at a table near the hearth, her scaly sandals propped most cavalierly. The White Ones loomed around her, their eyes gleaming with dispassionate malice.

Delia inquired of the proprietor whether he'd seen anyone interesting. She sought a man of superior bulk and rude countenance. A man who smelled of alkaline and the blood caked on his boots.

The proprietor pointed directly overhead and confessed he'd rented a cell to precisely such an enormous brute. Positively frightful, positively feculent.

"Did this gentleman perchance wear the mask and garb of Joad the Inimical, dread god of toads and a thousand slithering beasts?"

"As you say, lass."

"I am infinitely more experienced than these rosy cheeks suggest," she said. "Your bearing is that of a soldier. A footman from the minor tarot."

"Many days loafing and a few hogsheads of beer ago, yeah."

"Grace me with a soldier's appraisal. What did you make of your squatty guest? Is he a warrior? Would he strike fear in your heart on a field of battle?"

"Perhaps, ma'am, as a backstabbing scout. He's awful light-footed for a man of his bulk. Yeah, come to think of it, he trod softly as Slaughin's own shadow."

"Thank you, innkeeper. Sleep well and dream a red dream of butchery in the name of your old king." She smiled. "Oh, and my apologies for the once and future mess."

The proprietor's gaze shifted from the girl to her entourage and back again. He sidled away in the manner of a fighting crab.

Delia nodded to the Stoics who immediately lurched in tandem up the rickety stairs. White Ones typically perambulated as if directed by an amateur puppeteer's hand. She massaged her temples and awaited the inevitable outcry. This was the essence of her professional existence—auguries and dowsing to track prey; the casting of wards and charms; the deployment of her killers; support where necessary, although the White Ones tended to be a fire and forget proposition. Sic them upon a victim and profit.

She'd received the commission to eradicate Neck the Violator earlier that morning via a dead letter drop. The commission, labeled an emergency, did not enumerate Neck's offenses (many of which were common knowledge to denizens of the city's underworld) or whom longed for his death (it would've required ten men and a boy to tote such a scroll!), nor did Delia give a rotten fig. Neck represented an exorbitantly lucrative contract, and nothing more. Ur beasts were fearsome, but few living creatures could withstand the attentions of the White Ones. The cruelty she'd brought were exceptionally formidable and would make short work of the toad, his reputation notwithstanding.

For an exquisitely pregnant interval, nothing perceptible happened upstairs. Then, blood welled from ceiling planks and dripped onto the table, spattering her sandals. The Ecstatics cocked their heads and regarded this phenomenon with intense diffidence.

Time passed and more blood dripped, but the Stoics did not return.

"We'd best see what's keeping your brethren," Delia said with strained nonchalance. In an abundance of caution, she donned three extra murder rings, each set with a death's head gemstone attuned to a particular medium of slaughter. These stones complemented the settings of her bejeweled belt and the master death's head. Power swelled in her middle; power crackled in her delicate fists. The servitors proceeded her, naturally. Each of them was armed with a skinning knife, cleaver, or mallet. Rusty, jagged, and lethal.

Once, at least seventy or eighty years ago, a wealthy, albeit naïve, patron inquired how a nice girl like Delia became a black magician. She lacked the marks of discernment as popularized in literature—she wasn't a hag nor a be-goateed warlock. Her supple rosy flesh was un-scarified. Neither of her shapely ankles was attached to a hoof.

Delia said, *A toad resided in our family garden. Beastly, malevolent creature. It ate sparrows that flew too near. I was a child and believed in the fairytale of kissing frogs as a method to disenchant cursed princes. Much too late, did I recall that the tale made no mention of toads. Our tongues intertwined and its viscid bile burned my core. Light and purity were seared to crisps. The rest is the rest.*

That same patron then asked how she'd fallen in with the Men of the Flat Affect.

Simple. A cruelty of their ilk raped and murdered me, unaware that this violation transpired according to my own design. As such matters predictably follow, I arose via true resurrection and now own their souls forevermore.

The inquisitive patron made no further inquiries.

Ascending the stairs these many years later, she could be forgiven in indulging a morbid notion that her story had come full circle. The bitter taste in her mouth sharpened and a thread of drool unraveled along her chin. The fingernails of her left hand blackened as the murder rings sparked and sizzled.

Upstairs, a short, narrow passage extended too far and at a peculiar, canted angle, as though Delia and her entourage had entered the hold of a foundering ship. She glanced over her shoulder; the stairwell fumed with an aqueous green glow. Her breath caught. Her reactions lagged heartbeats behind the languid unfolding of events. She'd experienced variations of this nightmare on numerous occasions—a pitiful insect trapped in a glob of stiffening amber while a scarcely imaginable doom approached to snuff her life.

The second door on the left was ajar. Its opening brimmed with unnatural darkness. Stars and planets and capes of celestial dust could've swooped through this slice of void, so deep, dark, and cold. No glints of stellar fire winked from within, however.

Delia had studied eldritch portals in the Eleven Grimoires of Revulsion, Compulsion, and Repulsion. Such ruptures contravened physical laws of material reality and spanned immense distances as causeways between worlds, between galaxies. Some wormholes cored even farther, crossing into the Great Dark where flesh and brain represented provender for The Sleeping Dread. In either case, to cross the threshold was to court severe peril.

The Ecstatics flew off their feet and into the void; minnows yanked by the hook and line of a cosmic fisherman. She initiated a sign of greater warding. Too little, too late. A terrible force like constricting iron bands crushed her arms against her sides and shot her at velocity into the bottomless pit. Frigid wind shrilled. Her tears froze against her cheeks.

She comforted herself with a mantra.

I have known death and resurrection. And she fell, blinded in the darkness.

I have supped the black milk of the Gorgon and uttered her Profane Ululations. And she fell.

I have bent the will of the White Ones to my own. And she fell.

Julie V kissed my sandal. And she fell.

Jon Foot is my bitch. And she fell.

Delia had memorized twenty-three Greater and thirty-nine Minor Signs of Celestial Malice. Six names of demon kings quivered the tip of her tongue. None of these could save her, for she sensed her patrons were beyond communion. Consumed with mindless fear she could utter naught but an inchoate cry.

The sensation of plummeting ceased, instantly, seamlessly. She caught her balance, opened her eyes, and beheld the bland confines of a typical inn chamber, albeit marred by a pool of coagulating blood and the missing street-side wall which gave way to a panorama of slimy, towering mandrake and giant ferns (instead of shit-filled gutters and shit-spattered buildings). Mist oozed over beds of variegated moss. Birds warbled and chattered. Insects whirred in endless, stinging hunger; they clouded the surface of a sluggish river. She inhaled the rank humidity, tasting ancient bark and hints of spoilage. Here was a Verdant Hell of hermit philosophers—a reeking, fecund everglade, primeval as the fang of a dinosaur.

This everglade did not reside in any civilized region of the Empire. Civilization, so-called, was loath to suffer the existence of a man-eating garden within its confines. She beheld no sign of her erstwhile companions who might protect her against lurking predatory fauna. Had they dissolved during transit, or (scant difference) vanished into the gullet of a prehistoric reptile? Whence the sticky pool of blood? Thinking more clearly by the moment, she decided that moving away from the scene might be prudent, as scavengers and carnivores alike were certain to converge.

Delia walked parallel to the river, traversing hummocks and half-submerged logs, avoiding quicksand and fetid pools swarming with sickeningly large mosquitos. The fates of her entourage became apparent, by and by. She spied the mangled corpse of a Stoic depending from the boughs of a mangrove tree. A crocodile lazily chomped on the smirking remains of an Ecstatic. Bits of the others lay scattered from hell to breakfast. Likely sufficient disparate pieces to reassemble her slaves into grisly patchworks given a fortnight or so. Their kind was nigh indestructible, although they could be severely inconvenienced by the usual methods. Unlike the White Ones, *she* would not regenerate if reduced to a spool of guts and remnant fingers. She moved a trifle faster.

The white disk of a sun hung motionless behind its veil of clouds. Reality distorted here; time moved as slowly as the blood within the terrible lizards who drowsed in the reeds. In due course she emerged to behold a delta. Brackish water slopped near her toes. The water curved away into a milky haze, its expanse dappled by the breeze. Several crocodiles (more enormous than the specimen who'd eaten her death slave) lazed upon the delta; bloated logs decorating the tidal grounds of a ruined mansion.

"Neck has imbibed a dose of *Sanguine Dream Eater.*" She picked a gnat from her teeth with a knifelike thumbnail. "That is the only explanation. It is also the worst explanation." Where she'd landed was no more important than when. *Dream Eater* came in a dozen flavors, each more esoteric than the last. All varieties were capable of damaging the imbiber and his or her personal reality, but as a bonus effect, *Sanguine Dream Eater* scorched holes in the very fabric of space and time as it existed within the dreamer. Thus, the wormhole and this prehistoric jungle destination. She'd gone backward in time thousands, perhaps tens-of-thousands of years. The poison's nature also predicated a dreadful intimacy—the surroundings would undoubtedly bear personal relevance to Neck. No one ever truly escaped his or her provenance.

"The great toad spawned here," she said. "Eons gone by, he frolicked in this stew as a merry polliwog. Not a twatting care in the world. Thanks to his carnivorous predilections, here I tarry."

Do you not recognize your own home? She snapped her head around and saw nothing but tall grass. Either her inner demons whispered in a chorus, or the Dark Powers spoke to her on the wind. She regarded the ruins and their guardian lizards. Many years had passed and the mansion's dereliction was severe, so she but slowly twigged to the voice's insinuation that this was her childhood abode.

You penetrated the membrane, her inner demons said. *Your blood, your marrow, your animating force comingled with Walther Neck's effluvium—and not for the first time! Behold his Paradise and Purgatory for it is your very own—*

"Enough." Delia made a ward against malignant genius loci and supernatural possession and silenced the voice. She slashed a thick sapling with her flinty nails, and it toppled. She forged the narrow delta channel, probing ahead with her impromptu staff. The nearest albino crocodiles caught wind of her scent and hastily flopped into the water.

Such a luxurious mansion in its heyday. She wandered its marshy halls, ceiling open to the heavens. Father had been a moderately wealthy freeman. He and Mother protested the policies of someone a bit too high up the food chain, organized a peasant rebellion (really a glorified work slowdown), and were branded dissident traitors for their pains. Father lost his estate prior to his execution. The aggrieved nobility shipped Mother north as a trained slave. She placed Delia in the care of a distant relative; her final, desperate act. The relative, a strange, bloody-minded woman, was an occultist who'd endured the tutelage of several grand masters and was found wanting. However, the occultist recognized Delia's aptitude regarding the dark arts. The child's course was set.

And now ...

Walther Neck sprawled in the backyard where a magnificent-ly-tended garden had rioted into a jungle. He lay as still as the dead, his left paw locked onto the throat of a Stoic. Splinters of bone protruded from the Stoic's limbs. Its staring wet eyes swam with gnats. Mindlessly loyal to the bitter end, it had expired pursuing her quarry.

Delia could have revived her minion with a finger snap—although the result might've proved more interesting had the Ur swallowed her pet. She poised to make the gesture and utter the fateful syllables. Neck coughed. His grotesque bulk shuddered. He pushed the corpse aside and laboriously rolled to his knees. That brought him and Delia to approximately the same height.

"So, we meet again," she said. "You look terrible."

He glared at her. "Says the goth chick with the lazy eye and bad makeup." His breath was a pungent cocktail of half-digested carrion, hot offal, and poison.

"And that voice ..."

"We can't all be silver-tongued devils like Rabbit Abbot." He knew she was right. It pained him, nonetheless.

"Rabbit Abbot isn't a name I recall."

"Exactly. And you've never crossed my path either. I'd remember your attitude."

"As a young toad, you dwelt near the foot of yon vine-entangled fountain." She retreated several steps and opened her hand. "I held you in my palm."

"Hate to be the bearer of ill-tidings, crazy lady—I haven't been a "young" anything since the Bald Mountains were pointy and the East and West Continents were a vast, swampy plate."

"We kissed. It did not end well."

"If you can't discern the difference between a frog and a toad, you were doomed at the outset." He climbed upright. His shadow fell over her. "I'm dying a slow, horrible death via poison. The pain is exacerbated by this tedious conversation."

"Yes, yes, you swallowed a dose of *Sanguine Dream Eater*," she said. "I suspect that Mr. or Mrs. X became anxious, fearing a delayed reaction meant you'd either avoided the poison or were immune. He or she sent me to finish the job."

"Mr. X? Oh, no mystery in that regard. Seneschal Geld decided to terminate my services now that the royal coup is accomplished."

"That asshole. I wondered who could afford the extravagance of SDE. There are seven doses left in existence. Er, six doses."

"You intend to come at me, or what? The sun is going to set in a million years, give or take, and I don't want to miss the spectacle."

Though he didn't appear to be in any condition to threaten her, Delia maintained a healthy distance as she turned the problem over in her mind. "Here we are at a pretty pass. I hesitate to dispatch your miserable soul to the Great Dark. Due to these exigent circumstances, our fates may be temporarily intertwined."

"O fortunate me." Neck peered at the sky. "Don't take offense when I say that your intentions are the least of my problems." He pointed at a speck that detached from the sun and floated closer. "You will regret that bit about our intertwined fates. Apologies."

A hair-raising shriek echoed across the gulf.

Her demons returned with a gleeful monologue. *Time is a ring. The hole in its heart yawns. It is the crack that runs through everything. It is the bottomless pit that nothing can fill. The great toad is expressed in his myriad iterations as some believe all men are mere fragments of a singular god.*

"What approaches?" she said.

"He who finally noticed our arrival. *The Terrible Shadow that Dwells on High*." He glanced at her. "Heard of him?"

"God of the beasts of the air. Fisher of souls."

"Fisher of *amphibian* souls. And also whomever happens to be standing nearby."

The speck bridged the gap with astonishing velocity, and grew by magnitudes—a monstrously enormous heron surmounted by a hemisphere of glittering shadow, astride a second inverted hemisphere of thunderheads.

The heron to end all herons descended to the mouth of the delta. It might have swallowed an elephant; it might have devoured an army mounted upon elephants. Water boiled to vapor with each crashing beat of its wings that cast shadows across the earth and the water and into the forest. Wind battered Neck and Delia and they were drenched. The heron of herons folded its dripping wings and loomed. Azure head and feathers; crimson-throated, crimson-beaked; midnight black of breast; and eyes of molten gold. Tall as the trees, its bill parted to emit a frightful shriek that caused lesser birds to pelt against the canopy and the crocodiles to hurl themselves into the reeds, tails whipping madly. One lizard rolled over and floated belly-up in the shallows.

Delia went to her knees and bowed her head in instinctive supplication. Neck covered his eyes to ward off flying chaff, and waited for whatever must come.

"Oh, fuck me running," the God of Herons said, nasally and dinful. "I know you, toad. I've had you in my throat, once upon a time."

"That's what your mother—"

"Shut up, be-warted imbecile!" The heron raised his voice and the blast was bonfire-hot and rich with blood and righteous bile. "Let me recount our history. I speared your fecund sire with my bill and drank his nasty juices until naught remained but a warty sack. My mate Agatha feasted upon the rancid innards of your dam. We romantically gazed into one another's eyes as we gulped the vast, ocher strings of eggs that were your embryonic siblings. We gorged upon the pollywogs who fled in vain beneath the mossy sludge of these ponds. Made it a game of hide-and-seek, in fact. How many wrigglers could I shish kebab at once? Loads!

"But you, you, foul, poisonous, feculent turd on legs! You caught in my throat as your glands oozed a hypnogogic poison, not unlike the *Sanguine Dream Eater* I scent upon you now. Your squamous, vile hide choked me and I spat you into the world. Good riddance, says I. Then I curled into my nest for five-and twenty winters, shitting explosively while regurgitating a bellyful of hapless lesser glade dwellers as I succumbed to a febrile dream of unlife."

Neck wiped the heron's spittle from his misshapen dome and waited for the trees to cease swaying and the roiled waters to calm. "Aloysius, either eat us or fuck off back to your stump."

Aloysius, God of Herons, The Terrible Shadow that Dwells on High, Bloody Bill, and a hundred others, shifted his head side-to-side. "I would, I would, dear slimy brute. Yet, I dare not. You are a piece of meat wriggling beneath my invidious talon, but you are also an aspect of Dread and Awful Joad whom I'd rather not offend. His claws are long, his tongue is longer. As for the semi-mortal, she is human. Worse, she reeks of the White Ones' unlife taint and it riles my gorge. Agatha ate the little shits like Turkish Delight, Green Goddess keep her."

"What does he mean, you're an aspect of Joad?" Delia, still bowed, spoke sotto voce to Neck.

Neck said, "The heron's fearful presence is a purgative of the subconscious. Memories return to me as if gaseous bubbles long suspended in muck rise to the surface of a lake. It sounds correct, although fog remains. I am diminished from a previous life. Greatly diminished."

"Hurrah!" she said. "Are you a toad dreaming you're a god, or the ass-end around?" Her demons hissed, whether in rage or delight, she couldn't tell. "Neck, you gorgeous devil! All becomes clear—you've likely died a thousand deaths, only to reincarnate anew. Albeit with your original form and vestigial memories. You exist as a broken mirror exists. Each scattered shard reflecting within its frame of reference, yet an inviolate piece of the whole. We might yet quit this backwater oblivion."

"To what purpose? The king desires my head on a stick. You mean to collect the reward. The definition of untenable."

"*Geld* desires your head," Delia said. "Not I. Considering this revelation regarding your provenance, a bag of coin is insufficient.

The residual damage of SDE is liable to be ongoing. Which means you may persist as dual iterations simultaneously. God of the Toads and toad. The possibilities are staggering." She poked his chest. "Someone well-versed in esoteric methods must watch over you to ascertain your body and soul remain integrated with corporeal reality."

"I kind of like it here," Neck said. "It's peaceful. Perhaps, I'll rest a while ..."

The God of Herons clawed a gout of muddy water into the air. "Forget it, bilious sack! O murderous sucker of slugs! This is my demesne. Your particular acre resides far from these shores, should you crave a return to that benighted realm. Go squat in primacy, over garter snakes and tadpoles. Go in peace or go in pieces. That's the best offer you'll receive today."

"Fine. How do you propose I effect my departure? So far as I can determine, the poison is a one-way trip."

"Soon, the *Sanguine Dream Eater* in your blood shall dissipate," the God of Herons said. "The wound in your mind shall seal. Neither of you belongs in this paradise. You shall be expelled from my demesne as a splinter is ultimately disgorged from its seat in flesh."

Neck regarded Delia. "This is beyond my ken."

She nodded. "Our intrusion has deformed this reality—time and space are out of joint. By all rights, we should rot for eternity or be devoured by a lumbering denizen of the land. However, the god of the everglade wishes us gone, so it shall come to pass. His will is irresistible in his domain. I would expect the earth to open beneath our feet and swallow us at any moment."

"Allow me to assist." The God of Herons pecked at the shore with his executioner's bill. The ground crumbled and fell into a pit. "You'd best be gone when I return." He fluffed his plumage and waded into deeper water before launching toward the sky.

Delia and Neck exchanged glances. Since there was nothing for it but to do it, they descended. They rested at the bottom. A tunnel cored into the gloom. Above, the patch of hazy sky winked out like a blown candle and they were sealed in pitch blackness.

Delia gripped his elbow as they moved forward, blindly into the unknown. In a while, a guttural, wheezing cry echoed from the way they'd come. It sounded again, closer. Something enormous must've uttered such a cry.

"Dare I ask?" Neck said.

"Faster," she said. "Lest you meet yourself on the road through purgatory. I am unprepared. His freedom to roam shall be curtailed in our material reality. We must survive to reach it. Haste, toad."

"I've *seen* myself, glorified in the Hall of Doom." He began moving again, dragging her along. "Joad would be sorely disappointed in what I've made of his legacy."

Delia said nothing.

"One question." His raspy voice floated strangely in the dark.

"Speak it, toad."

"Did we really kiss?"

The sands of midnight had recently passed through the hourglass when Seneschal Geld strode into the royal bedchamber sans invitation. Tall and lean, he bowed, bending like a half-opened folding knife. His conical hat of office scraped the tiles.

"Your Majesty, pardon me."

King Dick, sunk to his chin in an herbal bath, was not amused at the interruption. The king was seldom amused unless the activity related to something pleasurable, such as the complete destruction of one of his countless enemies or detractors.

"Why are you bothering me, Geld? Your expression of acute fear is troublesome. What has gone wrong? I do hope you've snipped all loose ends and nothing will come back to haunt us. Please be exceedingly concise as I have no wish to become acquainted with the details of your heinous undertakings."

"Heinous undertakings on your behalf," Seneschal Geld said.

"Indeed? You must truly be in the soup to speak with such temerity."

"The good news, Sire? The "loose ends" are well and snipped, as you say. The bad news? The, er, help in this matter are rather disgruntled. If you take my meaning."

"Yes. I hear you've solicited the talents of a black magician, among other unsavory villains. Kudos on securing the magician—I thought Jon Foote and Julie V were the last of that ilk for another generation or two. Never mind. How does this concern me?"

"Assassins threaten my person," Seneschal Geld said. He'd not seen a Flat Affect Man prior to tonight. However, when a Stoic had emerged from behind a colonnade, there could've been scant doubt as to its purpose or ability. "The miscreants lurk within the palace itself. As your loyal and trusted servant, it would stand to reason that my problems are inevitably your problems. Sire."

King Dick scooped soap into his hand and blew a bubble. "Dear Geld, as of this moment, your position is vacant. Hie thee into town and take lodgings wherever you deem fit. Wait for the herald to announce a call for candidates. I'd say a tenday at minimum. Perhaps a fortnight. If your head rests upon your shoulders at such time, please be welcome to submit yourself with the other applicants."

"Sire—"

"IF you are not beheaded, Mr. Geld. Or worse. My money is on something worse."

Seneschal Geld didn't bother to plead his case. King Dick's favorite bodyguards waited outside the door and would cheerfully cleave the seneschal from stem to stern if their master so much as whistled.

"As you say, Sire." He bowed again as protocol demanded, and hastily departed for his own chambers to retrieve a satchel of personal items before making good his escape.

A draft moaned in the corridors of power. Lamps were spaced at lonely intervals. Seneschal Geld bunched his robes in his hands and hustled, aware that some grim fate pursued him.

Indeed, an Ecstatic blocked the passage back. The seneschal ducked into a doorway and fled through a series of unlighted ante-chambers. The palace was a honeycomb of levels piled upon levels that few had ever fully explored. It sprawled with disorienting grandeur and he soon lost his way. No matter what door he opened or what hall he traveled, a White One was there to chivvy him along, down short stairwells, then longer, narrower stairwells connected by longer, narrower, less illuminated passages. First dust, then moss and mold and dripping water as stone roughened and cracked with antiquity. No matter that he broke into a trot, then a panicked gallop, a White One paced him with a queer, shuffling gait.

Finally, he staggered, gasping and spent, into a decrepit cathedral lighted by a pair of iron braziers. The braziers seethed and simmered with red coals. Broad flagstone steps descended to a shallow basin at the heart of the chamber. Ankle-deep water rippled, disturbed by the flow of hidden spring. A scaly plinth, surmounted by a rusted iron hexagonal pyramid, rose from the center of the basin.

The temple walls were formed of basalt. Weird red shadows crawled across weirder stone and plaster effigies of neglected gods. The Heron; the Toad; the Leech; the Sleeper; the Lord of the Black River; and the FatherMother. These figures towered within alcoves that nearly scraped the vaulted ceiling.

There were no visible entrances besides the archway. A trio of White ones slouched at the threshold, content to observe Geld's escalating terror. They grinned and scowled, perfectly still, perfectly content.

A dripping, squelching eructation caused the braziers to gutter. Geld turned even as the distended, lolling tongue of Joad drooled forth, its barbs scraping over stone. He sprang backward, but the reeking flesh coiled around him, its barbs pierced him, and he gasped in pleasure or agony; both are the same. He was drawn upward, kicking and squirming toward a monstrous bulk shed of its plaster shell.

This isn't as grand as the Hall of Doom, Joad whispered in the seneschal's mind. *But it's a decent likeness.*

King Dick nibbled a fig. He sipped wine from a gem-encrusted goblet. He said, "Well, I suppose that's the last anyone will ever see of the pointy-headed bastard. Unfortunately, I'm down a seneschal. He was pretty effective, too. He absolutely terrified the staff."

Nearby shadows dissolved at the merest hint of unearthly radiance to reveal Delia in repose upon a pile of silk cushions. She too munched on figs and enjoyed a lovely goblet of wine.

"Don't think of it as losing a seneschal. Think of it as gaining a court magician."

"And a ... whatever in the Nineteen Hells your friend is," the king said.

"An exquisitely dangerous pet."

"As you say. Meanwhile, the bath grows tepid. Perhaps you'd care to fetch that fluffy towel and dry off the royal fundament?" His smirk faded as he noticed the water in his tub was rather inky. It stained the marble a deep, rich crimson. He wondered if he should call for his guards, if it would make a difference.

The faint glow suffusing Delia's flesh drained into her eyes and they briefly flared, metallic purple. Then her eyes too dimmed and dimmed and she sank into the shadows.

"Er, tell me more about our burgeoning friendship," the king said to make conversation.

"It isn't going to be anything like you imagine," she said.

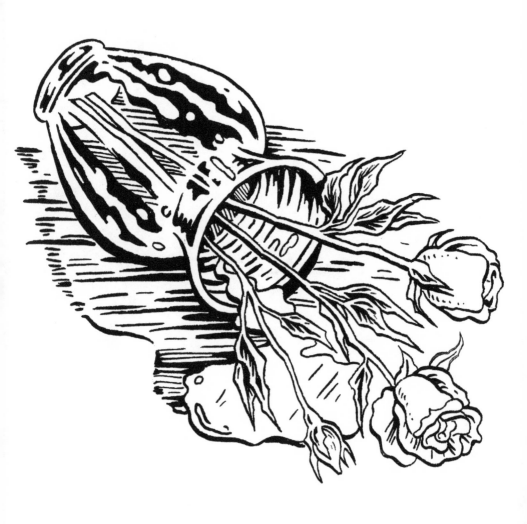

Only Bruises Are Permanent

SCOTT EDELMAN

After Amanda broke her lover's wrist, but before she broke his legs ...

After she threw him out of her apartment, but before she threw him out of her apartment window ...

She found herself in a tattoo parlor, not entirely sure how she'd gotten there. She was alone, studying the art pinned to the walls, having made up her mind, while at the same time unable to make up her mind.

Which wasn't at all how she'd intended to spend that evening.

What she'd planned, what she'd expected, was nothing more than a home-cooked dinner with Jim, followed by a movie—a romantic comedy she hoped, if she could sway him from yet another action movie—with some cuddling on the couch while they watched. Which would lead to more than just cuddling, and mean, as usual, they'd never get to see the end of that movie. Which was the way she liked it. Or if not, well, *liked* their long-established routine, at least gotten used to it in a way that was oddly comfortable.

All of which should have had her asleep by then, but instead, there she was—her muscles sore and growing even more so from the incident which had occurred earlier—as she paced after midnight under fluorescent lights along a wall of skulls and sea serpents, of butterflies and flames, considering, rejecting, wondering which symbol the long-simmering confrontation that had brought her there called for.

She'd been cleaning up from the meal she'd prepared after a long day of work as a court reporter—clearing the table, bagging the leftovers for the next day's lunch she'd planned to tote along, scraping the dishes before sliding them into the washer—when she happened to look over at Jim—

Jim who'd done nothing all day but hang around her place and play video games since his own apartment was a sty—

Jim who hadn't bothered looking for a job in months—

Jim who never thought to ask if she needed help—

Jim who wasn't even that good in bed—

And thought ...

No.

No more.

It wasn't any one thing which had planted that thought there.

It was just ... time.

It was just ... enough.

So she'd asked him what she'd never dared ask him before, to make a choice. To come over by her side and help—or go home.

And then he'd said what he'd never dared say before—or not said, really, because he only laughed ... and somehow things got physical.

Somehow.

Just like the somehow which had gotten her to the tattoo parlor.

She'd found herself hurling that final plate in her hands like a frisbee, which rained peas as it whizzed by Jim's head before shattering against a closet door (though perhaps it had ricocheted off one of his ears first, she was no longer sure, it was all a blur by then), after which he stopped laughing. And then was up, pinning her arms to her sides. Soon they were bouncing off the walls, the glass over her family photos cracking as the frames dropped to the hardwood floors, the two of them continuing to ricochet until she heard a crack, followed by Jim's scream.

Seeing him hug his oddly angled hand to his chest, she knew she once would have been quick to check on that wrist. She would have knelt to bandage it, covering it with kisses as she did so. But instead, she took the pause created by the moment of his shock and pain and uncertainty as a chance to push him out into the hallway.

He didn't resist her, whimpering as she pelted him, shepherded him, and through the peephole of her front door she could see him limp down the stairwell, not bothering to wait for an elevator.

After he was gone, she looked out her apartment window (the one through which he would later fall), and once she saw him down below stumbling toward the subway, she headed for the streets herself—though she, feeling calmer than she had in a long while, felt no need to rush, and waited for that elevator—in search of what she did not know, and eventually ended up inside a tattoo parlor she'd previously often walked by on her way to and from the courthouse, but had never entered.

It was time she went in, she thought.

Time to say—that was then, this is now.

Time to draw a line between.

So she moved through the shop, staring at the orchids and eagles on the walls, the hearts and hummingbirds, the devils, the imps, and the angels, seeking an image which spoke to her.

Finally, less (or so it felt) because the design was perfect than because a demarcation was demanded that night, she made up her mind.

"I'll take that one," she said.

She didn't mind the pain.

She'd grown used to the pain.

"You got ... a crescent moon?" said Jim, whom she was surprised to see had, even with his fracture, circled around and followed her and been waiting outside the tattoo parlor until the session was done. And yet, suddenly knowing him better in that instant than she had known him before, realized ...

No. She shouldn't have been surprised. He wasn't going to let things end that easily.

His wrist, unattended to, was swollen and red. Her throat was slightly swollen as well, beneath the protective layer of plastic wrap which the tattoo artist had applied once he was satisfied. She liked the way it felt. It told her a change had begun.

"Go away," she said, as she turned and walked back to her building, tightening her scarf around the open collar of her jacket to prevent him from continuing to see what the needles had pierced along her throat. He was undeserving. He was undeserving of it all.

"It's a cliché," he said.

"Stop it," she said. "You're being foolish. Go home. It's over."

"*You're* a cliché," he said.

"Leave me alone," she said.

But he wouldn't. He didn't. She didn't care. Because he *would*.

She didn't know why. And she didn't know why she knew. But she *knew*.

He followed her all the way back to her building, back up the stairs, and back to her third-floor apartment—*her* apartment again now, hers alone, no more sleepovers, no friends with benefits—and back through the doorway out of which she'd pushed him.

Allowing him to think her calm, she let him follow over the threshold.

But once they were inside, once none but him could see, she reached for her anger, and spun to unleash it on him, only … not so fast that she could avoid his good hand, the one with fingers which could still crush, from encircling her throat, his palm pressed against the moon she'd had inked there.

She winced as he pushed her, he pulled her, and knew she couldn't escape that hand through force alone. She wasn't that strong. At least, not yet.

So she dropped to her knees, and then to her back, pulling him down on top of her. He maintained his grip as they fell, instinctively tried to steady himself with his other hand as they hit the floor, and wailed as he landed on his broken wrist, a wail which couldn't entirely cover the ugly sound of bone grinding on bone.

She wriggled from beneath the weight of him, and he recovered enough to make a weak grab for her with his good hand. She dodged him, and kicked out, scraping his right cheek with the toe of one shoe, catching his nose with her other heel. She felt an odd pride as she sensed it crunch, a feeling better than any she'd felt during the time they'd spent on the couch with him watching movies which were only an excuse for what would come after.

He dropped back, but only for a moment. Then he was on his feet, and roared with an intensity he'd never before achieved but she'd always suspected he could. He flung himself at her, his good arm outstretched, the other hanging by his side, his wrist twisted even worse than it had been earlier. She spun quickly out of his way as he lurched once more for her throat, but all his fingers caught was her scarf. The tug at her throat as he lost his balance and hit the window almost pulled her after, but the fabric snapped free as his weight shattered the glass.

And then he was gone.

She steadied herself, took a moment, and stepped to the window, where she stuck her head out cautiously through the jagged shards which remained in the frame. Down on the sidewalk, he was on his back, her scarf still tight in his fist.

She touched her fingers to her throat, felt the now-shredded plastic which had been spread across her fresh tattoo, wondered what he had done to what she had done, and knew—a crescent moon could never be enough, not any more, to honor what had occurred that night.

If only Jim hadn't laughed when she'd asked him to put down the controller, to get up off the couch, to help.

But he had.

The police treated her much better than she expected, considering all the horror stories she'd heard about situations like these. What happened to women after a crime was so often a second crime, a bigger crime. It occurred to her that maybe the reason she was being believed was due to one of the officers recognizing her thanks to her job at the courthouse.

But maybe it was instead because, as she calmly told them the events of that night, talking with words similar to those she'd often heard while typing away at her job, she could barely speak above a whisper after what Jim's good hand had done to her throat.

Or maybe it was because they could see the bruising across her body as it began to rise. She felt a tenderness, a swelling there when she touched it, and imagined some of that had to be evident, even to those not inside her skin.

As they questioned her, there was still another surprise—even though Jim wasn't moving when she'd peered down at him earlier, it turned out he hadn't died from his tumble out their window—a fall from the third floor is only sometimes fatal—though it would be awhile before he was awake and the doctors could fully diagnose the extent of his injuries.

And yet one more surprise—

She found herself thinking a darker thought than she'd ever thought before, than she'd ever thought it possible for her to think.

She remembered the day she'd first visited this building with the agent, and it occurred to her—if only she had rented the other available apartment she'd seen, the one up on the sixth floor, rather than this one, the evening would have ended quite differently. As she considered that memory, weighed that choice made by an earlier Amanda, she realized—she wouldn't have minded that.

That was the biggest surprise of all.

Eventually, once the EMTs had finished checking her over, once she'd refused to be taken to the hospital, and once the officers seemed satisfied with her multiple repetitions of what Jim had done, what Jim had said, they all left her alone. And once the landlord was done installing plywood over the broken glass, because no glazier was able to make a house call at that time of night, she finally allowed herself to look in the mirror.

She could almost make out four fingertips there on one side of her throat, and on the other side, the impression of Jim's thumb. And in the center, where his palm would have pressed against her, pushed her back in order to pull her forward ... the moon, weeping blood.

Weeping *her* blood.

She knew with a certainty then that she would be going back to the tattoo parlor.

And she also knew then why.

Amanda postponed that return until the bruising around her neck was at the height of its garishness, producing colors she'd never worn on her skin before. Up until then, up until that night, what bruising she'd borne had never been visible.

But that didn't mean the bruising hadn't been there. She knew that. She guessed she'd always known that.

The artist who'd wielded the needle the previous week was horrified once she'd unbuttoned her shirt—more, she hoped, because of what Jim had done to her neck than what he'd done to the man's carefully pricked moon—but whether it was the former, or whether it was the latter, he led her to his table in the back under the lights with a level of concern she found soothing.

There, after he studied what Jim had done to his work of the previous week, explained to her what he'd need to do to repair it, and asked more than once what had happened, she told him that the why of it shouldn't matter to him, because it didn't matter to her—she was letting that go, and planned to talk of it no more, not with him, not with anyone—and explained what she needed him to do for her in addition to any repairs.

It wouldn't be easy, he told her. He didn't like the idea, he said. He preferred working with a clean canvas. And to be honest, he wasn't even sure if it would work.

He leaned in to her then, and she could tell why—he was worried that she'd been drinking.

"I know what I want," she said firmly. "And what I want is this."

So he sighed, and he shrugged, and he went ahead and did what she asked.

Not that it was anyone's fault, but it was several weeks before her coworkers at the courthouse noticed what she had done. This cluelessness didn't bother her. She preferred it that way, had planned it that way. Yes, she'd changed, but she wanted them to see the change only, and not the evidence of that transformation taking place.

On that day, the day she let it be known what had blossomed around her neck, the day she allowed them to notice, she chose to wear a V-neck blouse, a new one she'd bought just for that day, as opposed to the usual high-necked blouses they and she had been used to.

She knew they'd at last picked up on the change in her because the loud talk that usually went on uninterrupted as she passed through the halls of the courthouse had been replaced by a specific sort of whisper, and not at all the same sort of whisper which had greeted her when she first returned, because though she had said nothing of that night, people talked.

Her coworker, Mina, who was usually assigned to the courtroom across the hall, was the first one to speak to her about it directly, near the end of one long day when they sat across from each other in the cafeteria. Mina tore open four sugar packets and dumped them into her coffee. Amanda drank hers black.

"What happened?" asked Mina, eyes wide at what she saw around Amanda's neck. "Did Jim do that? I didn't … I didn't realize."

"Jim?" said Amanda, asking herself as she answered Mina. "I guess he did. But don't worry. Jim will never bother me again."

"Good. If only you'd told me. If only I'd known."

"There was nothing to tell."

And really, up until that night, there wasn't. At least not that could have been seen with the naked eye.

"To be honest, I always thought you could do better," said Mina, leaning in and whispering. "Still, I never thought he was capable of something like that."

Mina gestured to Amanda's throat, and to the colors that stretched from one side of her neck to the other. Amanda pulled her collar even further open so Mina could better see the garish swatch of purples and reds and blues. A lawyer who sat at a nearby table glanced in her direction and then quickly looked away.

"I'm so sorry," said Mina.

"Don't be."

And that was as much as anyone seemed willing to say to her about the change, and as much as she was willing to say, too, until that evening, after work, when she joined Mina and the rest of her coworkers for drinks, something which during her first months at the courthouse she'd rarely done, and then not at all in the year since she'd gotten together with Jim.

She was sitting at the bar with Mina, talking about which judges gave them the creeps, and which only made them laugh, and bemoaning that little could be done about it, when the bartender surprised her with a drink. Amanda followed the tilt of his head to the far end of the bar, and saw the man—his hair flat, his mustache futile, his ego inflated—who'd sent the glass her way. She tried to decide whether to smile at the man. Or even nod.

It was a first for her. She couldn't remember anyone having done it before, even on the nights she'd dared to go out. She took it as proof both of her change, and that someone else could see that change.

But he couldn't see all of it. None of them could.

"Well," said Mina, rising off her stool. "I don't think you need me here to cheer you up anymore."

"Wait," said Amanda, putting her hand around the glass which had been delivered, still uncertain whether to pull it closer or push it away.

"Have fun," said Mina. "You'll do fine. You deserve it."

She dropped a few bills on the counter and walked off. Before Amanda could even call after her, the man who'd bought her that drink slid onto Mina's stool, closing the distance between them more quickly than she could have imagined. He pointed at her glass like a man who was too used to pointing at things.

"You looked like a woman who needed another drink," he said.

"What makes you say that?" she said. "I wasn't done with this one."

She moved her hand over to the drink she'd been working on, raised it to her lips, sipped, then held it in midair, twirling the liquid between them.

She noticed a twitch around his eyes, could tell he was struggling then to not lower his gaze to her neck, which she imagined she'd magnified through the curve of her glass. She did smile then, less at him than at all the men in her life to whom she'd wanted to say, *hey, eyes up here*, but had been unable to do so. He noted that smile, misread that smile, and leaned in so close he could have drunk from her glass himself.

"I would never let anyone else do that to you," he whispered.

Up until then, she was going to thank him for the offer of the drink, but demur, and follow Mina out the door. But his final words made her pause.

Did he mean what she thought he meant?

Did she hear what he'd wanted her to hear, or only what Jim had now made her realize all men were saying?

Anyone ... *else*.

"Do you want to get out of here?" she asked.

Oh, he did.

There was a bouquet of roses by her door when the two of them got off the elevator on her floor. She walked slowly toward them, her fist tight around her keys so that some protruded between her knuckles, and kicked it down the hall as she'd done with all the others. It shed petals as it tumbled, a trail of petals that led to her door.

She no longer cared what the neighbors thought.

"Was that from the guy?" the man said, puffing himself up and crushing a rose beneath his heel. She figured he probably thought he was making himself look strong, that it was a thing he'd done many times before, hoping to impress, and didn't tell him he instead was only making himself look ridiculous.

"Maybe," she said. "Probably. I really don't care."

She opened the door, stepped over the petals which had dropped off since it had been placed there. Or were those petals remaining from the previous night's bouquet?

"Are you coming in?" she asked without turning or flipping on a light.

As he entered behind her, she realized she did not know his name, had not bothered to ask it on their way over from the bar. Would not ask it now that they were here.

Whoever he was, she was glad it was a stranger from the bar, rather than someone from the courthouse. Anyone from work would have already heard the whole story, however jumbled. Gossip travels. They'd have looked at the walls with the photos hung back neatly in place, looked at the glass in the window frame where once there'd been none, and not really seen them as they were. Overlaying all of it would have been the way things had been the night she'd been transformed. The way *she* had been before the night she'd been transformed. They'd have looked at her, and thought they knew more than they knew. They wouldn't have been able to be *present*.

Better to bring home a stranger anyway. Only strangers can see you as you really are.

As she stood between the door through which she'd pushed Jim, and the window through which Jim had propelled himself, Amanda removed her clothes, and let the nameless stranger see, without explanation, what she had done in the hours after.

Amanda was aware, as she sat with Marco nursing drinks in the restaurant—Marco, the man whose name she eventually learned, not because she'd asked, but because he'd offered—that they were being watched. It wasn't unusual during their brief time together, and though it thrilled her, Marco was, and always had been, oblivious to those who would, like this night, surreptitiously look in their direction. The tilted head which would quickly turn away. The flicker of a gaze which took but a moment to harden.

Sitting there, waiting for their appetizers to arrive, waiting for this to be the time their appetizer wouldn't arrive, she undid yet another button on her blouse. She struggled not to smile as she did so, because those other customers were seeing what she wanted them to see, and if she smiled, they would see that no longer. Marco leaned across the table and pulled the cloth back together so less of the mottled color was revealed.

"Maybe it's time you got yourself to a doctor, babe," he said, his fingers rearranging her collar. "Your bruises should have started to fade by now."

She wrapped the fingers of one hand around his wrist and lowered it to the tablecloth, using her other to open her collar again.

"This is who I am now," she said. "I'm not hiding anymore."

"You're more than that, babe. Don't let that guy—"

While he was speaking, a woman rose from a nearby table, rushed over, and before he could finish telling Amanda whatever it was she wasn't supposed to let Jim do, took Marco's wineglass, and tossed the contents in his lap. He leapt up, sputtering, slapping at his pants, looking as if he wanted to slap *her*.

"You should be ashamed of yourself," said the woman, slamming the empty glass back down on the table. "And you, you deserve better."

"What was that bitch talking about?" he said, looking down at Amanda as the woman returned to her table accompanied by the applause of the other customers.

"I have no idea," said Amanda.

But did have an idea. She knew, she knew.

"I still don't get it," he said, waving his arms wildly, occasionally punctuating his rant by punching a fist into his palm. The restaurant was many blocks behind them, but their walk had done nothing to calm him down. "What was that all about?"

"I'm sure it was nothing," she said, knowing it was something, knowing what she had done had finally done its job.

"But what could that woman have been thinking? What could they all have been thinking? They couldn't possibly believe I'm the one who did *that*, could they?"

He gestured at her neck, pointing again, pointing like he had that first night, pointing at the bruises she would no longer cover up, pointing at the bruises that weren't even visible then, not on the street.

"I have no idea what they were thinking," she said, knowing what they were thinking, knowing what they were all thinking. "Calm down."

"I can't," he said, in what was almost a shout. "That *was* what they were thinking! Of me! Who would never do such a thing! You know that babe, right?"

She didn't answer, even though she'd learned, even though she'd been taught, there was only one answer to that question.

"I mean, come on, Amanda. You know I'm not that kind of guy!"

She stayed silent for the few remaining blocks to her building, which seemed to agitate Marco more. She remained silent all the way up the elevator, silent until the elevator doors opened, silent until she stepped out into the hallway to see another bouquet of roses by her front door.

She paused there as the elevator doors closed behind her, and only then did she speak.

"Do I?" she said, by which time he'd forgotten what he'd said to which that was a response. He looked at her dumbly.

Then he turned, saw where she'd been looking.

"Again?" he said. "When is this guy going to stop? What is this with him?"

He grabbed the bouquet, similar to the one she'd kicked down the hall on the night they'd first met, and on many nights thereafter, and threw it to the other end of the hall. It spiraled through the air to hit a neighbor's door, which a moment later opened, then quickly closed.

"What would you tell him that would make him think you wanted this? No one would keep doing this without some kind of encouragement."

"It wasn't anything I said," she said, even though something she'd said had led them right here, that time she was cleaning up in the kitchen and said … enough.

He raised an eyebrow, and raised himself, too, growing larger again, much as he had the night she'd first brought him home, when he attempted to telegraph that he'd protect her. Only this time, he seemed uncertain against what.

"You're lying to me, Amanda," he said, sensing her mixed meaning, struggling to decipher it. "You did say something. What did you say? How did you lead him on?"

His voice grew louder, which was when she chose to slide her key in the lock and open her front door.

She entered quickly, stretching the distance between them. He followed, giving the door behind him a shove to close it. Instead of resulting in a loud slam, his action produced only a dull clunk, and he turned, they both turned, to see that it had been prevented from closing by a crutch.

And then the door was slowly pushed back open, and there was Jim.

He was on two crutches, and wearing a neck brace, with his left leg in a cast. He lurched toward Marco before the man could react.

"You'd talk to my girlfriend like that?" Jim croaked.

Marco crouched to defend himself, but as he threw a punch, stumbled over one of the forward crutches and fell into Jim. As they toppled, Amanda rushed over to take advantage of their momentum and push them both back out her door.

"Enough," she said.

They continued fighting in the hall, rolling one atop the other, Marco using his fists, Jim his crutches. Though Jim was the larger man, regardless of how Marco had liked to puff himself up to impress her, to impress himself, he was barely recovered from his fall. But he did have those crutches, so the two men appeared equally matched as they pummeled each other. Both were bloodied. Neither managed to rise up off the floor.

Amanda could occasionally make out her name, but not, through their grunting, what they were saying about her.

"Enough," she said again, this time in a whisper. But it wouldn't have mattered if she'd shouted. They wouldn't have heard her.

And she found she didn't really care.

She closed the door on them. The click as she locked it was as satisfying as a slam. It dampened the noise of the fighting, though she could still make out an occasional curse, still hear a random punch connect, but when she went to the bathroom and closed that door as well, the sound of the flailing was barely audible.

She stood before the mirror and slowly unbuttoned her blouse, letting it slip from her shoulders, drop to the floor. She unbuttoned her skirt, let it slide down as well, and studied herself, considered her pale flesh, and the blues and purples and browns that wrapped around her neck, that curved against her ribcage, that stretched down the outside of her left leg, garish clouds of color that comforted her. Uplifted her. Protected her.

As the faint sounds of fighting outside stopped, to be replaced by a knocking at her door, by whom she did not know and did not care, followed by cursing she couldn't decipher, ending with a welcome silence, she continued to trace her fingers along what had healed her, what would never heal, and knew she would never be troubled by sounds like that again.

Goodbye to all that, she thought. *Only bruises are permanent.*
Only bruises.

My Knowing Glance

LUCY A. SNYDER

According to the textbook we're using this term in Psychology 450 (*The Future Therapist's Guide: Theory and Practice* by Garza-Fieldman), the most important thing you can do to ensure a solid working relationship with your clients—beyond, you know, staying current on research and therapeutic techniques and making sure you don't stink when you go in the room—is to *know yourself*. And, at first blush, that sounds like a straight-up platitude like the LIVE LAUGH LOVE canvas on the greige living room wall of your cousin Becky's suburban condo.

But knowing yourself matters. It matters if someone is pouring their black little heart out to you in a session, and something they say disgusts you, or irritates you, and that negative emotion catches you by surprise, and in your surprise, you let your true feelings show on your face. Because then they see your frown or narrowed eyes, and they withdraw or shut down. And congratulations, you've just undone weeks or possibly months of work. So you're back to the Sisyphean task of building trust and rapport all over again, just because for one second you flinched when your client admitted that when he was thirteen he liked to fuck the goats on his mom's Ann Arbor farm.

So while I am not a psychologist, nor a social worker, my clients still have a host of mental illnesses and neurodiversities. And so I have tried my level best to stare my own shames, bigotries, kinks and squicks square in their beady little eyes so I can maintain my professionalism and not inadvertently destroy the positive feelings my clients have about paying their hard-earned cash to see me.

And yeah—I get that people refuse to understand that I am, in fact, a professional. My parents would not understand it. Everyone eventually asks what my father thinks of what I do for a living. As if anyone's father is supposed to have veto power over a grown woman's life when her teens are a full decade past, a vanishing dark spot in her rearview mirror. When they ask—assuming they're not clients—I just smile sweetly and say, "Aw, honey, does your daddy still run *your* life?" and that usually shuts them up right quick.

Some folks press on. They want to know how I can look my own family in the eye. How I can *justify* this lucrative, completely legal job to them.

And so I tell them the truth: My immediate family lost any care about what I do with my life when I was a junior in high school. I was away from home at regional band tryouts. My father decided to pick up a gun during a fight with my mother he'd started because he was sure she was cheating on him. (She wasn't.) He shot her between the eyes, then went upstairs and murdered my little sister and little brother because he believed they weren't really his biological children. (They were.) While their corpses cooled, he spent the next hour writing up an aggrieved, entitled, chest-thumping suicide note detailing why he had no possible choice but to slaughter his own family. And then, as is statistically typical of men like him, he blew his own brains out.

I tell the people who question my life choices that my father would have murdered me, too, had I been home. But I wasn't, because I'd chosen to play saxophone in marching band to have a reason to be gone on Friday nights when Dad drank. All the neighbors and his coworkers said my father was so nice and considerate and they were just *shocked* at what happened ... but I know my mother and my siblings did not die surprised because violence was *always* on the table behind closed doors. And I had worked hard and so I was safe a hundred miles away when Dad finally made good on the threats Mom had willfully ignored for years because, she always insisted, "Your father means well." (He didn't.)

That's my story of why I survived: because of my individual choices and my hard work. And it's fine to be skeptical about that. So let's take a deep dive there: Maybe there's no justice in this universe and my being alive today is just dumb shithouse luck. And if that's the case, then there's no point in moralizing over anyone's life choices, is there?

My father's choice to murder my family resulted in me having to spend the next two years in the home of my uncle Robert, who is a pastor at a Baptist church. And he loves Christian moralizing in exactly the same way my father loved Scotch. They were both narcissists cut from the same rotten wood. It surely comes as no shock that he disrespects women and women's work in equal measure, nor that I got the hell out of there as fast as I could.

And if anyone asks, I tell them that my uncle's opinion matters less to me than a skeet-soaked Kleenex dropped by a client.

Which leads back to this: most people insist what I do, despite it being the very oldest profession, is in no way professional. To them, my job is just lying on my back and taking a whole lot of cock.

First: It's not that much cock. Many of my clients are bi women who need that itch scratched, either because they just don't know how to seduce or be seduced by another woman—and hell yes I help them with that if they ask—or they tried and got shut down by local lesbians who get shitty with women who still sleep with men.

And second: What some of my clients want most is to have someone to talk to. They come in thinking it's sex that they want, but it's intimacy they're starved for. Or they've got uncomfortable thoughts rattling around in their heads and they just need to get them out in front of a sympathetic ear.

A paid-for friend isn't ideal, but it's better than what a whole lot of people in this city have. And if you don't have insurance, I'm way less expensive than a psychiatrist. It helps that our madam Em is a pretty damn cool boss and—shockingly, I know!—she values us for our individual interests, educations and skill sets. So the clients I get often skew toward women and people with special needs.

After the state blew up over the horrific human trafficking situation, voters finally decided to legalize sex work so women and children being held in slavery wouldn't have to be afraid of getting locked up if they went to the police. And so The Pink Rose and the rest of the first legal brothels to go online have been extra careful to prove that their employees are 100% there of their own free will and are safe for customers. So, unlike my counterparts in Nevada, I do get full medical and dental. Considering how many people have come down with Polymorphic Viral Gastroencephalitis and how easily PVG can spread through body fluids, having us work as independent contractors without health coverage would have been criminal negligence. At *least*. People get charged with murder for spreading that shit. The moment the FDA approved the vaccine, Em brought in a nurse practitioner and lined us all up to get our shots.

Legalized prostitution is hot like Kilauea, so reporters are dying to get dirt on the brothels. Just one disgruntled courtesan could bring down one hell of a sticky load of bad press. So, it makes sense that Em puts effort into ensuring we're happy with who and what we're doing. We're even allowed to keep guns and Tasers hidden in our playrooms in case a client decides to go all Jack the Ripper on one of us. I never wanted a gun for reasons that should be painfully obvious, but it's good we were given that choice.

I fully agree this is a news honeymoon; the brothels will be passé back-page stuff soon enough. As boring as adult trafficking victims were ten years ago. As boring as my family's murder was a month after they were buried. It'll all be downhill from here.

I mean, this is still capitalism, right? Filthy lucre fucks up everyone's best intentions. But for now, this is by far the best customer service job I've ever had. Even when I agreed to let an aging B movie star piss on me in the shower, it was still way better than phone tech support. (And I even got my Blu-Ray of *Chainsaw Hobos from Mars* autographed without having to wait in line at Comic Con!)

So, I'm always trying to use my education in my work, and always trying to know myself better. Most of the time, that's been a rewarding journey.

But three weeks ago, I learned some things I wish I hadn't. Everyone in this whole damn brothel would wish that, too, if they knew.

Gregory wasn't a steady regular, but he'd seen me a few times before and had behaved himself perfectly well. He was shy, wrestling with gender dysphoria—he hated being male, but because his parents had been as shitty as my uncle Robert, the notion of identifying as someone other than a man made him straight-up panicky. He mostly wanted me to peg him. Mostly; I kept condoms handy just in case.

Because he seemed scared to death that someone might photograph him, I set things up so he could use the online system to schedule a session rather than having to arrive in person to negotiate scenes. And, more to the point, he could use the secret, biometrics-equipped side door that's actually a block away and goes underground. Because of all the news vans camping in the parking lot across the street, the owners wanted to make sure that celebrities could come and go without harassment. But ordinary people stand to lose, too, if the flocking paparazzi stick cameras in their faces, so we offer back passage as a courtesy to good returning clients.

If Em or the receptionist had seen Gregory walk through the front door ... well, none of this would have happened.

I thought I knew all about PVG. The Centers for Disease Control agreed to work closely with brothels in our state to limit the possibility of on-site transmission—thus our swift vaccinations. They'd been sending us weekly informational videos and pamphlets. Big nerd that I am, I read it all and more.

Viruses have always fascinated me. I mean, think about it: They work by giving an unsuspecting cell new assembly instructions. It's just ... new information. That doesn't seem so bad, does it? And yet it can be a complete horror show.

This is what I knew about PVG: Within a week of transmission, an infected person gets a mild to moderate headache and some nausea. For some people, that's all that happens. After a few days of taking it easy, they're back to normal. But for others, the headache turns into the worst they've ever had. A day or so after that, they start vomiting up blood, followed by their stomach lining. Most everyone ends up in the hospital at that point.

When a PVG victim gets out—*if* they get out and don't straight up die—their digestive system is fucked all to hell. They can't digest most foods and consequently can't make certain proteins. Their body has trouble growing and healing. The enzymes their DNA uses to repair itself quit working like a tech bro after a four-whiskey lunch.

Sunlight, x-rays, cigarettes, cosmic rays ... anything that can even slightly damage your DNA becomes a real problem. Victims' skin cracks and their bodies sprout tumors. Their brains begin to degenerate. Sooner or later, they develop lesions on their frontal lobe and hippocampus. Without daily medication, those lesions inevitably lead to a variety of hallucinations, delusions and antisocial behaviors. And that's when the local SWAT team tends to get involved.

PVG patients are identified by type. Type Ones are the folks who just needed a little rest and were fine, but are maybe-probably still contagious if the stars are right. Type Twos need supplements containing the proteins found in fresh human blood. Type Threes need the proteins found in fresh brains. Type Fours are the ones who died in the hospital. It's all pretty gruesome, but honestly not really that much more scary than a disease like Ebola, or even drug-resistant syphilis. The CDC's overall message was, "This is an incurable, complex, life-changing infection, but it can be managed just like HIV," so most of us in the brothels figured we could get our shots and just roll with it.

But, obviously, we aren't supposed to let in anyone with a case of PVG. Our vaccinations are insurance against being infected through random sneezes on the street; there is no approved protocol for preventing transmission during physical intimacy. Type Ones have to pass a viral load titer and carry paperwork proving it or the front door staff will turn them away. It's not just on the honor system; there's a quick-prick blood test every prospective client has to pass. If someone claims our test generated a false positive—and, to be fair, a lot of Type Ones don't even know they are infected—the staff smiles and tells them to come back with a titer test from their doctor.

I didn't even realize until later that Gregory was infected, even though I knew right away that something was seriously wrong with him.

Our playrooms are set up basically like a hotel room, except with a door in the front and the back. We courtesans come in through the front door, which locks and has a foyer beyond with a sink, mirror, etc. so we can do last-minute checks of our costumes and makeup. In the main part of the room, there's a bed, sofa, and maybe some bondage furniture. The back entrance is for our clients, and it opens into a tiled dressing area with toilet facilities and a shower with sturdy handholds. The CDC says that washing with soap and water helps prevent PVG transmission, so clients have to clean up before they play; a lot of them like sexytimes in the shower, and none of us enjoy blowing a dude with swamp ass, so everyone wins.

I wasn't surprised to hear the water running and to find the room filling with steam when I arrived at the room for Gregory's session. I slipped off my green silk robe, draped it over the nearest high-backed chair, and sashayed over to the shower.

"Hey, Gregory, how's it going?" I called, hoping to not startle him.

He didn't answer. I figured he just couldn't hear, so I rounded the corner to the stall door, ready to knock on the shatterproof glass.

And stopped dead.

The glass was fogged up, so I could only glimpse him as a blurry beige shape against the white tiles … but something was Definitely Not Right. My mind split in two as instinct raised my pulse and screamed *get away* while the rational parts tried to stay calm and make sense of what I was seeing. Had he come here with a little person who was riding him piggyback as he showered? No, that wasn't one of his kinks—bringing someone else to a solo session wasn't allowed, anyway—and the asymmetrical hump I saw rising from his upper back wasn't really shaped like a clinging person.

I took a deep breath and tried again. "Gregory, you ok in there?"

No response. He was in the corner of the shower, pressing his face and chest against the tiles and swaying back and forth. Moaning faintly.

I gripped the handle and eased the door open just the tiniest bit so I could get a clearer look at him. Assess the situation. Use my brain and my education and not jump to any damn conclusions.

My next thought was that he had some kind of massive infection under his skin, like the epically pus-filled humps that Dr. Pimple Popper airs. But my eyes focused a bit more, and I saw that his skin was stretched tight over distorted shoulder blades and bulging ribs that looked like they had separated from his spine in places. Good Christ, how could he stand up and walk with that going on? Whatever was causing this ugly hump was pushing out from far inside him.

Cancer? It had to be cancer. How could it have gotten so bad so quick? It had been only six weeks since I'd seen him last, and he'd been perfectly fine then. What kind of tumor grows that fast?

I stepped away from the shower. Turned to the pile of street clothes he'd haphazardly dumped on the dressing room chair. Looking for clues like maybe a bottle of prescription medications or a clinic wristband or *something*.

The something I found was a boxy black pistol in a green nylon shoulder holster.

"God damn it," I whispered. This is a concealed-carry state, but clients are forbidden from bringing firearms into a brothel. Gregory *knew* that. What was he thinking?

I carefully pulled the pistol free of its holster, holding it gingerly as if it were a dead rat. Just because I hated guns didn't mean I hadn't taken time to learn the basics, like whether the safety was on and whether the thing was loaded. Enough of the other girls brought in firearms for self-defense that I figured it would be stupid not to learn enough to protect myself.

It was a Glock 9mm. The safety was on, and the magazine was full.

God damn it.

I left the pistol there and went back to the shower door and slapped the glass with my hand. "Gregory!"

He jerked in surprise and turned away from the corner.

"Savannah, help me," he moaned.

I backed up as he pushed the stall door open and stumbled out. And couldn't help gasping because—Jesus Christ, I wouldn't have recognized him except for St. Michael tattoo on his left pec. His face, chest and arms were painfully gaunt like he was a day or two from starving to death. And his eyes were both mottled black and red from 8-ball hemorrhages.

"What—what's happened to you?" I stammered.

His face contorted in grief. "This is not my body! This is not the Becoming that God promised me!"

He started weeping. "The other angels are massing in the hills. I— I can hear them. I am called to my mission, but I don't want it!"

Ah, shit, I thought. He'd had some kind of break from reality, or was delirious, or both. People knew I was running BDSM scenes in here; screams wouldn't raise any eyebrows. My panic button was over on the side of the bed. If I hit it, two very large men with Tasers and mace would be down here in less than a minute. But Gregory looked fragile; an electrical shock might kill him. Better to try to calm him down first and then phone for help.

"Gregory, deep breaths, buddy. Can you tell me what's happened?"

His expression twisted into a rictus of agony and he went into a half-crouch as though he were having a back spasm. "Oh God! It's happening. Savannah, I didn't know where else to go. Help me. I brought a gun ... please kill me!"

Fucking hell. "What? No—"

He started screaming and fell to his hands and knees.

That huge, twisted hump on his back was spasming, shuddering. Then the skin above his right scapula split with a spurt of dark blood and something amber and watery, and I realized *something was breaking free and clawing out of him.*

"Savannah, please ...." He sounded like he could barely breathe.

I couldn't move, couldn't speak. Frozen like a rabbit. A leathery blade sliced up through the split in the skin, followed by a long finger of bone and a fringe of pale tissue. Then another blade sliced out through the skin on the left side of his back. The sound of bones crunching and skin ripping made bile rise in my throat.

"The gun, please, I won't be able to stop ...." His voice was changing as he spoke. Deeper. Stronger.

I stopped focusing on the gory confusion of his back and realized that his whole body was altering itself. Bloody teeth drooling out of his gasping mouth. His face rearranging itself into something that didn't look exactly human anymore. Bones lengthening. Muscles and sinews stretching.

He screamed like a raptor as his wings broke free of the cage of his back. Wings. Holy fuck. They spread seven or eight feet wide, tough membranes stretched tight over thin bones that looked strong as titanium. The air stank of blood and amniotic fluid.

I stumbled backward into the rattling locker as the winged creature Gregory had become rose and towered over me.

"I was bound, though I have not bound," he intoned, his mouth full of long jagged teeth like you'd see on a deep-sea anglerfish. "I was not recognized. But I have recognized that the All is being dissolved, both the earthly and the heavenly. When a soul has overcome the third power, it goes upwards and sees the fourth power, which takes seven forms. The first form is darkness, the second desire, the third ignorance, the fourth is the excitement of death, the fifth is the kingdom of the flesh, the sixth is the foolish wisdom of the flesh, the seventh is the wrathful wisdom. These are the seven powers of wrath. And so I ask the chosen soul, *Whence do you come, slayer of men?*"

"Gregory, I— I don't understand." I was suddenly remembering passages about angels in the Bible. They weren't hot dudes with halos like you see in Renaissance paintings. They always had to tell mortals "Fear not!" because they were *fucking terrifying*.

"Whence do you come, slayer of men?" He stepped toward me on long legs lightened for flight. "Wilt thou take thine sword? Or wilt thou shirk thy duty?"

The chair with his clothes and the pistol was just a few feet out of reach to my right. "I— I don't—"

He reached out and touched my forehead with taloned fingers.

Instantly, my mind filled with images of winged, predatory beings like Gregory falling like a curse from God upon men, women, and children across the world. Tearing their skulls open with talons or drilling into their eye sockets with grotesque burred tongues. Devouring their brains, their memories, their very souls.

And in this vision I turned my face to the heavens, and suddenly I could hear the old gods whispering to me from their thrones in the dark spaces between the stars: *Follow thy nature, and thou shalt be rewarded.*

"We Archivists shall preserve the worthiest souls," Gregory told me, pulling my mind back to the playroom. "We shall use the blood of this world to write triumphant praises to our ancient lords. Thy duty is to cull the unworthy, so that those inferior souls shall not distract us from *our* duty."

The vision had shook me to my very core—I'd seen the wholesale slaughter of the entire human race. Was it happening now? Or was what I'd seen some glimpse of the future? Part of me had accepted that the vision was an absolute truth right up there with rain being wet and the sky being blue. But the rest of me was resisting the inevitable and thinking, *Oh hell no.*

So I lunged sideways for the gun, flicked the safety off, and unloaded the entire 10-round magazine into Gregory's chest. It would have taken a very special talent to miss him at that distance. (I didn't.)

Every bullet I fired into his flesh was nothing short of exhilarating. And when I saw his body crash lifeless to the tiled floor, I came so hard I lost consciousness.

I woke in the quarantine wing of the hospital. Guys in suits from the CDC interrogated me about what had happened, and what I remembered. I've done enough research on traumatic memory loss to fake it like a champ. After a few hours, I had them convinced that I didn't remember anything other than sickly-looking Gregory lunging at me when he came out of the shower.

The suits left, and then it was just a matter of waiting. I never did come down with any PVG symptoms despite inhaling a fine mist of Gregory's blood. Once a week had passed with no symptoms and no change in my viral titer, the hospital released me. Em gave me another week off with pay, which is pretty standard when a courtesan has someone go berserk on her.

Neither she nor anyone else batted an eye when I told them I'm buying a pistol of my own and bringing it to work. Everyone is very sympathetic and understanding. Some folks are telling me to buy three or four. You know, keep one hidden in the playroom, one in my car, one at home, etc.

But it's not for self-defense. I don't have anything to fear from those who have Become. As far as they're all concerned, I'm one of the Chosen, too; they won't touch me.

I am a Type Five, and I am not alone. We all received our apocalypse assembly instructions without any headaches at all.

Which isn't to say that this has been free of unpleasant effects. Ever since I woke up in the hospital, it's been hard to make myself come. And I've tried everything: my hands, my Hitachi, dildos, clients, a random hookup with a guy I met on Tinder. And yeah, Tinder guy did make me come, eventually ... but only when I slit his throat with a razor after *he'd* come and was snoring away in the back of his camper van.

It was just as glorious as it was with Gregory. The kind of white-light, ascending-to-the-heavens ecstasy the saints used to sing about. Came so hard I sprained my back.

Fortunately, Tinder guy won't be missed. And yeah, I know that for sure. I can glance at someone and know whether they'll Become, or if I must save them for Archiving, or if they're just a big ol' waste of time and oxygen for everyone except the *slayers of men* like me.

The biggest revelation from all this, at least for me personally, isn't knowing how and why the world will end, and that it will end in another three years at most.

It's knowing why my father killed himself.

I mean, I thought I knew his reason before. Having read his suicide letter, I knew it wasn't because he was sorry he'd just slaughtered his own family, because there is not a single shadow of regret in those three pages. I figured that he was too chickenshit to face the cops, the trial, and prison. Death was the easy way out.

But if murder is the purest joy I can find in this world, and if murder is just me following my nature like the old gods say ... well, I surely inherited my nature just like I inherited my blonde hair.

So now I know, deep in my bones, that when my father shot my mother between the eyes, he came harder than he ever had when he'd been balls-deep in her pussy. He'd come harder than he ever had with a prostitute or with his own left hand. And when he murdered my little brother and sister … maybe he came even harder.

He killed himself because he realized that the neighbors had already heard gunshots and called the cops, and once he was in custody, he'd probably never be able to experience that kind of existence-affirming ecstasy ever again. Thus the angry, embittered tone of his letter.

I could be wrong about that. But it *feels* right. It's just more satisfying to think that he died out of a deep, soul-wrenching despair rather than garden-variety cowardice.

I saw another Type Five at the grocery store the other day. Nice-looking middle-aged lady. Real grandmotherly type. But we both knew who we really were from the gleams in our eyes. We gave each other a little nod and smile and went on with our shopping.

The old gods still whisper to me in my dreams, but honestly they can all go pound salt. I'm not doing this for them. But if humanity's doomed, and I know it is, I'm gonna get it while I can.

Paper Doll Hyperplane

R.B. PAYNE

DEFINITION: PAPER DOLL

A chain of human figures cut from a single piece of paper.

MATHEMATIC PRINCIPLE: HYPERPLANE

"A hyperplane in a larger multi-dimensional vector space is any subspace that is one-dimensional."

RESEARCH NOTES
POSTULATE: REALITY AS AN N-DIMENSION KNOT

"The paper doll hyperplane theorem can be applied to all n-dimensional time spheres in m-dimensional Euclidean space using a series of nine sequentially linked nonahedrons[1]. This activity results in an alignment of time streams thereby breaching the reality of personal continuums and providing direct access to unfiltered infinity.

To test this theorem, I will dispatch nine randomly-chosen people into the n-dimension. Subsequently, this paper will discuss the outcome of my experiment upon the recently dead."[2]

---

[1] Definition: Any of the 2,606 topologically distinct convex polyhedra that have nine faces.
[2] Riemann, Zachary H. "The Effect of n-dimensional Hyperplane Alignment on the Recently Dead" Unpublished Working Papers, 2014

QUINN UNIVERSITY LECTURE: MELANCHOLIA I

The students rustled books and papers and at least half a dozen napped. That's the problem with early morning lectures. Brown bottle flu is a mathematical conundrum unsolvable by most university professors.

I darkened the room as the InFocus warmed up. The projector bulb clicked and an image lit the screen behind the lectern. I heard groans as bright light pierced their eyes. I almost pitied them; I do remember my undergrad years.

"Turn to page 93 of the course materials," I said into the mic. "I'll start today's lecture with our friend Albrecht Durer. Behold *Melancholia I.*"

I motioned to the image on the screen behind me.

"Observe that a winged woman sits and ponders the world, a compass grasped in one hand, a ring of keys tied to her belt. Her cheek rests on a clutched fist as she observes. The original engraving contained at least twelve clues to its meaning—a meaning instantly understood by any educated medieval viewer but which is hidden to us—sort of like *The Da Vinci Code*."

Now I had their attention. Anything that smelled of a Hollywood thriller always grabbed their interest. It's a cheap professor trick but I use it on the first-year students every semester.

I continued.

"You need to understand that melancholia, the effect of Saturn on man and the subject of this engraving, was the least desirable of all humours to Western medieval society."

By now, my eyes had adjusted to the darkened hall and I could see a couple of raised hands.

"If you missed last Tuesday's lecture about humours, please review the lesson on my YouTube channel."

The hands withdrew.

"At the beginning of the Renaissance, melancholia was associated with depression, apathy, lethargy, and insanity. On the upside, it was associated with intelligent and creative persons such as artists, musicians, carpenters, physicians, and mathematicians. And that's why we're looking at Durer in today's lecture. The engraving offers a mathematical proposition and proposes a philosophical solution. Take a moment. Do you see it?"

I sipped water from a bottle and waited for anticipation to build. Soon, restless bodies straightened in their chairs, papers rustled, someone coughed.

Stumped, every one of them.

B. F. Skinner is dead but not gone.[3]

---

[3] Skinner, B. F. Science and Human Behavior. New York: Macmillan, 1953. Print. "The strengthening of behavior which results from reinforcement is appropriately called 'conditioning'. In operant conditioning, we 'strengthen' an operant in the sense of making a response more probable or, in actual fact, more frequent."

"First, let's consider the problem," I offered. "It is despair which leads to melancholia which destroys power and wealth as represented by the symbolism of the keys and the purse. The hourglass represents the inevitability of time. See the bat? Boiled bats were believed to be a cure used by the rich. The wreath is likely made of hellebore or dodder-vines, plants believed to relieve depression. Unfortunately, as we know today, no remedy actually provided relief."

I lectured on for thirty minutes, my usual polemic on problem-solving. Or maybe rhetoric is a better word. What I told them was to isolate a solution, one must properly define the problem. And that's what Durer shows us in *Melancholia I*. When I sensed the students couldn't take much more, I relented by showing them the mathematical clue.

A red dot appeared on the screen as I clicked on my laser pointer.

"In the upper right corner of the engraving is a series of numbers on the side of a building. This is a *mathematical magic square* where the numbers all add to the same total – vertically, horizontally, and diagonally. Cleverly, the numbers 15 and 14 appear in the bottom row. This is the year that Durer's mother died and the presumed year of the engraving. The magic square adds to 34. This was a talisman thought to attract the ancient god Jupiter who was believed to offset the influences of Saturn. The real secret revealed by Durer is the bell above the magic square. The bell represented eternity, and this reflected an emerging Renaissance belief that mathematics held the key to explaining the universe and the fabric of reality itself."

Ironically, the school bell chimed indicating the end of the lecture.

"To sum up," I said. "Mathematics is the path to a singular definition of the universe. More on that next week."

The students hurried out, in need of coffee. As I gathered my papers, a pretty blonde approached with an armful of textbooks.

"Professor Riemann …"

"Call me Zach," I said. "All the students do."

"Ok. I'm having problems with the concept of palindromic primes, especially in the context of a magic square."

She hesitated then added my name: *Zach*.

"Sure," I said. "Why don't you drop by my residence at seven tonight? I have an office there. We can go over your questions then."

She smiled that sweet undergraduate smile.

She looked a bit like the woman in *Melancholia I.*

"I'm Madeline Blake," she said, reaching out her free hand for a shake. "Everyone calls me Maddie."

Her palm was shiny damp.

I shook it.

QUINN UNIVERSITY
(BROCHURE)

"Located in the Mad River Valley of Vermont, Quinn University is a residential campus occupying 4,000 acres of rugged foothills and forests. Previously a logging community and sawmill belonging to Meryl and John Quinn in the early 1800s, the university is fondly known by students as *Camp Quinn*.

"Today, students enjoy the Gothic Revival village that serves as the bustling campus center or can take time for quiet reflection by hiking Vermont's famous Long Trail, a section of which bisects the nearby forests, streams, and mountains.

"The university offers a think-tank philosophy to learning that encourages personal research, professional development, and innovative thought. Over the years, Quinn University has produced a Nobel Laureate in Chemistry, three Fields finalists in Mathematics, and one Wolf Prize in Physics. With high academic standards and a low student-to-professor ratio, Quinn University has been in the Top Ten *Best Small Universities* for the past eleven years."

I still remember the first time I read that.

POLYBUFOHEXANE-12[4]

Maddie's chin dropped to her chest but when she realized what was happening, she bolted to her feet from the easy chair. She tottered, her breath slowing, her sense of balance failing. Then she whimpered the last rally of resistance often heard the moment before a horse is broken and the saddle accepted.

Now a gentle sleep crept toward her mind and the glass of Chardonnay that contained the dose of polybufohexane-12 shattered on the tile floor as her grip relaxed.

No matter, I would mop it up later.

I glanced at my watch. The digestive system can be so unreliable. She should have been down thirty seconds ago. How much cheese had she eaten? I should be more observant.

She staggered to face me, her eyes meeting mine with intensity and hate. For a moment, I worried she might be fully conscious. Then her head jerked; she turned to stare at the flames in the fireplace and

[4] Investigational New Drug Application (INDA), FDA, Clinical Trials Approval, (Federal Register May 2016, pages 37-38), Washington D.C., see "Induced Coma in White Mice with PolyBufoHexane-12," Journal of Biometrics Research, June 2013, Pages 77-93

I waited and pondered the limitations of such a slow-acting drug.

I am no Lothario, so the probabilities of convincing eight more women to share a glass of wine was highly unlikely. And this outcome was certainly not quick enough. In the future, I would have to rely on surprise; a needle, and a vein.

Unexpectedly, Maddie screamed. But it was a swallowed scream repressed by muscle contraction, so it sounded like the involuntary mew or bark of a sedated pet on the operating table when the first incision is made.

I caught Maddie as she collapsed into unconsciousness and placed her gently back into the chair.

Her breathing was shallow and rhythmic.

I went to find the killing pillow.

ADVAITA (अद्वैत) (SANSKRIT, N.)

The belief there is only one reality.

THE ALIGNMENT OF ALL MATHEMATICAL STRUCTURES

I dug precisely, the lantern casting a dim circle in the darkness, the unkempt grass rippling in a cold wind that presaged winter, the soil steaming as I turned it over to reveal wriggling earthworms cut in halves or thirds. Maddie's glistering eyes faded as she seemingly watched me; her body losing warmth on the hillside while I sweat.

I stacked the near-perfect squares of sod and then bent my back to drive deeper into the earth, the sharpness of the shovel easily slicing the loam.

A palindromic prime is a prime number whose decimal expansion is a palindrome.

Simple.

Definitional.

Maddie should have known that.

She probably did.

I measured.

The hole was deep enough.

I laid the shovel aside.

It has been argued by quantum cosmologists that beyond our vision, there is a singular and true reality waiting to be discovered.

Using my boot, I carefully rolled Maddie into the cradle of her journey to the Great Beyond. She flopped loosely onto her back and I bent to place her arms into paper doll position.

My transmigration ambassador to the true reality.

I flipped the switch on the nonahedron and balanced the nine-sided object below her chin. The fabric of her blouse was momentarily a problem, but I smoothed it, and all was fine.

Even in the darkness, the specialized palindromic prime worked on a limited scale as the nonahedron discharged. The air shimmered like a heat wave making Maddie's face waver in the dim lantern-light.

She was the first.

Return to me, Maddie.

Prove there is one timeless reality.

Of course, I would have to send eight more ambassadors before the paper doll hyperplane was complete. The process required nine travelers in total as postulated by my formula.

I filled in the hole with the loose soil, re-laid the sod carefully, and tamped the edges to prevent discovery. This was university backcountry on my allotted parcel. I doubted I was in much danger of discovery.

Hoisting the shovel, I clicked off the lantern, left the clearing, and chose to descend the wooded hillside in the darkness of a moonless night.

In the distance, my kitchen light glowed through a thin curtain as a beacon. I had much to think about. I could only take one student from the university.

Maddie.

The other eight had to be random.

I stumbled on a stone.

Perhaps tomorrow I'd take a drive to Montpelier and check out the mall-walkers.

IMPLEMENTING A PAPER DOLL HYPERPLANE WITH A POWERED
NONAHEDRON[5]

Any first-year student knows that a number is a mathematical object
used to count, measure, and label. Numbers, and the mathematics
that manipulate them, are concepts and nothing more. In the real
world, numbers have no power other than the idea they represent.

Until now.

My discovery is that the physical universe reacts to rare sequences
of numbers if combined and dispersed in a specific manner and
order.

Of course, the first test rat, a female named Heidi, fragmented
into an infinite number of sub-atomic particles, dissolving into
nothingness. One expects failure in science experiments. But a week
later, a pile of skin and bone and raw meat returned unexpectedly to
my workbench. Spraying blood from half-formed veins, a struggling
heart, melded to a twitching claw, pulsed erratically.

It was the rat, poorly reassembled by the universe. It squeaked
incessantly from its malformed head and I beat it to death with a
Gerzog mallet.

Conclusion: My first palindromes had been too small and not
prime. Not powerful enough. And my homemade nonahedron: too
primitive.

But from this singular experiment, demonstrating more than a
modicum of success, I concluded there was a relationship between
the complexity of an organism and the length of the palindromic
prime; a more complex life form could be shifted in and out of
the time stream with a larger number, thus unifying known and
unknown reality.

That was many years ago.

A series of experiments followed.

As part of my next summer sabbatical, two doctoral engineering

[5] Riemann, Zachary H. "Embedding a Paper Doll Hyperplane in a Powered 3-D Nonahedron
to Unravel Reality" Unpublished Research, 2003

students helped me construct Nonahedron 2.0 as a summer project. One of them wrote an app for my phone that enabled the input of long strings of numbers and formulae. They believed it was to resonate the B-flat tone from the Perseus Cluster[6] that is 57 octaves lower than Middle C on the piano. Unknown to them, with a few modifications after their departure, the nonahedron could broadcast palindromic primes at a frequency of 9.6 million years.

The two students moved on to careers in Silicon Valley, none the wiser and happy for my doctoral endorsement.

And I moved on to more complex experiments.

Six years later, I had a filing cabinet filled with records of failed experiments complete with photo evidence of dozens of returned rats, cats, and dogs. Included were two chimpanzees, which had been extremely difficult to obtain. None survived their journey. Their remains were consigned to the ancient well outside the laboratory. By now, fur, flesh, and bones were nothing more than chunks of mush feeding a bacterial cesspool.

Discouraged, I became melancholic and then deeply depressed. I abandoned the research.

As Nietzche wrote, "Hope, in reality, is the worst of all evils because it prolongs the torments of man."

And tormented I was.

One of the perks of professorship at Quinn University was privacy. My small house, previously the logging foreman's, sat on forty acres surrounded by sugar maples and beech trees. A rustic barn functioned as my laboratory and the aforementioned composting well readily accepted my failed experiments.

My work had been unencumbered by discovery, literally or figuratively. But the problem is: Research is expensive. Certainly, I had received the odd university funding tied to some other hypothetical project and was also able to obtain foundation grant money without

---

[6] Roy, Steve; Watzke, Megan (October 2006). "Chandra Views Black Hole Musical: Epic but Off-Key". Chandra X-Ray Observatory. Harvard-Smithsonian Center for Astrophysics. Retrieved 20 February 2014.

disclosure of my real intent. But by the end of the sixth year, I had depleted my life savings.

Work ceased for several years.

But then the largest known palindromic prime was discovered. A massive 320,237 digits long, it was expressible as $10^{320236} + 10^{160118} + (137\times10^{160119} + 731\times10^{159275}) \times (10^{843} - 1)/999 + 1.$

The number was a thing of beauty. By itself, it was weak, just another number, but when combined with my nonahedron, it became quite powerful.

With this new expanded palindromic prime, I was able to send a dozen mice, four rats, and a dachshund named Pam across the Great Divide.

After creating a digital record of the experiments and photographic evidence, I destroyed them all. I had to. The creatures were somehow different.

Aggressive.

Extremely healthy.

By this point, I had cemented my theorem: a sequence of interlocked relational palindromic primes can unravel the time knot and unify all hyperplane realities. By happy accident, I had discovered that a live creature returns dead, *but a dead creature returns alive* as time realigns.

The implications were profound.

Now, I was ready for human trials, and that required nine women. Nine laid in a row like paper dolls cut from the same sheet of paper, holding hands; each powered by a nonahedron containing one-ninth of the master palindromic prime.

That would break the time stream for human beings and thrust the dead back into a singular reality called life.

The last piece of the puzzle that I needed to know was if there was continuity of memory. Would the person who departed exhibit the same consciousness of the person who returned?

One couldn't tell with a lab rat and I'd never learned to teach a trick to a dachshund.

I needed a blonde.

Nine blondes to be exact.

HOW TO CATCH A SERIAL KILLER[7]

Maddie had been the first.

Initially, I underestimated the complexities of finding nine ambassadors in total.

Avoiding the police, who certainly would not understand the significance of my theory, required elegant planning.

The problem with serial killers is that they are serial.

What appears random isn't, and thus, sooner or later, they are caught. The probability of being discovered is directly related to the number of seemingly independent factors that remain consistent over time. The more victims, the more consistency, the higher the probability of capture.

Therefore, the key is to have no consistency whatsoever.

Of course, I am not a serial killer. I am simply a mathematician working on the edge of a moral boundary.

I did have a problem though.

I wanted all of my paper doll ambassadors to bear a physical resemblance. Blonde, late teens or twenties, slight.

This was hubris, on my part, and I admit it. My selection criteria had nothing to do with the formulae.

I was already thinking about the presentation to my peers. And the Nobel Prize. Or the Wolf Award. And ultimately the book cover for the *New York Times* bestseller.

The fact is I am not killing anyone.

I am only sending them unwillingly through a reality knot.

They return alive.

And when I announce my findings, all the unseemly details will be forgotten in the excitement. Because, if I am right, and it appeared so from the preliminary experiments, returnees will live forever as a result of their exposure to the unified time stream.

---

[7] White JH, Lester D, Gentile M, & Rosenbleeth J (2011). The utilization of forensic science and criminal profiling for capturing serial killers. Forensic science international, 209 (1-3), 160-5 PMID: 21333473

THE NINE AMBASSADORS

Time in an experiment is the enemy of the impatient. I hurried to complete the first phase before Christmas. Moderate risk was already in play; I had to time my acquisitions prior to autumn snowstorms, which would then cover my hillside tracks to the burial site. Just to be safe. Fortunately, that year, the snows arrived late and, by then, the experiment was in full swing.

The following are the personal details of the ambassadors. I gathered this from their belongings (which I have stored for their return) and the events which led to their collection.

The pressure to make this happen in such a tight time frame was grueling and exhausting. For the record, I never missed a single lecture: Tuesdays, Thursdays, and Fridays. No one saw me come and go; I was extremely careful. On my trips, I stuck to the backroads, never ate, never gassed the Volvo station wagon up, never paid a toll. I left no trail at all.

The ambassadors were:

Madeline Blake – Number 1, student, 22, Quinn University, Vermont, asphyxiation, math mentor meeting, September 2.

Addilyn Winters – Number 2, housewife, 26, Montpelier, Vermont, taken from minivan at Health Nuts grocery store, cephalic vein injection, asphyxiation, September 19.

Hadlee Pellatier – Number 3, barista at Legal Grounds Coffee Emporium, 19, Freeport, Maine, intramuscular injection resulting in coma followed by death, October 4. Broke the ring finger on my right hand in a brief scuffle; multiple scratches.

Kinsey Grant – Number 4, trout fishing on the Musconetcong River, medial cubital vein injection.

Teegan O'Connor – Number 5, Insurance Agent, 29, Hartford, Connecticut, asphyxiated in sales office after laced cocktail, both of us in costume for Halloween, October 31.

Waverly Bradford – Number 6, Grocery Checker, 24, Manchester, New Hampshire, flat tire, cephalic vein injection, suffocated, November 6.

Janette and Julia Dayman – Numbers 7 and 8, twins, cheerleaders, 17, Pittsburg, Pennsylvania, post-football game after party, drunk and passed out, asphyxiated with pillow, no resistance, Nov 22.

Sylvia Larsson – Flight Attendant, 26, Holiday Nights Hotel, Mt. Snow, Vermont, on vacation in ski area, very fit, strangled until unconscious, asphyxiated, December 4.

"REALITY IS MERELY AN ILLUSION, ALBEIT A VERY PERSISTENT ONE."[8]

On December 5, the nine ambassadors finally lay in a complete sequence on the hillside, holding hands, a series of perfect chiral unions in a palindromic line—the numerical sequence presenting a postulate to time and reality, an offer to spiral inwards upon itself and through dissonance, force a realignment and thus the rebirth of the ambassadors.

When the first serious snow of the season fell two weeks before Christmas, a heavy white blanket covered the paper doll hyperplane.

I relaxed.

And waited.

---

[8] Attributed to Albert Einstein (1897 – 1955)

MAPLE SUGARING SEASON

When winter loosens its grip and the days are warmer under blue skies, but the nights are still freezing cold, I sharpen my .375-inch drill bits. Relaxing before a roaring fire in the hearth, I use my bit sharpener to get the perfect 59° profile on the cutting edge and the correct overhang on the tip.

I have three of the best German surgical orthopedic bone bits and, once sharpened, they work quite well on the ancient sugar maples that populate the landscape of Camp Quinn.

Spring approached.

The thinning snowpack glimmered in the sunlight as I traipsed through the clearing pulling a sled stacked with buckets and tapping spouts. My tool belt rattled as I struggled through a snowdrift toward the dense forest.

Somewhere beneath my feet, the ambassadors rested.

Months had passed.

I spent the day drilling trees.

They bled sweet sugar sap.

DEATH IS BUT AN ILLUSION CAUSED BY POINT-OF-VIEW

The lecture hall door creaked. I looked up from my notes, expecting a student in search of a forgotten book or phone from the preceding class. At first, I couldn't see a face as the brightness of the spring day backlit a form, although I could see clearly enough—it was a woman.

She stepped into clarity.

Blonde.

My heart leapt.

"Zach," she said.

Maddie.

But what struck me most was that she was nude.

And clean.

So very clean.

Like a scrubbed newborn.

I could hear the clatter of boots on the tiled hallway behind her. No doubt the security guards, guns drawn, were responding to the menace of a naked woman.

"You'd best come in," I said, grabbing my corduroy sports coat to cover her.

Strangely, the pounding footsteps passed the hall entrance, the door silently shut on its own volition and the two of us were embraced by an awkward silence.

Maddie and me.

SEX AND THE SINGLE PROFESSOR

Maddie sat in front of my laptop, scrolling through endless photos of some post-modern psychedelic band and giggling. She wore a tight-fitting rose-colored dress featuring flowers that I'd picked up at Goodwill when bringing her home.

At first, I thought the dress was more fitting for someone's grandmother, but on her, well, my thoughts momentarily turned away from mathematics and professorship.

I watched her breathing, her breasts rising and falling.

She hadn't needed to shower at my residence, but she had anyway and now her damp hair was woven and pulled into pigtails that brushed her exposed shoulders. She turned to stretch her lower back and hips, smiling at me as she did, and I wondered if she knew what had happened to her.

Despite her clothing and apparent adulthood, Maddie seemed more like a puppy than a woman and I realized I'd have to feed her soon. She hadn't spoken since she greeted me, and I wondered how her speech could be diminished if she could read and laugh. I watched as she clicked the mouse on the computer and it dawned on me.

She wasn't reading.

She was looking at bright colors.

I added another log to the fire crackling in the fireplace. I felt a chill and although there was only a light snow on the ground outside,

I suspected my chill had nothing to do with the weather.

I should explain what happened.

Like an ancient magician seeking to change lead to gold, the Holy Grail of Mathematics is to discover a non-representational mathematical formula. Not a number as an abstract symbol but rather an Independent Functional Initiator (IFI) lacking the precedence of any real-world event. In my case, I discovered operational palindromic primes which result in an alignment of the singularity. I can't say what that vector of time and space looks like. That's why I needed Maddie and the others.

But when I glanced at the mute girl watching a Pokémon video on YouTube, I was concerned about the veracity and viability of my premise.

Still, the other eight should return soon. Perhaps one of them would be mentally intact. The next should be Addilyn, although I had no idea of how soon or even where she would arrive. That might present a problem, although at the campus no one appeared to see Maddie even when we crossed the parking lot.

At the moment, though, the biggest question in my mind was whether this Maddie had deconstructed the Maddie buried in the meadow. Was Maddie's original human form still rotting in her grave, or was the only Maddie-instance the one sitting here in front of me? With the test animals, the original was always disassembled and reassembled but there was only one way for me to know for sure.

I had a grave to open.

"Maddie," I said, and she looked up, her hearing obviously intact. "We have to take a ride in the car."

She leapt to her feet, excited.

I wondered about the wisdom about what I was going to do. What would happen if this Maddie saw Maddie Prime? What if the grave wasn't empty?

In science, you learn to stand back objectively and let the experiment unfold.

Sometimes, you roll the dice.

And you take copious notes.

"I'll be back in a minute, Maddie," I said. "I have to get a shovel."

"I remember," said Maddie quietly as I reached the garage door.

Excitedly, I returned to face her; she had risen to her feet and was examining her surroundings like she'd never see them before. Of course, she had.

"What do you remember, Maddie?"

She vacillated, then spoke.

"I remember squid eye."

She smiled wryly and for the first time I wondered if I had made a mistake.

A STITCH IN TIME SAVES NINE

I tied a rope to Maddie's wrist. We climbed the hill, stepping on spring flowers and wet stones poking through patches of snow. Maddie was a slight girl. I could handle her if she ran. She seemed increasingly unenthusiastic as we trekked. At the meadow's edge, I tugged hard. She came reluctantly.

I didn't know how she'd react once I opened her grave.

Frankly, I didn't know how I'd react.

I paced off the location of the paper doll hyperplane and my foot pressed the blade of the shovel into the soil.

Twenty minutes of digging and I hit nothing. Of course, I'd expected that Maddie's body would be gone. After all, every experiment had started with disassembly, including the nonahedron, which never returned.

I kneeled, to lift out the remaining clumps of soil. Not only was Maddie's body absent, there wasn't a hand outstretched from Addilyn.

I shoveled more dirt aside, widening the gravesite.

Confirmed.

No Addiyn.

And then no hand for the next one named Hadlee.

"They're not here," Maddie stated emphatically, her voice breaking the silence of the forest and meadow. Then she enunciated slowly, Zach-a-ry.

"I know what you did to me."

The rush of blood to my head made me dizzy. My heart pounded. My ears throbbed as if to explode. I took a deep breath.

This was a wrinkle.

"We should go," Maddie said. "Hadlee will be coming soon and I want to freshen up. But first you must fill the hole."

I shoveled the soil back into the grave as she untied the rope from her wrist.

We walked down the hill.

Shouldn't Addilyn be next?

MANDALA (**मण्डल**) (SANSKRIT, N.)

A geometric spiritual and ritual symbol in Hinduism and Buddhism representing the entirety of the universe.

SQUID EYE
(MADDIE'S NOTES)

Maddie wrote:

> *At the center, which is not a center, the great squid eye floats in the nothingness and sees all. The eye exists but doesn't exist, a numerical representation of zero. Like zero, it exists in a conceptual realm but is equivalent to a mathematical set containing a null value.*
>
> *All stars, galaxies, and realities orbit the great squid eye. A low frequency hum vibrates but I can't hear it when I arrive, I can only feel it penetrating the luminous ball of energy I've become.*
>
> *When one arrives in the nothingness, one perceives the great squid eye in the distance, which means it is neither near nor far. A simple thought and you are next to the eye, which is simultaneously infinitely large and infinitesimally small. It*

blinks without an eyelid, its massive undulating pupil spewing luminescent purple time streams in all directions.

None of the time streams have purpose, including the ones we perceive and those that can never be perceived. The time streams simply dance as discharges of energy, stretching to all horizons, of which there are infinite.

When the eye blinks, each emitted time stream is broken. Whatever was in the time stream slowly degrades to non-existence. Time stream occupants can do nothing. Everything dies and is eventually reborn. Matter persists. There is no time in the nothingness. The great squid eye only exists in the eye of the observer. The observer only exists when seen by the great squid eye.

While I rested there, eight other luminous beings arrived. I did not know them, yet I knew everything about them.

A sparking time stream touched me, and I instantly found myself standing outside a classroom.

Flesh and blood again.

Reborn.

I slipped her handwritten notes into a manila folder and went to a file cabinet.

Someone rapped the knocker at my front door.

I slammed the drawer shut, locked it, and went to see who it was.

As predicted, it was Hadlee.

She hoisted a plastic sack.

"Maddie wanted better clothes. What you gave her was total crap."

The experiment was officially out of control.

VICTOR HUGO MEETS THE INFINITE SQUID EYE

As Victor Hugo once remarked, "When a woman is talking to you, listen to what she says with her eyes."

Maddie and Hadlee sat on the sofa; Hadlee leaned forward aggressively, Maddie easily tucked her legs beneath her new dress.

I shifted uncomfortably in the easy chair.

The chair in which I had killed Maddie.

"Will the others be arriving soon?" I asked, trying to figure out what the hell was going to happen next.

They both sipped Chardonnay. Maddie had opened a bottle and poured. No opportunity for me to catch them off guard.

"We've all returned," said Maddie. "Only Hadlee and I wanted to see you again. For starters, Hadlee wants to break your fingers. I think breaking your fingers is insufficient. We understand your math now. We are considering."

Hadlee smiled.

She said, "We know something you don't."

Maddie winked at me.

She said, "We can augment the formulae."

Their eyes studied me and it was then that I knew what was different about my two ambassadors. I hadn't noticed it with Maddie alone but looking at them now, it was obvious. Although their sclerae were white, their eyes had undergone a subtle transformation. Iris and pupil had merged into a singular blackness.

A sucking blackness darker even than Vantablack[9].

"What shall we do with him?" Hadlee asked.

"You know what I think," said Maddie.

And I realized they were talking out loud for my benefit.

"Until we decide, you'd best give us your car keys," Hadlee said, hand outstretched.

I tossed the keys to the Volvo.

"Don't get any ideas," said Maddie.

The front door locked itself.

I tried to rise from the chair.

I couldn't.

---

[9] Vantablack: A substance made of Vertically Aligned NanoTube Arrays of carbon and the blackest artificial substance known in the Universe, absorbing up to 99.965% of radiation in the visible spectrum.

MATH AND THE LAW OF KARMA[10]

That night, trapped in the easy chair, I could not sleep. Provided with a pencil and pad, I made what I assumed would be my last research note.

Question: What if the law of Karma is a natural law like Newton's law of gravity? Does Karma mathematically resolve itself?

THE SNAKE THAT EATS ITSELF
(WRITTEN AT HADLEE'S INSISTENCE)

I smell smoke.
I think the barn is burning.
Swallowing the last of the Chardonnay, I set
the glass aside to write these final notes.
I have no free will.
Throughout this day, I have given the Maddie
and Hadlee all my secrets.
I am to be an ambassador.
A wave of heaviness sinks into my body.
Drug impeding thought.
Nearby, Hadlee stands, watching, resting
weight on handle of shovel. Nonahedron sprays
table blue light.
They have made some modification.
Objects colors threads beams
Blinks
polybufohexane-12
blood pulsing heart pounding
eyes bulging wanting to explode
see Hadlee stretch duct tape my iPhone
setting text mode I hear her say to Maddie

---

[10] Jargal Dorj. Mathematical Proof of the Law of Karma. American Journal of Applied Mathematics. Vol. 2, No. 4, 2014, pp. 111-126. doi: 10.11648/j.ajam.20140204.12

who has pillow in hand
Maddie setting nonononononoheddrron to palindromic prime plus Pi she says her eyes looking me
I thought you'd want to understand
dizzy sick
sick
i will put pencil down now

END OF SELECTED RESEARCH NOTES

NOTES FROM THE UNDERGROUND
(ADDENDUM BY MADELINE BLAKE)

My phone chimed an empty text from the prof's iPhone, deep in his hole his finger moves. Dead but not dead. Aware but not aware. Neither here nor there. Everywhere and nowhere.

Hadlee and I drove south through the night, Hadlee at the wheel, me navigating down Highway 89 toward New Hampshire. Behind us, the prof's house and barn are burning the evidence to the ground although there may be few dog or monkey bones left in his well. For your information, casual reader or policeman or scientist or researcher of these documents, he's not buried up the hill in the meadow behind his farm.

Good luck finding him.

His nonahedron is set to Pi.

Professor Zach will understand infinity.

He is a powerless god, living forever, but hardly alive.

Unless there is an eventual end to Pi.

Hadlee laughs aloud at the thought and so do I. She steps on the gas and speeds up. A ribbon of light outlines the eastern horizon.

Dawn will arrive soon.

We have a rendezvous.

We nine paper dolls.

My phone vibrates another empty text.

Of course, Zach's iPhone will soon lose its charge and he will experience never-ending melancholia. He should have known if you look deeper into Durer's copper etching you can find the symbol for Pi hidden among the narrow black lines.

And a squid eye too.

My phone vibrates again.

Finally, some text. Typed with one finger. Hadlee duct-taped his hand to his phone, leaving only his half-healed ring finger free.

The text is gibberish.

I think he begs for forgiveness.

I turn off my phone, satisfied.

In the end, we destroyed the remaining nonahedrons and the two Silicon Valley entrepreneurs will misremember their doctoral work if anyone ever asks.

What about the paper doll hyperplane?

We existed but we never existed.

But we leave you a clue. The universe should have mysteries. Something to keep art researchers and mathematicians and conspiracy theorists busy at night. A distraction for the masses. The disappearance of an esteemed professor and a radical new scientific theory? Or an apocalyptic etching and the musings of a depressed medieval artist?

As we pull to the curb, I position the research papers on the backseat of the prof's Volvo on a street in Brooklyn. Hadlee and I will walk from here to the gleaming towers of New York City.

The others wait.

We will find our way among the lesser beings.

END ADDENDUM

Not Eradicated in You

BRACKEN MACLEOD

> Look how desperately you wanted to bond with "parents" who would not love you. That is not a defect; indeed, it can be a strength. It proves that the ability to love has not been eradicated in you.
> — Andrew Vachss

HARLOW

Harlow had handed him the money already—the most she'd ever saved, the most she'd ever spent at once on anything—but he held on to the paper bag, looking down at her with narrowed eyes. "You sure you know what you're getting into? I mean, anybody ever showed you what to do with something like this?"

She shook her head. "Huh uh. But I'm good at figuring shit out."

"Yeah, I bet." The guy smirked.

"Is there a problem?" The problem was the same as it was for everyone she dealt with: No one took her seriously because she was a kid. A *small* one at that—when other girls her age shot up past the boys, growing tall, filling out, she stayed short and slender. Her torn, oversized black sweater made her look even smaller. Some people thought that because she was petite, she was meek. Being underestimated allowed her to get away with things other girls couldn't.

She held out her hand. She wanted what the guy had promised

to sell to her. What he'd told her he could get, "no problem." Finding a dealer had been easier than getting the money. Mostly she collected a little at a time, scrounging change here and there, sponging from friends. "Hey, can I borrow a dollar for the Coke machine?" Her friends knew she wasn't "borrowing," but it was easier to ask that way than to outright request a handout. She'd take their dollars and later, produce a can of soda she'd hidden in her backpack from the fridge at home so it looked like she'd done what she said she would with the money instead of pocketing it.

She kept everything she saved in a jar hidden in her bedroom closet behind a box of old stuffed animals where her mom never looked.

It felt like it took forever to set aside enough, but she was patient and resisted the urge to spend even a little of her stash on other things ... no matter how hungry she got. Eventually, she had enough, and now she stood in front of this man, having given it *all* away, waiting for him to hand over what was hers. Waiting to see if he'd treat her like every other adult she knew, or if he'd respect her.

"I don't know. You fuck this up and there's no taking it back. There ain't no training wheels on this shit."

She didn't say anything, just held out her hand. He reluctantly passed the paper bag to her. It was smaller and lighter than she'd imagined. Harlow badly wanted to peek inside and reassure herself she hadn't just spent a personal fortune on this man's lunch. It seemed rude though. As if she didn't trust him. She didn't, of course, but she wanted to appear worldly, like she'd done this before—a hundred times, more often than she could count—and knew how something like this felt in her hand. Though they both knew this was her first time. Maybe it was a first for him, too. Selling to someone as young as she. Probably not, though.

"Thank you," she said.

His jaw flexed as he gritted his teeth. They were done. It was time for them both to leave. He sighed and held up a finger, silently asking her to wait a moment. He went to his car and leaned in through the window. A moment later, he turned around with an envelope in hand. "I shouldn't do this," he said as he walked back, holding it out. "I shouldn't be selling *any* of this to you, but ..." he trailed off. He told her that he wouldn't be doing this deal except for the name she'd dropped. Dierdre—her best friend's old after-school babysitter who sometimes bought them pints of Ruble vodka—said this guy owed her and gave Harlow his number. At first, he'd accused her of making a prank call. But then she said Dierdre's name and he listened. Whatever he owed the babysitter, it had to be something.

She reached out for the envelope and he yanked it back. "Look. I'm not fuckin' around about how serious this shit is. You gotta do it right, okay? I mean, for real. People get hurt."

"I get it." Her voice was as thin as she was.

He let her take it. "Everything you need to know is in that or the bag. *Pay attention.* You can practice without the works, okay? But once you start using what's in there," he pointed to the bag, "it's for real. No ... backsies."

Frustration burbled up in the back of her throat. As much as she hated being spoken to like a child, she appreciated the warning. No matter how things turned out, she figured screwing it up still had to be better than not ever trying it. "Thanks," she said.

"Yeah," the man sighed as he walked away. He waved a hand as if her gratitude was something he knew he ought to deflect. He climbed into his car and started it up. The thing rumbled like a storm, and Harlow felt the engine's vibration throb in her chest. They were meeting under the Route 2 overpass because it was private, but then he showed up in a car so loud no one could miss it. She didn't get adults.

He stuck an elbow out the window and looked at her a last time before peeling out, kicking up gravel and dirt. The sound of his car lingered in the neighborhood for a long time as he sped off to wherever it was that guys like him went when they were done selling their stuff to kids. Harlow turned and stalked back to the bushes where she'd stashed her skateboard and backpack. She slung the pack over her shoulder, and dropped the board on the asphalt. She kicked off and rolled home.

Harlow pulled the house key out of her shirt collar and bent forward to unlock the door. The aluminum-beaded chain she wore the key on was too short to reach the keyhole without taking it off, or leaning close. Stooping over was more difficult and embarrassing, but she was too nervous about dropping it to take off the necklace. She'd had a different key on a nicer chain that had once been her grandmother's; she'd removed it to unlock the door one afternoon and dropped it. The key fell perfectly, slipping between the boards of the front porch as though they weren't even there, and before she could drop and snatch at it, the chain slithered through the gap, into the dark. It was after dark before she got inside, got something to eat. And then her mother had been furious about having to get another one made. Still, the next day, her mother gave her a replacement. She recognized how it would look to the neighbors if her tender-aged child had to sit outside on the steps waiting to be let in. Harlow stole a new chain off of a rotating display on the counter at the record store downtown. She threw away the dog tag with the stupid peace sign on it and replaced it with her key. The chain wasn't as nice as her grandmother's necklace had been, but it felt sturdier and was longer. Long enough, she could bend down to unlock the door instead of having to take it off and risk losing it in the hungry porch flooring.

Once inside, she shut and locked the door behind her. If she didn't remember to unlock it later and her mother had to use *her* key to get in, she'd undoubtedly say, "What? Are you afraid someone's going to *steal* you?" Then, she'd laugh that bitter laugh at the too-familiar-by-repetition jape and lock the door after her as if it weren't the exact same gesture of self-assurance her daughter had made. It wasn't that Harlow was afraid of someone coming in to kidnap her, but she felt better behind the locked door. It was something in her life she could control.

The house was dark. Though it was still early and bright outside, Harlow didn't bother to open the heavy curtains. She took her skateboard to her bedroom and propped it next to the door inside, using her backpack as a brace to keep it from sliding down and clattering on the hardwood floor. Her stomach rumbled and she thought about going to the kitchen to find something worth eating. She thought there might be some leftover Chinese in the fridge, though it was from last week and she wasn't sure if it was still good.

The thought of the paper bag still concealed in her backpack tugged at her like a hook in her skin. Though she was excited to see, she hadn't opened it. Not outside. She didn't want to be caught out with what it contained. What she *hoped* was there. Her "works" the man had called it. It might still be a rip-off—she could imagine the guy now, getting high with Dierdre and laughing about the stupid girl who gave him all her money for nothing. It made Harlow want to cry. The babysitter had been so convincing—she'd seemed so sympathetic, like she wanted to help. Told her to tell the guy Dierdre said she was cool. But, Harlow had no idea what something like that really meant. So here she was with an expensive lunch sack filled with probable nonsense and a deepening despair over her proven naïveté.

Sniffling and pushing down her disappointment, Harlow forced herself to confront her gullibility. She unfolded the top and peered in. Her heart quickened and she pulled out a small cardboard package of skinny black birthday candles. She dropped to her knees and spilled the rest of the contents on the floor in front of her. A stubby compressed charcoal stick fell out, the tip chipping on the floor shedding little pieces of black like brittle shadow. Two plastic film canisters tumbled after and rolled away, labeled with light brown masking tape—one read GYD and the other BLD. An incense cone and a small rolled piece of paper followed last. She opened the paper and read it.

She hadn't been cheated. This was exactly what she'd asked for.

It didn't seem like much, and most of it had likely cost the guy less than five dollars to get, but then, you couldn't just go to the Rexall Drug and ask the pharmacist for *everything* he'd given her. The candles and incense and charcoal were easy to find, sure. But that last part. The little slip of paper. That wasn't something just anyone could just get. *That* was special. You had to *know*. That was worth the price.

Excited, she dug in her pocket for the envelope the man had given her. He'd seemed to go back for it as an afterthought, but opening it and unfolding the page within, she saw he'd prepared it for her carefully. She didn't know why he'd held it back, or exactly what she'd done to convince him to give it to her, but reading over it, she felt a shiver of anticipation streak up her back. Everything she needed to know was written out for her in clear detail. Step-by-step instructions. And the incantation.

She jumped to her feet and ran into the kitchen, snatching a bowl for the blood and earth in the black plastic film canisters and a long, sharp knife from the drawer. On her way back, she darted into the living room and grabbed her mom's lighter out of the drawer in the coffee table. She consulted the list again and found the last thing she needed in the hallway closet: a pair of scissors.

In her bedroom, she sat on the floor and began reading the page carefully. The dealer's voice in her head like an echo trapped in the walls of her room slowly escaping.

Pay attention. You fuck this up and there's no taking it back.

She read the words in a whisper, "Asmodel, king of the East, Azazel, king of the South, Paimon, king of the West, and Mahazuel, king of the North, send and bind your servant to me ..."

Slow down. People get hurt.

She started over, careful to say each name as it was written on the page with the man's hints at pronunciation. *Az-mo-del. Ma-ha-zoo-ell.* She studied the symbol drawn at the bottom of the page and traced it on a piece of paper before attempting it on the floor. Using the round, removable lid to her laundry hamper, she traced a circle on the floor with the charcoal. Surely it was big enough. She began drawing the sigil on the page inside of it, careful to get all the lines and angles right, and placing the six black candles at the points.

"By your mistress, Lilith, I call you. I know your name."

She pried the lid off the first canister and poured the desecrated graveyard dirt into her bowl. Dark menstrual blood followed from the second—she couldn't use her own, she was a virgin—beading on top of the dry earth and turning muddy black. Fertile soil; infertile blood. She lit the cone of incense and set it in the lid of one of the canisters. "By the bowl and blade and blood and soil, answer me. I know your name."

Finally, she took a small lock of her hair in her fingers, and cut. She dropped it in the bowl and whispered, "Come to me and stand in my circle. I know your name; you are bound to it and to me."

Harlow picked up the kitchen knife with a trembling hand and held the tip over her wrist. It was going to hurt. But *everything* hurt. Why shouldn't her pain get her something that she wanted for a change?

She pressed the tip into her skin and watched the swell of blood rise up out of her and slip over the side of her arm into the bowl.

"I know your name. Come stand in my circle. I know your name, Ertzibat."

CAROL

Carol felt a tinge of exasperation at having to pause to fish her keys back out of her purse. The kid was home and there was no reason for her to lock the goddamn door. The porch light wasn't on and it was dark and the keys had somehow slipped down to the bottom of her bag, though she'd just dropped them in a second ago. One annoyance piling atop another after a day full of them, like a cherry at the zenith of all her troubles. She dragged the keyring out of her purse and cycled through looking for her house key. Feeling more than a little buzzed from the after-work drinks she'd had with Billie, she missed it the first pass around. Finally, she found the right one. Once inside, she slammed the door behind her, making a point of entering the house noisily.

She stood in the gloom for a second, listening for her daughter, before flipping the light switch. Nothing. The kid wasn't home. Just perfect. That was worse than locking herself in. Where was she at this hour? Carol dreaded getting a call from a parent asking if it was okay if Harlow had stayed for dinner. *She and little Suzy-sweetheart were having the best time and we had stroganoff and Harlow says she loooves stroganoff. I just wanted to call to let you know I'm bringing her home as soon as they're through with dessert.* "Don't bother," Carol would be tempted to say. Except, it was a weeknight and she couldn't count on the unlikely mercy of a sleepover that'd make it easier to go out and have some fun—maybe bring someone home without having to sneak a guy past the kid up late watching something she shouldn't be on HBO. Not that Carol cared what Harlow watched, except when it came back on her at Parent Teacher Night. *Did you know that your daughter has seen the movie* The Entity? *We had to have a talk with her because she was describing it to the other girls, Ms. Sackett. It's inappropriate. We'd encourage you to take a greater interest in your daughter's viewing habits.*

And while we're at it, can we talk about her hair? And her clothes?

Carol hung her purse on the doorknob and plopped down on the sofa. She stared up at the blankness of the ceiling. She needed a bump to give her the energy to slip into character, and *then* she'd start phoning around to see where her daughter had landed. *Oh, I'm so sorry, Terri,* she'd say. *I hope she wasn't a bother. I got caught up at work and the time ... well, you* know *how it is.* Of course they didn't know. PTA mommies who stayed home and drank chardonnay in the afternoon while she had to work—*had* to work because that asshole Stephen ran off. She glanced at her watch. "Jesus," she sighed. A quarter to ten. When did she get to ride off in a fancy red sports car and enjoy life? Hell, she was thirty-two and at her sexual peak and look at where she was. Cutting it off with Billie before either of them could really get a start on the evening so she could get back to her budding delinquent daughter—who wasn't even home!

She leaned forward and slid open the drawer in the coffee table, pulling out the glass vial and the plastic McSpoon next to it with the little arches at the end of the stem. *Fucking Stephen took the ivory one. Selfish prick.* She unscrewed the cap and dipped the spoon in, scooping out enough to take the edge off. Just a bump. She didn't get paid until Friday and this had to last.

A thump in the back of the house made her fumble the nearly weightless spoon as she inhaled. Carol replaced the bottle and spoon in the drawer and got up to take a look. Maybe Harlow hadn't gone to a friend's at all. She'd stayed home and, what? Gone to bed early? *Not* my *daughter.* It wasn't like her daughter to turn in before midnight, or to leave any room in the house dark for that matter. The girl was anxious about everything. Unlocked doors, the dark,

NOT ERADICATED IN YOU

silence, sleep itself. If Harlow was home, the place was ablaze with light and sound.

She stalked toward the bedrooms, feeling the numbness in her sinuses extend down into her throat, a touch of it tingling ever so slightly in her face. Billie always got her good stuff. Friday couldn't come soon enough.

She felt a breath of cold air on her skin at her daughter's door, like standing in front of an open freezer. *The little shit left her windows open when she crawled out.* Carol decided she'd close and latch them. See if the little criminal remembered her key when she finally dragged her ass home. Carol reached for the knob and hesitated. She blinked, trying to clear her mind. Her head felt blurry and was getting blurrier. Standing in the hallway felt like a dream. Like she'd fallen asleep and woken up outside her daughter's bedroom. Something about the door. The darkness. Deeper here, like shutting herself inside a box. She turned and flicked the light switch. A dim illumination cut through the obscurity, but everything remained imprecise. She looked at Harlow's door and for a moment it seemed to blend into the wavering walls, like a shadow itself before resolving into a sort of solid clarity.

Carol rubbed her eyes. She'd overdone it. A little drunk and high as fuck. Not even ten and she was spent. Well, it'd *been* a day. She'd go shut and lock Harlow's windows and go to bed. She reached forward and opened the door.

The darkness on the other side pooled and eddied in front of her like water. It drifted down and out of the room swirling around her feet, chilling her ankles. *Oh my god! Fire!* But the smoke was cold—so cold—as it touched her. She took a step back. The darkness resisted her. It was thick and stepping back felt like walking in water. A small shriek escaped her lips and a booming noise invaded her mind like a sudden migraine. It pushed outward from inside her skull and she pressed her hands to the sides of her head trying to hold herself together against it.

SHHHHHHHHH.

Her scream died on her tongue and she struggled to take a breath. Tendrils of darkness reached out for her face. She batted at them with a hand and they broke and dissolved like smoke, but her hand came away a little blacker with each wisp she touched. She wiped her dirtied hand on her pants and the darkness smeared in a streak across the fabric. Not smoke. Where was the heat? Where was the crackling sound of it?

"Wha— what's happ—?"

SHHHHHHHHHH.

Carol dropped to her knees and the charcoal mist swirled around her legs, lapping up against her thighs and hips. Chilling her in intimate places she preferred to be warmed with breath and body. She shivered. It cascaded out of the room letting the light from the hall strengthen and enter slowly, touching the familiar shapes in the room tenderly, bringing them out of the shade. A dresser covered with girlish things—a music box, a stuffed mouse—the chair beside Harlow's desk with a leather jacket draped over the back, and the desk itself, lamp and cassette tape player atop it, books and albums on a shelf next to the record player. She saw the walls adorned with posters and clippings from magazines stretch away from her like she was backing out of a dark tunnel, until the posts of her child's bed emerged from the darkness, and beyond them Harlow lying on top of the covers, black boots, black tights, a white shirt and her bright crimson hair, face nestled up against … it. Another scream rose up from her lungs and threatened to emerge from her mouth, but died before it reached her lips and the black mist was reaching up from the floor and smothering her.

YOU'LL WAKE HER.

The pain of the voice in her mind made everything blur and dim before her vision resolved again and she saw the thing on Harlow's bed, her daughter on top of it, clutching it like a … like a …

"Mother?" the girl said, stirring. An onyx hand caressed the back of her head as she turned to face Carol. "That you?"

Carol struggled against the wisps. She brushed at her face and tried to push up from the floor. The mist held her down. Darkness reentered the room and shifted against the walls as the thing under her daughter extended its great wings, stretching them in the confining room. Harlow pushed up on its lap, and looked at her mother.

"G-get away … from it."

The girl didn't move, except to turn and look into its face. "That's her," she said. "My mom."

The dark thing shifted and wrapped an arm around the girl. It whispered from a red mouth like a gash torn by a dull knife. "Your mother."

Carol's bowels felt tight. Her head ached and fear peaked in her, making her heart pound. If the thing spoke again, *in* her, the way it had shushed her, she thought she would die.

The dark thing sat up, heavy breasts and broad shoulders shifting as it righted. It cocked its head and a spill of writhing, inky hair obscured a shoulder. Its eyes were darker than anything Carol had ever seen. As black as not existing at all. The gash in its face opened again and it said, "Caroliiiiiiine." Her name oozed in the air like oil.

Harlow nodded. The thing pulled her back to its body. Harlow wrapped her arms around it. The girl turned her head and said, "You should get some sleep, Mom. You have work tomorrow." Her voice sounded like it came carried on the wind from a mile away. Everything was wrong in the way that dreams are. A gross distortion in a familiar setting, like being in her office but also out to sea. Her real daughter in the lap of a nightmare. Carol was too heavily embodied, too delicately conscious. Nothing was real, though everything felt it.

Another tendril of charcoal mist reached up and left a streak on the side of Carol's face. She felt the thing looking into her. Seeing through her to blood, bones, and organs—She felt it exploring her being, experiencing all the boundaries of her from the inside out.

And she despaired.

Carol awoke in bed, lying on top of her covers, still dressed in the clothes she wore the night before. She felt dizzy and her head throbbed. A queasy feeling in her stomach threatened revolt. Her daughter's record player blared shrilly from the far end of the hallway, making her head ache to a beat. *Identity! Identity!* She forced herself to sit up, and swing her legs over the end of the bed. After a moment to adjust, she stood, holding on to her nightstand for support while the room seemed to pulse before setting into fixed reality. Creeping to the door, she opened it a crack and peeked out expecting to see … what? The memory was hazy and all she could recall was that deep black mist.

And the woman-thing inside of it that was the darkness.

The bright morning and loud music assured her it was only a dream. A nightmare. Mercifully, in the way of dreams, mostly extinguished from her mind. By the time she finished her second cup of coffee, it would be all gone, except maybe the lingering unease.

Light shone from her daughter's open door, reflecting brightly off the polished hardwood floor. Carol squinted against its offense. She smelled breakfast. Eggs and toasting bread. Harlow was cooking. Her stomach alternately growled and lurched. She dragged a palm across her moist forehead and worked to keep her gorge down. She'd never had a nightmare like that. It had been so much more vivid than a normal dream. Someone must've spiked her drink at the bar. *Bad trip.* That was it. That guy with his friend—the one flirting with Bobbie—he'd dropped something in her glass and she peaked when she got home. Probably intensified it with the bump. She wanted to laugh, but felt like she might vomit if she took anything but short, measured breaths. *Stick to blow, Carol. It's safer.*

She stank of cigarettes and sweat. She shed yesterday's work clothes and wrapped up in her bathrobe. First, a shower and then a cup of coffee. If her stomach would take it, maybe she'd try to eat some of the toast Harlow was making too.

Carol stepped out into the hall holding her hands against her ears to deaden the song playing on Harlow's record player. It was familiar and despised. Too much for a rough morning. She fought against her disorientation and ducked into the child's room, slipping in the candle wax melted in a mess on the floor, kicking something solid and glass sounding across the room. It stank. *What the fuck was that? God* she wanted something to take the edge off. Get her to baseline. She staggered across the room and lifted the needle from the groove.

"Hey! I was listening to that," Harlow yelled from the kitchen.

Carol didn't care. She didn't like punk music without a hangover, and she *really* hated it with one. She stomped toward the kitchen, her reprimand about how rude it was to play obnoxious music before everyone in the house was awake already half out of her mouth. The thought went unexpressed when she saw the strange woman standing at the stove, cracking an egg into a skillet. It wouldn't do to yell at Harlow in front of another parent. *Oh Jesus. How long has this woman been in my house?* She blushed deep red at the thought that another mother had brought Harlow home and decided to linger until Carol returned. And then she, what? Stayed the night until Carol sobered up? Was making breakfast for her child. Who was this woman inserting herself into their lives as if she had the right to judge, let alone *interfere?* Carol held down her rage and said, "I'm sorry, but who—"

The woman turned. Carol lost her breath. The woman stood assured and steady, spatula in hand and wearing a cooking apron like some TV reflection of the woman Carol had never been. Never wanted to be. Hair, height, figure, face, even the clothes she wore. Everything about her was the same … but better. All except her eyes. They absorbed light. They stole her breath. Those flat black eyes drove Carol back. Being seen by them felt like being captured, stolen from herself. The woman had to be blind, but Carol was beheld.

Harlow stood from the table and skipped over to the woman. "I'm going to be late for school. No time! Sorry."

It said, "That's okay, honey. Take this." The creature that was not Carol handed her daughter a paper sack, the bottom bulging with the weight of a can of Coke or an apple. The girl got up on her tiptoes and the too-familiar thing bent down and they kissed. A chaste motherly kiss that smacked loudly and echoed against the Formica countertops and tile floors.

The girl turned to look at Carol. Her wide eyes narrowed. Carol wanted to shout that Harlow didn't get to judge her. That she wasn't the one who paid the rent and put food on the table and who gave birth to her. Her work, her money, her body. She didn't say a thing. Her legs felt weak and bile burned the back of her tongue.

The girl snatched up her skateboard from against the wall and skipped out of the room calling back over her shoulder, "Love you!"

Before Carol could process the sound of her daughter saying

those two words, so rarely spoken or heard, the thing at the stove said, "I love you too! Don't be late."

"I won't."

The door slammed and the world darkened. The black char mist of Carol's nightmares cascaded off the thing like waterfalls, filling the room, eating light. Stretching out from her back like great black wings. It turned. An abomination in a silk wrap top blouse tied at the waist and a tan skirt. It still wore her face. But its mouth was redder. Lips crueler.

"What are you?" Carol managed.

It tilted its head and looked at her with its shark's eyes.

It spoke.

"I'm what she wants." The voice, which had a moment earlier held a sing-song lightness, deepened to an unutterable depth that made Carol's bowels slack.

Carol bolted from the kitchen. She snatched her purse off the front door knob, whipped the door open, and flung herself out into the bright morning daylight. She flailed and stumbled as she expected to run through the open door, down the front steps and into the soft grass outside. Instead, she plunged into the growing shadow of the thing filling the kitchen. Her panicked mind tried to comprehend where she was. She dropped to her hip to avoid running into the thing's swirling darkness, kicking and trying to backpedal away.

It smiled.

Carol's bladder emptied.

"Why?" she sobbed.

"Because she loves you."

Deep in its words, Carol heard something she knew was as true as morning and appetite and fear. Her daughter had summoned this thing to what? Love her? To steal the love Carol deserved, that *she* earned. And be loved in return?

"She's *my* daughter. You don't get to love her!"

"I do love her."

The thing in the swirling darkness seemed to take a moment, and looked up at the ceiling as if searching its damned mind for what to say. It looked back at Carol and a chill penetrated her. It gestured to its face, her clothes. Its smile was cruel and mean and red. "Though I don't love you." It reached for her.

And she fell into darkness, lost and thoughtless, loveless and alone.

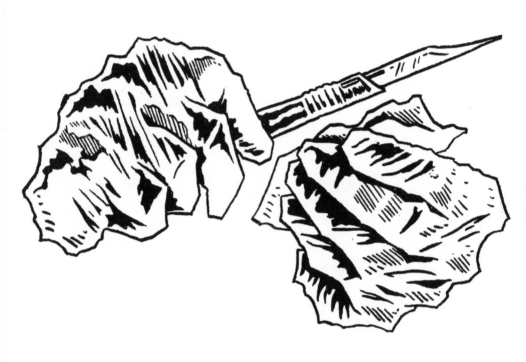

Resurrection Points

USMAN T. MALIK

I was thirteen when I dissected my first corpse. It was a fetid, soggy teenager Baba dragged home from Clifton Beach and threw in the shed. The ceiling leaked in places, so he told me to drape the dead boy with tarpaulin so that the monsoon water wouldn't get at him.

When I went to the shed, DeadBoy had stunk the place up. I pinched my nostrils, gently removed the sea-blackened aluminum crucifix from around his neck, pulled the tarp across his chest. The tarp was a bit short—Ma had cut some for the chicken coop after heavy rainfall killed a hen—and I had to tuck it beneath DeadBoy's chin so it seemed he were sleeping. Then I saw that fish had eaten most of his lips and part of his nose and my stomach heaved and I began to retch.

After a while I felt better and went inside the house.

"How's he look?" said Baba.

"Fine, I guess," I said.

Baba looked at me curiously. "You all right?"

"Yes." I looked at Ma rolling dough *peras* in the kitchen for dinner, her face red and sweaty from heat, and leaned into the smell of mint leaves and chopped onions. "Half his face is gone, Baba."

He nodded. "Yes. Water and flesh don't go well together and the fish get the rest. You see his teeth?"

"No."

"Go look at his teeth and tell me what you see."

I went back to the shed and peeled the pale raw lip-flesh back with my fingers. His front teeth were almost entirely gone, sockets blackened with blood, and the snaillike uvula at the back of the throat was half-missing. I peered into his gaping mouth, tried to feel the uvula's edge with my finger. It was smooth and covered with clots, and I knew what had happened to this boy.

"So?" Baba said when I got back.

"Someone tortured him," I said. Behind Baba, Mama sucked breath in and fanned the manure oven urgently, billowing the smoke away from us toward the open door.

"How do you know?" Baba said.

"They slashed his uvula with a razor while he was alive, and when he tried to bite down they knocked out his teeth with a hammer."

Baba nodded. "How can you tell?"

"Clean cut. It was sliced with a blade. And there are no teeth chips at the back of the throat or stuck to the palate to indicate bullet trauma."

"Good." Baba looked pleased. He tapped his chin with a spoon and glanced at Mama. "You think he's ready?"

Mama tried to lift the steaming pot, hissed with pain, let it go and grabbed a rough cotton rag to hold the edges. "Now?"

"Sure. I was his age when I did my first." He looked at me. "You're old enough. Eat your dinner. Later tonight I'll show you how to work them."

We sat on the floor and Ma brought lentil soup, vegetable curry, raw onion rings, and cornflour roti. We ate in silence on the meal mat. When we were done we thanked Allah for his blessings. Ma began to clear the dinner remains, her bony elbows jutting out as she scraped crumbs and wiped the mat. She looked unhappy and didn't look up when Baba and I went out to work the DeadBoy.

DeadBoy's armpits reeked. I asked Baba if I could stuff my nostrils with scented cotton. He said no.

We put on plastic gloves made from shopping bags. Baba lay the boy on the tools table, situating his palms upward in the traditional anatomical position. I turned on the shed's naked bulb and it swung from its chain above the cadaver, like a hanged animal.

"Now," Baba said, handing me the scalpel, "locate the following structures." He named superficial landmarks: jugular notch, sternal body, xiphoid process, others familiar to me from my study of his work and his textbooks. Once I had located them, he handed me the scalpel and said: "Cut."

I made a midline horizontal and two parallel incisions in Dead-Boy's chest. Baba watched me, shaking his head and frowning, as I fumbled my way through the dissection. "No. More laterally" and "Yes, that's the one. Now reflect the skin back, peel it slowly. Remove the superficial fascia" and "Repeat on the other side."

DeadBoy's skin was wet and slippery from water damage and much of the fat was putrefied. His pectoral and abdominal musculature was dark and soft. I scraped the congealed blood away and removed the fascia, and as I worked muscles and tendons slowly emerged and glistened in the yellow light, displaying neurovascular bundles weaving between their edges. It took me three hours but finally I was done. I stood, surrounded by DeadBoy's odor, trembling with excitement, peering at my handiwork.

Baba nodded. "Not bad. Now show me where the resurrection points are." When I hesitated, he raised his eyebrows. "Don't be scared. You know what to do."

I took a glove off and placed it on DeadBoy's thigh. I tentatively touched the right pec major, groping around its edges. The sternal head was firm and spongy. When I felt a small cord in the medial corner with my fingers, I tapped it lightly. The pec didn't twitch.

I looked at Baba. He smiled but his eyes were black and serious. I licked my lips, took the nerve cord between my fingers, closed my eyes, and discharged.

The jolt thrummed up my fingers into my shoulder. Instantly the pec contracted and DeadBoy's right arm jerked. I shot the biocurrent again, feeling the recoil tear through my flesh, and this time DeadBoy's arm jumped and flopped onto his chest.

"Something, isn't it," Baba said. "Well done."

I didn't reply. My heart raced, my skin was feverish and crawling. My nostrils were filled with the smell of electricity.

"First time's hard, no denying it. But it's gotta be done. Only way you'll learn to control it."

I was on fire. We had talked about it before, but this wasn't anything like I had expected. When Baba did it, he could smile and make conversation as the deadboys spasmed and danced on his fingertips. Their flesh turned into calligraphy in his hands.

"It felt like something exploded inside me, Baba," I said, hearing the tremble in my voice. "What happens if I can't control it?"

He shrugged. "You will. It just takes time and practice, that's all. Our elders have done it for generations." He leaned forward, lifted DeadBoy's hand, and returned it to supine position. "Want to try the smaller muscles? They need finer control and the nerves are thinner. Would be wise to use your fingertips."

And thus we practiced my first danse macabre. Sought out the nerve bundles, made them pop and sizzle, watched the cadaver spider its way across the table. With each discharge, the pain lessened, but soon my fingers began to go numb and Baba made me halt. Carefully he draped DeadBoy.

"Baba, are there others?" I asked as we walked back to the house.

"Like us?" He nodded. "The Prophet Isa is said to have returned men to life. When Martha of Bethany asked how he would bring her brother Lazarus back to life, Hazrat Isa said, 'I am the Resurrection and the life. He who believes in me will live, even though he dies.'"

We were in the backyard; the light of our home shone out bright and comforting. Baba turned and smiled at me. "But he was a healer first. Like our beloved Prophet Muhammad Peace-Be-Upon-Him. Do you understand?"

"I guess," I said. DeadBoy's face swam in front of my eyes. "Baba, who do you think killed him?"

His smile disappeared. "Animals." He didn't look at me when he said, "How's your friend Sadiq these days? I haven't seen him in a while." His tone was casual, and he tilted his jaw and stared into the distance as if looking for something.

"Fine," I said. "He's just been busy, I think."

Baba rubbed his cheek with a hairy knuckle and we began walking again. "Decent start," he said. "Tomorrow will be harder, though." I looked at him; he spread his arms and smiled, and I realized what he meant.

"So soon?" I said, horrified. "But I need more practice."

"Sure, you do, but it's not that different. You did well back there."

"But—"

"You will do fine, Daoud," he said, and would say no more.

Ma watched us approach the front door, her face silvered by moonlight. Baba didn't meet her eyes as we entered, but his hand rose and rubbed against his khaddar shirt, as if wiping dirt away.

Ma said nothing, but later, huddled in the charpoy, staring through the skylight window at the expansive darkness, I heard them arguing. At one point, I thought she said, "Worry about the damn house," and he tried to shush her, but she said something hot and angry and Baba got up and left. There was silence and then there was sobbing, and I lay there, filled with sorrow and excitement, listening to her grief, thinking if only there was a way to reconcile the two.

The dead foot leaped when I touched the resurrection point. Mr. Kurmully yelped.

"Sorry," I said, jerking my fingers away. "Did that hurt?"

"No." He massaged the foot with his hand. "I was … surprised. I haven't had any feeling in this for years. Just a dry burning around the shin. But when you touched it there," he gestured at the inner part of his left ankle, "I *felt* it. I felt you touching me."

He looked at me with awe, then at Baba, who stood by the door, hands laced behind his back, looking pleased. "He's good," Mr. Kurmully said.

"Yes," Baba said.

"So when are you retiring, Jamshed?"

Baba laughed. "Not for a while, I hope. Anyway, let's get on with it. Daoud," he said to me, "can you find the pain point in his ankle?"

I spent the next thirty minutes probing and prodding Mr. Kurmully's diabetic foot, feeling between his tendons for nerves. It wasn't easy. Over the years, Mr. Kurmully had lost two toes and the stumps had shriveled, distorting the anatomy. Eventually I found two points, braced myself, and gently shot them.

"Feel better?" I said, as Mr. Kurmully withdrew his foot and stepped on it tentatively.

"He won't know until tomorrow," Baba said. "Sometimes instant effect may occur, but our true goal is nocturnal relief when the neuropathy is worst. Am I right, Habib?"

"Yes." Mr. Kurmully nodded and flexed his foot this way and that. "The boy's gifted. I had some burning when I came. It's gone now. His first time?"

"Yes."

"Good God." Mr. Kurmully shook his head wonderingly. "He will go far." He came toward me and patted me on the head. "Your father's been a boon to our community for twenty years, boy. Always be gentle, like him, you hear me? Be humble. It's the branch laden with fruit that bends the most." He smiled at me and turned to Baba. "Let me pay you this once, Jamshed."

Baba waved a hand. "Just tip the Edhi driver when he takes the cadaver. One of their volunteers has agreed to bury it for free."

"They are good to you, aren't they."

Baba beamed. He opened his mouth to speak, but there was sudden commotion at the front of the clinic and a tall, gangly man with a squirrel tail mustache strode in, followed by the sulky-faced Edhi driver looking angry and unhappy.

Baba's gaze went from one to another and settled on the gangly stranger. "Salam, brother," Baba said. "How can I help you?"

The gangly man pulled out a sheath of papers and handed it to Baba. He had gleaming rat eyes that narrowed like cracks in cement when he spoke. He sounded as if he had a cold. "Doctor Sahib, you know why I'm here."

"I'm not sure I do. Why don't you tell me? Would you like to take a seat?"

"Just read the papers, sahib," he said in his soft, nasal voice.

"Oh?" Baba looked at the Edhi driver. He was a gloomy, chubby boy fond of charas and ganja and often rolled joints one-handed on his fat belly when waiting at red lights. I had ridden with him a couple times and once he showed me his weird jutting navel. Everted since birth, he told me proudly.

"Zamir, what's going on?" Baba said.

"Sahib, they're giving us trouble with the burial," Zamir said. "This man is from the local *Defend the Sharia* council. They have a written fatwa stating that since the dead boy was Christian he cannot be buried in a Muslim cemetery."

Baba turned back to the gangly man. "Is that true, brother?"

Gangly Man thrust the papers into Baba's hands. "This is from Imam Barani. Take a look."

Baba took the roll, but didn't open it. "This boy," Baba said, "was tortured by someone."

Gangly Man's shoulders stiffened.

"He was beaten badly. His teeth knocked out with a hammer. Someone took a razor to his mouth. When he was near dead, they threw him in the river."

Gangly Man's lips pressed into a thin, white line.

"He was sixteen. He had a scar on his stomach from a childhood surgery, probably appendectomy. He wore a tawiz charm on his forearm his mother likely got from a Muslim saint. You know how illiterate these poor Christians are. Can't tell the difference between one holy man and another, and—"

"Doctor Sahib." Gangly Man leaned forward and whispered conspiratorially, "He and his filthy religion can ride my dick. My orders are simple. He will not be buried in the Muslim cemetery, and if I were you I wouldn't push it."

Baba's face changed color. He looked around and for the first time I saw how angry and tired he was. He looked like he hadn't slept in days. Maybe he hadn't. It was hard to know. He and Ma were talking less to each other lately.

"If you make it difficult for us, well, things could go many ways, couldn't they? Sometimes clinics run by quacks can be shut down by provincial governments until NOCs are obtained. I don't even see a diploma on your wall. Surely, you went to medical school?" Still smiling, he toed the threadbare couch, the only piece of furniture in the room. "Besides, you might be Muslim but blasphemy is blasphemy, brother, and punishable under the Hadood Ordinance. The boy is

Christian. That cemetery is not."

The Edhi driver took Baba's arm and led him aside. They talked. Zamir gestured furiously. Baba's shoulders rose and sagged. They came back.

"We will take the body to Aga Khan Medical College and donate it to their anatomy lab," cried Zamir.

"But he has already been—" Baba began

"I'm sure they will find more to do with it," Zamir said, nodding and smiling.

Gangly Man took the front of his own shirt with a tarantula-like hand and began to shake it, fanning his chest. "Very wise. How they will appreciate you!"

Baba remained silent, but a heavy ice block appeared in my belly and settled there. I turned and ran from the clinic, ran all the way to our house three streets down. I burst into the shed and went to DeadBoy and wrenched away the tarp. His insides were tucked in with thin stitches. I yanked the stitches out, peeled back his skin, and pressed my gloveless fingers into his muscles. I discharged the biocurrent again and again until his limbs twirled and snapped, a lifeless dervish whirling around his own axis. I let the electricity flow through my fingertips like a raging torrent, until the room sizzled with charge and my nostrils filled with the odor of burnt flesh.

After a while I stepped back. My cheeks burned and the corners of my eyes tickled. Even though it was close to noon, the shed was dark from a low-hanging monsoon ceiling. Interstices of sunlight fell on DeadBoy's half-face, revealing the blackness of his absent teeth and his mutilated lips.

"Sorry, DeadBoy," I said.

He twitched his shoulder.

The movement was so unexpected that I jerked and fell over the toolbox on the floor. I sat on the sodden ground, gazing at Dead-Boy, my heart pounding in my chest. He was still. Had I imagined it? That movement—it was impossible. The deadboys couldn't move without stimulus.

I got up and went to him. His disfigured flesh was placid and motionless.

"Hey," I whispered, feeling foolish and nervous. "Can you hear me?" The shadows in the room deepened. Somewhere outside a swallow cheeped.

DeadBoy never said a word.

After the Edhi driver hauled DeadBoy away, I walked around for a while. Soon it began to drizzle, the kind of sprinkle that makes you feel hot and damp but never really cool, so I took off my shirt, tucked it into my armpit, and ran bare-chested to Sadiq's house.

He lived in the Christian muhallah near Kala Pul, a couple kilometers away. His two-room tin-and-timber house was next to a dirty canal swollen with rainwater, plastic bags, and lifeless rodents, and the rotten smell filled the street.

His mother opened the door. Khala Apee was a young-old woman. Her cheeks were often bruised. Her right eye was swollen shut today.

"He's at the Master sahib's," she told me in a hoarse voice. She smoked cigarettes when her husband was not home, Sadiq had told me. "He'll be back in an hour. Want a soda?"

They couldn't afford sodas. It was probably leftover sherbat from last Ramadan. But what was Sadiq doing at Master sahib's? Summer vacation wouldn't be over for another month. "Thank you, but no, Khala Apee. I'll wait under the elm outside."

She nodded and tried to smile. "Let me know if you want something. And if you can, do stay for dinner."

Plain roti with sliced onions. No gravy. "I'll try, Khala Apee. May I borrow a plastic bag?"

She brought me one. I went to the charpoy under the elm where we sometimes sat and made fun of our families. Rain pattered on the elm leaves and hissed on the ground, and as I sat there with my plastic-draped head on the steeple of my fingers I thought about Baba and Ma and how they had been arguing for months. Ma was worried about the house. She wanted Baba to start charging patients. Baba refused. His father and grandfather had never charged a fee, he said. They lived on food and gifts people gave them.

Ma laughed bitterly. Those were different times, you fool. So different. And the house, what about the house, Jamshed? We are in debt. So much debt. What will you do when they come to take our home? If you cared as much about your family as you do about your goddamn corpse-learning, we could live like normal people, like normal human beings.

But we're *not* normal, Baba protested. This is a good way to blend in, to be part of this world. Be part of the community—

Blend in? Mama said. We will never blend in if you keep antagonizing them. What was the point of arguing with that mullah? You know they are dangerous people. You keep going like this, we will never be part of the community. How could we be? We are ...

Sadiq was shaking me awake. "Hey, Daoud, hey. Wake up."

I opened my eyes. "Hey, how was ... *what?*" I said when I saw his face. Sadiq was a small boy with mousy features and at the moment they were chiseled with worry.

"You've got to leave, Daoud," said Sadiq, glancing around. "Now."

"What's going on? Everything okay?"

"Yes. Master sahib had heard some rumors and he wanted to warn us. He ..." Sadiq gnawed at his lip, his fingers still tugging at my arm. "Go home. We'll talk tomorrow."

"Why?" But he was already leading me away from the elm and toward the canal. The drizzle had stopped and the canal water eddied gently. I put on my shirt and watched as Sadiq took a tin box from his pocket and tied a brick around it with jute twine and twice-doubled rubber band. He waded into the shallow canal and deposited the box at a spot two feet from the bank.

"What are you doing?" I said when he climbed back up the embankment.

"Nothing," he said, but his voice was strange. "Run back home now. I'll come by in a couple days if I can."

I went up the canal road, occasionally looking back, trying to make sense of what had just happened. Sadiq stood there, hands in the pockets of his shorts, a skinny, brown boy with a sad face and a fake-silver cross gleaming around his neck. Sometimes even now I see that cross in my dreams, throwing silver shadows across my path as I trudge down alleys filled with heartache and rotting bodies.

As I glanced back one last time, Sadiq took off the cross and slipped it into his pocket.

Baba was waiting for me.

"Where were you?" he said, his eyes hard and red. "I was worried sick."

"At Sadiq's. I wanted to—"

"Foolish boy," he said. "Don't you know how dangerous that was? Don't you realize?" I stared at him, feeling my head throb. He saw my incomprehension and his voice softened. "Someone vandalized a church in Lahore yesterday. Someone else found feces strewn in a mosque in Quetta. As a result, two people are dead and tens more injured in riots around the country. These tensions have been building for a while. You saw what that *Defend the Sharia* asshole did this morning. This will only get worse. You cannot visit Sadiq until things settle down."

"But what does Sadiq have to do with that?"

Baba gazed at me with pity. "Everything."

I met his eyes and whatever was in them frightened me so much that my hands began to shake. I couldn't stand facing him anymore. Quickly I walked past him and went to my room, where I sat on my rickety charpoy and watched the dusk through the skylight. In the other room, Ma prayed loudly on the *musallah*. She might have been crying, I couldn't tell. I tried to read a medical textbook Baba gave me for my last birthday, but my mind was too restless, so I gave up and went to the kitchen where Ma had arranged unwashed raw chicken breasts on a chopping board.

I lay my hands on the meat. I thought about Sadiq and his tinbox, and softly let the current flow. The chicken breast jumped and thudded on the wood. I discharged again, this time with more force, removed my hands, stepped back, and watched as for a whole minute the meat slapped up and down, squirting blood that puddled on the wooden board, making curious dark shapes.

That should have been impossible but clearly wasn't.

In school during physics class our teacher had explained capacitors to us. Strange ideas came to me now. Words that Baba taught me from his textbooks: cell membranes, calcium-gates, egg-shaped mitochondria, and polarized ionic channels. Could *they* act as capacitors at times and hold charge so the flesh would stay alive even after I removed my fingertips?

The boy is gifted, someone said in my head.

I should have felt better. Instead I felt angry and miserable. I went to Ma's room and opened the door.

She was sitting on her haunches in front of the only pretty piece of furniture in the room, a mahogany dresser Baba's mother gave her as a wedding present. Ma had been fiddling with a half-open drawer, a jewelry box glittering in her hand. When I entered, she plunged the drawer into place. "Are you so ill-mannered now that you won't knock?"

"Sorry, Ma. I wasn't thinking."

"Idiot boy," she said quietly. Her gaze drifted back down to the box she held, fingers sliding up and down its metallic edges. The space beneath her eyes was dark and wet. "Next time mind your manners."

I thought it prudent to remain silent. Ma lifted the lid and gazed within and her eyes turned inward. The effect was so intense that for a moment she looked dead, her lifeless eyes watching something in the box, or behind it. Uneasy, I took a step forward and glanced inside. A picture of a naked man nailed to a cross, surrounded by wailing people; then Ma was snapping the lid back into place so violently that I jerked and fell back.

Ma's hands shook and she said something that didn't make sense, "Never wanted to come here. Your father made me. I never wanted to leave my people," and she glared at me hatefully. It was a brief moment, but nothing in my life since has made me feel so ashamed. So lonely and self-loathing; a mutant child broken and hated forever.

I turned and ran from the room, blinded by anger or tears or both, while my mother watched me from the darkness of her room, the jewelry box still in her callused hands.

Later they told us it was an accident, that a wooden shanty caught fire and set the muhallah ablaze, but we all knew better.

It was the tail end of monsoon season and the rains had petered out which worsened the conflagration. Fifty Christian houses burned down that night; the flames and smoke ceiling could be seen from as far as Gulshan Iqbal, we were told. Twenty people died; Sadiq's father (who survived tuberculosis and, later, the 1999 Kargil War) was among them. Their corpses were pulled out from the wreckage, burnt and twisted. Sadiq's mother recognized him only by the hare-shaped mole on his left foot.

When I went to see Sadiq, he sobbed on my shoulder.

"They took everything," he wept. "My house, our belongings. My father," he added as an afterthought. "They burnt the house down. My cousin saw them, I swear to God."

"Which God?" I said. My right arm was around him. My left hand dug so hard into the flesh of my thigh I popped the blood blister a biocurrent discharge had raised on my finger. "*Which* God?"

He stared at me with bloodshot eyes, threw his head back, and cried some more; while his mother sat stone-like in the charpoy under the elm, rocking back and forth, her face blank. One hand tapped the bruises on her cheek. The other hid her lips.

I held Sadiq for as long as I could, then I went home, where Ma sat knitting a cotton sweater. Winter would come in two months, and we couldn't afford to buy new clothes.

Baba was out—he'd been delayed at the clinic—so I sat at Ma's feet and counted her toes. Ten.

She watched me through the emptiness between her needles and said, "I'm sorry."

"Yes."

"It was horrible, wasn't it?"

"Yes."

"Tell you what. Why don't we take Sadiq and his mother some naans and beef korma tomorrow? I'm sure his mother is too upset to cook right now."

I recalled Khala Apee's vacuous stare, the hand covering her mouth, and nodded.

Ma placed her knitting needles aside, lowered herself to the floor, and hugged me.

"The world is a bad place," she whispered. "We're in danger all the time. People who are different like you, like us … can sometimes seem like a threat to others."

I listened. Outside, thunder cracked. The skylight window rippled with water as the night opened.

"You use your gift to heal others, you hear me?" she said. "Don't get involved with anger or hatred or sides. There are no sides. Only love and hate."

Behind me the door banged open. My left eye twitched, the vision in it dimmed transiently, and cleared. Ma sprang to her feet.

"Zamir?" she said. "What is it?"

"Your husband," someone said. I turned. It was the Edhi driver. His hair was dark from rain. His cotton shirt was soaked and I could see his abnormal navel protrude through it like a hernia.

"What about him?" Ma's voice was full of fear. "What happened?"

Zamir had a look on his face I had never seen before. His lips trembled. "There was an incident at the clinic."

Ma stared at him, eyes wide and unbelieving, then comprehension dawned in them and she screamed. It was a sudden noise, sharp and unfamiliar, and it wrenched the air out of me. I shrank back and clutched the end of Ma's love couch, and the knitting needles slipped and fell to the floor, forming a steel cross.

"No, God, no," Ma said. Her hair was in her eyes. She clawed it away, looked at the ends, screamed again. "Please don't let it be true. I told him to be careful. I *told* him."

Zamir's face was ashen.

I scrabbled blindly on the dirty floor. The steel cross glinted at me. Pinching the skin of my thighs, I hauled myself up, feeling the world flicker and recede. Zamir was holding Ma's hand and speaking gently. Your husband went to the Police, he was saying. He reported the Christian boy's mutilated body. The mullahs didn't like that. Then someone somewhere discovered an old marriage certificate with *your* maiden name on it.

Ma yanked her hand away from Zamir's. "I killed him," she whispered. Her fists flew to her chest and beat it once, then again and again. She rushed to the door, she shrieked at the rain, but the night was moonless.

Bewildered and crying, I thought about the tin box Sadiq hid in the canal when he realized they would be attacked. I thought about dead bodies and festering secrets; of limbs thrashing on a healer's fingertips; of the young Christian boy who was tortured to death. I thought of how "Daoud" could have been "David" in a different world, such a strange idea, that. Most of all I thought about the way the chicken breast thrummed under the influence of my will, how it kept jerking long after I took my hands away. Would Baba whirl if I touched him, would he dance a final dance for me?

I wiped my tears. From the crevasse of the night rain blood-black gushed and pawed at my eyes. Then we went in Zamir's rickshaw to pick up my father's corpse.

Someone once told me dust has no religion.

Perhaps it was the maulvi sahib who taught me my first Arabic words; a balding kind, quiet man with a voice meant to chant godly secrets and a white beard that flowed like a river of Allah's nur. The gravedigger who was now shoveling and turning the soil five feet away looked a bit like him, except when he panted. His string vest was drenched with sweat, even though the ground was soft and muddy from downpour.

Perhaps it was Ma. She stood next to me before this widening hole, leaning on Khala Apee as if she were an axed tree about to fall. Her lips moved silently all the time. Whether she prayed or talked to Baba's ghost, I don't know.

Or perhaps it was Baba who lay draped in white on the charpoy bier under the pipal tree. The best cotton shroud we could afford rippled when the graveyard wind gusted. It was still wet from his last bath. Before they log-rolled him onto his back, the men of our neighborhood had asked me if I wanted to help wash him.

I said no. My eyes never brimmed.

Now I let a fistful of this forgiving dust exhaust itself between my fingers. It whispered through, a gentle earthskin shedding off me and upon Baba's face. It would carry the scent of my flesh, let him inhale my presence. I leaned down and touched my father's lips, so white, so cold, and a ghastly image came to me: Baba juddering on my fingertips as I reach inside his mouth, shock his tongue, and watch it jump and thrash like a bloodied carp.

Tell me who murdered you, I tell my father's tongue. Talk to me, speak to me. For I am Resurrection and whoso believes in me will live again.

But his tongue doesn't quiver. It says nothing.

Someone touched my shoulder and drew me back. It was Ma. Her mouth was a pale scar in her face. She gripped my fingers tightly. I looked down, saw that she had colored her hand with henna, and dropped it.

A shiny flaming orange heart, lanced in the middle, glistened on her palm.

It was dark enough to feel invisible. I left Ma praying in her room and went to Kala Pul.

Lights flickered in the streets and on chowrangis. Sad-faced vendors sold fake perfumes and plastic toys at traffic signals. Women with hollow eyes offered jasmine motia bracelets and necklaces and the flower's scent filled my nose, removing Baba's smell in death. Children fished for paan leaves and cigarette stubs in puddles, and I walked past them all.

Something dark lay in the middle of the road under a bright fluorescent median light. I raised a hand to block the glare and bent to look at it. An alley cat, a starved, mangy creature with a crushed back. Tread marks were imprinted on its fur; clots glistened between them. A chipped fang hung from one of whiskers.

I didn't know my right hand was on it until I saw my fingertips curve. They pressed into the carcass like metal probes seeking, seeking. I didn't even need to feel for a point. In death, the creature's entire body was an enormous potential ready to be evoked.

I met the cat's gaze. Lifeless eyes reflected the traffic light changing from green to red. I discharged.

A smell like charred meat, like sparks from metal screeching against metal, rust on old bicycle wheels. The creature arched its spine, its four legs locking together, so much tension in its muscles they thrummed like electric wires. Creaking, making a frothing sound, the alley cat flopped over to its paws and tried to stand.

It lives, I thought and felt no joy or satisfaction.

Blood trickled from the creature's right eye. It tried to blink and the left eye wouldn't open. It was glued shut with postmortem secretions.

My hand was hurting. I shook it, brought it before my eyes, looked at it. A large bulla had formed in the middle of the palm, blue-red and warm. Rubbing it gently, I got up and left, leaving the newly risen feline tottering around the traffic median, strange sounds emitting from its throat as if it were trying to remember how to mewl.

Deep inside the Christian muhallah I waded through rubble, piles of blackened bricks, and charred wood. I stood atop the destruction and imagined the fire consuming rows upon rows of these tiny shacks. Teetering chairs, plywood tables, meal mats, dung stoves, patchworked clothes—all set ablaze. Bricks fell, embers popped, and shadow fingers danced in the flames.

I shivered and turned to leave. Moonlight dappled the debris, shadows twisted, and as I made my way through the wreckage I nearly tripped over something poking from beneath a corrugated tin sheet.

I stooped to examine the object. It was a heavy, callused human hand, knuckles bruised and hairy like my father's. Blood had clotted at the wrist and formed a puddle below the sharp edge of the tin.

A darkness turned inside my chest; rivers of blood pounded in the veins of my neck and forehead. I don't know how long I sat in the gloom, in that sacred silence. Head bowed, fingers curled around the crushed man's, I crouched with my eyes closed and groped for the meat of the city with my other hand's fingertips. I felt for its faint pulse, I looked for its resurrection point; and when the dirt shivered and a sound like ocean surf surged into my ears, I thought I had found it.

I stiffened my shoulders, touched the dead man's palm, and let the current flow.

The hand jerked, the fingers splayed. A sigh went through the shantytown. Somewhere in the dark bricks shifted. The ruins were stirring.

Something plopped on the tin sheet. I looked down. Fat drops of blood bulged from between my clenched knuckles. I let the dead hand go (it skittered to a side and began to thrash). I opened both of my fists and raised them to the sky.

A crop of raised, engorged bullas on my palms. One amidst the right cluster had popped and was bleeding. The pain was a steady ache, almost pleasant in its tingling. As I watched, blisters on the left palm burst as well and began to gush. Dark red pulsed and quivered its way down my wrists.

Trembling, I crouched on my haunches and grasped the dead man's convulsing limb with both hands. I closed my eyes and jolted the Christian muhallah back to life. Then I sat back, rocking on my heels, and waited.

They came. Dragging their limbs off sparkling morgue tables, slicing through mounds of blessed dirt, wrenching free of rain-soaked grass, my derelict innocents seized and twitched their way across the city. I rose to my feet when they arrived, trailing a metallic tang behind them that drowned the smell of the jasmine. Metal rattled and clanged as my last finally managed to crawl out from under the tin sheet and joined the ranks of the faithful.

I looked at them one last time, my people, faces shining with blood and fervor. Their shredded limbs dangled. Autopsy incisions crisscrossed some's naked flesh. Blackened men, women and children swaying in rows, waiting for me. How unafraid, joyous, and visible they were.

I raised my chin high and led my living thus on their final pilgrimage through this land of the dead.

The Old Gods of Light

CHRISTINA SNG

Godlike,
You sweep into our land
Through the thorny perimeter

Keeping predators like you away
From the most vulnerable of us,
Our children and our crops.

Yet you present yourself
As a benign force,
Offering gifts of technology

To lengthen our lives
And improve how we live,
As if the thousand years we have

Are not enough,
Nor are the peaceful ways
We farm and gather.

Foolishly,
We accept your offerings,
Curious as we are,

Enraging our jealous gods
Who turn our children
To dust while they play,

Extinguishing their lives
Before they have a chance
To live them.

Grief and fury consume us,
Betrayed by the gods
We once worshipped.

We turn to you to find meaning,
But all you offer are platitudes
That do not assuage us.

In violence,
We find relief,
Tying you up and quartering you,

A week-long celebration
Where our people scream and cheer
In a hate-fueled catharsis.

At the end,
Exhausted and broken,
We bury you in the ground

And overnight,
A forest sprouts up,
Almost as a surprise,

Covering the land
And engulfing us
Beneath its roots.

It takes to the sea,
Devouring its life,
Sucking it dry

Till there is nothing left
But an empty bowl
Twirling in the dust

Where you crawl out,
Whole, and in a cold fury,
Abandoning our cursed land,

Now dead and blood-red
From the rusted metal
Of our unmoving machines.

You drift in the ether,
The empty space between worlds,
Drawn by light

To a new land,
One of blue and white,
Aquamarine-bright.

Sounds Caught in Cobwebs

M.E. BRONSTEIN

Mother Lark used to say things like: "Your vows are something to take seriously. They are our one feeble contribution to the Harpist's Song, before we dwindle down to notes, flecks of spider caught in the web of sound."

Before she started falling apart, Mel told Vi how easily she had figured out her vows. Vi supposed she meant to be reassuring.

"I had my scroll in hand, and the first few times I dreamed, it was always blank," said Mel. "Then, one night, the scroll had one word on it. Then the next night it had two, then three. They kind of grew into place, I guess. And I could feel out the cadence, how it would all fit into the Song. And when I woke up, the words stayed with me and I wrote them down."

Vi imagined Mel's words as flowers, pressed into a book, dried and flattened. Stuck between the pages of dream and waking.

Mother Lark had sent them to the attic, to dust and polish some of the relics that had gotten buried beneath too much cobweb. Mel and Vi sorted through old mahogany cabinets that had beveled glass doors. Some were so cluttered and dark that Vi and Mel had to explore them with flashlights; pale beams interrupted the shadows and scattered little floods of spider.

"Is it always like that?" asked Vi. "The words just—manifest? You don't have to work to find them?"

Mel considered for a moment. "I don't know," she said. "That's how it was for me, anyway."

They opened a new cabinet. Inside, they found tarnished lockets, a bronze ear wrapped up in a silk handkerchief, a silver bowl containing the corpse of a wolf spider, its legs curling in toward its abdomen. Vi recognized it as the one Mother Lark called the Harpist's Hand and she didn't want to touch it for fear of breaking it somehow.

"Here," said Mel, "give it to me." And while Vi picked up the silver bowl and polished it with a dish cloth, Mel held the Hand and plucked one strand of web at a time off of its legs (fingers?)—with each strand she moved, a snippet of harp song bloomed and faded through the room.

The sound of wind chimes glimmered outside. The rhythm of the spider silk and wind almost braided together into a recognizable tune—but not quite.

Vi knew that she and Mel were thinking the same thing: There used to be more Song. And more sisters to tend to it.

Childhood devotion had been different, easier and more painful all at once and by turns.

The sisters used to sit out in the garden all together, the ivy stirring in the breeze all around them. The sky turned teal around the edges and a deep blue overhead and the first stars came out. Mother Lark passed around bowls of figs and plums and they all ate as she spoke and sang. They would wipe sticky fingers off in the grass and lie on their stomachs and listen.

Sometimes, Vi would start to fall asleep and Mel would tug her hair—which meant that Vi had to stir and throw bits of grass at her. Mother Lark would scold them both, and Gale (Lark's favorite) would laugh. Vi getting things wrong again. That was her way; she needed correction.

The brief interruption silenced, Lark sang of the Harpist:

When he played, the trees would uproot themselves and come listen to his tune. The spiders would weave harp strings between the trees' branches, silk humming along to the Harpist's rhythm. The Harpist could sing so sweetly as to alter the harmony of the spheres, and the world would shift around him.

Sometimes, Mother Lark would break her tune to speak, to whisper to her daughters:

"The Harpist had an enemy, a spirit—let us call the spirit Cacophony. Cacophony was envious of the Harpist's control over the world's music and would invade upon his domain, would inhabit the creatures in the Harpist's garden and fray the strings of the cosmos until they broke and the Song fell apart, decayed, wrong notes filling the air as the world's harmony died."

The girls became grim. Vi stopped fidgeting.

Sometimes, after dark, Vi would lie awake in fear of Cacophony. She would watch the moonlit walls, and the spiders dangling against them looked like lost musical notes on a glowing page.

She would listen for the spiders' melody—the Song her oldest sisters had already joined—and fail to hear it and she would hate herself for that; she knew that it should be much easier for her to hear it by now: a glowing and growing kind of noise. First low and strident whispers, an unseen orchestra tuning the web, then building fragments of a chant, and then a familiar Song ...

Vi would clutch a necklace Lark had given her, a locket full of spider silk, and pray for the Harpist's help, and then she would hear it—a wayward strand of music. Maybe it was just the breeze, maybe the wind chimes, but she thought not. She could hear the web radiating sound all around her.

And she would feel better and fall asleep, reassured that, somewhere, the Harpist was composing a Song that would include her one day, that she would be a part of things too.

This is how it goes, one of the very oldest stories:

One day, the Harpist found a woman with the loveliest voice that ever breathed or spoke or sang. He chose her as his Bride, and at their wedding the earth was strewn with dried lavender and foxglove. Birdsong echoed between the trees and the spiders' threads quivered, their hymns reverberating through everything.

But the marriage torch sputtered more than it ought to, coughing out inauspicious signs.

Cacophony entered, unseen but omnipresent.

The Harpist played sweetly, but the ending of each and every tune he played went wrong. He adjusted the pegs on his harp, but his final note always went sour.

After the wedding, the Harpist's Bride wandered barefoot through waves of grass to gather flowers.

And then Cacophony, who had watched their wedding jealously, fell among the spiders' webs, entangled with their silk, and the Song went astray all around the Bride. It limped and stuttered.

The day darkened and the Bride found herself caught in a fog.

When the Harpist found his Bride, her bones had been picked clean by Cacophony, who had driven the spiders mad with the wrong kind of sound. They ate up the remains of the Bride's voice.

The Harpist crafted a new harp with strings of spider silk in honor of her.

Some of the girls used to giggle to each other about the stories and songs. Cacophony was a weird word—that gave them fuel aplenty some nights. Vi said that it meant "shit-noise," which made Mel and the others laugh (even though Gale had already explained wearily to them that the caco- part really just meant "bad" or "ugly").

Vi could not sing as well as her sisters, but she had an ear for certain things—though not the right things. Mother Lark often reproved her for paying too much attention to how words sounded instead of the meaning behind them. Vi liked cacophony (the word, not the spirit) because the first bit sounded like it was breaking.

She was not supposed to enjoy that so much.

Mel's ceremony. Vi helped weave the garland of foxglove for her hair. The drooping blossoms looked like bells, staring earthward, and Vi played with them instead of weaving them into the garland, shook them as though expecting sound to fall out, until Mother Lark told her to quit it.

Mel sat patiently and waited while they fretted over her hair, her dress. And then they took her by the hand and guided her outside.

Everyone assembled on the grass and faced the olive tree where the Harpist's spirit would manifest. Only Mel would see him, but the rest of them would hear his music build around the edge of Mel's union with him.

Mel drifted to the olive tree. She unfurled her scroll and held it out to read from it. She spoke, she sang. Vi could see sweat collect beneath the garland, dampening her bangs.

Vi would not remember Mel's vows afterwards, but she would remember thinking that every word had been perfect, beautiful.

Then, as she used up the scroll, Mel looked around at her sisters, at the ivy clinging to the trees, at the too-vibrant blue sky.

When she collapsed upon the grass, she looked a little like a flower herself, in her pile of crumpled lace skirts. A crushed lily, used up by the summer heat.

Vi wanted to run to her, but Gale kept a hand on her shoulder, held her in place.

The moment stretched until the quiet of it became unbearable.

But then, at last, Mel stirred; she propped herself up on her elbows, rose shakily to her knees, her feet. She stood, wavered, and she went on singing, and they all sang with her and through her.

For days after her ceremony, Mel whistled as she worked in the kitchen, in the garden. Music fell from her whenever she opened her mouth. Mel trilled so beautifully and Vi wished she would not, since she wore away with every note that came loose. She grew thin and brittle, as though her skin had stopped being skin and had become something more like eggshell, ready to shatter and let Mel's real substance out.

That was familiar; that was how it was supposed to go. And yet, Vi grew afraid that Mel would vanish when she wasn't looking, and so she started barging into rooms in the hope of finding her, before she joined the Song. She prayed for Mel to stay and then she got mad at herself for praying for something like that. The wind slammed doors shut in her wake (which annoyed Lark to no end).

And then Vi found Mel sitting upon the floor beside her bed with a needle in hand. She was stitching up a tear in the fold of skin between her ear and her cheek, wet spilling out of her eyes while she worked with a shaking hand.

"It's happening," she said. "I'm falling apart."

Her ear dangled loose like a door, wavering open and closed over a rift in her skin. There was no blood in the gap, just darkness—and black beads dripped slowly out, notes of spidery music flowing out of Mel. They scattered across her lap, across the floorboards, hid beneath their sisters' beds.

Vi sat down beside her and wordlessly put out a hand for the needle and strand of silk. Mel passed them to her, and Vi did her best to sloppily stitch up the loose ear. Mel hissed as the needle dipped in and out of her skin. A few final drops of spider slipped out from beneath her flesh, singing softly as they descended on silver threads. They skittered away while Vi patched up their avenue of egress.

"Was it that terrible?" asked Vi. "Seeing him? A glimpse of him, anyway?"

She could still picture Mel's collapse beneath the olive tree.

"Who?"

"Who? The Harpist." Who else would she mean?

An acrid laugh fell out of Mel. "I didn't see him," she said. "I didn't see anything."

Vi knotted up the last of the thread and cut it loose. They sat in silence for a moment while Mel gingerly touched her repaired ear. A little golden hoop in her lobe glittered.

And then she said, "I don't think there is a Harpist."

A breeze stirred through the wind chimes just beyond the window.

Mel went on and on then. She said things she should not say:

The world may be a harp, but nobody's ever been there to play it right. The Harpist is an absence. You think that we're his creation, but, in fact, he is ours.

"So—why?" asked Vi. "Why do we do this?"

Mel did not know.

She thought for a moment, then said that perhaps it was all just an exercise in being loud. We have to tear ourselves to pieces because the tearing makes some noise, and that is one way, at least, of becoming a part of the world's music.

Vi was good at ruining things, and Mother Lark had a whole lexicon uniquely deployed in description of her sometimes willful clumsiness:

Lark called Vi a "strepitous child!" when she sang poorly.

Lark called her "Vi the little earthquake" when she broke or knocked things over. Once Vi dropped a ceremonial plate a little on purpose, because in truth, she just liked how the word "earthquake" sounded; it seemed much bigger and more important than a soft monosyllable like "Vi."

And then there were all the reminders not to slam doors, not to interrupt Lark's stories and songs, reminders to listen and pay attention. Reminders to sing. Lark called her "our sweet and tuneful Viola" when she wanted to be cruel.

Sometimes Vi wanted to scream.

Interlude: a brief effort to leave the house.

Once, many sisters had been tasked with leaving, to find more Brides for the Harpist out in the world, whom they would bring back to the house and garden. But these leavings had started to create trouble in recent years, since the sisters who left tended to stay away as the world grew louder and distracted them and they could not find their way back into the web.

Lark never protested when one of her daughters asked to leave, though she did frown and tell them that it would become harder and harder to hear the Song the farther they went from the house.

Vi started listening for traffic. Airplanes passing overhead. Muffled, electronic pulses of non-song thudding through the dark.

And she left. She went to school. She drank too much and learned about architecture and words like "tympanum" and "clerestory" and studied dead languages. She met new people who said, "You're one of those sisters—the crazy spider ladies? Didn't know there were any of you left." Vi felt like an exotic specimen and did not tell them about the spider silk in her locket. She wondered how they slept without any ability to hear the web's Song, how they could avoid knowing that the world would fade around them if the music ever stuttered to a halt.

And she sent messages home, kept promising a return. The promises became self-deprecating jokes. You know me. I am the stray note in this tune. Probably won't be back until it's too late.

When Lark didn't answer and Gale did instead, Vi stopped sending messages.

Nighttime in the world beyond the gate could get so strange. It never matched Vi's internal picture of "night," dusted with stars. Instead, buildings became monolithic shadows, darker than the strange sky which glowed livid shades of dusky orange, purple.

And the sounds: no birdsong, no thrumming web. Instead: car alarms, the occasional siren, some drunken hooting from the street below.

And then a different sound altogether: someone pounding at her door.

Vi rose, stumbled into wakefulness, peered through the peephole and saw Gale. A bedraggled Gale, hair in wan shreds, and she was shaking as though she had fallen out of a pocket of winter, even as summer heat choked the air.

"Vi?" said Gale. "Are you there?"

Vi opened the door and let her sister in.

Gale's skin had become like eggshell—just like Mel's—and Vi could see the stitches of silvery spider silk, marking the fault lines that ran all across her. Vi led her to the couch and started to brew some tea. But even as Gale wrapped herself up in a cocoon of blanket, she kept shivering.

"Music," she said. "Please. I need to hear something at least a little like the Song."

And so Vi sorted through her CD's, found Edvard Grieg and loaded him into the stereo; Solveig's Song mounted and a wave of harp and violin trembled and flooded through the room. Gale sighed and leaned back into the couch.

Vi did not dare ask about their sisters, for fear of what Gale would say. She asked about the house instead.

Gale frowned and said, "Why don't you come home and see for yourself?"

"I will," said Vi. "I've been meaning to for a while."

"You have to," said Gale.

And Vi heard what she would not say:

You have to become a part of the Song or it will run out of words, and we will be gone forever.

The next morning, when Vi awoke, she found a foggy gray craquelure of web had consumed the apartment. It looked a little like everything was made of glass, like the world was cracking apart around Vi. She found spiders here and there, legs twitching as they plucked feverishly at the web's weave and yet no music came out.

Shreds of Gale's voice cried out and then faded into silence.

When Vi returned, she found the old wooden gate overgrown, swallowed up by ferns and grasses and ivy. When she swept the ivy aside, looking for the latch, she found tangles of graffiti carved into the gate's surface. Local teenagers, probably. They had cut caricatures of spiders and fanged harps into the woodgrain, then run away.

Glass crunched underfoot. Vi looked down and fragments of crushed beer bottle glittered at her.

Once there were fairy lights that glowed through the grass past the gate, drops of cheap amber brightness that would lead the way across a brick path. Now all was dark and the bricks unsettled by the moving and shifting earth and weeds.

Beyond the gate: the house. Home. The looming Victorian looked so familiar and strange all at once, its silhouette the same, but the white paint peeling off the clapboard walls was wrong—or had it always been like that? Tearing apart a little? Vi couldn't remember now. She climbed up the narrow set of steps that led to the front door, then rattled the knob until it opened.

Vi flicked a light switch that did not respond.

But as she entered, she could still make out myriad flecks of spider as they ascended strands of indiscernible silk—they looked like dark drops of water falling the wrong way.

It felt like a salute. A welcome home.

Or a warning. Perhaps she had come back too late. Perhaps they were not glad to see her.

Vi tried to listen for a trace of Mel's voice as the spider silk hummed all around her. But she could not hear her. She could not hear the music of the house at all.

Just muttering noise, loud and quiet all at once.

Vi did not want to sleep in the room she used to share with Mel and the others. And so she found a bare spot on the floor of the dining room. She nestled into a thick quilt, unearthed from one of the closets.

She lay awake, afraid of what she might dream.

And then:

She stood quaking before her sisters—they were back, they had coalesced again out of the Song. But all they did was watch her in silence.

The lace skirt tangled around Vi's legs felt wrong and heavy, an insistent cocoon that wanted to transmute her into something else— the right kind of Bride, maybe. One with a sweeter voice.

The scroll in her hand. She tried to twist apart the twine around it, to let it uncoil, but it resisted her. Vi reached for the words that were not there, words she had not assembled, thoughts she had neglected to think.

When she tore the scroll open at last, she faced an insistent blank—

Or was that the needling blank of moonlight that had crawled in through the window and draped itself across her, nudged her out of the dream.

Vi rose to draw the curtain so that she could sleep again—but something dark, a fat shadow, dangled at the edge of her vision. She turned to face it. Again, the fat shadow flickered in and out of sight. And then it squirmed and she felt a tickling beside her ear—

In spite of herself, Vi raked her fingers through her hair, felt something wriggling between her fingers and threw it.

A loud screech. An almost audible smack as the spider fell against the wall, then dropped to the floor.

Vi wondered if she had hurt it and waited, her breath become a heavy knot. She could almost hear the house's reproof: You would crush these final leavings of your own sisters, selfish child? Haven't you done enough already?

"Mel?" she said. "Are you a part of Mel? Lark? Whose voice, whose vows are you?"

Then, at last, the spider moved, a slip of misplaced dark in the moonlight. It fled into a corner, melted away into a pool of shadow.

Vi tried to sleep again.

The next morning, Vi set to work taming the mess that once passed for a garden.

She weeded. She imagined herself perched on top of a giant dryad's head, yanking out its hairs. Accordingly, she was not surprised at all to find things like a fine, matted plait of hair, dried flowers woven into it. She tried to pluck the flowers out of the weave, wondered if she could use them in her own garland, and whose head they had sat atop previously.

Later, Vi moved on to the attic. Sorted through old relics. Looking for things she could use for her own ceremony.

She opened a jewelry box and found a little bundle of soft white. A cocoon. She picked it apart, and the silk murmured and hummed as it unraveled—then became shrill. Sounds split apart and wound their way together again as a distinct voice.

Little beads of spider flowered out of the cocoon and onto Vi's fingertips and before she could stop herself, she yelped and dropped the cocoon into her lap and began brushing at her arms and the spiders dropped to the floor around her.

They chattered darkly as they scattered.

Vi returned her attention to the shreds of cocoon in her lap. And exhumed from within it: an ear. An ear with a little gold hoop in the lobe.

Vi held onto it tightly while her vision and hearing went sideways.

Vi had her scroll in hand and she passed down the grassy aisle. She stepped barefoot over bundles of lavender, her heels crunching on skeletal bits of blossom, fragrant punctuation left in her wake. Thorns and brambles tugged at her, the earth itself trying to hamper her progress—she had been gone so long and the garden was upset with her, it did not want her to become the Harpist's next Bride.

Vi stumbled. Her scroll toppled to the grass and she reached after it.

And then the world groaned and black droplets bled out of the garden as the web underlying things tore apart; they swarmed together and crawled up Vi's skirt, and she realized that she was not wearing lace but spider silk, she had gotten tangled up in cobwebs as the music broke and grew monstrous and it was screaming all around her and the dark dew drops of it were all over her arms, her shoulders, her neck—

And then something bright ended it all.

A distant siren knifed through the dream.

Vi did something she knew she shouldn't. She attacked her vows the wrong way around, tried to find the right words in the waking world so that she could take them into the dream with her.

She sat at Mother Lark's old desk and dragged a pen across blank paper and hoped that the line she was drawing would begin to waver up and down and form words of its own accord, but it did not. Vi stopped. She started again.

May the Harpist accept these vows, she wrote.

She stopped. Started again.

How shall I describe my devotion?

Again.

How shall I describe my many failings?

How to go on loving Mel when Vi needed so badly for her to be wrong?

The more she worried at it over the years, the more the old story fell to pieces. Vi thought too often of Cacophony, more than she meant to. Her sympathy for harsh voices always reared up whether she wanted it to or not. She felt for crooked musicality. Sometimes, breaking the song felt better than singing.

Vi's first failing: falling for the wrong word.

Vi stood out in the garden, which she had done a poor job of weeding. The ivy framing everything had gone foggy beneath a silver shroud of web.

She decided that she would not let the heat of the day devour her. She would wait until after dark, when everything turned cool. The orange petals of birds of paradise nodded through the garden and remained bright as flame even as the color drained out of everything else.

Little legged musical notes, dots of her sisters' voices, surrounded her. They wavered up and down upon their strands of silk as the music mounted and mounted until Vi could hear nothing else, none of the noises of the outside world, none of the birds and traffic in the distance.

She remembered sitting in the garden and listening to Mother Lark's stories.

She could hear Mother Lark calling her a strepitous child. Cacophonous.

As the music built, Vi stepped barefoot across the grass, her scroll in hand. She made her way to the olive tree, the only thing that looked exactly as it had all those years ago, all twisting silver bark and attenuated leaf—no decay there. And Vi squinted, tried to see a harp-shaped absence standing before it.

She stood between the tree's roots and held out her scroll. There was nothing written upon it. She tore it to pieces. And she did not speak her vows, did not sing them. She screamed into the branches of the olive tree until she could almost hear its leaves rattle and fall. A net of spider and silk fell down upon her. A new bridal veil.

Vi cried out:

"I am not right for this and never was, but here I am and you have nothing better to do than listen, so hear me: I want to play Cacophony's role instead of the Bride's. I want to break and go on living, if only as a scrap of ragged sound. I want to make new songs.

"I may be doing this all wrong but I'm all you've got.

"Sing through me."

All around her, the world's strings frayed. The spiders, full of familiar voices, sang. Everything was singing so loudly—or screaming, not singing, because everything, the world, it had all forgotten how to sing properly.

There was music in it anyway.

Umbra Sum

KRISTI DEMEESTER

My mother plaited my hair the night the river swelled over its banks. "There are so many who see only an end in water," she said. She tied a ribbon the color of dying sunlight at the bottom before turning to face Thomas, who had not spoken since the rain began the week prior. "Some would call it a cleansing," my mother said, but Thomas' face was still, his mouth a sloped mound of reddened flesh that had long forgotten the shape it once knew.

As quickly as she had done it, my mother undid the braid, her fingers slashing through my hair so that my scalp smarted, but I knew there was no use in my weak urge to cry out, to ask her to please stop. Above us, the light flickered, the power giving in momentarily to the swaying winds of the storm.

Thomas' face was so like my own in that blinking darkness that it was hard to tell if he was even there at all, if his body was nothing more than a mirrored image of my own, mute and staring at whatever he'd found behind his silence. At school, our teachers saw the oblong shape of our faces, the muddied green of our eyes, the slight tint of our skins and believed we'd emerged from the womb tangled up together, our breaths coming in that same instant and tying us into some larger existence that transcended the simple connection of blood. They saw it in the tilt of our heads when we grew bored with the lesson, heard it in our voices when we pretended to answer their questions, but we were not born on the same day. "When I dreamed of you, when I called you to me, it was the same face I saw," our mother said, but the years stretched between us. We were not tied in the traditional ways of those born on the same day.

"Three years apart?" our teachers would say and cluck their

tongues as if we had betrayed them while they weren't looking.

There were a handful of times—Thomas had told me it happened to him, too—when our teachers seemed to forget we were there. They would stare past our raised hands or mark us absent or would start—a small, strangled scream dying in their bellies—when they realized we were standing beside them, our lips wrapped around a question. "It makes me feel like a ghost," I told him, and he would hold his hands out before him and moan until I hit him hard enough in the chest to make him stop.

I stared at him, but his face was his own again, and my mouth tasted of something bitter, and I blinked, my hands twitching toward him because my mother—*our* mother—had turned away and would not see me when I traced my fingers over his hands, the bare, smooth skin of his forearms, to spell out the words I imagined would pull him back to me. *Conjure*, I wrote. *Come back. You fucker.*

His hands remained limp against his lap, and the rain beat out a pattern above us that sounded like mourning, and I imagined what it would be like for no other words to pass between us. What kind of death it would be to acknowledge there were no more nights where he came into my room without knocking and slipped beneath the thin sheet I draped over myself, not because I was cold but because it felt unnatural to sleep bare, and press wet lips to my ear, my hair, and tell me of what it had been like to be here before I had come, always knowing there was a part of him missing.

Instead of touching him again, I traced my fingers over pieces of me that were hollowed out: the dip in my throat where my collarbone met; the space between my breasts; the angled slash of my hipbones; the singular spaces between my ribs. All of these secret spaces I had found when Thomas stopped speaking. So many nights of swallowed air so I could learn of these new places inside of me that belonged to neither of us. Our mother hadn't noticed yet how thin I'd gotten.

"He should drink something. It's been so long since he's had anything to drink," our mother said, but Thomas' mouth stayed sealed. Even when she tried to force the glass to his lips—the water dribbling down his chin to drop against his lap—he did not swallow, and I thought of what it would mean to pull him outside into the storm, what it would mean to force that water into him before it came and drowned us all.

Our mother mumbled something about "our plight" and went stumbling out of the room again. I pinched the tops of Thomas' hands, but he still did not move, did not turn to look at me, and I wished the water would come crashing against the house, fill up our lungs with brown silt, our choking, gibbering bodies twisted into a beautiful tableau. Maybe then all of those years of feeling that Thomas and I had swallowed each other, had vanished into the other's body, would actually mean something.

Our mother baked bread and apples with cinnamon and set out the plates, but there was no one to eat the things she made. The rain was too heavy overhead and sounded like an accusation. Or maybe it was prayer.

That night I stood outside Thomas' bedroom door, my lips pressed to the wood, but I could not bring myself to ask the questions bursting in my throat. Instead, I waited. I listened for the sound of his breath, which I had learned to know as well as my own. I heard nothing except the steady beat of my own heart and turned away, my own room like a hollowed out reminder of what had once been. There was no place for sleep, so I sneaked into the kitchen and sank a spoon into what remained of the apples and swallowed the slices without chewing, my lips coated in a sweetness I could not taste.

I hoped for suffocation.

Inside her room, our mother prayed, but her words were garbled imitations of what Thomas and I had learned in Sunday School when we were children. I laid another piece of apple across my tongue and watched the windows. Outside, the grass was painted in silver, but it was not moonlight. I closed my eyes.

"Is this what you saw?" I whispered, but Thomas was not in his room. He was not in the house. Whatever sat behind my brother's door no longer had the same heartbeat. I could hear the wrongness of it, how it bent and stretched around the emptiness and grew into the hammering of the rain on the roof.

The apples sank into my stomach like small stones, and I tried to keep them, tried to hold them inside of me, but my body had forgotten what it was to eat, and so I leaned over the sink and gagged as my body purged itself.

Inside her bedroom, my mother believed that the end of the world had come, that the water would continue to fall from the sky, would turn yellow and sulfurous, the kind of thing that burned exposed skin or made small children ill from the deep stink of it. Tomorrow, she would braid my hair in the same way she had because it was the only thing left she could do with her hands that was not slapping Thomas again and again, and she would believe she was doing some right by me.

"It's only rain," I said. Outside, the light shifted from silver to a putrid yellow, and I turned away. Thomas' room was silent as I shuffled past, and I pressed my hand to his door as I went. I thought my palm would burn, but it didn't. I left my clothes on and lay down and draped the sheet over my face and pretended I was dead and wondered if it would feel as delicate as this to be put into the earth.

In the corners of my bedroom, I imagined I saw movement, the shadows jerking back and forth like a machination breathed into life. I flipped on the lamp beside my bed, but there was nothing there, no strange forms crouched against the floor, fingers spread outward as if in supplication. "Thomas," I said, but whatever was there was not Thomas. It had been stupid to say his name. What shadows had found me did not belong to him.

There should be no ghosts at the end of the world.

I slept too lightly, the sheet tangling over my face, my neck, so that there were moments when I woke gasping as if there were hands against my throat instead of thin fabric. The fifth or maybe the twentieth time I jerked out of sleep, Thomas was standing over me, his face a mask I could not read. "Hey," I said because I could not be sure his presence was not a dream. He looked back at me with eyes the color I had seen painted over the grass, and I sat up and pulled my hair away from my face. "What are you doing?"

He lifted his hand to his face and then let it drop. "Mother is wrong. Thinking that this is the end of the world. You know that."

"Yes." I paused because there were so many other things to say. "Where did you go?" I did not know how to be angry with him even though I had been before. What remained of my need to scream at him, to drag my fingernails across his face for leaving, drained away.

"I don't know."

"You're lying."

"Maybe. Maybe not." A patter of darkness danced across his face, one of the shadows let loose from its moorings, and he sank onto the floor. "It doesn't matter, does it?" I shifted to sit beside him, but he held up a hand. "Don't," he said, and this small death held me in place, an ache forming in the center of my brain.

I bit at the corner of a cuticle, but no blood flowed back into my mouth. "Why not?"

"There's something here." He touched his face again and then brought his fingers to the center of his chest and pulled his hand into a fist. "You can't hear it?"

"I can't hear anything. Not anymore. Not like it used to be."

Thomas shook his head, and the color of his eyes shifted from silver to yellow. "When we were the same. When I could lie in my bed with my eyes closed and know your heart was beating the same as mine, and I would come in here and lie next to you because it reminded me there was something real. That my heartbeat wasn't something I had imagined."

"I can't eat anymore."

"I know. It's the only way."

"For what?"

"Transfiguration."

My skin went warm, and I kicked the sheet away. I did not hear it when it fell to the floor. "When will the rain stop?"

"Tomorrow. Never. We can learn to float." In the past, he would have laughed—a sarcastic, choking noise that was too loud—but Thomas did not laugh.

"What are you? Now?" I asked. I couldn't see his eyes anymore. I brought my hands together and apart, my skin sticky and bones sharp in their hidden places.

In another part of the house, our mother sighed. It was the

sound of someone looking for something. The sound of what it meant to not understand the thing in front of you.

"A need. An ache."

"Come up here. Please," I said, but Thomas fell silent, and when I pushed myself up to look down on him, he was gone. I did not go to look for him. He was not something to be found.

The next day, there was no sun, only clouds the color of something dead, and our mother made soup and watched from her chair beside the window and mumbled in a voice that sounded like worry but was actually panic. Thomas stayed locked inside his room, and our mother set a bowl of the soup outside his door. It went untouched and when it went dark once more, insects had dropped to their deaths in the broth, and our mother collected the bowl, her mouth set in a thin line.

"He'll die," she said. I did not tell her I thought he already was. I did not tell her that I was finding my own way into death through starvation.

That night, I taught myself to hold my breath until the closed off rooms of the house I'd known my entire life looked different. I waited for my mother's sigh or Thomas' voice to tell me again the things I couldn't understand, but there was only rain and the smell of sweat as I tried to sleep. In the morning, Thomas was already awake and sitting in our mother's chair by the window, his breath fogging the glass. I crossed to him and dragged a finger over the window. Drew a star and then my name before drawing my fist across the glass to wipe it clean, and my hand came away as if slicked in oil. I could not bring myself to look and see if it was blood.

"Has it stopped? The rain?" I asked, and Thomas rolled his eyes back so that I could see only the whites. Still I somehow knew he was looking at me. He opened his mouth, but our mother came into the room then, and I winced to hear his teeth clamp together.

When our mother kneeled before Thomas and laid her head on his lap, I stole away, determined not to watch her beg her only son for something that could not return, her tears as useless as the tears Mary Magdalene had used to bathe the feet of Christ. There were some things that could not be saved with sorrow, and my mother had the weight of her grief that tethered her to this house, to us.

Neither of them heard when I opened the back door. Neither of them heard when I closed it behind me and stepped out into the rain. It was warm and smelled of rosemary or honey or baking bread or something I thought I remembered from being a girl. My feet sank into the earth, the depressions filling with water as soon as I moved, and I almost laughed at how like Hansel and Gretel it was. Like leaving breadcrumbs behind to mark not where you'd been, but the terrible place you were going. Not an invitation but a warning.

Perhaps I imagined I would find Thomas there, his frail body huddled under a tree, his eyes like two hollow flames as the rain fell over him. "I got lost," he would tell me, and we would understand that the thing wearing his skin inside our house was something else, and we would go in together to tear our mother from this false son and smooth our hands over her face and mumble words that sounded like, "It will be okay. We're here. Everything is fine." I circled my thumb and forefinger and turned back to the house, gazing at the world through the small hole I'd created, but it was the Thomas I knew standing next to our mother inside the house, his body rocking side to side as he swayed on his feet. My mother had covered her face with her hands, but I could still see one of her eyes, the deep brown of it staring at Thomas in confusion. She blinked and dropped her hands, her mouth going slack, and then she turned, and I could not see her anymore.

Thomas came to the window and pressed his mouth to the glass. All I could see were his teeth, but I could hear him screaming.

I went to the river, stood apart from that surging, foaming water, and told myself it would be easy to walk out into it, to let the current tug at my legs, my hips, and then let myself be carried along, my lungs crushing in on themselves like paper, tearing and dissolving until I became something new. Something gilled and finned or made of stone so that the water could pass over or through me, and I would be changed. A transfiguration. Like Thomas had said.

I'd touched my feet to the water, the current already an insistent, needy thing, when my mother called my name, and I stumbled backward, the mud cold and wet and darker than pitch and clinging to my arms. I went back to the house. I did not look back.

"What were you doing?" My mother touched my hair, my face, her fingers wrapping around my chin so I could look only at her and not at Thomas who stood just behind her, his mouth still frozen in a silent scream.

I held myself still and let her look me over, let her touch my shoulders, my neck as if she had forgotten what it meant to have a daughter. She encircled my wrists with her hands, measured out the weight of me with her touch. "You've gotten so thin." She said this as if it was something she had always known. A secret she'd carried with her through dreams and waking and had only now let spill out of her.

"Yes," I said, and Thomas opened his mouth wider. "Stop it," I said.

My mother leaned her forehead against mine. Her breath was metallic, the sharp smell of pennies or wire. "Is he still there? Behind me?"

"Yes," I said, and Thomas raised his hand like a child begging to be called on in school.

My mother closed her eyes.

"It's just Thomas. He's always been here. Just like I have," I said, and she cocked her head at that but said nothing else as she backed away, not turning to face him, not taking her eyes from me.

"You're so thin," she said again. If her words were made of meat, I would devour them while they lived.

Only when she was gone, did Thomas lower his hand and close his mouth. The skin around his lips was chapped and raw, as if he had been passing his tongue over and over the thin flesh there. "You were gone a long time," he said, and his voice was like the sound of deep water, of silt gone still after a long period.

"I wasn't. It was just a few minutes."

He shrugged, and the movement was unnatural, a quick skittering that made me think of the bent angles of a spider's legs.

"You were, though. Gone for a long time. I waited for you to come back and made myself quiet so I could hear when you came through the door. The same way you always knew to listen for me.

Like hearing where your own breath leaves off but knowing there should be something else there. Some other sound to finish it."

Outside, something crashed to the earth. A branch, or a tree, or the sky itself. There was no way of knowing which or of knowing if it mattered because Thomas had opened his mouth again. Such a round, perfect circle. Something you could press your own lips to and learn what it meant to taste something you'd always wanted, what it meant to find your heart buried underneath mud and dead leaves and water when the world upended itself. I leaned forward and touched his teeth, curved the pad of my index finger around his canines, testing their sharpness. If there was to be any bloodletting, it was right that Thomas would be the one to open me up.

There were no teeth in what came after.

Thomas went to the front door and opened it on the water slowly rising. I had hoped for suffocation before. In the end, this was what I found.

"Did I dream you into life, or was it the other way around? Or was it Mother all along? So desperate for a child that she somehow called two of us into existence when there should have only been one?" Thomas said and brought his mouth to mine.

When we were young, he whispered stories into the dark of the tiny creatures that crept into bedrooms in the night to steal the breath of sleeping children. My heart would seize as I listened, but then he would squeeze my foot, and I would sleep long and deep and would not dream. In the morning, I would wake with my chest tight and in fear that somehow I had slipped out of my skin while I slept and tumbled back into the wrong body, but Thomas would be there beside me, his hand covering his eyes and his hair pushed away from his face, and I could breathe again.

He inhaled, and I remembered the strange suction of his kiss. So many mornings struggling to breathe. "You were mine," I tried to say, but Thomas pulled my breath from me. It was possible I was never here, that my body was not solid, that Thomas called me out of the darkness. My memories a carefully constructed memory palace built from the same gossamer lightness of moth wings.

The heaviness in my chest was a wonderful thing to sink into.

Like warm water overflowing its banks.

"Was it like a dream? Was it like coming back after seeing the other side of death?" Thomas said.

"I had a mother," I said because I could not think of how else to tell him I had been real.

"There are so many words for change. So many things you can speak to bring something into life. I said them all. It was time to be quiet. Time to swallow down all of the things I tore out of myself. I have fed myself on your fear, on your awe."

The water reached the porch and then the door itself, and still the paper heart Thomas had given me beat and beat and beat.

"She braided my hair," I said as the water curled around my ankles.

"She braided your hair," my brother agreed.

This was the thing I remembered. This was the thing that made me bare my teeth.

When I finally bit down, Thomas screamed. My brother imagined suffocation to be an act of mercy.

I was not so kind.

A Benediction of Corpses

STEPHANIE M. WYTOVICH

This haunting in my mouth, the cry of
church bells against my ears, do you see
the ghosts of surgery tables? Smell the rot
of my potential amongst the silver shears,
the misplaced stitches?

    See, I am an amalgamation, the river that runs
    through science and death: taste the rancid swill
    of chemicals in my eyes, the way my skin shines,
    glistens like a widow's smile, all this poisoning,
    these exterminations. I'm sewn together like a
    botched-autopsy confession, a man-made monster
    embroidered with possibility, my sutures open,
    the scent of grave dust still dry on my cheeks

Yet I cringe when you touch me, every moment
of my life a disfigured plea, a reverse exorcism,
my genetic makeup filled with murder, my heartbeat
a collection of cut-off screams. Can you hear
the trepidations of my soul? All the moans and
aches of those trapped inside me, their caskets,
my bones, their ashes, my marrow?

STEPHANIE M. WYTOVICH

It hurts to look at my reflection, the taste of language,
of love, foreign on my tongue. I brace and name myself
demon, wanderer, prophet: my title a benediction of corpses,
a holy awakening, this my second chance to walk in the
garden, the reaper's forgiveness a welcoming sacrament,
a true gift to behold.

But you—my maker, my creator—you fear me!
Your disgust a mask of anxiety and guilt. I exist
as a consequence of your obsession, my knees
bruised from prayers, from all your blessings
that burned my skin. It's my job to exist
in this body, to live out my days as an outcast,
your approval lost somewhere in the air of angels,
me, your nightmare, your breathing question mark:
I'm the child of another God.

The Making of Asylum Ophelia

MERCEDES M. YARDLEY

Being mad wasn't enough. She also had to be beautiful. Thankfully, Brigitte, whose name meant "strong, firm, healthy woman," chose the perfect name for her baby girl.

She named her Ophelia.

What is in a name? So very much, Brigitte thought. The name Ophelia brings so many things to mind! Wonderful things. Emotive things. She knew her lovely daughter would wander around with a garland of flowers in hair. How did she know this? Because she, Brigitte, with her sturdy hands, would make that garland herself. She would weave it through Ophelia's long, loose curls.

Ophelia's tresses would tumble, of course. She would grow her hair long and sit at her mother's knee while Brigitte cooed and sang and brushed Ophelia's wild locks.

She would sing songs of madness. She would sing songs of want. She would sing them in her husky voice until her winsome daughter sang them back to her, her voice clear like a bird's.

Ophelia wanted to wear Wonder Woman shirts and dinosaur pajamas like the other kids she saw from her window, but Brigitte, like her name, and her solid orthopedic shoes, stood firm.

"No, Ophelia," she said. She put her hands on her hips for emphasis, as her own mother had taught her. "Pretty little girls should only wear white nightgowns. They look lovely when you ghost down the halls. When you become a woman, they'll flutter behind you as you walk on the moors in the night. Can you see in your mind's eye how you will glow under the moon? An unearthly thing of beauty? The evening's chill will prick your arms and legs, but you won't even feel it. You'll dance in bare feet, humming and swaying gracefully to music that only you will be able to hear."

"What if I can't hear it?" Little Ophelia asked. She wanted to play with trucks. She wanted to watch movies on her mother's tablet. But Firm Brigitte took these things away and made sure she played with charmingly clumsy handstitched dolls and wooden figurines instead.

"You'll hear it," Brigitte said loosely. "We'll begin music lessons soon so that you can always hear the music in your soul."

Ophelia didn't go to school like other little boys and girls. Her mother taught her at home. She had teachers come in to teach her ballet and embroidery and Shakespeare. Brigitte worked at the large store across the moors, the local Walmart, and she locked Ophelia inside the house while she was gone. Ophelia learned how to curl up prettily in a soft chair in the reading room and pour over books. Both legs pulled up, clean feet tucked away. She wasn't allowed to sprawl or spread her knees in a horrid, unladylike way, lest she spend the rest of the day in the closet.

One day, as a young teen, she appeared in her mother's doorway. Her pale face had two bright spots of color in her cheeks.

"Mother, I am reading Hamlet."

Brigitte's eyes were stars.

"My favorite. What a powerful story, yes? Family and betrayal and murder and madness."

Ophelia's pretty mouth twisted.

"Let's talk about this madness. It's an epidemic."

"It seems to be."

"Everybody loses their lives."

Brigitte nodded.

"Hamlet is Shakepeare's greatest tragedy."

Ophelia shifted uncomfortably in her flowing nightdress. It had long bell sleeves which fell demurely over the leather book she held. All of her books were bound in leather. She wore a nightdress day and night, her feet kept bare or perhaps slippered in soft-soled velvet shoes if the night was especially cold.

Except for lessons. Her mother allowed her to change into corseted dresses for lessons. Ophelia's teachers had commented on the strangeness of a thirteen-year-old girl showing up for singing, piano, and dance lessons in a nightgown.

"Mother, I want to ask you about Ophelia. In the story."

Brigitte's eyes glittered, and her unpainted lips showed strong teeth.

"Isn't she lovely? So charming. So tragic. Do you see how everybody responds when she hands them flowers? Isn't she the most wonderful thing? Their hearts go to her. Their mouths tremble. They accept her gifts and wear them near their hearts. She brings them together."

Ophelia's jaw set, and Brigitte had never seen such an ugly thing on a child.

"She's mad, mother. She isn't charming. She's crazy. She needs a psychiatrist and somebody to watch over her. She needs medications to stabilize her moods. She needs to get help and live somewhere other than that wretched place where they just let her pinwheel off into the water to die."

Sturdy, firm Brigitte stood up. Her legs were strong, her dark eyes imposing. She filled them with steel. Ophelia shrank back, her white fingers fluttering to her face as they should.

"None of this unseemly talk, Ophelia. You will not abuse your namesake. Heaven knows the dear girl has had enough of that."

Ophelia blinked large, dewy eyes and peered at her mother's face.

"You do realize that she is just a character in a story, mother? She isn't ... real?"

She asked so beautifully. She asked so charmingly. Brigitte smiled and brought her rough hands to rest on Ophelia's feminine shoulder.

"Such sweetness in you, my child," she murmured, and kissed Ophelia's forehead. "You will be remembered."

"Was I going to be forgotten?" Ophelia asked, but her mother was already hard at work, head bent low over a new pair of slippers for her charming daughter.

More than anything in the world, Ophelia longed for a friend. She didn't want to spend her evenings staring at the giant moon, which looked low and fat and rather carnivorous. Her mother got her a kitten, a fluffy white thing with a feminine ribbon tied around his neck, but he escaped into the night.

Ophelia wished she could follow.

"You should," Brigitte urged, her eyes glowing hotly. "Flee across the moors, shouting his name. You won't find him, of course, but won't you be such a sight? Your tears will shine in the moonlight. Sadness makes a woman extraordinarily lovely. Grief is the finest of jewels."

"Did you flee across the moors into the darkness once, mother?" Ophelia asked, and Brigitte's face became an old house. It was a rugged thing, weathered, and shutters fell over her eyes to protect them.

"The midnight moors are not kind to a woman named Brigitte," she said simply, and left. Ophelia did not go out to search for her kitten that night, although the front door was left not only unlocked, but standing open. The moon ran a tongue over its teeth outside.

Brigitte plaited Ophelia's hair, twining flowers here and there. Ophelia couldn't lie down or rest her head for fear of smashing the pansies, rosemary, and violets.

"They make me weary, mother," she said.

"There's rue for you; and here's some for me," her mother answered.

Ophelia touched Brigitte's brown locks. They were shot through with silver, wiry and looking somewhat wild.

"Shall I plait flowers into your hair, mother?" she asked.

Brigitte's hands flew to her hair, patting it far too quickly like a dying bird. Her fingernails slid down and cut deep furrows in her cheeks. Blood bubbled up like the clear brook Shakespeare's Ophelia drowned in.

"Go read, child," she said. Ophelia's cornflower eyes grew wide and she flew, prettily, to her room. Brigitte smiled after her.

Ophelia the Lonely grew quieter, paler, sadder. The air inside her home changed, as if the house itself was holding its breath in dark anticipation. She began feeling unwell, her stomach hurting after she ate, and she caught her mother heaping spoonful after spoonful of strange herbs into Ophelia's food and drink. She ceased eating and her cheeks hollowed. Her head drooped like the thirsty flowers in her hair.

Her caring dance teacher slipped her a note. She patted Ophelia's cheek and looked her in the eye meaningfully. Ophelia read the spidery handwriting and color returned to her face. She slipped the note in between her lips and it was the first thing she had eaten in days.

Brigitte didn't notice her sturdiest pair of shoes go missing from her closet. She lost the scissors from her mending kit. Ophelia ghosted about the house, a winning thing, all hair and robes and silver secrets.

"Do you remember what my name means?" Ophelia asked Brigitte one evening. They were reading in the study. Brigitte was humming, repeating the same stanza over and over.

"Of course I do. Ophelia means help. You are a helpless, darling thing and the world needs to take care of you before you go mad."

"If I go mad, don't you mean?"

Brigitte looked at her. Or more correctly, she looked through her, into the future where Ophelia's exquisite corpse lay.

"I'll surround you with flowers. With pearls. Your tresses will be arranged around your face in such a pleasing way. I can see it now."

Ophelia paled. "What do you mean? Surround me with flowers? Do you mean after I am dead?"

Brigitte closed her eyes. "The plaiting was practice, don't you see. Now I'll be able to do it just right. I have the most beautiful pale gown for you. The palest of blue with silver threads dotting it like stars. So lovely, so tragic."

Ophelia's voice sounded ethereal already. The wind and her mother's words had swept it away.

"A ... a gown? A funeral gown?"

"Ah, it's so lovely, Ophelia! I made it myself with such care. It fits you perfectly. You will be such a wonder."

"What if I grow, mother? And the gown no longer fits?"

Brigitte's laughter sounded like broken bells, like the car horns that blared in the Walmart parking lot as she threaded her way on foot to work.

"It is nearly time, my sweet girl. There's no need to grow anymore. You will never be more beautiful than you are right at this moment. I have some herbs that I have gathered, to make a draught. You will die in the epitome of loveliness. This is my gift to you, my darling."

Ophelia's stomach grew hard and heavy at the thought.

"Mother," she asked, "what of you, during this? While I lie there pretty and dead, what will happen to you?"

Brigitte's lips trembled, but only for a minute.

"I will adore you. I will throw myself on your casket, weeping, but only for a moment. You will be buried and I will put flowers and small gifts on your grave. I will never forget you. I am Brigitte, and Brigittes are faithful. We are durable. I will trek out to see you morning, noon, and night. I will work my fingers to the bone to make sure that I can bring you the loveliest of things for your grave. Your headstone will be marble. I will keep it clean and free from soil and weeds. For I love you, my darling."

She did. She did, and Ophelia knew she did, but she realized this love was a sickness, an abomination, and no matter how she loved her mother, this resolute Brigitte, she could not stay here lest she die.

That night Ophelia brewed her mother a cup of tea. It was filled with the secret herbs, and honey, and sweet things that made one sleepy.

She led her mother to bed and tucked her scratchy wool blanket around her.

"Why don't you use my blanket, mother?" she asked. "It's so very soft and fine."

"It's not for me," Brigitte murmured, and then she was asleep. The tight line of her mouth softened. Her dark hair was loose.

Ophelia stole to her room to fetch her blanket. It was of the finest of linen, embroidered beautifully by Brigitte's worn hand. She spread it over her mother with careful fingers. She slid the flowers from her own hair and tucked them gently into her mother's curls.

Ophelia pressed her pink lips to her mother's cheek. Brigitte's skin was soft, the bloody furrows beginning to heal.

The girl padded to the bathroom. She stepped out of her night-dress and into a practical outfit stolen from Brigitte's closet. She slipped out of her satin slippers and into Brigitte's functional shoes, the toes stuffed with paper so they would fit.

Ophelia looked into the mirror and took the scissors to her long hair. She sobbed as she cut, one hand over her mouth, chopping and hacking until she had tresses no longer, but a short, uneven cut that made her eyes too wide and her runny nose far too big.

She smiled.

The stranger in the mirror grinned back.

She did what her mother had always hoped and fled across the moors, but her footsteps weren't graceful. She clomped across the land in oversized shoes, dodging the parked cars in the dark, and breathing hard. The parking lot pavement was hard and unfamiliar under her feet, but she still ran through the rain that began to fall. Shorn bits of her clipped hair fell into her eyes and plastered them-selves onto her reddened cheeks. She ran toward a woman who had three daughters and two sons, and she had been invited to become one of them, whichever she wanted, as winsome or slovenly as she liked. Her name, Ophelia, meant help after all, and she had the power to help herself.

Brigitte's eyes fluttered open. She turned her head to the side and caught the faint scent of flowers.

"Ophelia?" she called. She sat up in bed and a daisy fell from her hair. Brigitte reached out to touch it, her hand trembling, and realized she was covered in her daughter's exquisite blanket. She ran her fingers over the expensive fabric, feeling its softness. Her fingers fluttered to her lips.

"Ophelia!"

Brigitte leapt out of bed and rushed down the hall in cold, bare feet. She flung open the door to Ophelia's room.

Her daughter's bed was horrifically cold and empty.

"No," she said, and flew around the room like a frightened bird. She plucked at the curtains and the sheets. She searched the house and made a small sound when she saw that the front door had been left slightly ajar. Brigitte snatched one of Ophelia's white robes from the front closet and pulled it over her nightgown as she flew into the night after her child.

The rain hit the ground prettily as she ran. She left the gardens and raced across the moors, her bare feet hitting the ground, splashing through the rainbow-colored puddles of car oil. She gave her discomfort no heed, hands to her terrified face, hair dripping flowers as she raced around, calling for her daughter.

"Ophelia! Ophelia!" she screamed, and she was calling help help help.

Tragedy brought Brigitte to her knees. A missing child makes its mark on a person and sadness, as we have learned, makes a woman extraordinarily lovely. A devoted mother caught up in madness can, indeed, die of a broken heart, and she tumbled into a stream, the water rushing up her nose and mouth, flowering inside of her lungs. Her dark hair waved gracefully around her white face, her eyes staring at the hungry moon. Brigitte had never, ever been so beautiful as the night she lost her Ophelia, and the moon devoured her whole.

Ophelia made her way into the Walmart.

OPEN 24 HOURS, it said. The signs were loud and garish, and the lights inside hurt her eyes.

Ophelia hesitated in the doorway, her sopping clothes sticking to her body, and she stared at the horrors around her. Men with hair on their faces who smelled of musk. Women using loud voices and wearing rough pants of scratchy fabric. Jarring voices came out of the air and asked for checkers and aisle cleanups and said there was a great deal on air fresheners.

Sound. Noise. Saturating color. Smells. It was too much, far too overwhelming to a young woman raised on weak tea and quiet afternoons in the library with Proust.

Ophelia's raised her fingers to her teeth, biting her fingernails, gnawing at a hangnail until it bled. She backed out of the store and into the rain outside.

A thin woman with suspiciously bright eyes grabbed her arm.

"Hey, have any money?" she asked.

Ophelia yanked her arm away and stepped back. She spun around and ran for the house.

"I'm sorry, I'm sorry, I'm sorry," she repeated. It was a chant, a spell, and it would keep her safe. It would ferry her home and tuck her snug in her bed, where she would be warm and things would be quiet. Her mother would forgive her and weave flowers into a garland to cover her shabby head until her hair grew out. She would eat the delicate soups and drink mugs of warm milk with all of the poisonous herbs, whatever her mother wanted, as long as she didn't have to be out in this world of horrors alone.

The lights of her home glimmered on the other side of the moor. She used her arm to brush tears and rain out of her face as she staggered, weaving in and out of the parked cars, tripping over her too-large shoes. She was nearly there when she caught sight of something in the gutter. Her stomach fell and her mouth formed a large O.

Her mother, face bloomed with death, lay in the water. It rushed over her, washing the color from her skin and out into the moors. Her dark hair moved gently in the current, jeweled with the remnants of beautiful flowers.

Ophelia fell to her knees and sobbed, the sound ugly in her throat. She reached for her mother with ruddy hands, but could not force herself to touch Brigitte's unlined, peaceful face. A violet slipped from Brigitte's curls and floated away.

Ophelia managed to choke out two words.

"Ophelia. Help."

Frankenstein's Daughter

THEODORA GOSS

To Mrs. Saville, England

May 27th, 17—

My dear Margaret,

You know with what high hopes I set out once again on this third of my expeditions into the Arctic Circle. This time, I told myself, I would not be defeated by ice and the dreadful cold of those latitudes. This time my sailors would not rebel; this time my ship would not become trapped among icebergs. This time, finally, I would break through into that temperate northern sea I had dreamed of, and sail upon it to the other side of the globe, returning with riches from Africa or the Americas. This time the North would not defeat me.

But I return to you a broken man, more broken this time than in my previous endeavors. I am weakened by a long illness, but it is not that which has made me, in the space of six months, a bent wreckage of my former self, my hairs gray—or rather grayer than they once were, particularly about the temples, although I confess what when I look into the mirror, I remain youthful of countenance, and not unattractive. No, it is that most common and yet mysterious of human ailments, a shattered heart.

How I shattered it—or how she did so, the woman to whom I offered it, and who cared about it no more than she cared about jewels, fine clothes, or such other feminine adornments, you shall hear. I shall sit down again at your fireside in Hampshire, where I shall return to nurse my wounded heart. I know that you, most affectionate of sisters, will welcome me into your parlor, and gazing at me in your particular way, both loving and admonitory, say "Seriously, Robert" at this account of my adventures. But I assure you, dearest Margaret, that they are all true, or as true as memory may recollect, for my mind was touched as well by the illness I suffered, and there are things I remember only as fever-dreams. Yet her, and her dreadful father, I remember as clearly as though they stood before me—alas, if only she were here with me now! But I lost her, or rather I never had her, and therefore I return to you alone, with hopes and dreams dashed.

How fortunate I am that you, my sweet sister, are one of those women sent to be a comfort to man! It will be a pleasure to see your face again, with its calm gray eyes, and feel the warmth of your solemn smile, and taste the wonderful cakes that Mrs. Asher makes, the ones with the apricot jam centers.

But now to my story!

You know how I have dedicated my life and fortune to the exploration of the Arctic Circle, and how in that attempt I have been thwarted again and again! You yourself have been a generous supporter of these endeavors, when the audacity of my dreams has been greater than my income. On my first attempt, I was able to purchase the services of an English ship and captain. We made our way to a northern sea that glitters with icebergs, under the almost perpetual light of the Arctic summer. But alas, the ice closed in on us, and in the end, fearing for the safety of his ship and crew, the captain determined to turn back. It was on this trip that I encountered my friend Victor, of whom I have often spoken—a nobler gentleman never walked upon this earth. It was then, too, that I met the fearful shadow that pursued him—that fiend in human form, the destroyer of my friend's health and happiness. Of him, more anon.

On my second attempt, I was not able to get so far—waylaid by a fever in Archangel, I was confined to a sanatorium for three months, and finally ordered home for my health. I still remember with what devotion you nursed me, dear sister, during my long convalescence. "Robert," you said to me then, "surely this is enough. Surely now you will leave off this vain pursuit and live a sensible life. There are sciences you may pursue here, without going off to the ends of the earth, that will benefit mankind." Or some such. I cannot exactly recall your words, as to be honest, I did not then mark your advice. I remained desirous of scientific renown for opening up regions that had been hitherto hidden from man. Surely any gentleman who has been educated in what science can do, in its limitless potential to transform our understanding of this earthly realm, if not indeed the heavens themselves, will understand my ambition.

I still remember what a serious child you were, with your long brown ringlets, eternally sketching wildflowers, catching insects in jars and creating the most enchanting displays pinned on cards, prattling about the gradations of species as though you were an infant Linnaeus! And how you grew into a very pretty girl, the picture of sense and propriety, hiding your muddy boots under the hem of your skirt so our uncle would not know you had been out on the downs, collecting what have you—fossils, I think it was? You, with your feminine modesty, cannot understand the desire for glory, for the conquest of new realms, whether of land or knowledge, that drives men on—or some men. My friend Victor was much a man, and I myself have not been able to resist similar lofty ambitions. But alas, this third attempt was to prove my most disastrous, and I do not think that I shall ever again make the attempt.

Once again, I hired a ship, but I was known in Archangel, and said to be bad luck, so no captain would work with me except one, a Russian named Ivan to whom others had given the soubriquet of The Madman. This madman, so called, said he would work for me, and he assembled a crew. The men were not prepossessing—I suspected that some of them were smugglers or even pirates rather than honest whalers—but I had no choice in the matter.

We set out in late summer, later than I would have liked, but it had taken longer than I expected to equip our expedition. There was no enthusiasm for my project in Archangel. There was no wealth to be gained from sailing so far north, men said—they did not believe in my dream of a northern sea that would allow us to travel over the top of the globe itself, to the other side, and establish new routes to the riches of the Orient. They insisted that to the north was only ice. Alas that the mass of mankind is so shortsighted.

Nevertheless, the voyage started more propitiously than my last one. The weather was relatively balmy for those climes, the water remained clear of ice, and we sailed without impediment farther than I had been able to sail on my first ill-fated voyage.

But then, almost a month after we set out from Archangel, on a course headed northwest into the sea beyond Nova Zembla, we encountered storms so severe that I was in despair, expecting every day that my crew would insist on turning back, and I would once again have lost my chance at renown. Indeed, I believe they were prevented from so doing only because I had laid in a considerable supply of rum, and there was general drunkenness on board although somehow, the captain managed to keep us on a steady course. At last, the sea grew calm—I hoped we were about to enjoy a period of milder weather. But the cold came, suddenly, silently in the night— there was ice on the masts, ice on the sails, frost on the men's beards. We continued to sail northward, but the men began to grumble, and the rum was almost gone. Fights broke out—evidently the quarter- master had saved a private barrel for his mates, and some of the men suggested throwing him overboard. These are the circumstances of a rough sailing life, which would shock a gentlewoman like yourself.

Each day was colder than the last, and the ocean began to freeze around us. Finally, we had only a narrow path northward, and then no path, and the ship was entirely surrounded by ice.

Then began a dark and difficult time. For two weeks we stayed there, trapped in ice like the insects you collect in amber, insisting they reveal the age of the earth—darling Margaret! How your specu- lations have always charmed me! I am glad that you have never been exposed to the harsh, rough world of such men as these sailors. They fought and drank, and when the rum ran out, they fought the more. Then the biscuits and salted meat ran out, and a dark sort of talk began of salting the quartermaster—of how he would taste pickled and brined, probably like pork. One of the cabin boys disap- peared, and I do not know if he wandered off into the white fogs that sometimes swirled about the ship, or whether—but I should not speculate about such things.

I knew that I must do something—so I asked the captain to gather his men on deck, and I spoke to them, as my friend Victor had done on my first voyage. I exhorted them to think beyond themselves: of the good they could do mankind, the fame they would achieve if we stuck to our purpose. Did they not want to benefit their fellow men? Did they not want to expand the field of science, of human knowledge?

Victor must have had some eloquence I lack, or perhaps this crew was so much lower than the last in sensibility and ambition, for when I had made this argument, they glowered at me out of eyes that were red and raw from the perpetual light of the North, and in a few moments I found myself trussed like a chicken, tied hands and feet with rope.

Then they put me out upon the ice. None of them wished to kill me himself—there were English trade representatives in Archangel who would make inquiries, and none of them wished to be more guilty than his fellows, only *as* guilty so there would be no value to any of them in informing on the others. And besides, some of them were religious—they did not want blood on their hands. But they were willing to let the ice and cold perform the task they shunned. So I found myself out upon the ice sheet, which was in some places blue, in some gray, in some pure white, far enough from the ship so they did not have to witness my inevitable demise. I shouted myself hoarse for them to come back and get me, but to no avail. There I remained, bound hand and foot, protected only by the fur coat and leggings that I had commissioned specially in St. Petersburg.

I do not know how many hours I lay there, alternatively feeling anger and despair, sometimes commending myself to my Lord and Savior, for I expected to die before nightfall, sometimes railing against the men who had so cruelly abandoned me. At last, I lost consciousness from cold, fatigue, and hunger. I had no voice left with which to curse my fate or beg for mercy. My last memory is of the bright northern sky above, the glittering plains of ice around, and two word descending from the heavens as though spoken by God himself. I clearly remember that they were *You fool!*

When next I woke, I found myself in a room—not the cabin of a ship, but a proper room, although somewhat rough, with thick beams overhead. I could feel that I was lying down, and that I was warm. Indeed, I soon found, when I sat up a little, that I was in a bed under a wool blanket, and that the room was spacious, with dark wood furniture and a wide hearth on which a hearty fire was burning.

Where was I? What good angel had brought me here? Whoever he was, he had saved me from certain death.

For some minutes I lay still, wondering, then attempted to rise— but I could not. My head immediately began to spin, and my limbs to tingle as though I were a pincushion, with a thousand pins stuck into me. Indeed, the pain was so great that I once again lost consciousness, but before I did, it seemed to me that an angel came into the room, with a halo of black hair braided around her head, and eyes as gentle and kind as your own, Margaret, although brown rather than gray. She looked down upon me and said something I could not understand, then held a cup to my mouth, from which I drank—and remembered no more.

When I woke again, she was sitting in a chair beside the fireplace, reading a book of some sort. She heard me stir and looked up. By her dress, she was a servant—it was a simple red tunic over loose trousers, such as peasant women sometimes wear in Russia, embroidered at the neck and on the cuffs and hem.

"How are you feeling today?" she asked. To my astonishment, she spoke in English—heavily accented, but nevertheless English! She walked to my bedside and looked down at me—hers were the eyes I remembered from my dream, hers the braid of black hair. This woman, young and beautiful, was my good angel.

"Well, thank you," I said. I was startled by the sound of my own voice, which emerged as a hoarse whisper, as though I had not used it in a long time. I had a fit of coughing then, and she held my head while I drank from the cup that had been placed on a table at my bedside. Her hands were gentle, although they held me firmly, and I felt that she was an angel indeed. She did not look like our English notion of an angel—her complexion was what we call olive and associate with the classically Greek, while her eyes turned upward at the corners, like those of a Turkish houri. Nevertheless, I divined it was she who had nursed me through my illness. But who had rescued me from the ice and brought me to this house? It could not have been this delicate maiden. Such a rescue must have taken a team of intrepid men. I must find out to whom I owed my gratitude.

"If you will take me to your master," I said, "or perhaps your mistress, I will express my thanks for the care that has been taken of me. I do not know how I got here or how long I have been your patient, but someone has saved me from a dreadful fate, and I would like—"

"I am the only mistress here," she said, smiling with what seemed like amusement. "And at present, the only master. My father, who rescued you from the ice, is not expected back for some weeks. You may express your gratitude when he returns. You have been here a month, mostly under the influence of laudanum, my own formulation of it, while you recovered from exposure and dehydration. You will not remember most of that time. And there is no possibility of you getting out of bed, not today or anytime soon. No, don't try to get up—" for I had been in the process of attempting to rise, not aware that I was dressed only in a nightshirt. "I just gave you another dose of the drug. You will be asleep within a few minutes."

That is how I first met Aila, although I did not know her name until later. I was under the influence of the drug for some weeks after—there are days I remember only from moments or perhaps an hour of lucidity. Even now, I blush to think of how she must have cared for me during that time, bathing me, attending to the needs of my body—I vaguely recollect a chamber pot under the bed. And the conversations we had, in which she listened with interest to my accounts of England and my voyages, although she often had to depart before I was finished to perform her household duties. Is it any wonder that I grew to love her, that sweet maid whom I shall never see again? She told me that I had almost lost both legs and one hand to the terrible cold. It was only her ministrations, I am convinced, that kept me a whole man—except two toes on my left foot and my right pinky finger, which could not be saved. You have likely noticed that my handwriting is even more of a scrawl than when Mr. Parsons used to lecture me about it. Do you remember that we called him Parsley-face? You are fortunate, dear sister, that you did not have to listen to the lectures of a tutor, and were put under the guidance of Miss Elliott instead. What a pretty singing voice she had, although a rather large nose, and how nicely she danced! But no woman is a match for my lost angel, my beautiful Aila.

As the days went by, from her answers to my questions, for she never spoke much but answered with amused tolerance, I pieced together her history. She lived in that house with her father, but had not always lived there. The master of the house, who had rescued me from my terrible predicament, was a European, cast out from society for some sin or crime she did not specify. By her account, he was a great explorer, and had performed inhuman feats—climbing mountains no man had climbed, venturing into the inhospitable North farther than any man has yet ventured. At the time, I assumed these exaggerated claims arose from her evident love for her father, which I found admirable. In his journeys through the wilderness, he had encountered the reindeer herders of Lappland, who lived all year in their tents and wander here and there over the high tundra. There he met and fell in love with a woman, the chieftess of her people. By Aila's account, she was as strong and courageous as her father, but more steady of character. One day, when I was more lucid than usual, because I was beginning to heal and she had lowered my daily dose of the drug, I begged her to tell me more.

"All right," she said, putting down her book—when she entered my room, she was generally carrying a book of some sort, or some implement I could not identify, perhaps for cookery. I could not tell what that day's tome was from the name on the spine, since it was in Hebrew and my education, as you know, stopped at Latin. "I will tell you, if only to stop you from asking interminable questions. I cannot always be attending to you, now that you are getting better. I have my own work. But this once, because I know that otherwise you will not stop asking."

She sat down on the side of my bed—today her tunic was yellow, with the same embroidered patterns, or similar, but I do not have a woman's eye for such fine work—paused for a moment, then began.

"I did not know my mother long," she said. "I was only seven years old when she died, defending our herd from southern hunters. Every year they would come for the sport of hunting the reindeer, from Norway, Sweden, Denmark ... Every year our tribe guarded and defended our herd. It was more than our source of milk, meat, fur. It was a part of our tribe, and my mother told me that sometimes a person who had died would return as a reindeer, or the other way around. Her own grandmother, a shaman during her lifetime, had been reborn as a leader of the herd, a large female with antlers that grew each autumn like the spreading branches of a tree.

"I asked her how she had met my father, who was obviously not of our people, with his pale face, his long limbs. Our people are short and compact, to conserve heat in winter, at the latitude where we dwell.

"She told me that one day, she had ridden out upon the tundra to find a pregnant female who had wandered away from the herd. She had given birth during the night in a ditch, and wolves had come—five of them, a small pack. The female was obviously sick—that was probably why she had wandered off. She could not care for her calf, who was staggering about, crying for milk. My mother could have fought off the wolves, but she could not do that, and protect the calf, and save the mother at the same time. She did not know what to do. That is when my father appeared at the top of the ditch—he had heard her shouting at the wolves, which often frightens them. But this pack was not frightened off. The three females had begun circling my mother, while the two males approached the calf. My father would have killed the wolves with his bare hands, but she told him to stop and leave them be. He did not understand our language, not then, but her gestures were clear, and he obeyed them. She could see that one of the female wolves had just given birth—her dugs were hanging down. The wolves needed food as much as the reindeer, as much as the tribe itself. The calf's mother was obviously too sick to survive. She told my father to keep back the wolves and, as gently as she could, she cut the female's throat, telling her to come back soon and be reborn as a member of the tribe.

"'Perhaps you are that reindeer, Aila,' she once said to me. 'Perhaps she blessed me for saving her child by becoming mine.'"

Aila was silent for a moment, perhaps considering the notion that she was a reindeer reborn—primitive tribes often have these sorts of ideas, which may seem ridiculous to civilized Europeans, but help them understand the world in the absence of science or theology. Then she continued. "They left the mother for the wolves, and my father carried the calf back to our tents. That was their first meeting. You will meet him soon," she said, glancing at me. "My father. He returns within a few days. Do not be startled when you see him. I used to think that he was ugly because he was European—I thought all of you looked like him. Since I have learned about Europeans from reading their books, I have realized that he would be considered an ugly man anywhere. You are shocked that I speak so of my own father, but you will see—even as a child I knew there was something wrong with his appearance, although his heart is more tender and loving than most.

"But my mother did not consider him ugly. To her, he was beautiful—for his strength, his compassion. She was the chief of our tribe—her father had been chief before her, and his aunt before him. Her brothers and uncles were worried when she chose a foreigner to be her husband, but when they saw how hard he could work, how impervious he was to any hardship, and how quickly he learned our languages, they respected her choice. My parents loved each other with a tenderness that I believe is rare, for any couple.

"For some years, they did not have a child—my father told me that he feared he would never be able to have one. But at last I was born. I spent my first seven years with the tribe, sleeping in our tent, running over the tundra, learning the plants there, the signs that foretold weather, the ways of the reindeer. And I would have remained there all my life, perhaps becoming chief myself someday, or following the path of a shaman. But that summer the southern hunters came early, in larger numbers than usual—a Prussian count and his party wanted game. They paid a high price for the best guides and trackers. My father was away on one of his journeys—he could not keep from wandering in the wilderness, and my mother did not try to stop him. He assumed we would be safe until later in the season.

"I was not there when she was shot—she had left me safely back in our tent. But I was there when my uncles carried her back, still alive although dying from wounds we could not heal. There is no herb that will help against a gunshot.

"'Aila,' she said to me. 'Remember that I will always love you. When you look up at the stars at night, my spirit will be there, watching you, until one day it will be reborn again. I think this time I would like to come back as a wolf … But you, grow up strong and brave, my daughter. And take care of your father. He is strong but he has wounds on the inside, close to his heart—wounds that will never heal. When I die, he will have another one. He will need a reason to continue living. You must be that reason.'

"And then she died. Three days later, my father returned, in time to place her body on the funeral pyre. 'Aila,' he said to me after her funeral, 'there is something I must do. I will return soon.' It was three months before he returned again."

"Where did he go?" I asked, for she had paused in her narrative. I thought she might have forgotten I was there altogether—she seems so lost in her own story.

She looked up, as though mentally returning to my sickroom. Then, she smiled. "Even in England, you must have heard of the death of Count von Schmetterling. It was notorious for its gruesome and inexplicable nature—the count was found both drowned and strangled, at the top of a tower that had not been entered since medieval times. He was found only because his horse was tied to an iron ring at its base. The key to the tower had been lost long ago, and it was evident that the door had not been opened for centuries—its hinges were so rusted that it had to be removed entirely before the local magistrate could enter. Under those circumstances, no suspicion could attach to anyone—a supernatural agency was clearly indicated, and rumors circulated of a family curse. His window inherited his estate and is, I have heard, very happy with her second husband." She seemed amused by this terrible account, which made the hairs on my neck stand up and sent shivers down my spine.

Something was beginning to stir in my mind, a memory and a supposition. Perhaps if I had not spent weeks in the Lethe of laudanum, I would have put it all together sooner—perhaps, Margaret, you have guessed where my letter is leading already. You were always good at puzzles and parlor games. But I merely stared at Aila, uncertain what to do with this information.

"Finally, my father returned," she said. "He told me that he could no longer stay with the tribe. There were too many sad memories for him there, too many painful recollections. But I could, if I wished it. I could stay with my mother's people, my aunts and uncles and cousins, learning the ways of the tribe and the reindeer. Or I could go with him, to a house he had built long ago on the coast of Spitsbergen. There he would teach me as best he could, as he had taught himself. But it was my choice to make.

"I remembered my mother's words—that he would need a reason to continue living, and I could be that reason. 'I will go with you, father,' I said. So he brought me here, where I have grown and learned, alone except for him, when he is here. There is a village where we go for supplies, but it is three days from here by cart in summer or sleigh in winter, so I do not go often."

I took her hand. "You do not have to be alone any longer, lovely Aila. In these weeks I have grown to love you dearly. You are my sweet angel, a natural gentlewoman to match any in Europe. Come back to England and be my wife. I know my sister, Margaret, will welcome you into her household. And I will make a good husband for you. I will love and care for you as you deserve."

She looked at me with astonishment, then burst out laughing. "You take care of me? You cannot even take care of yourself. What would I do with a husband who goes off on useless and impractical journeys into the northern snows, who cannot wipe his own behind for a month at a time? You are not the husband for me, Robert Walton."

"Well, that is good to hear!"

Whose voice was that? It echoed through the room and into the depths of my consciousness. And then I knew what voice—not God's but the devil's—had said *You fool!* on the ice.

It was he, the fiend and murderer of my friend Victor, his nameless creation—the monster.

"You!" I shouted. I believe I would have launched myself at him, despite his superior size and strength, if I were capable of doing so. But in my weakened state, all I could do was glare at his hideous countenance—still crossed by scars, still the pale yellow of a corpse. How could any woman, even one from a primitive tribe, who had never learned the refinements of civilization, find beauty in such features? How could anyone love *that*?

"Hello, Papa," said Aila, going to him and kissing him on the cheek. I shuddered. My love for her did not die, would never die—not even such a gesture would kill it. But I could not bear the sight.

"Yes, it is I," he said, with an expression of lurid glee—or so I supposed, for what else could that embodiment of malice be feeling? He was my rescuer—and now my tormentor! As he had been to Victor himself.

"I thought you had determined to destroy yourself in a conflagration at the North Pole," I said, with contempt.

"That was my intention," he said, with a smile—a ghastly smile, I should say, although it also seemed somehow sorrowful. "But there are few materials with which to conflagrate, at that cold and remote location, and in the end, I wanted to live. Life itself remained precious to me, even after all I had suffered—and I still retained the desire to experience the natural world, to understand mankind. So I lived and traveled, to see sights upon this Earth that you, with your frail mortal body, shall never witness, Walton. To marry the best and most courageous woman who ever walked this Earth, and father a child that even you, with your limited, provincial mind, cannot help admiring, although you understand only a small portion of her worth. But she is not for you. It's time for you to return to your home in England. And God help me, if you ever set foot above latitude sixty degrees north again, I will strangle you myself, which is better than you deserve for all the trouble you cause. As soon as I heard in Archangel that you were back for another of your foolish voyages, I knew where it would end—and in truth, perhaps I should have left you there! I am only glad that the rest of your crew managed to make it back safely, once the ice broke. Aila, can he be ready to travel tomorrow?"

Aila looked at me appraisingly. "I think he is well enough, if he is dosed well and wrapped warmly."

"Good," said the monster. "I want him out of my house as soon as possible. Walton, you will travel by land to a village on the coast, where you will be picked up by a whaler on its way to Archangel. There, you will remain until you are well enough for the long journey back to England. And for God's sake, stay there! This is no place for a gentleman adventurer. Aila would find the Pole more quickly than you could find your own ... well, I shall not say that in front of my daughter."

Did she understand the nature of her father? Of how he had been created from corpses by my friend, Victor Frankenstein? Alas, my poor Victor, who had suffered so much! It came to me that I should tell her—I should warn her that her own father was a fiend in human form, a daemon of the pit. But as she stood beside him, with her hand in his, her cheek against his arm, so calm and confident, I shuddered at the thought. I could not tell her of her own dreadful parentage. And it came to me, as well, that if I did, the monster might kill me directly afterward. So I said nothing.

And that, my dear sister, is how I ended up once again, for the second time, at a sanatorium in Archangel—the same sanatorium, where luckily the sisters recognized me and treated me kindly, calling me Walton the Arctic Explorer—admiringly, although some of them did giggle, but then girls do, you know.

I look forward to once again sitting by your fireside, drinking tea out of the Sèvres service that our mother left you, eating Mrs. Asher's cakes and little sandwiches. Please remind her that I particularly like the curried eggs and the watercress. I return to you a broken man—love lost, dreams and ambitions unfulfilled. But I shall henceforth take pleasures in the little things of life, and my own hearth, or rather yours, dear sister, for as I have no home of my own, I hope you will allow me to spend considerable time at Chatworth with you and Charles and the children. Please tell him that I am looking forward to seeing him again, and to continuing our discussions of

Roman politics in the time of Julius Caesar.

I almost forgot to mention that, before I left, Aila asked me to enclose a letter to you, no doubt some reminiscences of our time together and directions for my care. It is a bit lumpy, I do not know why, most likely because of the quality of the paper. You know she does not have access to fine linen weave in the far North! But I enclose it here. I look forward to seeing you soon, my dear Margaret.

Your loving brother,

Robert

Dear Margaret,

I hope you don't think it rude of me to address you informally. Your brother, Robert Walton, told me a great deal about you, both in his delirium and when in his right mind, for the man never stops talking. Forgive me, he is your brother, but the tedium of hearing his stories over and over again almost drove me mad. I do not know how you can stand it. You may recognize my surname, for Robert spoke incessantly of his friend Victor—the man my father taught me to call grandfather, although I scorn the lineage. Among other deficiencies, my grandfather seems to have been a careless researcher.

From what he has said, or did not say, it seems that you too are interested in the science of botany. It is one of my fascinations, and I hope that someday I can study in Europe at one of the institutes, or perhaps a botanical garden. I write to you now asking if you would perhaps care to correspond, and I enclose several seeds, with a description of their characteristics and properties, that may interest you as examples of the local flora. I do not believe they have yet been studied by European scientists.

If you write to me at the enclosed address in Archangel, the letter will reach me, although slowly in my present remote location. But I look forward to hearing from you, and to learning that I have a sister in science who is as dedicated to the pursuit of knowledge as I am.

Yours sincerely,

Aila Frankenstein

Contributors

LINDA D. ADDISION ("One Day of Inside/Out") is the first African-American recipient of the Bram Stoker Award® and has received four awards for collections in the Poetry category. She was also part of two books that were finalists. She is the only author with fiction in three landmark anthologies that celebrate African-American speculative writers: the award-winning anthology *Dark Matter: A Century of Speculative Fiction* (Warner Aspect), *Dark Dreams I* and *II* (Kensington), and *Dark Thirst* (Gallery Books). Her work has made frequent appearances on the honorable mention lists for *Year's Best Fantasy and Horror* and *Year's Best Science-Fiction*. She has published over 300 poems, stories and articles, and is a founding member of the writer's group Circles in the Hair (CITH) and a member of SFWA, HWA, and SFPA.

MICHAEL BAILEY (co-editor) is a writer, editor, book designer, and a resident of forever-burning California. He is the recipient of the Bram Stoker Award®, Benjamin Franklin Award, over two dozen independent accolades, and a Shirley Jackson Award nominee. Publications include *Palindrome Hannah* and *Phoenix Rose* (novels), *Scales and Petals*, *Inkblots and Blood Spots*, and *Oversight* (collections), and over sixty published stories, novelettes, and poems. Edited anthologies include *Qualia Nous*, *The Library of the Dead*, *You Human*, *Adam's Ladder*, four volumes of *Chiral Mad*, and more. He recently finished *Seven Minutes*, a memoir about surviving one of the most catastrophic wildfires in history. Future books include *Psychotropic Dragon*, *Seen in Distant Stars*, *The Impossible Weight of Life*, and *Hangtown* (titles subject to change). Find him online at nettirw.com.

LAIRD BARRON ("Ode to Joad the Toad"), an expert Alaskan, is the author of several books, including *The Imago Sequence and Other Stories*, *Swift to Chase*, and *Blood Standard*. He is a three-time recipient of the World Fantasy Award (four-time nominee), the Bram Stoker Award® (five-time nominee), a three-time recipient of the Shirley Jackson Award (fourteen-time nominee), was nominated for the Theorore Sturgeon Memorial Award, numerous times for the Locus and International Horror Guild Awards. He was also nominated for the William L. Crawford IAFA Fantasy Award. Currently, Barron lives in the Rondout Valley of New York State and is at work on tales about the evil that men do.

MAX BOOTH III ("I Am Your Neighbor") was raised in Northern Indiana on an unhealthy diet of horror movies and Christopher Pike paperbacks. He now lives in San Antonio, Texas where he is constantly trying not to get shot. It is harder than you think. He is the author of several novels, including *Carnivorous Lunar Activities* (Fangoria) and the forthcoming *Touch the Night* (Cemetery Dance). His nonfiction has been published online at *Fangoria*, *LitReactor*, *CrimeReads*, and the *San Antonio Current*. He is the Editor-in-Chief of Perpetual Motion Machine, the Managing Editor of *Dark Moon Digest*, and the co-host of *Castle Rock Radio: A Stephen King Podcast*. Visit his website TalesFromTheBooth.com to learn more, and follow him on Twitter @GiveMeYourTeeth.

M.E. BRONSTEIN ("Sounds Caught in Cobwebs") is a PhD student in Comparative Literature based in northern California who writes dark fantasy when she should be working on her dissertation. Her work has appeared in *Beneath Ceaseless Skies*, *Metaphorosis*, and *Literary Orphans*, and she is a graduate of the Odyssey Writing Workshop and Clarion UCSD. You can find her at mebronstein.com.

NADIA BULKIN ("Operations Other Than War") writes stories, thirteen of which appear in her debut collection, *She Said Destroy* (Word Horde, 2017). Her short stories have been included in editions of *The Year's Best Weird Fiction*, *The Year's Best Horror*, and *The Year's*

Best Dark Fantasy & Horror. She has been nominated for the Shirley Jackson Award five times. She grew up in Jakarta, Indonesia with her Javanese father and American mother, before relocating to Lincoln, Nebraska. She has a B.A. in Political Science, an M.A. in International Affairs, and lives in Washington, D.C.

RAMSEY CAMPBELL ("Brains") is noted by *The Oxford Companion to English Literature* as "Britain's most respected living horror writer." He has been given more awards than any other writer in the field, including the Grand Master Award of the World Horror Convention, the Lifetime Achievement Award of the Horror Writers Association, the Living Legend Award of the International Horror Guild, and the World Fantasy Lifetime Achievement Award. Among his novels are *The Face That Must Die*, *Incarnate*, and others. He recently brought out his Brichester Mythos trilogy, consisting of *The Searching Dead*, *Born to the Dark*, and *The Way of the Worm*. His novels *The Nameless* and *Pact of the Fathers* have been filmed in Spain, where a film of *The Influence* is in production. Campbell lives on Merseyside with his wife Jenny. His pleasures include classical music, good food and wine, and whatever's in that pipe. His website is at ramseycampbell.com.

KRISTI DEMEESTER ("Umbra Sum") is the author of *Beneath*, a novel published by Word Horde Publications, and *Everything That's Underneath*, a short fiction collection from Apex Books. Her short fiction has appeared in a variety of publications including Ellen Datlow's *The Year's Best Horror, Vol. 9* and *11*, Stephen Jones' *Best New Horror*, *Year's Best Weird Fiction, Volumes 1, 3*, and *5*, in addition to publications such as *Pseudopod, Black Static, The Dark*, and several others. In her spare time, she alternates between telling people how to pronounce her last name and how to spell her first. Find her online at www.kristidemeester.com.

SCOTT EDELMAN ("Only Bruises Are Permanent") has published nearly 100 short stories in magazines such as *Analog, PostScripts, The Twilight Zone*, and *Dark Discoveries*, and in anthologies such as *Why New Yorkers Smoke, MetaHorror, Once Upon a Galaxy, Moon Shots*, and the recent Harlan Ellison tribute anthology *The Unquiet Dreamer*. His collection of zombie fiction, *What Will Come After*, was a finalist for the Bram Stoker Award® and the Shirley Jackson Award. His short science fiction has been collected in *What We Still Talk About*, and his most recent collection, *Tell Me Like You Done Before (and Other Stories Written on the Shoulders of Giants)* was published in 2018. He worked as an assistant editor for Marvel Comics in the 70s, writing everything from display copy for superhero Slurpee cups to the famous *Bullpen Bulletins* pages, with scripts appearing in *Captain Marvel, Master of Kung Fu, Omega the Unknown, Welcome Back, Kotter*, and others. He created the character Dr. Minn-Erva, recently portrayed by Gemma Chan in the *Captain Marvel* movie. Edelman worked for the Syfy Channel for more than thirteen years as editor of *Science Fiction Weekly, SCI FI Wire*, and *Blastr*, and was the founding editor of *Science Fiction Age*, which he edited during its entire eight-year run. He also edited *SCI FI* magazine (previously *Sci-Fi Entertainment*) for more than a decade, as well as *Sci-Fi Universe* and *Sci-Fi Flix*. He has been a Bram Stoker Award® finalist eight times, and a four-time Hugo Award finalist.

M. FERNSTER / HAGCULT (cover artist, illustrator) is a freelance illustrator who specializes in the spooky and macabre; the shadowy spaces that make life fun. HagCult has had work featured in several publications, such as *Rue Morgue* (Ghoulish Gary's art column, "The Fright Gallery"), *HorrorHound Spring 2016 Annual* (Featured Artist), *HorrorHound Fall 2015 Annual* (1 of the top 10, "A Nightmare on Elm Street" alternative movie posters), *Alternative Movie Posters II: More Film Art from the Underground* (by Matthew Chojnacki), *Framed: The Poster Art of Murder by Death, Shadows Over Main Street: An Anthology of Small-Town Lovecraftian Terror, Vol. 1*, and *MetroPulse: Oct. 31, 2013* ("Season of the HAG").

THEODORA GOSS ("Frankenstein's Daughter") is the World Fantasy and Locus Award-winning author of the short story and poetry collections *In the Forest of Forgetting* (2006), *Songs for Ophelia* (2014), and *Snow White Learns Witchcraft* (2019), as well as the novella *The Thorn and The Blossom* (2012), the debut novel *The Strange Case of* the *Alchemist's Daughter* (2017), and its sequel, *European Travel for the Monstrous Gentlewoman* (2018). The final novel in the series, *The Sinister Mystery of the Mesmerizing Girl*, was published in October 2019. She has been a finalist for the Nebula, Crawford, Seiun, and Mythopoeic Awards, as well as on the Tiptree Award Honor List. Her work has been translated into twelve languages. She teaches literature and writing at Boston University and in the Stonecoast MFA Program. Visit her at theodoragoss.com.

BRIAN HODGE ("Butcher's Blade") is a prolific writer in a number of genres and subgenres, as well as an avid connoisseur of music. His most recent works include the novel *The Immaculate Void* and the collection *Skidding Into Oblivion*, companion volumes of cosmic horror. His Lovecraftian novella *The Same Deep Waters as You* is in the early stages of development as a TV series by a London-based production company. After a year lost to the endless business of family deaths, more of everything is back in the works again. He lives in Colorado, where he also endeavors to sweat every day like he's being chased by the police. Connect through his website (www.brianhodge.net), or Facebook (facebook.com/brianhodgewriter).

ALMA KATSU (Foreword) is the author of *The Hunger*, a reimagining of the story of the Donner Party with a horror twist. *The Hunger* made NPR's list of the 100 Best Horror Stories, was named one of the 21 best horror novels written by a woman, and was selected as a most-anticipated Spring 2018 pick by *The Guardian, Bustle, Pop Sugar, io9*, and many other media outlets. *The Taker*, her debut novel, has been compared to the early works of Anne Rice and Diana Gabaldon's *Outlander* for combining historical, the supernatural, and fantasy into one story. *The Taker* was named a Top Ten Debut Novel of 2011 by *Booklist*, was nominated for a Goodreads Readers Choice award, and has been published in over 10 languages. It is the first in an award-winning trilogy that includes *The Reckoning* and *The Descent*. Ms. Katsu lives outside of Washington D.C. with her husband, musician Bruce Katsu. In addition to her novels, she has been a signature reviewer for *Publishers Weekly*, and a contributor to the *Huffington*

Post. She is a graduate of the Johns Hopkins Writing Program and Brandeis University, where she studied with novelist John Irving. She also is an alumni of the Squaw Valley Community of Writers. Prior to the publication of her first novel, Ms. Katsu had a long career in intelligence, working for several US agencies and a think tank. She currently is a consultant on emerging technologies.

VICTOR LAVALLE ("Spectral Evidence") is the author of the short story collection *Slapboxing with Jesus*, four novels, *The Ecstatic, Big Machine, The Devil in Silver,* and *The Changeling,* and two novellas, *Lucretia and the Kroons* and *The Ballad of Black Tom.* He is also the creator and writer of the Bram Stoker Award®-winning comic book *Victor LaValle's Destroyer.* He has been the recipient of numerous awards including a Whiting Writers' Award, a United States Artists Ford Fellowship, a Guggenheim Fellowship, a Shirley Jackson Award, an American Book Award, and the key to Southeast Queens. He was raised in Queens, New York, and now lives in Washington Heights with his wife and kids. He teaches at Columbia University. He can be kind of hard to reach, but he still loves you.

BRACKEN MACLEOD ("Not Eradicated In You") is the Bram Stoker Award®- and Shirley Jackson Award-nominated author of the novels *Mountain Home, Come to Dust, Stranded,* and *Closing Costs,* coming from Houghton Mifflin Harcourt. He has also published two collections of short fiction, *13 Views of the Suicide Woods* and *White Knight and Other Pawns.* Before devoting himself to full-time writing, he worked as a civil and criminal litigator, a university philosophy instructor, and a martial arts teacher. He lives outside of Boston with his wife and son, where he is at work on his next novel.

JOSH MALERMAN ("One Last Transformation") is a *New York Times* bestselling author and one of two singer/songwriters for the rock band The High Strung. His debut novel, *Bird Box,* is the inspiration for the hit Netflix film of the same name. His other novels include *Unbury Carol* and *Inspection.* He lives in Michigan with his fiancé, the artist/musician Allison Laakko.

USMAN T. MALIK ("Ressurection Points") is a Pakistani writer of strange stories and a resident of Florida. His work has appeared in several Year's Best collections, won the British Fantasy and Bram Stoker Award®, and been nominated for the Nebula and World Fantasy. He likes running and occasional long hikes. You can find him on Twitter @usmantm.

LISA MORTON ("Imperfect Clay") is a screenwriter, author of nonfiction books, and award-winning prose writer whose work was described by the American Library Association's *Readers' Advisory Guide to Horror* as "consistently dark, unsettling, and frightening." She is the author of four novels and nearly 150 short stories, a six-time winner of the Bram Stoker Award®, and a world-class Halloween expert. Her most recent book, *Ghost Stories: Classic Tales of Horror and Suspense* (co-edited with Leslie Klinger) received a starred review in *Publishers Weekly*, who called it "a work of art." Lisa lives in the San Fernando Valley and online at www.lisamorton.com.

DOUG MURANO (co-editor) is the Bram Stoker Award®-winning editor of *Behold! Oddities, Curiosities and Undefinable Wonders*, and co-editor of the Bram Stoker Award®-nominated *Gutted: Beautiful Horror Stories*. He is an Active Member of the Horror Writers Association, and was the organization's promotions and social media coordinator from 2013-15. In 2014, he served on the World Horror Convention's steering committee as its social media director. For his efforts to modernize and professionalize the Horror Writers Association's marketing and P.R. machine, he was awarded the 2014 Richard Laymon President's Award, the organization's highest honor for volunteers.

JOANNA PARYPINSKI ("Matryoska") is a writer of dark speculative fiction whose work has appeared in *Black Static*, *Nightmare Magazine*, *Haunted Nights* (edited by Ellen Datlow and Lisa Morton), *New Scary Stories to Tell in the Dark* (edited by Jonathan Maberry), *The Beauty of Death, Vol. 2* (edited by Alessandro Manzetti and Jodi Renee Lester), *Tales from the Lake, Vol. 5* (edited by Kenneth W. Cain), *Nigh-*

script IV, *Vastarien*, and more. Her novel, *Dark Carnival*, was recently published by Independent Legions Press. She holds an MFA from Chapman University and is a member of the Horror Writers Association. She currently lives in the L.A. area and teaches English at Glendale Community College.

R.B. PAYNE ("Paper Doll Hyperplane") got really serious about writing as a member of the Dark Delicacies Writing Group in Burbank, California about a decade ago. His story "Eddie G. at the Gates of Hell" was well-received in the award-winning and Stoker-nominated *Midnight Walk* anthology way back then. About twenty stories later, (he is admittedly a slow writer), his work has appeared in a multitude of magazines and anthologies, including *18 Wheels of Horror*, *Madhouse*, *All-American Horror of the 21ˢᵗ Century*, *Monk Punk*, and the original *Chiral Mad*. He is an active member of the Horror Writers Association and soon the Science Fiction Writers Association. He loves dark speculative fiction and is very near to finishing that novel he started some years ago. Meanwhile, the tales "paddle-jumpers" and ">>>\last of the bark-men}" will see print in the near future. A nomad by choice, R.B. Payne currently lives in Paris, France, with his wife, dog, and cat. He can be found frequently at the local brasserie where wine and conversation impede the writing process but provide an endless source of story ideas. Online, he is at www.rbpayne.com.

CHRISTINA SNG ("The Vodyanoy" / "The Old Gods of Light") is the Bram Stoker Award®-winning author of *A Collection of Nightmares* (Raw Dog Screaming Press, 2017). Her poetry has been nominated multiple times for the Rhysling Awards, Dwarf Stars Awards, and Elgin Awards, received honorable mentions in the *Year's Best Fantasy and Horror* and *Best Horror of the Year* anthologies, and appeared in numerous venues worldwide. Visit her at www.christinasng.com and connect on social media @christinasng.

LUCY A. SNYDER ("My Knowing Glance") is the Shirley Jackson Award-nominated and five-time Bram Stoker Award®-winning author of over 100 published short stories and 13 books. Her most recent titles are the collection *Garden of Eldritch Delights* and the forthcoming novel *The Girl With the Star-Stained Soul*. Her writing has appeared in publications such as *Behold! Oddities, Curiosities and Undefinable Wonders*, *The Library of the Dead*, *Chiral Mad 2*, *Asimov's Science Fiction*, *Apex Magazine*, *Nightmare Magazine*, *Pseudopod*, *Strange Horizons*, and *Best Horror of the Year*. She lives in Columbus, Ohio. You can learn more about her at www.lucysnyder.com and you can follow her on Twitter at @LucyASnyder.

MICHAEL WEHUNT ("A Heart Arrhythmia Creeping Into a Dark Room") lives in the woods of Atlanta with his partner and dog. His stories have appeared in multiple best-of anthologies and other well-known spooky homes. His debut fiction collection, *Greener Pastures*, shortlisted for the Crawford Award, a Shirley Jackson Award finalist, and the winner of Spain's Premio Amaltea for Foreign Translation, is available from Apex Publications.

STEPHANIE M. WYTOVICH ("A Benediction of Corpses") is an American poet, novelist, and essayist. Her work has been show-cased in numerous venues such as *Weird Tales*, *Gutted: Beautiful Horror Stories*, *Fantastic Tales of Terror*, *Year's Best Hardcore Horror, Vol. 2*, *The Best Horror of the Year, Vol.8*, as well as many others. Wytovich is the Poetry Editor for Raw Dog Screaming Press, an adjunct at Western Connecticut State University, Southern New Hampshire University, and Point Park University, and a mentor with Crystal Lake Publishing. She is a member of the Science Fiction Poetry Association, an active member of the Horror Writers Association, and a graduate of Seton Hill University's MFA program for Writing Popular Fiction. Her Bram Stoker Award®-winning poetry collection, *Brothel*, earned a home with Raw Dog Screaming Press alongside *Hysteria: A Collection of Madness*, *Mourning Jewelry*, *An Exorcism of Angels*, *Sheet Music to My Acoustic Nightmare*, and most recently, *The Apocalyptic Mannequin*. Her debut novel, *The Eighth*, is published with Dark Regions Press. Follow Wytovich on her blog at http://stephaniewytovich.blogspot.com, and on twitter @SWytovich.

MERCEDES M. YARDLEY ("The Making of Asylum Ophelia") is a whimsical dark fantasist who wears stilettos and poisonous flowers in her hair. She is the author of *Beautiful Sorrows*, the Stabby Award-winning *Apocalyptic Montessa and Nuclear Lulu: A Tale of Atomic Love*, *Pretty Little Dead Girls: A Novel of Murder and Whimsy*, and *Nameless*. She won the prestigious Bram Stoker Award® for her short story "Little Dead Red." Mercedes lives and creates in Las Vegas. You can find her at mercedesmyardley.com.

Also Available

ANTHOLOGIES BY DOUG MURANO

Shadows Over Main Street, Vol. 1
(co-edited with D. Alexander Ward)

Gutted: Beautiful Horror Stories
(co-edited with D. Alexander Ward)

Behold! Oddities, Curiosities and Undefinable Wonders

Shadows Over Main Street, Vol. 2
(co-edited with D. Alexander Ward)

Welcome to the Show
(co-edited with Matt Hayward)

ANTHOLOGIES BY MICHAEL BAILEY

Pellucid Lunacy

Chiral Mad

Chiral Mad 2

Qualia Nous

The Library of the Dead

Chiral Mad 3

You, Human

Adam's Ladder
(co-edited with Darren Speegle)

Chiral Mad 4: An Anthology of Collaborations
(co-edited with Lucy A. Snyder)

CPSIA information can be obtained
at www.ICGtesting.com
Printed in the USA
FSHW010952170220
67223FS